SHOT LIST

THE DOUGLAS FILES:
BOOK FOUR

NATHAN BIRR

Published by BEACON BOOKS, LLC

Beacon Books LLC

Cover Images Copyright ©
Aneese/iStock/Thinkstock
basar17/iStock/Thinkstock
inigofotografia/iStock/Thinkstock
John Roman/iStock/Thinkstock
nevodka/Shutterstock
Photographer1773/iStock/Thinkstock

THE HOLY BIBLE, NEW INTERNATIONAL VERSION®, NIV®
Copyright © 1973, 1978, 1984, 2011 by Biblica, Inc.®
Used by permission. All rights reserved worldwide.

ISBN: 978-0-9967691-6-7 (hc)
ISBN: 978-0-9967691-7-4 (sc)
ISBN: 978-0-9967691-8-1 (e)

www.nathanbirr.com

Also by Nathan Birr

Overnight Delivery
The Douglas Files: Book One

Black Male
A Douglas Files Short

Three's a Crowd
The Douglas Files: Book Two

WinterKill
A Douglas Files Short

All An Illusion
The Douglas Files: Book Three

God, Girls, Golf & the Gridiron
(Not Always in That Order)
... A Love Story

To you, the readers,
who make this
struggle worthwhile.

Chapter One

Monday, December 31, 2012
10:01 p.m.

ONLY A FEW specks of light managed to penetrate the canopy of trees in the center of the cemetery. It was enough to reflect off the barrel of the Glock 19 pistol trained on Jackson Douglas, but not for him to identify the figure holding the gun or make out facial features. He saw only a rough shape, as might be formed by baggy pants and a sweatshirt with the hood pulled up. That, and the unmistakable polymer barrel of the gun.

A minute ago, the gun had been in Jackson's hand. Like now, he had been unable to identify more than the general shape of the figure in front of him. Unlike now, the two of them had been separated by only a few paces, close enough that a slight moment's hesitation had cost Jackson.

Time stopped. Both of them panted for breath, staring at each other like gunfighters in an old Western. Only Jackson couldn't see the grit in his opponent's eye, and he didn't have a six-shooter strapped at his waist.

He licked his lip, tasting blood. And rain. It had been falling steadily all night, and succeeded where the light failed in making its way through the tree cover overhead. The drops that didn't fall directly through found their way onto leaves and branches, then dripped in syncopation on the road below. All around the little canopy, the rain fell with perfect rhythm, pelting the grave markers while drowning out any ambient noise.

And, perhaps, acting as a natural silencer to keep noise in.

Jackson considered his options. He was at least a dozen feet away from the gun. With it already raised and with him being stationary—even with the cloak of rainy darkness—he had no shot to rush the shrouded figure. To his right or left, he had just as much ground to cover to reach the slightest shelter. Beyond the tree line, there was nothing but open ground and small headstones. He had only one choice.

Jackson exhaled slowly. "You don't have to do this."

1

The gun didn't waver.

Maybe this was it. Maybe Jackson's time was up. He'd dodged a few literal bullets already. Maybe this really was the end of the line. It hadn't been a long journey, but the final few miles had been torture. Maybe he was the old, sick hound about to be put out of his misery . . .

"Are you Jackson Douglas?"

He swallowed hard, eyeing the officer. "I am."

A cloud passed over the officer's blue eyes, and Jackson's heart sank. Plummeted. A visceral growl—a death wail—rose up from within him, but he bit it off, clamping his teeth into his bottom lip. His throat constricted in a gulp, and he blinked the moisture from his eyes.

"I'm very sorry to have to tell you," the officer said.

Beside him, Hillary mouthed a quiet, "No . . ."

Jackson's heartbeats were like pile drivers. His teeth nearly drew blood as he waited for the sentence, one he hoped against hope wasn't coming.

"But your parents and brother . . ."

"No," Hillary moaned again, a little louder.

"They didn't make it," the officer said. "They're dead."

His last words came in slow motion as Jackson's legs gave out. He collapsed to his knees, oblivious to the smoke and flashing lights and voices all around him—oblivious even to the officer's crisp pant legs in front of him or Hillary in her heels at his side. He was consumed by an ache so sudden and so powerful that nothing else existed.

With a sigh, hoping Ryan maintained some modesty while she slept, Jackson reached for the doorknob. It was locked.

Jackson quickly swallowed the panic that tried to rise up into his throat.

"Ry-an!" he said, pounding the door.

Jackson stepped back and kicked the door.

The lock snapped, and the door banged open.

Ryan was under the covers, eyes closed, peaceful as could be. On the end table, next to a dimmed lamp, was her journal and an empty pill bottle.

"Oh, no."

Jackson hurried over to the side and felt for a pulse. It wasn't there.

He half carried, half dragged her onto the floor and began administering CPR. But he knew before he started that it wouldn't do any good. Her golden face had drained of color, and her body was as still as could be.

"Don't let her go!" he begged. "No!" he screamed, beating on her chest. He bent to give her breaths again, trying to will life back into her hollow frame—to bring her soul back from the brink.

"No. No, no, no, no! Do not let him have her!"

There was no response. Ryan's eyes were shut, the mystery unsolved. Her flirtatious, fun, feisty face was now a blank canvas.

Eventually, the paramedics arrived and pushed him out of the way. He heard their questions, heard Stephanie's answers, heard their futile attempts to resuscitate Ryan's lifeless body.

But all other sounds faded to the pounding in his head, a hundred whys and how comes that he knew would never have an answer.

A cell phone lay on the floor, a picture of a man on the screen. Jackson bent to look at the picture and the name above it, and that's when he saw the arm.

Slowly he stood and advanced toward the open closet door. The arm gave way to a shoulder and a head, and then the rest of a body clad in a silk robe that, like the body, was spattered in blood. Several bullet holes were clearly visible through the fabric and in the flesh above the collar. The face, drained of blood, showed panic and pain. The eyes were rolled back into the head. Wet, tangled hair was splayed in every direction—across the face, onto the floor, and over some of the wounds. Even so, Jackson had no difficulty recognizing the corpse.

It was Arielle Coal.

"Your turn," Hillary said. "I want to know what happened. How did you find me, how did you track me from Kingman to Blane and Lake Mead?"

Jackson told his story yet again, hitting the high points. When he was finished, Hillary made him pull over. She got out of the car and bent down, hands on her knees, losing her hospital breakfast. Jackson got out and joined her on her side of the car.

"I had no idea," she said.

He brushed loose hair off her cheek. "I did what I had to."

Raindrops started to fall. Big, splotchy droplets that kicked up dust as they pelted the ground. Hillary slowly turned back to Jackson. "How many?" she asked.

"How many what?"

"How many people did you have to kill to save me?"

"Twenty, give or take."

"Oh my goodness," Hillary said, and she sagged against the door of the car.

"But it was the only way."

She turned and buried her head in his shoulder, and he held her for several minutes while the rain became a steady shower. Eventually, he became aware of Hillary's body shaking, heaving in sobs. He'd never seen this reaction from her—weakness.

"How did this happen?" she asked, wiping her eyes. "How did we get here?"

Jackson swallowed, eying the black figure. "We can work this out."

He shuffled his foot a half step forward. If he could close the gap in half, he'd have a chance to make a lunge. With some skill and a little bit of luck, he could avoid being shot altogether, or at least take a bullet in the arm or leg instead of the heart or head. Assuming the figure was a decent shot.

And capable of actually pulling the trigger.

Jackson exhaled again and took another small step, hoping the rain would muffle any sound and the darkness would obscure his tiny movement. In front of him, the figure was like granite. Like another tombstone in the graveyard.

Shaking his head ever so slightly, Jackson inched his foot forward again. "Why don't you put the gun down? Tell me—"

The gun discharged, emitting a brilliant white flash and a deafening report. Jackson's mind processed both the sight and sound in the instant before he felt a bullet tear into his flesh, commanding all of his brain's attention.

He spun backwards from the blow, staggered once, and fell to the ground. His brain was pummeled by neurons that jostled for position to announce new and unheard of levels of physical pain. Despite the agony, he was aware of three things as he rolled onto his back.

His Glock had clacked on the pavement.

The shooter had darted across the cemetery lawn and disappeared into the shadows.

And the rain fell with renewed intensity and complete apathy.

Chapter Two

10:05 p.m.

JACKSON WAS PRETTY sure he wasn't going to die. The bullet had hit him in the shoulder, too high to have punctured any vital organs and too far off to the side to endanger his aorta or jugular or anything of real significance. It had not been a fatal shot.

Assuming he didn't bleed out on the cemetery road. He had no idea how long a single bullet wound to the shoulder took to drain all the blood from a human body. Or if it even would. Certainly not in the movies, where guys took bullets in the leg and arm all the time, wrapped a makeshift tourniquet around their limb, and fifteen minutes later were chasing down baddies and making out with the girl.

Making out with the girl . . .

Jackson closed his eyes as a fresh wave of pain washed over him. He'd seen no one else upon arriving at the cemetery. The shooter was gone, meaning Jackson was alone in the rain and darkness. Maybe somebody had heard the gunshot, but with the rain, with revelers shooting off firecrackers, and with the fact that it had been a single gunshot in L.A., the chances of a passerby stumbling upon him were slim.

He knew he should try to stop the bleeding by putting pressure on the wound. He raised his right arm, and the slight movement several muscles away from the wound felt like a new bullet biting into his flesh. The fabric of his T-shirt stretched, pulling across and out of the bullet hole. Jackson thought he might faint. He'd been in pain before—real pain. But nothing even close to this.

He collapsed onto his back, breathing in gasps, hoping the pain would subside slightly. He felt the rain puddling around him, soaking his clothes and hair. Fresh drops splattered down on his face. He closed his eyes against the rain, steadied his breathing, gritted his teeth, and, in a swift motion, reached his right hand across his body and pushed his palm into the wound.

5

He growled then screamed in pain. It infuriated him, and instead of removing his hand, he pushed harder. Neurons set world records transmitting commands to his brain, insisting he release pressure. When they overwhelmed him, he surrendered, dragging his hand back across his stomach and onto the pavement.

He rolled his head to the side, away from the wound and the rain that continued to beat down. Jackson clenched his right hand into a fist, his legs tense as he waited for endorphins to flood him and ease his anguish.

Instead, the wound throbbed, and unconsciousness tugged him toward safety. Maybe he would wake to a Good Samaritan standing over his shoulder, or to morning when a jogger or paper boy could hear his cries for help.

Or maybe he just wouldn't wake at all.

And maybe he didn't deserve to.

Jackson reached for the gun, still tucked into the back of his pants, doing a somersault into the middle of the aisle while he grabbed it. As he rolled, he clicked off the safety, and came up on his back, feet up in the air. Between his legs, he aimed at the blur of blackness that was moving. He squeezed the trigger.

Jackson had no idea how many shots he fired. He just kept pulling the trigger, varying his aim up and down, left and right, shooting anything inside the V formed by his outstretched legs.

Finally, he stopped. Slowly, shakily, he got to his knees and then his feet. His shots still echoed through the warehouse, which otherwise had gone eerily silent again. It was still dark, except for a small ray of light cast by the flashlight that was now rolling back and forth on the floor. The glow reflected off smoke hanging in the air and illuminated a growing puddle of blood on the concrete.

Gun still drawn, arm shaking, Jackson bent for the flashlight and confirmed his suspicions.

The man was dead.

Sanders appeared in the cabin stairway, gun drawn in his right hand, his left shoulder sagging and bleeding profusely. His face was gray and his eyes wide. How he was still conscious Jackson had no idea. And at the moment, no concern.

Jackson dived to the side as several shots spit into the deck of the boat. He rolled behind the galley counter and looked up to see a small fire extinguisher attached to the side of the counter. He ripped it off the hook, pulled the tab, and began spraying in the general direction of Sanders.

While Sanders was momentarily distracted, Jackson scampered around the right side of the counter and popped to his feet. He unleashed another spray of foam while running in the general direction of Sanders. When he saw him through the mist, he swung the fire extinguisher, aiming for the gangster's head. He missed, connecting instead with his shoulder. His left shoulder. His bleeding shoulder.

Sanders' howl of pain woke the valley. He fell to the deck, and Jackson slipped in the foam. He slid once before rising to his feet, again reaching for his gun. Somehow, despite the pain, Sanders had risen, his gun still in hand.

Like in the movies, the mist in the air seemed to separate, giving Jackson a clear view of his target. He squeezed the trigger, and felt the small kick as his Glock discharged.

One pull of the trigger.

Two almost simultaneous shots.

Jackson looked down to see where he had been hit, but he was clean. He looked back up as Sanders slumped to the deck, the gun falling from his lifeless hand. Jackson turned his eyes to the shore where Dylan stood, gun drawn, still slightly crouched as he aimed toward the boat.

Jackson approached the fallen drug dealer, kicked the gun away, and made sure he was indeed dead.

As a doornail.

Uttering something between a guttural growl of frustrated resignation and a war whoop, Jackson squeezed the trigger.

His first bullet tore into the man's shoulder. The second sailed wide as the guard reacted to the first and spun. Jackson shot quickly again, hitting the guard in the arm, causing him to release his weapon. He was still standing and began to charge, and Jackson shot two more times, both bullets tearing into flesh but not hitting center mass.

The man continued to charge, himself growling in pain and rage. Jackson stepped out fully from behind the building, planted himself, and took aim. He had one shot before the man was upon him, and he had no choice.

His hands were shaking, and he again missed center mass. His bullet was high, penetrating just below the neck. Blood immediately bubbled to the surface.

The man dropped to his knees, then facedown into the sand, blood gushing from his wounds.

Then the hangar was turned a stunning white, the bang reverberating in Jackson's ears. He spun around the side of the van with the rifle. It took a second to identify a target, a man crouched in the wake of the detonation. Jackson screamed viscerally as he unloaded a dozen rounds, shredding the man where he stood.

He stepped over Hillary and switched the gun to his left hand, looking down the driver's side of the vehicle. He saw a figure running for the corner of the hangar, and chased him there with another half dozen bullets.

Jackson walked over to Margaret Moore and placed the gun in her leg, just above the knee. Senator Moore swore at him.

"Do not make me do this," Jackson said.

Moore scowled and called him a litany of dirty words.

Jackson gritted his teeth. He was in it pretty deep. Extenuating circumstances might explain some of his actions away. He was hoping for lenience once the truth came out. But if he put a bullet in Margaret Moore, he would cross another line, beyond the reach of clemency. The court's or his own soul's.

"I shot Quinn," Jackson said. "I killed over a dozen men at the base. I drove up to your house in the burbs and took you and your guards captive. Do you really want to take the chance that I'm bluffing," he asked, "that I'll just say 'aw, shucks, you win' and hand over the gun?"

Moore stared at him intently.

"Three seconds," Jackson said, still unsure what to do if Moore called his bluff. "Two . . ." He couldn't shoot her, but if he backed down . . . "One . . ." He pushed the gun deeper into Margaret's leg, and she stifled a yelp.

"Wait!" Moore yelled.

Jackson turned the gun back on him. "Confess!"

Jackson sat in the dark, staring at nothingness on his TV. Some lame cable action hero dodging bullets in a burning building. Revulsion and apathy played to a draw, and the remote remained on the couch cushion beside him.

His eyes were glazed over; his ears unreceptive. Somewhere in the house, his phone was ringing again. It had been ringing for two days, playing the assorted ringtones assigned to his various friends. He let them play. Three messages from Sam. Two from Reggie and Leroy. One from Mouse. Six from his neighbor Connie.

And it was probably her banging on his front door.

Jackson thought again of the sedatives he knew were upstairs. All the way upstairs. Farther even than the remote.

Something on TV blew up in spectacular fashion. Debris and bodies flew everywhere. The action hero made a clichéd, vulgar gesture. Then he grinned as he walked away.

The banging on the front door had ceased, but gave way to a new, more terrifying sound. Soft clicks.

The door was thrown open, light flooding the room. Jackson closed his eyes against the assault.

"Jackson!" Connie's boisterous voice echoed through the room. "What are you doing sitting on the couch? And what is that filth you're watching?"

The hero was about to get some action of a different kind. Jackson felt for the remote and popped off the TV.

"How long have you been like this?" Connie asked.

Jackson rolled his head. "Depends," he muttered, the first words he recalled speaking that day. "It's Thursday, right?"

"I don't know what you and that young lady did in Las Vegas, but do you realize my lawn hasn't been mowed in two weeks? I don't think you can even get that old mower through it anymore. And Sabrina's due in this afternoon. I was hoping maybe you could take her out tonight instead of tomorrow? I've got a Gourmet Gala meeting, and I—"

"No," Jackson said.

Connie stopped, almost in front of him. She scowled. "What do you mean, 'no'?"

"I mean I'm not showing your niece around town."

"But you promised. I fixed your little backstory—isn't that what they call it on TV?—and you agreed to take Sabrina out. I know it's a day early and short notice, but—"

"I know what I said," Jackson replied. "But things have changed."

"Jackson, this isn't like you. Is something going on with you and . . . what was her name, Hailey?"

"What's going on is that I killed twenty people and blew up an Air Force base in Nevada, Connie! I left more collateral damage than a Lethal Weapon *movie, and so I'm not really in the mood to mow your stupid lawn or show bipolar Sabrina around town or make good on any of my favors right now, okay?"*

Connie stared at him with bulging brown eyes. Then she huffed and stalked toward the door, mumbling curses in Italian as she went. Jackson waited until the door slammed behind her, then hurled the remote control at the TV with a yell.

Jackson heard footsteps on the pavement. The shooter was coming back.

He tried to raise his head, tried to reach for his gun. Where was his gun?

Somebody shouted. A girl, maybe a teenage boy. Jackson couldn't decipher the words. The footsteps grew louder.

Then the rain stopped. Or just moved. He could hear it falling all around him, slapping against the tombstones and the pavement. But it wasn't falling on his face anymore.

Suddenly, he felt another bullet tearing through his body, in the exact same place. This one didn't pass through. It just continued to tear, like a giant knot in his shoulder, growing both tighter and bigger at the same time. Jackson wanted to scream in pain. He wanted to reach for the wound, to somehow alleviate the pressure. And he wanted to shut up the babbling voice that may or may not have been only in his head.

But he passed out before he had a chance to do anything.

Chapter Three

10:18 p.m.

JACKSON AWOKE WITH a sudden stabbing pain in his shoulder. And pressure. So what was new? He was also shaking. That couldn't be good.

He heard multiple voices now, all lost in the darkness, all muffled by the rain. Some of them were talking to each other. Some were just talking. None of them made any sense. Maybe he'd been shot in the head too.

Then Jackson noticed lights flashing. Various shades of red. He thought he heard a siren.

His eyes finally blinked away the rain. He made out a face, and bright blue eyes.

Blue eyes . . .

More footsteps, now shouts and commotion, and finally the pressure stopped. He was able to breathe again, and tried to suck in lungfuls of air. He just choked on rain.

"Sir, can you hear me?" a thick, male voice asked.

Jackson nodded. He panned his eyes to look into a flashlight. "You . . . Youse . . ."

"Pulse is thready. Sir, can you hear me?"

Jackson panted. "Yeah." He winced as he felt the pressure on the bullet wound again.

"We're stopping the bleeding," the voice announced, "and I'm going to put you on oxygen. Just continue to breathe normally."

"UCLA," he muttered before the mask was lowered over his face. He saw heads and arms, but hadn't yet put the pieces together as to how many paramedics there were or where they were stationed.

The medic lifted the mask. "UCLA?"

"Medical," Jackson panted. "In Santa . . . Monica."

"That's where we're going. We'll have you there in a few minutes," the man said, replacing the mask.

11

"C-c-call S-Sam," Jackson uttered, but it was turned into a garble by the oxygen mask. He panted for a few breaths and then concentrated on breathing normally. In, out. In, out. As he was turned onto his side, his world was turned upside down by the pain.

A hand ran over his back, feeling, patting loosely. He yelped into the mask when it touched a sore spot he hadn't yet noticed.

"One exit wound in the rear," another mail voice stated matter-of-factly, as if describing a pimple or a birthmark and not a bullet hole. "Appears to have gone clean through."

You'll get that from a dozen feet away.

They rolled him onto his back again, onto a dry, softer surface. A gurney? They continued to chatter, using words like "blood loss," "controlled," "deformity," and "shock." Jackson tried to concentrate on breathing, but the movement had caused pain to reverberate through him with renewed ardor.

Next thing he knew, he was being fastened to whatever it was he was laying on. They had elevated him, and also covered him with a blanket. That's when he realized his entire body was soaking wet.

Jackson reached and tried to remove the oxygen mask. He succeeded for only a moment before his hand was restricted and the mask was replaced. His second exhortation to call Sam's name went as unheeded as the first. He resigned himself to the inability to speak and settled back, focusing on breathing and ignoring the pain.

Then he was airborne, and seconds later, rolling smoothly down the pavement.

And getting rained on again.

*   *   *

Saturday, August 18, 2012
4:04 p.m.

"YOU'RE NOT having fun," Maggie said.

Jackson looked at her. Blue jeans, mauve Henley open over a gray tee, wavy chestnut hair down—momentarily not swirling in the breeze—no jewelry, little if any makeup. And eating ice cream from a small plastic container via a wooden spoon as she leaned on the railing at the end of Fisherman's Wharf. She was the picture of carefree. Typical Maggie.

"I am," he answered.

"No, I can tell when you're having fun. It's in your eyes."

Jackson turned and stared at a pelican perched on the next pier over.

"Ryan?" Maggie asked.

Without looking, Jackson nodded. It had been three weeks since her suicide. Two and a half since the funeral attended by less than a dozen people. The rest of the world had already forgotten about her, just another orphan with a tragic tale.

"Maybe we should have postponed," Maggie said.

Jackson turned back to her. "No. I want to be here, with you. Really."

Maggie dug out some ice cream and slid it onto her tongue. She eyed him. "Turn around."

"Huh?"

"Turn around," she said.

With a sigh he did so, leaning on the pier railing.

"Look at this," Maggie said, gesturing at the panorama. The wharf, with its restaurants and shops, stretched to his right. Beyond it, the Presidio of Monterey rambled across the hillside. Ahead and to the left, green hills rolled under a bright blue sky dotted with tufts of clouds so close they appeared ready to engulf the treetops. And behind him, he knew sailboats skimmed across the surface of Monterey Bay and the Pacific Ocean.

Maggie moved to stand in front of him. "Right here, right now, in this moment, what's wrong?"

He lowered his eyes to hers. "Right now?"

"Right now."

He sighed. "Absolutely nothing."

Maggie spooned some more ice cream. "So . . . ?"

Jackson let a grin tug at the corner of his mouth. "So what's next?"

They had left Los Angeles before dawn that morning, making the five-hour trip up the coast (actually, through the interior on I-5 and the 101) to Monterey in time for lunch. After that had been a visit to the famed Monterey Bay Aquarium before a stroll down Cannery Row and then ice cream at the foot of Fisherman's Wharf. The day was Maggie's, which meant the rest of their agenda was up to her as well.

"I've got an idea," she said. "But first let me finish this."

"Weren't we supposed to share that ice cream?" he asked.

Maggie's gray-blue eyes sparkled mischievously. Then she scooped her spoon around the edge of the dish, digging out the rest of the ice cream in the container. She lifted it slowly to her mouth, moaning in mock delight as she extracted the spoon.

"This idea of yours," Jackson said.

Maggie swallowed. "A caricature."

Jackson mused. "It's kind of teenage girlish, but okay."

They started walking back down the pier, toward all of the souvenir shops, art galleries, and seafood restaurants. They stopped at a small stand where a guy with as much ink on his arms as on his canvas was finishing an airbrushing of a young boy and girl. Jackson and Maggie waited five minutes and then posed while the guy quickly sketched them. Jackson stood behind Maggie, his arms loosely around her, as she leaned back into him and he leaned against a pylon of the pier. The ocean was behind them, probably with some flitting seagulls. Definitely some barking sea lions.

The whole thing took less than fifteen minutes, and after Jackson paid the guy, he and Maggie continued to stroll along the wharf. They bought some saltwater taffy at Carousel Candies and sampled various pieces as they ducked in and out of a handful of shops. Still deep in debt to Connie after harboring three women at her place for a week, Jackson bought her a tiny glass sculpture of an emerged whale tailfin. It was the tacky sort of thing her house was littered with. He also bought Maggie a fifty-cent mood ring, claiming he wanted to see what color feisty was. It earned him an elbow in the ribs.

"You have the time?" Maggie asked as they stepped back out onto the wharf. She reached her hand into the bag of taffy and pulled out a piece.

"Do I ever have the time?" Jackson asked.

She shook her head in disgust.

"I can't help but notice your wrists are bare," he said.

"I didn't want to spend the day worrying about time," she answered, grinding her teeth into Neapolitan taffy.

"And yet here we are with you asking me for it."

Maggie held up the hand with the ring. "Hmm, it appears that orange correlates with annoyed."

"I think the clock in there said quarter after five," he said, reaching for a piece of taffy. Maggie snatched the bag from his reach before he could grab one.

"We'd better get to dinner then. If we're going to drive 17-Mile Drive and still hit Big Sur before dark."

They started walking, headed for the Red Snapper Restaurant & Bar at the south end of the wharf. Maggie had picked the place after peeking at a laminated outdoor menu on their way past earlier. It offered a wide variety of seafood, her favorite.

"You might as well say it," Jackson said. He was trailing Maggie by half a pace as she stalked ahead of him with the taffy, all in good humor.

"Say what?"

"This is my fault. Although it's not. You were the one to suggest a day trip."

She turned her head. "Only because I knew you wouldn't go for it otherwise."

"We've been over this, Maggie."

"I know. And I'm not mad. It's just . . ."

"Unflattering?"

"No."

"Because that's not it."

"What's not?"

"You."

She stopped walking. "Please tell me you didn't just give me the 'it's not you, it's me,' line."

He shrugged. "It's true."

Maggie resumed walking. Jackson rested the rolled up caricature on his shoulder and ambled after her. Maggie had the ability to make him the sweating, shaking, fidgeting recovering alcoholic. He could resist her wiles, but barely.

They beat the dinner rush and were offered a table overlooking the water and the marina. And a lot of seals whose barking was muted indoors. After they had ordered, Jackson leaned forward. "Look, Maggie, it really isn't you."

"I know. It's just . . ."

"What?"

She sighed. And licked her lips. "I feel like it never will be me."

He frowned.

"I'm not asking for a relationship commitment, Jackson, so you can stop perspiring."

"It's lack of airflow."

"Whatever. I'm just saying, there's nothing that will change your mind. There's nothing I could say or do that would get you to stay here and spend the night with me, is there?"

Jackson looked up from his well-fiddled-with straw wrapper. "There is one thing."

"What's that?"

He held out his hand and nodded. She extended hers, and he rubbed his thumb over her fingers . . . and the mood ring. "We'd need to trade this in for a slight upgrade."

Maggie rolled her eyes as she withdrew her hand.

"I know it's a crazy concept in this day and age," Jackson said, "but I'm saving myself for marriage."

"You and Tim Tebow, I know." She reached for her water and took a drink.

"I've never been so favorably compared."

Maggie leaned forward. "Okay, let's say I proposed to you and we ran off to the Justice of the Peace to make it legit. Don't I have to be a Christian too so we aren't unequally yoked or whatever?"

Jackson felt the sweat coming back. "Yeah."

"So what are we doing?"

He swallowed. It was one of those moments where the little voice that had been whispering for so long had just been given a megaphone. He swallowed again.

"Are you having fun today?" he asked.

"Until about ten minutes ago."

He nodded. "That's what we're doing. We're having fun. Maybe someday you'll become a Christian, we'll get married, and come to Monterey for a month-long honeymoon. But today, we're just having fun."

Maggie bit her lip. A smile fought to get out. Jackson encouraged it with one of his own.

"Fine," she said at last. "You win. For now."

Jackson sat back, the megaphone temporarily flicked out of the whispering voice's hand. He took a long drink of water, then leaned forward again. He peeked at Maggie's hand.

"Blue," he said. "Blue means peace and contentment."

"Blue means you're a dork," she said.

"Ah, there's that urbane articulation that's made you an ace journalist."

She mock-glared at him for a moment, then kicked him under the table.

Their conversation turned light over steaming plates of crab legs and shrimp. With full stomachs, and close to an hour of daylight remaining, they left the wharf. They had made the trip in Jackson's car instead of the back of Maggie's Yamaha motorcycle. Not that the idea of clinging to Maggie's midriff along the twists and turns of Highway 1 for five hours hadn't appealed to Jackson. But a car had simply made more sense, and with a chill settling in the air as the sun set, Jackson was glad they'd opted for it.

The first part of their journey home was along the serpentine 17-Mile Drive. The winding highway led them through Pacific Grove and Pebble Beach, along the jagged Monterey Peninsula shoreline, and beside world-famous golf courses and million-dollar mansions. Ancient Cypress trees dotted the landscape, framing spectacular views of the ocean and the explosions of foam and spray sent skyward as the cerulean Pacific collided with the rocky coast. It was mesmerizing, and Jackson had all he could do to keep his eyes on the road.

"This is incredible," Maggie said, watching as another wave slammed into the rocks and splashed into the air, the spray drenched in the evening sunlight.

"Yeah," he said. "You want to try to explain this all away on a 'we're an accident of the cosmos' theory again?"

"Sure," she replied evenly, flicking hair out of her eyes as she turned his way. "Then we can swing by Compton on the way home to get up close and personal with the impoverished and destitute, and you can tell me again about your all-loving, all-powerful God."

He met her eyes for a moment before turning his attention back to the road. 17-Mile Drive eventually emptied into Highway 1, which took them south past Carmel and back to the coast. They drove mostly in silence, captivated by the views of Big Sur. Fifteen minutes later, Jackson pulled off the road at a small, crescent-shaped overlook. He and Maggie both got out.

To the north, the coastline of Big Sur stretched out for miles, one promontory after another jutting into the ocean. Lush green vegetation covered the hillsides, running right up to and sometimes over the edge of the cliffs that towered over the Pacific. A wispy marine layer was moving in, but instead of ruining the magnificent scene, the clouds actually enhanced it by reflecting the yellow and orange light of the setting sun on the panorama below. As a result, the entire sky was lit up, shading the green terrain in a golden glow.

The scene was breathtaking. Thanks to the roar of the pounding surf below and the feathery texture of the low-hanging clouds above, it felt more real and vibrant than even the standard brilliant California vistas.

Jackson and Maggie were alone, at least for the moment, and cast against the setting sun, Maggie looked pretty good too. At first glance. But her jaw was set firmly, and her eyes distant.

He took a chance and loosely wrapped his arms around her, as he had when they posed for the caricature. He set his chin on her shoulder. "You mad at me?"

She took a moment to answer, turning her head slightly toward him. "No. Look at this . . . How can I be mad right now?"

He stepped back. "It would seem the California coastline can solve all of our problems."

Maggie turned her body to face him. "We don't have problems, Jackson."

"No?"

"No."

He nodded, gazing at the Bixby Creek Bridge off in the distance. Spanning a small inlet in the coastline, the reinforced-concrete arch bridge was one of the more famous along the Pacific Coast. As with the Golden Gate Bridge in San Francisco, the builders had managed to blend the perfect amount of human ingenuity as a complement to God's handiwork.

"And I do want to thank you for today," Maggie said. "It's been perfect."

"I did owe you."

She leaned over and pecked him on the cheek. "Consider the debt cancelled."

Jackson grinned and reached for her hand. She let him take it, and he twisted the mood ring off her finger. Then he heaved it over the side of the cliff.

"What'd you do that for?" she asked.

"You were right before—as a Christian, I'm not supposed to marry someone who isn't a Christian. But that bridge is a long ways off, and I agree that today was perfect, and the last thing I want to do is drive you away by coming off as holier-than-thou or something."

"So what, taking off my mood ring and heaving it into the ocean is symbolic?"

He nodded. "Yeah, something like that."

Maggie simultaneously shook her head, rolled her eyes, and smiled.

"Plus, with you it's more of a strobe light—I was afraid you'd break it."

She punched him in the ribs, and as he turned to deflect the blow, she twisted his arm behind his back.

"Agh—I like your moods, Maggie."

"Moods?" She twisted a little harder.

"I—Ow—I meant your personality. Good and bad moods. Temperament?"

She let go but continued to glare. Good-naturedly.

"I mean it, Maggie. I like that you're feisty."

18

"Feisty?"

"In the finest sense of the word. Spirited, lively, fun. And besides, you don't strike me as the keep sentimental trinkets kind of person. You'd rather have the moment, and chucking a fifty-cent mood ring into the ocean is memorable, right?"

Maggie stared at him, still with a trace of mock indignation. But her eyes said he'd hit the nail on the head. Slowly, she smiled. "And you thought through that all in the instant while you were sliding it off my finger?"

"More like been backpedaling ever since. Now can we watch the sunset?"

She stared at him for a few more seconds, then turned toward the ocean. The sun was big and orange as it slowly disappeared into an ocean that had been transformed to lava beneath it. As it dipped below the surface, a hush seemed to fall over the Big Sur coastline, accompanied by a chilly breeze. They lingered in the magic for a few more minutes, then headed for home.

Chapter Four

Monday, December 31
10:23 p.m.

"BP'S ONE HUNDRED over fifty. O2 sats, ninety-two. Pulse, ninety-six."

Jackson tried to focus on the eyes of the medic hovering over him, but his eyes didn't want to focus. Maybe they were rolling back into his head. Maybe he was going into shock or fainting or something. Or maybe the pain was literally blinding. It certainly was figuratively. Just a little bullet. Just a little hole. Nine millimeters, to be precise. And it hadn't even hit anything important. At least, he didn't think it had.

Around him, the medics were scurrying to hang this, unclip that, adjust this, remove that. It was all a blur. Maybe he'd hit his head when he fell.

They were both guys, the medics. Jackson would hate to vomit in front of a girl. And he felt as if that was a real possibility. Action heroes on TV took bullets that didn't even slow them down. And Jackson wasn't a wimp. Maybe the shooter had been some sort of kook, dipped his bullet in something. Poison. Mind-altering drugs. Salt. But no, that couldn't be; the bullets had been Jackson's.

One of the medics leaned over to get in Jackson's line of site. He removed the non-rebreather oxygen mask. "Sir? Sir, what's your name?"

"Jack . . . Jackson Douglas."

"Jackson, I'm Trent. Can you tell me how old you are?"

"Thirty."

"Do you know where you are?"

"Depends . . ."

"Depends on what?"

"How fast your guy's driving."

Trent actually smiled. "Do you remember what happened?"

"I was shot."

"That's right. I'm going to check you now for any other pain, bruising, bleeding, anything like that. Does anything else hurt?"

"If it does I can't feel it right now."

"How bad is the pain, on a scale of one to ten?"

"Seven hundred and eight."

Trent grinned again and began moving his hands from Jackson's head, down to his chest, torso, and legs.

"Any difficulty breathing?" he asked when he was finished.

"No," Jackson answered, but Trent reached for a stethoscope and listened to his lungs for a minute anyhow.

"Do you have any allergies?"

"No."

"Are you taking any medications, have any medical conditions?"

"Other than being shot?"

"When's the last time you had something to eat or drink?"

"Six-thirty, seven."

"Any drugs in your system?"

"Not unless you've given them to me."

"Just LR to replace fluids."

The ambulance turned suddenly, and Jackson tried to figure out where they were. The Santa Monica-UCLA Medical Center was at 15th and Wilshire. And he'd been shot at . . .

"Oxygen's dropping," the second medic announced.

Trent nodded. "Jackson, I'm going to replace your oxygen mask, all right?"

Jackson nodded, thinking back to being shot. He'd been at the cemetery. Woodlawn Cemetery, on 14th and Pico. But why?

It would come to him. In the meantime, the pain medication wasn't working, assuming they'd already administered more than a mental placebo. So he tried to drift off into unconsciousness, the best pain medication he knew of. Tried and proven, for the last eighteen months.

*   *   *

Monday, September 3
3:11 p.m.

DODGER STADIUM in Chavez Ravine was awash in sunshine on a splendid Labor Day afternoon. The sky was clear, the San Gabriel Mountains beyond the outfield fence had texture usually obscured by the smog, and the air was warm and alive with anticipation. The Dodgers were hot, having won ten of thirteen, and had trimmed the Giants' lead in the National League West to seven and half games. It was still a sizeable margin, but with San Francisco in town for three games, L.A. at least had hope. And hope smelled as good as peanuts and Cracker Jack and Dodger Dogs.

Maggie was her usual casual stunning self—blue jeans, charcoal T-shirt, hair in a high, bouncing ponytail. The seats were good, halfway up along the third base line, compliments of the *Los Angeles Times*. The occasional Lakers and Dodgers tickets were one of the perks of Maggie's job, at least for Jackson.

"Did I thank you for the tickets yet?" he asked as he joined the packed house in celebrating a strikeout of the Giants' first batter.

"A half dozen times."

"Well thanks again." He cracked open the shell of a contraband peanut. "We should really do this more often."

"Me use my pull to get you free entertainment?"

"Exactly. The Lakers aren't the Lakers of old, but how many times will we get to see Kob—"

The crack of the bat distracted him, and he turned to see a Giant batter on his way to first with a single to right. A fly in the ointment.

Jackson popped a few more peanuts. "I'm serious, Maggie. Summer flew by and we hardly saw each other. We should spend more time together. Dodgers, Lakers, sunsets from spectacular vantage points."

Another crack of the bat and another base hit to right. Suddenly the Giants had a rally, and Jackson turned his body and his attention fully to the game. Momentum seemed far more consequential in September, and the Dodgers couldn't afford to fall behind.

The pitching coach made a quick trip to the mound. Probably a tweak in the pitcher's mechanics, a quick fix that would lead to a double play and get the team back in the dugout. As the coach retreated from the mound, the public address system urged the crowd into a hand-clapping, foot-stomping fervor as the Giants' cleanup hitter dug in.

"Can I ask you something?"

"Sure," Jackson said, casting Maggie a quick glance between pitches.

"What do you really think of me?"

Jackson crunched on a peanut, sensing this was not just a casual question. The cleanup hitter reached on a cheap infield single, and suddenly the Giants had the bases loaded.

Jackson sat back, chucking a peanut, still in shell, to the ground. "I think you have lousy timing," he muttered. He turned her way. "What do you mean?"

"I've been thinking since our talk in Monterey. You're a self-proclaimed Christian, and you say that impacts everything in your life. You think God is real and belief in Him is logical and everything is black and white, true and false. So what do you think of me, then, as an unredeemed pagan?"

Jackson looked up as the next batter lined a ball into left-center field. Two runs came in to score, and the building anxiety among the fifty-seven thousand people in Dodger Stadium was released as a collective groan.

"Do we really have to talk about this now?"

"Yeah," she answered. "I want to know."

Jackson exhaled. The pitching coach was back on his way to the mound. Time for more tweaks. Jackson had a minute. "For one thing, I've never used the term 'unredeemed pagan.'"

"Call it what you like. Unsaved, a non-Christian, worldly. That's me, right?"

"Why do I have a feeling I should be looking for a bear trap around my ankle?"

Maggie stared at him.

"Okay, look," he said. "The Bible says that everyone who does not believe in Jesus will be condemned. That's not my thoughts about you—it's God's."

"Great, pass the buck."

"Maggie, everybody starts off in life with zero points. And zero points won't get you into heaven. And the problem is, despite what everybody and every religion seems to think, you can't score points for yourself. Only Jesus can. And He offers them to you, all you need. You want them, they're yours, case closed. But if you don't want them, then you're stuck at zero."

"Is this supposed to be a metaphor?"

"You asked what I think of you," he said. "I think that if you don't trust in Jesus—same goes for everybody—you'll go to hell when you die. I know that sounds harsh, but it's true, and it's not me, it's the Bible that says it."

"And you've done that, trusted in Jesus?"

"Yeah."

"Okay, so what do you in the trust circle think of me on the outside?" Maggie pressed.

The next Giant hitter was stepping to the plate, and Jackson tried to bring closure to this whole deal. "Beyond what I told you, I think you're great."

"Come on."

"I mean it. Whether you're the most wonderful person in the world or the wretch of the earth, you need Jesus. I believe that, and I've told you that before. We've had this discussion. What are you after, Maggie?"

"I mean, if you and I don't see eye to eye on something so important, how can you have any respect for me as a person? And if you don't have respect for me, how can we have . . . anything?"

"Anything. Like love, marriage, then a baby carriage?"

"Stop joking about everything."

"Sorry."

"And yes, that's what I mean."

Jackson shrugged. "Maggie, I never . . . I didn't know you were thinking long-term relationship. You said in Mont—"

"I'm not. But I know you'll never have just a casual relationship."

Jackson swallowed. The Dodger pitcher was laboring, behind two balls to no strikes. "What do you call what we have now?"

"Nothing we couldn't have if I was Mack instead of Maggie."

"You don't mean that."

She stared at him. "Face it, we're just pals unless I accept your worldview. And if I don't, you think I'm some kind of messed up degenerate or something."

"You're not a degenerate, Maggie. You're . . . blinded. And until those blinders—"

"I'm blinded? So what, I'm some ignoramus because I don't believe the way you do?"

"I didn't say that. What are you doing?"

"What am *I* doing?"

"Yes. Asking me antagonistic questions and jumping down my throat right away?"

"You tell me I'm going to hell because I don't believe the way you do and I'm the antagonistic one?" She shook her head in disgust and pushed herself out of her seat. Meanwhile, the Giant batter drew a four-pitch walk and jogged to first base. Jackson sat back with a sigh, wondering how things—on the field and in the stands—had gone so wrong so quickly.

Maggie returned at the end of the first inning, after San Francisco had scored five runs and the Dodgers had scratched out a hit that quickly was erased by a double play. She plopped into her seat, sipping on a soda, ignoring Jackson.

"Maggie . . ."

She merely shook her head to shut him down.

24

And so they sat without talking for five innings. The Giants scored six more runs, taking an 11-1 lead after the sixth. Despite the beautiful weather, many in the sellout crowd had begun to head for the exits. Maggie tapped Jackson in the knee, their first interaction since he'd asked if she wanted something from the concession stands after the third inning. "Let's go," she said.

He didn't argue, instead following her out into the parking lot. As they searched for his Granada, he tried again. "Maggie, I'm sorry if I came across wrong."

"You see, that's just what I'm getting at. You're not apologizing for what you said, just for how you said it. Which means you meant exactly what you said. I'm a big girl, Jackson. I don't need sugar-coating."

He quickened his pace to catch up with her. "Maggie, what if I was sick with some deadly influenza, and you had the cure? Wouldn't you be pretty adamant about not changing your belief that the cure was indeed the cure, and that without it, I'd die?"

"So now I'm sick?"

"We all are," he answered.

"No, you have the 'cure,' remember? So what do you think of me for not having it?"

"You're right. I do think you are sick. But we're not talking about being a leper at a fashion show. The whole world is sick, Maggie."

"Well excuse me for not being soothed by that thought."

Jackson sighed as they reached the car. They got in, sitting gingerly on blistering hot leather seats. "You still want to hit Fish Grill?" he asked.

Maggie folded her arms. "I'm not hungry. Maybe you should just take me home."

Jackson started the car, and without another word, drove Maggie back to her apartment. He parked and turned off the car. "I'll walk you up," he said.

"Don't bother."

"Maggie," he said, reaching for her arm. "Can we please talk about this?"

"We have nothing more to talk about, Jack." She pulled her arm away from his, at the same time opening the door. She gave him only a brief glance as she said, "Goodbye."

*   *   *

Monday, December 31
10:35 p.m.

ON TV, the doors to the ambulance bay always flew open. The gurney with the victim crashed through the doorway, medics and nurses and doctors running alongside it like rodeo clowns trying to corral a bull. They read off every vital sign and statistic imaginable, barked orders, punctuated everything with "Stat!" and usually stopped on the way to the ER to confer with their secret lover about a pressing personal problem.

In reality, Jackson was wheeled in calmly, having been handed off to hospital staff by the paramedics. The bay doors opened automatically, and the conversation by the nurses and doctors or whoever they were was calm and collected. Almost too calm.

Jackson wasn't sure what time it was, but Sam's shift had to be almost over. Was she still there? Had she heard the news? And if so, did she know anything other than that a male gunshot victim was en route?

"Mr. Douglas, I'm Annie," a female nurse announced.

Annie . . .

She had a simple, pleasant face, framed by wavy blond hair.

Wavy blond hair . . .

"We're going to check you for any other injuries, all right?"

Jackson nodded, his mouth and nose still covered by the non-rebreather mask. He waited as he was wheeled through the hospital and into a small side room, while nurses conferred several times, and while he was poked and prodded again. Where was Sam? She should have been here by now. What happened to Trent and the other guy? And why was Annie frowning?

"Mr. Douglas, how are you feeling?" She took his hand, looking up at a monitor as she did.

"I'm . . ."

When had she removed the oxygen mask? And when had that infernal beeping started? And why was his head spinning?

Annie hollered something and several more nurses joined her in the room. Now they were scurrying around, looking anxious, and Jackson thought he even heard the word "Stat!" His brain may not have been functioning at a high level, but he could tell something was amiss.

"BP's eighty-five over forty," Annie said.

"Heart rate's one-twenty," another chimed in.

Somebody mentioned sats at eighty-four.

"Face is pale. Is he losing blood somewhere?"

"Bandage is clear."

"Gurney?"

"Minimal."

"Might be internal. Call anesthesia and get him to OR right away!"

Chapter Five

THE PAIN WASN'T quite as bad. That was good.

Sam was still nowhere to be seen. That was bad.

Jackson tried to piece things together, assign faces to names, figure out what was going on. But he wasn't as coherent as he had been back in the ambulance, when . . .

The ambulance. Trent. He'd been shot, been in pain, and been on his way to Santa Monica-UCLA Medical Center. But he hadn't seen Trent in a while, just that new nurse with the wavy blond hair. Annie.

Not Sam.

Something had gone wrong. His blood pressure had dropped, something about being pale maybe. He may have heard the word tachycardic. So where was he now?

A large room, white walls, white ceiling, quiet. Except for the machines beside him, beeping and clicking and humming. And he was alone. Where was Annie? Or anyone?

He tried to speak, but was still wearing that blasted oxygen mask. It was just a mumble, even to him.

But it worked. From beside him, a blue form stirred, and he felt a hand on his wrist. A moment later he was looking into the brown eyes of a nurse with blond hair tinged with dark streaks.

"Mr. Douglas. You're in the operating room." Her voice was calm and soothing, a far cry from the anxious tone he'd heard a few minutes earlier. "We think the bullet might have nicked your subclavian artery and you've lost quite a bit of blood. But we've been able to control the bleeding, your vital signs have stabilized, and you're going to be in very good hands with Dr. Nelson."

Jackson managed a small nod.

28

"We'll be putting you under general anesthesia very shortly, so the next thing you know you'll be out of surgery, recovering comfortably. I know you've had a rough night, but just hang on a little while longer."

If Jackson could remember when he got out, assuming she was right and he made it, he would get her a fruit basket or something. If that was how normal people showed gratitude to a nurse with a good bedside manner. He still wasn't sure he was thinking clearly.

"Is there anyone we can contact for you?" she asked.

"Sa . . . Sam."

"Sam?"

"Mag. . ." He swallowed. "Maggie."

"Sam Maggie?"

His brain was scrambled and he tried to shake his head. "Mc . . . MacRaney."

"Sam MacRaney?"

Jackson swallowed in place of a nod. "Let her know."

"I'll see if she's on duty tonight."

"Till . . . till ten-th . . . thirty or . . ."

The nurse patted his wrist. "As soon as you're under, I'll track her down, all right?"

Jackson exhaled and relaxed. She replaced the oxygen mask and resumed the check of his vitals. He counted the seconds until general anesthesia.

*   *   *

Friday, September 28
9:31 a.m.

JACKSON WAS asleep on his couch when the door opened. Well, not really asleep. More like comatose, his eyes blinded from staring at the TV most of the night. He'd been watching an old John Wayne Western last he knew, laughing at how fake and cheap the violence was. Now it was a modern Western, a remake of a classic, and the violence was ramped up for the sake of violence. It was still a joke.

A shadow eclipsed the TV. It remained in place for a moment, then took form as it placed two containers onto the coffee table.

"What are you doing, J?" Reggie Cameron asked.

Jackson looked up at his best friend. "What are you doing here?"

"I brought you some breakfast," he said, nodding at the containers on the table. Styrofoam leftover boxes. The smell was nauseating.

"Thanks, but I'm not hungry."

"Been four days since you got back from Las Vegas, J. Thought I'd have heard something from you."

Jackson nodded.

"What with your having been accused of every crime short of treason and telling me you were going to James Bond your way out of things. I thought I might have gotten a call to let me know you were still living."

"That's debatable. And your intel is wrong. I was accused of treason too."

"So what happened?"

Jackson met Reggie's mahogany eyes for the first time. Only for a moment, then he broke away. "I got off."

Reggie sat his former football player's body down on the coffee table, causing it to groan. But it held. He sat there for several minutes, waiting until Jackson looked his way.

"Look, man, you and I've been through some stuff together. We've both been to rock bottom, and we've compared scars. Ain't nothing you can't tell me, J."

Jackson mashed his lips together, rolling his head to the side.

Reggie got up and walked into the kitchen. He returned with two forks. He clanked one onto the table beside the boxes, one of which he picked up. He sat down in Jackson's recliner and began to eat.

"You talk to your grandpa?" he asked a few bites later.

"No."

"Sam?"

Jackson laughed a laugh that turned into a sob.

The chair creaked. Reggie set down his open food container and sat again on the edge of the coffee table. "Remember when we met, J?"

Jackson nodded.

"You know how I looked all clean?" he said, stroking his well-manicured jawline. "I'd just shaved, hacking off the nastiest, *Duck Dynasty*-style beard you ever saw. Full-on Brett Keisel. I grew it because I literally could not look in the mirror after what we did." He looked out the window, toward the distant Pacific, obscured by morning haze. "Me and Keisha killed my baby, man. An innocent, defenseless person that we brought into this world, and we killed it for convenience." Now he pursed his lips. "There ain't nothing more evil than that, J."

He had Jackson's attention, his eyes damp. Very softly, he said, "Tell me what happened. If there's one person on this earth who can take it, who won't judge you for anything, it's me."

Jackson's lip trembled as he fought the tears that trickled from his eye. He couldn't stop them, and couldn't avoid breaking down into a long, messy cry. Reggie placed a hand on his shoulder, letting him get it out, waiting. Finally, his throat sore and his ducts dry, Jackson sat up. He was lightheaded, nauseous, weak. He wiped the last trace of tears and snot on his arm and sleeve. It didn't matter, it was the same shirt he'd worn for two days.

"I killed twenty people, Reggie. Murdered. Slaughtered. Massacred. I—I tortured . . ." He broke down again, finding a new wave of tears, doubled over on his knees. The big man placed two hands on his shoulders, his head bent low over Jackson's. After several minutes, Jackson realized he was talking. He sniffed away tears, trying to comprehend the whispered words.

Reggie was praying. It wasn't a great piece of oration, wasn't even coherent at times. Just phrases and words. Mostly, "Jesus," and, "Help."

After several more minutes, Jackson moved to sit up, and Reggie leaned back. He cupped both of Jackson's cheeks in his large hands, looking intently at him. "J, I know enough psychology not to force you to talk if you're not ready, but . . . this is going to eat at you, man. You need to get it off your chest sooner than later."

Jackson nodded, wiped his face on his sleeve again.

A shootout on the TV suddenly raised the volume, and he found the remote and silenced it. Then he walked Reggie through the previous two weeks.

He had been hired by Hillary McKenzie, his late brother's fiancée, to find a Las Vegas prostitute named Arielle Coal. Hillary claimed she was an important witness in a court case she was appealing. But after finding Arielle dead, Jackson discovered Hillary's true motives were to find what connection Arielle had to her father, Warren. Their pursuit of the truth led them to a massive conspiracy between Senator Carson Moore, Army General Ernest Reynolds, and Las Vegas resort mogul Richard Holloway.

They had gone undercover at Oasis Las Vegas, Holloway's resort hotel and casino on the Strip, in an effort to learn more about the conspiracy and how Warren was involved. They found ties to Kingman, a dot-on-the-map town north of Las Vegas, and a decommissioned Air Force base nearby. The deeper they delved, the more sinister the plot became. A thought-to-be-retired military project called Silver Dawn had been resurrected by Moore and Reynolds under the name Golden Dawn, its goal to study the effects of mind-control and genetics experiments conducted in the 1980s. Jackson and Hillary discovered that she had been born out of the project, and shortly after that revelation, she disappeared.

Jackson had tracked Hillary to the old base, which was being used by members of the Golden Dawn project. He infiltrated the base and rescued Hillary, only to have her airlifted from him by mercenaries posing as Army soldiers. He tracked her down again, to a houseboat on Lake Mead, where he again saved her in the nick of time. Along the way, he killed roughly twenty participants in Golden Dawn—members of a militia group named RASER and rogue CIA operatives—took a corrupt local sheriff as his prisoner, tortured him, and stormed the home of Senator More, taking his wife and staff hostage and threatening them with torture if Moore didn't confess and give him the information he needed.

When he recounted sticking a gun into the knee of Moore's innocent wife, he had to push himself up and run to the bathroom, where he emptied what contents there were in his stomach. He returned to the living room and flopped back onto the couch. He exhaled.

"I'm sorry, J. I'm sorry you had to go through that."

"The killings were justified, they tell me. And Moore's wife turned on her husband and refused to press charges. In the eyes of the law, I'm clean." He explained the terms of the deal granted by the DOD, DOJ, Air Force, and other parties that had convened the previous weekend in Las Vegas. Along with probation and the suspension of his private investigator's license, he was still subject to prosecution if further developments indicated his and Hillary's stories weren't entirely truthful.

"How's Hillary?" Reggie asked.

"I don't know. She was coping when I dropped her off Monday."

Reggie nodded.

"You want to know the worst part? It came easy. I mean, I wasn't even thinking. I was just acting and reacting, and when it's done, twenty people are dead. What kind of . . . What kind of person does that?"

"Jack, you were in an impossible situation. You did what you had to do."

"I know. I know I was acting to save Hillary's life. But I still killed all those people. I still beat the truth out of Quinn. I still put a gun to Margaret Moore's knee, and so help me, Reg, I was this close to pulling that trigger to get Moore to tell me where Hillary was."

Reggie looked down.

"How can I put that behind me?" He stood and paced, needing to expend some nervous energy. "How am I ever supposed to look in the mirror again? Look at my grandpa again? Look at . . . Sam again? I can barely look at you."

Reggie stood as well. "We're your friends, J. Your family. We're not going to judge you."

"How can you not? I'm judging myself!"

"Look, man, I can't imagine what you're going through. But these guys made the choice to be part of something evil, made the choice to kidnap Hillary. And they were trying to kill you right back."

"Margaret Moore wasn't. Her terrified housekeeper wasn't. Her bodyguard and Moore's protective detail weren't. I went full Bauer on everybody, Reggie, and I mean last few seasons, indiscriminately angry Bauer. I was a man without a conscience."

Reggie shook his head. "From where I sit, J, you're clearly not without a conscience." He leaned forward. "Look, I'm not going to write you a pardon for everything you did. But I know Someone who did. And no, you can't undo what happened. But I also know it doesn't define you. And I firmly believe you did what you had to do. I know you, J. If there was any other alternative—any!—you would have taken it."

"I know, I know. I keep telling myself I did what I had to do, that I didn't have a choice. But it doesn't make it any easier."

"No, I don't suppose it does," he said as Jackson dropped back onto the couch. Reggie ran his hand over his head and across his face. Then he sat beside Jackson. "Listen to me, J. You don't have to go through this alone. You don't have to go through anything alone, man. I'm here for you no matter what, you got that?"

"Yeah. And I'm sorry, I should have kept you in the loop. Things were just spiraling so quick and when I got back . . ." He looked up. "I haven't slept since I got home, Reg. I'm exhausted but I can't sleep. I'm starving but I can't eat. I don't know how to go on and I don't know if I want to."

Reggie placed his hand on Jackson's back.

"It was bad enough when Mom, Dad, and Grant died. Then Ryan. Now this. My life's just one train wreck after another."

"As someone who's been in a multi-car pileup, man, it doesn't stay that way. You made progress after the accident. You made progress after Ryan. You'll make progress after this. I know it's pitch black right now, J. But it won't stay that way, I promise."

Jackson shook his head. "You can only get up from a haymaker so many times. I fight and claw to make the least little progress, and then here comes another roundhouse. I'm losing the will to fight."

"That's where Angie comes in."

"Who?"

"Angelo Dundee. Ali's corner man. I'll pick you up, J. Every single time."

Jackson made eye contact with his pal and nodded.

Reggie cupped the back of Jackson's neck and squeezed. He withdrew his hand. "So what are you going to do for work?"

Jackson shrugged. "For now, nothing. Hillary won fifty grand in a poker game, so we split that."

"Hold on, J. Fifty grand?"

"Yeah. Well, forty really. Ten was hers. And not so much hers as a dead hooker's. And we had some expenses to take care of. But I cleared sixteen and change."

Reggie whistled. "Where is it?"

"In the safe in my closet."

"Are you for real?"

Jackson nodded.

"Well if you decide to put that away for a rainy day, you can work for me."

Jackson huffed. "Doing what?"

Reggie shrugged. "Security."

"Security?"

"Of sorts. Crowd control. Bouncer. Call it what you like."

"Sounds like charity."

Reggie shook his head. "On the weekends, private parties, it can get pretty rowdy sometimes. I could use an inside man."

"Right, an inside man who'll go to jail if he so much as asks a couple of drunks to take it outside."

Reggie shrugged. "It's an offer, man. If you need it."

"Thanks."

Reggie clapped his back again. "I hafta get going. You should get up, do something. Take a shower, for starters."

"Yeah."

"Voice of experience: Don't sit and wallow. Mow your lawn. Give Maggie a call."

"Haven't you heard, we're on the outs?"

34

"What?"

"Yeah. Apparently my prudish Christianity has morphed into bigotry."

"What are you talking about?"

"We were at a Dodger game on Labor Day, and she ambushed me about our lack of a future since she's not a Christian. It all seemed to stem from a conversation we had a few weeks back. Anyhow, now she won't return my calls, and I tried to stop in before I went to Vegas with Hillary. She wasn't there or wouldn't open the door if she was. I'm apparently off her friend list."

"Give her time, man."

"Yeah, time for her to see what a wonderful example of Christian behavior I've been."

Reggie stood. "Keep your chin up, J."

"Right. Give the other guy a good target."

Reggie extended his hand, and Jackson slapped it, clasping tight. "Thanks, Hoss."

"You need anything, you call."

"I will."

"Anything."

"I will. Thanks."

He sat on the couch as Reggie let himself out. Then, before what little willpower he had drained away, he stood up. He forced his legs to trudge up the stairs to take a shower and attempt to look into the mirror long enough to shave.

*   *   *

Monday, December 31
10:55 p.m.

JACKSON WAS vaguely aware he was in another room. What was this, three or four now? And he was immobile. And possibly naked under a bed sheet. He remembered them cutting his shirt off, but couldn't for the life of him recall when.

The pain in his shoulder was throbbing again, and he felt something in his arm. Just the IV? The onset of partial paralysis? Acute myocardial infarction?

The nurse with the dark-tinged blond hair had said something about a subclavian artery being nicked. Where was the subclavian artery? It sounded

Roman, brought to mind aqueducts and nasty strap sandals and a dagger in Russell Crowe's back . . .

Probably under the clavicle, seeing as that's where you got shot, chief.

"Mr. Douglas," a dainty male voice called out. He flicked his eyes to see a narrow, stern face. Was it connected to the good hands of Dr. Nelson? "We're going to begin now."

The stern face nodded, and a mask was placed over Jackson's face from behind.

"Please count down from one hundred," a female voice said.

"One hundred," Jackson said in little more than a whisper. "Ninety-nine, ninety-eight . . . ninety-seven . . . ninety . . ."

Chapter Six

Tuesday, January 1, 2013
1:51 a.m.

LIFE WAS SOMETHING of a haze. Jackson distinctly remembered the number ninety-eight, and a pretty face looking down on him. And a pair of glasses, but not on the pretty face. He also remembered Trent's chuckle, and still wasn't sure where his paramedic friend had gone.

The questions just kept flowing. Had somebody located Sam yet? And why did he get the feeling someone else had dressed him? And when were they going to start his surgery? Hadn't somebody said something about nicking an artery or a clavicle or something?

At least his shoulder didn't hurt anymore. Or was a painful shoulder part of the dream too?

Jackson's eyelids felt like the windows in his house, most of which had to be propped up. No matter how hard he tried to keep his eyes open, all he saw was murky darkness. Then it hit him. His eyes were open, the room was just dark. Duh.

Two more observations penetrated the fog around his brain. He was madly thirsty, and something kept beeping. He tried to look around, but his head felt like a rock. So he cast his eyes to the side. So that was it—he wasn't dressed at all. At least not from the waist up. Except for the padding over his left shoulder. Rats. He had been shot. That wasn't a dream. That meant the pain had been real. And would be coming back.

Jackson tried to open his mouth, but all he got was sticky dryness. How was that for an oxymoron?

"Hey, man, you awake?"

Jackson turned his eyes to the side and saw darkness distinguish itself from other darkness. The shadow turned into the Incredible Hulk, and then Reggie.

Jackson licked his lips. Nothing happened. "Water."

Reggie nodded and reached for a cup. "Ice chips. All they'll give you for now."

Jackson sucked on the chips for a moment. "Can you squeeze my IV then?"

"How you feeling, man?"

"Hole-ier than thou."

Reggie smiled. "You've got your humor, at least."

"I don't know. I can't tell if that was funny or not."

"Not really."

Jackson tried to raise himself up onto the bed, already at an angle. Movement wasn't easy. "I already have the surgery?"

"Yeah. The doc said it wasn't too bad. They originally thought the bullet had hit an artery, but it just missed. You got lucky."

"Yeah, I feel lucky. How long was I under?"

"Not long. You just got out of recovery a few minutes ago."

Jackson was processing Reggie's statements in snippets. "So am I good then?"

"You will be. Man, you remember what happened?"

"I got shot."

"Beyond that, bro."

Jackson reached for the ice chips, and Reggie spooned a few more into his mouth.

"Where's Sam?"

"In the waiting room. Your grandpa too. We didn't know how long you'd be out, so I drew the first watch."

"We . . . We had a . . . a date."

"You want me to get her?"

Jackson took several deep breaths. "No . . . No, I'm not decent."

"It's a hospital, man. Nobody's ever decent."

Jackson looked for a clock, saw none. "Is it still nighttime?"

"Not quite two a.m."

"Good. I'm bushed."

"Yeah, get some sleep. We'll be here when you wake up."

Jackson ceased holding his eyes open, bringing incredible relief. He was out before they closed.

*   *   *

Tuesday, October 9
8:24 a.m.

JACKSON SLOWLY got to his feet and shook the cobwebs. He'd never been hungover, but he wondered if it felt similar to waking up on half a night's sleep. Sixteen large in his safe, and here he was being a bouncer/chaperone/security guard/concierge for Reggie.

Last night had been bad. A dozen rugby players and their dates. They had closed down the bar, then moved to the upstairs banquet room for a private party. They drank some more, told filthy jokes, and made lewd advances on their women. Collective. There were about as many as the men, and Jackson wasn't sure who belonged to whom or if they were all channeling the '60s. He had been tasked with keeping an eye on the debauched group, making sure they didn't trash the place or decide to start a wrestling match in the parking lot at two a.m. or get behind the wheel after their binge. (Not that he could have stopped them from anything by force.) He had finally gone to sleep on the sofa in Reggie's basement office at close to three, mentally drafting his resignation and expecting to see sulfur raining down from heaven when he woke.

Jackson availed himself of Reggie's shower, then headed into the downstairs dining room. Part of his compensation was food and drink on the house before or after a shift. This still counted as after, he concluded. Katie, the head waitress and assistant manager, shot him a lopsided look when he walked in. With long blond hair and a bright smile, Katie was cute in a girl next door sort of way, and Jackson was glad he'd taken the time to shower. Shaving might have been a good idea too. He'd hacked off almost two weeks' worth of beard a few days ago, but the stubble was fast turning into a reprise.

"Bad night?" Katie asked.

"Don't ever date a rugby player."

"No?"

"The highlight of the evening was when I had to ask Brad—some springbok with a mohawk and a devil tattooed on his neck—to kindly not pee in the potted plants."

"Eww."

Jackson frowned. "No, actually the real high spot was having to repeat the request to his girlfriend ten minutes later."

Katie winced. "You want some breakfast?"

"No, just coffee. Hot. Black. Strong."

"Have a seat."

Katie returned a minute later with his coffee and, taking a look around, slid into the booth opposite him. "Want to take a guess on the bar tab?"

Jackson sipped the coffee. Piping hot, indeed. And strong.

"You're not the only one who likes it to kick in the morning," she said.

Jackson swallowed. "A grand?"

"Higher."

"Two?"

"Higher."

"You're kidding."

"Twenty-four hundred."

Jackson whistled. "Quite the celebration."

"I haven't told Reggie yet."

"I take it he's not in?"

"Not till noon."

Jackson nodded.

Katie reached out a hand, a purely friendly gesture. "You okay?"

"After a few more cups I will be."

"No, I mean . . . I heard what happened on the news. I can't imagine . . . Anyhow, you've seemed a little down lately. I wanted to see how you're doing."

Jackson took a long pull on the coffee, burning his throat. "Thanks. And I'm okay, considering."

"Really?"

He nodded, unable to muster the conviction to lie again. He was still working on his casual, polite "I'm okay" brush-off. It was getting a lot of play.

"I should get back to work."

"Thanks, Katie."

Jackson finished his coffee and hit the beach. He hoped a walk would energize his sluggish body and the fresh air would clear his head. If nothing else, it would help rid his nostrils of the pervading stench of expired (and recycled) alcohol. Not even a shower had managed it so far.

The sky overhead was cloudy, turning the normally brilliant Pacific a matching shade of gray. It muted everything and, combined with the cool air, kept the crowds off Santa Monica Beach. Which was fine with Jackson. Random people weren't his thing right now.

He had nowhere to be—no steady job, no work as a private investigator without a license, and no more work for Reggie anytime in the immediate future, as weeknights without rugby parties tended to be rather tame. Jackson walked without paying attention, his mind still on the events of a few weeks prior in Nevada. Somewhere, he'd definitely crossed a line. He just wasn't sure exactly where, or what he could have done to avoid crossing it.

The beach got a little busier as Jackson neared the Santa Monica Pier. It reminded him of Sam. And Maggie. He'd been there with each of them, memories that stood out like beacons in a sea of black. Beacons that weren't blinking anymore.

Jackson sidestepped a pair of mimes, not performing, but out for a morning stroll, talking and laughing. Wasn't that against the mime handbook, talking while in costume?

"Hey, watch it!"

Jackson turned over his shoulder and offered an apology to a young woman—a girl really—whose shoulder he had bumped. Blame the mimes.

"What's the matter with you?" she asked, throwing in an obscenity for good measure.

Jackson nearly kept walking. She wasn't the first brat to get irate because she'd been bumped in a crowd. But something—lack of sleep, the rugby players and their poor manners, his general bad mood—made him stop. He turned around, arms out. "I said I was sorry, all right? I hope your shoulder makes a full recovery."

The girl seethed. Her face was handsome—technically good-looking, but like so many supposedly "hot" starlets or actresses in L.A., this girl appeared to be trying too hard: a lot of makeup, dark brown hair that was over-styled, and a face a little too hard. Instead of sculpted, it looked chiseled out of marble. Speaking of marble, her eyes were gray and ominous. By comparison, the sky overhead was bright and cheery.

"How dare you!" she spat back. "And you made me spill my latte."

Jackson glanced at her loose, layered blouse and short skirt. Neither had any apparent stains. There was however a small puddle on the sidewalk, next to her stilettos. He also took notice, for the first time, of the guy who had stopped walking along with her. He was a few inches shorter than Jackson, surfer hair, a polo shirt over khaki shorts, flip-flops. If this got ugly, Jackson was not scared.

"Look, princess," he said, "I get that you're out a few sips of coffee. Life has thrown you a nasty slider. Have a pout, get some therapy, or cowboy up."

The girl huffed, her honor deeply insulted. "Shawn Thomas, are you going to let him talk to me like that?"

"Come on, Jess. It was just an accident."

She huffed again, then swore under her breath.

"Sorry, dude," Shawn Thomas said. "No hard feelings?"

"You're apologizing to him?" Jess exploded. "He's the moron who ran me over!"

Jackson again thought about turning and walking away. And he probably should have. But he was in the mood for a fight. "You're the one who can't walk and drink coffee at the same time," he said.

Her eyes took intensity to a new level. And if Jackson wasn't mistaken, Shawn Thomas swallowed a smile.

"You know what," she said, reaching for her purse. She came out with a phone. "Maybe I'll just put your face on Twitter and tell the world what you did."

"Oh no," Jackson said with mock alarm. "My image tarnished to all of those thirteen-year-old girls."

"Shows what you know. I have over ten thousand followers."

"So everyone you've ever been a jerk to in your life, is that it?"

Shawn Thomas had gone from hiding a smirk to staring to musing in Jackson's direction.

"Let's go, Shawn Thomas."

"Hold on a sec."

She sighed, practically stamped her stiletto-strapped foot. "What?"

"You mind if I ask what you do for a living?" Shawn Thomas said, still staring at Jackson oddly.

Jackson took a breath. "I'm sort of between jobs."

"Figures," Jess said, eyes down at her phone.

"You fight? You know, boxing, MMA, anything like that?"

Jackson shook his head. "Not unless I have to."

"You ever do any acting?"

Jackson chuckled. "Seriously?" He glanced over both shoulders. "This some kind of con or *Punk'd* spoof, because, really, I am not in the mood."

"No, man, I'm serious," Shawn Thomas said. "Really."

"About what?" Jess whined.

He finally took his eyes away from Jackson to look at her. "We need a Grayson."

"What? No, you're not . . . No."

Shawn Thomas extended a hand. Jackson shook it warily.

"Shawn Thomas Aaron," he said. "This is Jess Leigh. We're sorry about the mix-up."

"Forget it," Jackson said, soothed by Shawn Thomas's amiability. And strangeness. "Jackson Douglas," he answered.

"Thank you," Jess said with a smirk as she thumbed in a few more words on her phone.

"Come on, Jess. Let it go." He turned back to Jackson. "We're both shooting on the set of *Twenty Something* here in Santa Monica. And we're actually looking for a replacement for a bit part."

Jackson shook his head. "What's that got to do with me?"

"Slow and clumsy," Jess muttered. "He wants you for the part, stupid."

"Me?"

Shawn Thomas nodded.

Now Jackson was too curious to walk away. "Why?"

"It's a little complicated, but you fit the part. Call it divine inspiration."

Jess huffed again. "You've never been inspired in your life."

"We're shooting up at Palisades Park this morning, and then we've got some stuff around town this afternoon. Come meet V, see what he says."

"He'll say you're an idiot, Shawn Thomas."

"Come on. He does stuff like this all the time, Jess."

"That's because he's V."

"We need to shoot today, we need a Grayson. Let's just see what he says."

"Who is V?" Jackson asked.

"Viggo Polansky. He's the director. I'm sure you've heard of him."

Jess huffed. "You don't bring him to the director, idiot. He'd have to go through Casting first."

Shawn Thomas shrugged. "We're in a time crunch. V can make the decision."

Viggo Polansky. The name sounded vaguely familiar, but Jackson was still wondering if this was some sort of a setup or trick. Only he couldn't figure out what their angle would be. Still, he wasn't in the mood for acting. "No thanks. I'm flattered, but it's not my thing."

"It'll pay like five hundred bucks for an afternoon."

"Think how much weed you could buy with that," Jess said.

"What's the scene?"

Jess smirked again. Shawn Thomas nodded at her. "Her character gets attacked by some crazy ex. It's three lines, a quick choreographed fight, and then I take you out."

"You?"

"I'm sort of the hero."

Jess rolled her eyes.

Jackson thought about it. Five hundred bucks, plus a distraction for an afternoon. And he got to attack Jess's character. Who would fault him, a novice, if he failed to pull a punch?

"Okay, on one condition."

"Name it."

"You're both actors, right?"

"Yeah."

"Give me the filmography."

Shawn Thomas eyed him for a minute. "You ever seen *Crash Course?*"

"Why would he have?" Jess replied. "Nobody else has."

Jackson shook his head.

"Three freshmen from Berkeley end up in the Navy," Shawn Thomas said. "I was Dane, the party animal, always looking for some blow."

"Sorry."

He shrugged. "I was also in *Irish Suck, Out All Night, Scarlet, How High?*"

"All a bunch of frat boy movies," Jess said, her eyes back in her phone.

"*Irish Suck* was a vampire movie."

"Yeah, frat boy vampires."

None of the movies rang a bell, but then again, Jackson didn't watch a lot of frat boy movies.

"I was also on an episode of *CSI.*"

"The original?"

Shawn Thomas nodded.

"You guys are shooting in Palisades Park?"

"Yeah, right across from the Hotel Oceana."

Jackson knew of it. He nodded at Shawn Thomas. "You know where Cameron's is, up the beach a little ways?"

"Yeah, I've seen it."

"Meet me there, say twenty minutes."

Jess huffed.

"I'll go see this guy V with you."

"All right." Shawn Thomas extended his hand and Jackson shook it again. Jess merely shook her head in contempt and followed him down the sidewalk. Mini-skirt and stiletto heels for a walk along the beach, albeit on the sidewalk.

Either she was in costume or one of those people who didn't get situational dressing. Jackson leaned toward the latter.

As soon as they were out of earshot, he reached for his phone. Mouse, his tech wizard and online research "assistant," answered on the fourth ring. "Yeah?"

"Hey, Mouse."

"Dude, what's up? Haven't heard from you."

"Been working on a low profile. You got a minute?"

Jackson heard a few agonizing death screams, likely aliens melting in front of a phaser gun on some video game. Then Mouse said, "Sure."

"Can you Google a guy for me? Shawn Thomas Aaron."

"The actor?"

"You know him?"

"I've heard of him. What do you want to know?"

"Filmography."

"Sure. What's up?"

"It's kind of a long story."

"No problem. You at the beach?"

"Yeah."

"Any dolls?"

"Only one, and she was cold as ice."

"Okay . . . You want these in any particular order?"

"Just hit some of the main ones."

"Um . . . *Crash Course*, *Scarlet*, a *CSI*, *Irish Su*—"

"That's good enough. What's he look like?"

"I don't know, good, I guess. Brown hair, kind of messy on purpose."

That could be Shawn Thomas. Or half the male population of L.A. "Thanks, Mouse."

"You want to tell me what's going on?"

"Maybe later. One more thing. You ever heard of a Viggo Polansky?"

"Of course. He directed *Plasma Ridge*, one of the *Transformers* I think. Maybe not. A couple of teen dramas. He's pretty well-known, in the circle."

Jackson nodded. "Thanks, Mouse. I'll fill you in later."

"All right, dude."

Jackson closed his phone and sighed. He should have just kept walking. Should have broken his promise and gone home. But his car was at Cameron's anyhow. And something was telling him there was more to this than just a chance meeting.

So with another sigh, he tucked his phone back into his pocket and started after Shawn Thomas and Jess.

Chapter Seven

10:18 a.m.

ALL PRIVATE INVESTIGATORS—real ones Jackson knew and fictional ones on TV and in the movies—had little voices and gut instincts. They warned them when they were in danger, gave them hunches to follow certain clues, and told them when encounters were more than just random events. Jackson didn't believe in Fate or Luck or Chance, not as entities anyhow. He did believe that God could impersonate a little voice or a gut instinct, but wasn't ready to chalk up every hunch or whim to the Almighty. So as he strolled back toward Cameron's, the ocean on his left and the rising bluffs on his right, he tried to makes sense of the feeling that there was something to his bumping into Shawn Thomas and Jess.

Then he tried to figure out some way they could be messing with him. Two actors out for a stroll, run into a guy on the beach and think he's perfect for some bit part, and invite him to come meet the director. Did that really happen? The term "big break" did have to come from somewhere.

Jackson also considered the possibility that he went with Shawn Thomas and Jess, they weren't pulling his leg, he actually met this Viggo Polansky character, and Viggo told him to get lost. What did it matter? All he'd be out was a few hours of another meaningless day. And some defamation on a B-lister's Twitter feed.

He almost missed the rugby players.

"You're back," Katie said when Jackson arrived in the front entry of Cameron's.

"I'm back. You happen to see a frat boy and a diva around?"

"They're downstairs. Friends of yours?"

"Ish. Thanks."

Jackson found them at the bar, arguing about whether or not Jess could have a drink. "Relax, Shawn Thomas. I'm not in a scene until this afternoon."

"Hey, Douglas," Shawn Thomas called with a wave. "I wasn't sure you'd come."

"I checked you guys out first."

"Checked us out?"

Esteban, the bartender, wandered over. "Coffee," Jackson said. "Very black."

"Make it two," Shawn Thomas said. "Two creams, two sugars. Jess?"

"Forget it."

Esteban disappeared and Shawn Thomas turned on his stool to face Jackson. "You in?"

"Yeah."

"Great."

"He still has to pass V's eye test," Jess said.

"Come on, Jess. He's perfect for the part."

"You said that before," Jackson said. "What are you talking about?"

Shawn Thomas looked around to make sure no one was eavesdropping. Aside from Esteban who slid two mugs of coffee to them and then went back about his business, the trio was alone. "We had a guy, some bit actor, playing the role of Grayson. He's an old boyfriend of Cate's or something, who—"

"Cate?"

Without looking up, Jess raised her hand, clanging several bangles together.

"Jess's character. He showed up a few episodes ago, sort of threatened her, and she told him to get lost. Now he shows up again and attacks her before I save the day. We shot the first scene on the beach back in August, and then about a week ago, this actor comes down with mono or something. He's out, and now we need somebody to play the last scene as Grayson, for the attack in her room. And you, my friend, look enough like Grayson to pull it off."

"Enough like? Don't I pretty much need to be a ringer?"

"The first scene, on the beach, was at night, low light, shadowy on purpose. Never gave the audience a real good look at his face. We could just shoot it again with some other Grayson, but then we have to get the beach again at night, get the permits, all that crap. And we'd still need an actor to play the role."

"Key word being 'actor,'" Jess muttered.

Jackson tested his coffee. Black and hot. "She's got a point," he said. "I'm not an actor."

Shawn Thomas shrugged. "It's a couple lines. Piece of cake."

"Fair enough." He took another pull on the coffee. "So what's the plot of this *Twenty Something*?"

"It's about a group of millennials—twenty of them, originally—who are summoned by some unknown benefactor to L.A. They arrive but he never shows, so most of them split. A handful of us stay there and try to figure out who this guy is and why he summoned us in the first place."

Jackson nodded.

"That's the gist of it, anyhow. There's a lot of subplots, character development, romance." He put an arm around Jess.

She huffed.

Jackson had some more coffee. Shawn Thomas drank his as well.

"So if you're shooting in Palisades Park today, why are the two of you strolling on the beach?"

"Noelle's got a big scene this morning," Shawn Thomas said. "The episode's heavy on her character and Mario's. Kind of light for us, actually."

"So you're just killing time?"

"More or less." He shrugged. "We're shooting as much of it as we can on site, and I wanted to take in Santa Monica. Honing my craft, you know?"

"Your craft," Jess said with a laugh. "You're a once-cute face on a square body."

"And you're what, Aubrey Hepburn?"

Jess slammed down her phone. "It's Audrey Hepburn, you dimwit. And can we just get this over with?"

"You ready?" Shawn Thomas asked.

Jackson nodded, and the trio set out. Just a little ways up the beach from Cameron's, a pedestrian walkway crossed the Pacific Coast Highway and the California Incline. From there, a walking path led them up the side of the cliff to Palisades Park. Perched on a bluff at the western edge of Santa Monica, the palm-dotted park offered magnificent views of the ocean. At least, on days when the ocean and sky weren't complementary shades of gray.

Halfway up the hill, Jess began to complain about her shoes. Jackson kept comments about wearing stilettos to himself. Shawn Thomas continued to clop along in his flip-flops. Jackson sort of liked the guy. He seemed like a normal dude, not full of himself, no superiority complex. And, Jackson guessed, he played himself in most movies: messy hair, slacker attitude, beer and babes, a few punch lines here and there.

When they reached the top of the cliffs, Shawn Thomas was winded, Jess was barefoot and complaining, and Jackson was quadruple-guessing his decision. An actor, really?

"Over there." Shawn Thomas pointed, past a small pavilion to a tent erected beneath the palm trees. Jackson scanned the park, from the tent along Ocean Avenue to the edge of the cliffs. A walking trail and a wooden fence ran along the top of the bluffs. Sitting at a bench next to the trail was a small blond girl in black leather and a guy in a suit. They were surrounded by a dozen other people holding cameras, microphones, and scripts. Jackson had seen movie and TV shoots before—they were everywhere in Los Angeles. They had just never evoked nerves in him.

Shawn Thomas led the way across the grass to a tent where several other people were milling about. He grabbed a donut off a table, along with a bottle of water, and nodded for Jackson to do the same. He took a water.

"Shawn Thomas, leave my name out of this," Jess said. After complaining about the temperature of the bottled water, she stalked off.

"Don't worry about her," Shawn Thomas said, biting off a hunk of his donut. He chewed twice and gulped it down. "She's busy being the queen of Jess-Land."

Jackson shrugged.

"There's V," Shawn Thomas said, pointing with his donut. Jackson turned his head, and couldn't help but expect to see a Guy Fawkes mask. Else maybe Ed Harris' character from *The Truman Show*. Way off, in both cases.

Viggo Polansky was tall, over six feet, and heavy. Not fat, just thick. He had white hair, both in the ponytail that hung halfway down his back and on the very long, full goatee that obscured his chin. His eyes were dark and deep set, surrounded by bags that made him look like a raccoon. (Or Jess about three a.m. on a Sunday, if Jackson had to guess.) He wore cut-off khaki shorts and a baggy brown T-shirt, and had a pair of headphones around his neck.

"Didn't I see him on *WrestleMania*?" Jackson asked.

"Distinctly possible."

Shawn Thomas waved, and Viggo sauntered over. He reached for a Diet Coke and unscrewed the top before acknowledging one of his stars. "Mr. Aaron. How was your stroll along the beach with Miss Leigh?" He spoke with a trace of a British accent, accompanying the deep baritone of a man his size. It was a voice that belonged behind a lectern, or maybe reading audio books.

"Enlightening, Mr. P," Shawn Thomas answered with a smile.

Viggo frowned at the nickname as he took a swig of his soda.

"I'd like you to meet Jackson Douglas," Shawn Thomas said.

Viggo extended his hand. "Mr. Douglas, a pleasure."

"Same here."

Viggo turned back to Shawn Thomas. "Mr. Aaron, you know the rules. I assume this is either a close family member or your new agent."

"Actually, sir, he's your next Grayson."

"Ah, so you're in the Casting Department now, are you?"

"He looks enough like him that we won't have to reshoot at the beach and I think the guy's a natural."

"So he's not an actor?"

"No."

Viggo nodded. Turned to Jackson. "Mr. Douglas, I'm not sure what our intrepid young actor has told you, but we aren't generally in the habit of hiring people off the street."

Jackson shrugged.

Viggo crossed his arms, eyeing Jackson through slits. "However, in this case, we are somewhat behind the eight ball. And you do bear a rather strong resemblance to Mr. Hewitt." He leaned to the side, catching Jackson at profile. Then he turned over his shoulder, and it was only then that Jackson noticed a kid behind him. Kid in the figurative sense. He was mid-twenties, handsome enough to be an actor, and dressed to embarrass Viggo. He carried a tablet, wore a Bluetooth in his ear, and had the look of a major day trader working on a big score.

"Taylor," Viggo said, "get Andres and see if he can make it work. And check with Maura, see what she thinks. Also, better check with Michael."

"Yes, sir."

Viggo nodded and turned to Shawn Thomas. "What'd Miss Leigh think?"

"That I'm an idiot."

"Well, she's a smart woman. Mr. Douglas, hang with Mr. Aaron here. Try not to absorb too much of his behavior, and if Maura, Michael, and Andres are a go, we'll give you a chance."

Jackson nodded. He waited five minutes with Shawn Thomas, who had another donut in the meantime. The assistant director Maura, the casting director Michael, and the costume designer Andres all looked him over and questioned him. Maura then had the line producer Linda give her opinion too. Lastly, they took half a dozen photos of him to send to the editor, to make sure they could make Jackson look like the original Grayson. They all gave their approval, or something close to it, and Maura left, throwing a, "Now, we'll see if you can act," over her shoulder.

"So you want to walk me through this?" Jackson said to Shawn Thomas. "I've never done any acting."

"None? School plays, community theater?"

"Church Christmas play when I was nine. I was Wise Man Number Three."

"Fabulous."

Jackson turned over his shoulder to see that Jess had returned. Her hair was back in a ponytail, but she was still dressed for a night on the town.

"Acting's simple," Shawn Thomas said. "You've just got to let yourself go. Immerse yourself totally in the role, in the character. Take me, for example. My character, Braylon, is kind of this spoiled rich kid from Boulder. Gets by on good looks and charm." He held out his hands. "I've become Braylon."

"Aside from the good looks and charm," Jess said.

"So based on that model," Jackson said, "I take it Cate is the offspring of House and that lady from *Glee*?"

Her reply was interrupted by Viggo's return. "All right, Mr. Douglas, it seems you have Maura's approval. Now let's see what you've got."

"Well, first, sir, I just have to say I appreciate the opportunity and want to compliment you on your cast and crew. They've been very courteous and helpful. Shawn Thomas here, and especially Miss Leigh."

Shawn Thomas clapped his hands. "That settles it for me."

Jess huffed.

"Thank you, Mr. Aaron, but perhaps we could have him read a few lines anyhow?" Viggo then turned to Jackson. "I thought I told you not to absorb any of his behavior."

"Sorry."

"Do you have a wife, a girlfriend, Mr. Douglas? Particularly a jealous one?"

"No, sir."

"Surprise," Jess mumbled.

"Excellent," Viggo said, clapping his hands. "Instead of reading from a script then, perhaps you could do a little impromptu audition for us all." His voice dropped. "Convince us you have romantic feelings for Miss Leigh."

"So this is science fiction then," Jackson muttered.

"It's up to you, Mr. Douglas. We're in a bind, but not entirely out of options. We can find someone else. And we've got another scene to shoot in about five minutes, so do make your decision promptly."

Jackson took a deep breath. "Jess, I'm sorry. I was out of line. It was a long night, and . . . It's no excuse, but . . ." He swallowed for effect. So far, he had taken Shawn Thomas's advice and decided to genuinely—as genuinely as possible—apologize. Now he had to wing it. "Will you take me back? We can make it work, just give me another chance."

"Is that all you've got?" she asked, hands on her hips.

"You're all I've got," he answered. He took a step forward. "Please, Jess. I need you."

Jess turned to the director. "Really, Viggo? Can't we make him go away?"

"On the contrary, I don't think it was too bad, for a beginner. We only need him for a few lines, and with a little coaching from Caroline, I think it can work. Congratulations, Mr. Douglas."

Jackson nodded his thanks, then smiled widely at Jess as Shawn Thomas clapped him on the back.

Chapter Eight

1:28 p.m.

CAROLINE HAD MISSED her calling. By seventy-five years and a continent. She had the hard features and equally hard edge that would have made her perfect as one of Hitler's paranormal psychologists. Instead, she was Jackson's acting coach.

He rehearsed his lines with her fifteen times, being trained on inflection and timing and speaking clearly and half a dozen other things he forgot. Then he watched raw footage of Grayson's first interaction with Cate. He had showed up on the beach, at night, and threateningly announced that she couldn't run away from him so easily. Jackson tried to copy his voice, style of speaking, mannerisms. After all, he did a killer Vin Scully and a near perfect Hawkeye from *M*A*S*H*. But there wasn't much of Charles "Grayson" Hewitt to imitate, and Caroline assured him they could clean up the discrepancies in editing as long as he was decent. It was the closest thing to encouragement she offered.

During lunch, Shawn Thomas gave him a few pointers while wolfing down a sandwich. Jackson tried to walk through the scene with Jess afterwards, but she said she prepared on her own. Fair enough. He also signed a contract, provided by Linda, after reading it for all of five minutes. A lot of jabber about likenesses and royalties and blah, blah, blah. Whatever. If he got his five hundy he'd be happy.

They whisked him off to Wardrobe, where he traded in his jeans and long-sleeved tee for a different pair of jeans, a plain tee, and a leather jacket. They did what they could with his hair, applied a little makeup, and sent him to Viggo.

The first afternoon shoot was actually in the courtyard of the Hotel Oceana. Viggo Polansky was known for trying to film on location as much as possible, and *Twenty Something* was taking that to a new level. It cost more and could be a major hassle, but it added to the realism. So said Viggo, according to Shawn Thomas.

Viggo was also known for some unusual and creative camera angles and takes. For this scene, he chose to have a camera positioned outside Cate's door. He explained beforehand that since Cate would encounter Grayson in her room in the following scene, having the camera fixed there would serve as foreshadowing of what was to come. As she and Braylon returned from lunch together, Braylon wasn't just leading Cate to her room—he was leading her to the climax of the scene and the "oh, wow" moment of the act. (Viggo chose different language to describe it.)

Jackson was surprised as he watched the scene play out. Since the camera was a hundred feet away from Shawn Thomas and Jess as the take began, it couldn't pick up their words. Those would be dubbed in later, he figured. They still said their lines, so that their mouths would be moving at the right times and to pace themselves. Viggo, Maura, and Caroline all gave tips and pointers as they slowly crossed the courtyard, ascended the steps, and took the catwalk to Cate's room. It took seven takes before Viggo was satisfied, followed by four more takes of their exchange outside her room. It was filmed from inside her room, through the window, for more foreshadowing.

They cut for a break, and Shawn Thomas found Jackson in the crowd. "You ready, man?" he asked. He was, of course, snacking.

"Yeah, I suppose."

"Remember, just be Grayson."

"Yeah, sure."

One of the stunt coordinators walked through the scene with Jackson and Jess, and when Viggo was satisfied, they began shooting. Jackson stood just off camera, a glass of something from the minibar in his hand. The camera was in the back of the hotel room, aimed at the door. A second camera was in the window, ready to shoot at Jackson.

Viggo offered Jackson a quick word of encouragement and then called for places. Jackson took a deep breath and tried to transform himself into Grayson. Being upset with Jess wasn't too hard of a concept to grasp.

"Action."

The door opened, and Jess walked through, a sly grin on her face. The previous scene had concluded with her and Braylon talking about a possible lead in determining the identity of "Mr. X," their unknown benefactor. The conversation had segued to plans to meet at the beach later that afternoon, with a little innuendo thrown in. Hence the grin.

Maura gave Jackson his cue.

"Hello, Cate," he said.

"Cut."

Jackson stopped.

Jess stared at him.

Viggo stepped in. "Mr. Douglas, you need to be threatening. In the last scene, you showed up and told her there would be consequences for running away from you."

Jackson nodded.

"Convey that in, 'Hello, Cate.'"

He nodded again. "What kind of consequences?"

"Excuse me?"

Several in the crew exchanged glances.

"Am I going to kill her, beat her, financially ruin her? Is it just an idle threat? How mad am I?"

Viggo stared at Jackson for a second, his jaw set. Great, he was about to be fired before finishing his first take. Then Viggo smiled. "I miss this kind of devotion to craft." He looked straight at Jackson. "Grayson is violent. He's going to physically assault Cate after slight provocation. And he's stalked her, so we can assume it is not momentary passion. He's smart enough to find a way into her hotel room without her knowledge, so it isn't just uncontrolled rage." Viggo clapped his hands. "Imagine that you are here with the calculated intent of bringing physical harm to Jess. Short of murder, but far more than an idle threat."

Jackson nodded.

"Okay, let's run it again," Viggo said.

The actors and Jackson returned to their places.

"Action."

Jess entered the room again, same sly grin. Maura flashed Jackson his cue again.

"Hello, Cate," he said with something akin to vengeance in his voice. He took a step forward, so that his shoulder and head would be caught by the camera behind him. It was the same first image the viewer would be getting of the previous Grayson on the beach, Viggo had explained while setting up the scene.

"Grayson," Jess said, immediately trembling. "Wh-what are you doing—"

"Who's the stiff?"

"Cut!"

Jackson exhaled.

"Disinterest, Mr. Douglas. You're cutting her off because you couldn't care less about her question. It's all about you and your agenda."

He nodded again.

"And can we do away with 'the stiff?'" Viggo asked. "Who says that? Broderick, tell me we can come up with something better?"

"Loser?" a voice in the distance suggested.

"Loser is more Grayson vocabulary, but no."

"Tool?"

"You're a tool."

"Girlfriend," Jackson suggested. He received several incredulous looks.

"Girlfriend?" Viggo asked.

"I take it Grayson's a tough guy, macho. To him, Braylon's an effeminate sissy. The necklace, polo shirt, frankly not real manly jeans."

Viggo slowly put his hand over his nose and mouth, then slid it down his chin. "Try that. 'Who's your girlfriend?'"

Jackson repeated the line, in his best Grayson voice.

Viggo turned to Jess. "Your response?"

She huffed, either at Jackson's idea and Viggo's acceptance of it or in character. Whatever the reason, Viggo clapped. "You're not getting extra or writing credit," he said with a quick wink at Jackson. Then he notified Broderick of the script change, had everyone take their places, and called, "Action," again.

"Hello, Cate."

"Grayson. Wh-what are you doing—"

"Who's your girlfriend?"

Jess huffed. Gained some courage. Placed her keys on the dresser. "I told you it was over between us."

Jackson spiked his glass into the floor. It was plastic and the floor was actually a pillow, so no harm was done. The clanking of shattering glass could be added later.

"It's over when I say it is!" Jackson bellowed, grabbing Jess by the neck and forcing her into the wall.

"Cut! You're growling, Mr. Douglas."

"Sorry."

"And you're anticipating his attack, Miss Leigh. His blow is to strike you completely off guard. Run it again."

They started again from "the top." When Viggo interrupted this time, it was to inform Jess that she had forgotten to stutter when seeing Grayson. They started over yet again, and this time—the fifth take—was perfect. Viggo called,

"Cut!" with a clap of his hands, and after checking with his camera operator, declared they had the shot.

In the next scene, Braylon heard the sound of struggle, called for Cate, then broke down the door and attacked Grayson. The stunt coordinator again walked the trio through each step in the fight sequence, and they practiced with increasing speed until they had it right. Again, Viggo called for action.

Braylon burst through the door and threw Grayson off Cate. They grappled. Grayson landed one punch, and then the effeminate sissy blocked a second and landed a combo that knocked him back onto the bed, unconscious. It took six takes, at the end of which Jackson was getting winded. Fake fighting was no less stressful than real fighting, and this fight had lasted to the middle rounds.

"Excellent! Well done, Mr. Douglas, Mr. Aaron, Miss Leigh." Viggo clapped several times. "All right, everyone. One more scene and we are off to the beach. Let's go."

Braylon and Cate had a discussion about what had happened and what they should do next and who was that guy I just knocked out and is your eye okay and so on. Jackson lay "unconscious" on the bed through it all. Nine takes worth. And then, as soon as Viggo got the take he wanted, the entire crew packed up and headed out. In five minutes, the Hotel Oceana was deserted, and Jackson was left by himself.

Viggo had congratulated him, Shawn Thomas had said it was a pleasure, and Linda had taken his name and address so they would know where to send his check. And just that quickly, Jackson's acting career was over.

He shrugged mentally. He had killed half a day. And earned "like five hundred bucks." And now he had a story to tell his grandpa.

*   *   *

5:21 p.m.

RAIN PUMMELED the normally tranquil waters of Marina del Rey, where Leroy Douglas's houseboat *Marsha* was anchored. Named for his late wife, the houseboat, along with a black Vespa, had taken the place of Leroy and Marsha's house and his car—a well-maintained Ford Granada that was now Jackson's—after her death. That had been fifteen years ago, when Leroy was still an ordained minister. Now he was retired, and instead of preaching, he just offered his wisdom free of charge to his only living grandson.

Jackson parked at the end of Bora Bora Way at the southwest edge of the harbor. He ignored the rain as he got out and trudged toward the houseboat. Leroy met him at the door, an uncharacteristic baseball cap on his head and a light rain jacket over a T-shirt and jeans.

"You're wet," he said.

"I'll dry."

"I suppose so."

"Sorry it's been a while, Grandpa," Jackson said, stepping out of the rain. "I've been . . ."

"Moping. Yeah, Reggie told me."

"You talked to Reggie?"

"He was worried about you."

"Past tense?"

Leroy waved his hand. "You ready?"

"Yeah."

Leroy reset his cap on his head and trudged along with Jackson back to the car. Having only a Vespa for transportation meant Jackson occasionally played chauffer. Today, it was just back to his place for dinner and a long overdue explanation.

"I'd ask how you've been, but that seems a little trite," Leroy said as they started for Pacific Palisades. Jackson's house, bought out of foreclosure, was up in the hills overlooking the ocean. A steal. And it was only a fifteen-minute drive—on a good day—from Marina del Rey.

"You ever heard of *Twenty Something*?" Jackson asked.

"Isn't that one of those drinking games kids play?"

"It's a cable TV show."

"This one of your crazes?" Leroy asked with a sideways glance.

"Crazes?"

"*Lost*, *24*, the psychic detective, those Fillmore Girls."

"*Gilmore Girls*, and that was seriously like eight episodes over a weekend."

"Um-hmm."

"Anyhow, this is different. It's a new job."

"Come again."

Jackson explained his chance meeting with Shawn Thomas and Jess, and how a near altercation had turned into a bit part on the show. Leroy raised his eyebrows as he removed his cap, revealing graying brown hair. "You're telling me you're now an actor."

"Not anymore. One-time part."

"There a punchline coming here soon?"

"That's what I thought," Jackson said, and walked his grandpa through the day. It brought them back to his house, a small one-bedroom place that he had renovated after buying it a little less than two years ago. Compared to most on his block, it was puny. But there was enough room for him.

"You want something to drink?" he asked when they were inside and out of the rain. If anything, it had intensified on the drive over.

"Nah, I'm good," Leroy said, settling into Jackson's couch. Jackson grabbed a cream soda from the refrigerator and joined his grandfather in the living room.

"What have you been up to?" he asked, popping the top on his can.

"About the same as always," Leroy said. "Fishing, watching the playoffs at Eddie's, reading the newspaper to see if my grandson is alive."

Jackson looked up. "I deserved that one."

"You kind of went off the grid, kiddo."

"I didn't want to scare you."

"Is that it?"

"And I didn't know what to say. 'Hi, Grandpa, I'm a mass murderer'?"

"Not all killing is murder."

"I know. I've had this talk with Hillary and Reggie and myself a hundred times. Still feels about the same."

Leroy nodded. "I had a military vet in my church once, a guy who served in Vietnam and then for twenty years fighting gangs in South Central with LAPD. He said the worse you felt after a killing, the more justified it probably was. His theory was the cold-blooded killer doesn't think twice about his crimes whereas the cop who shoots in self-defense is racked with guilt and second-guessing." He shrugged. "Not sure if he was right, but it sorta makes sense."

"Well then my killings were indeed justified."

"Look, kiddo . . ." Leroy leaned forward. "I know you better than anybody, and I know how your mind works. I especially know how it grieves. You can't beat yourself up over this. The Accuser does enough swinging of his own—you don't need to help him."

"How do you recognize accusations from convictions?"

"Number of ways. Mostly on what they're trying to accomplish. You're not some hardened soul spurning a call to repentance. You're overcome by what happened. Beating you down and shaming you is most definitely the Accuser."

Jackson took a drink of soda.

59

"I don't know all the details of what happened," Leroy said. "I read bits and pieces in the papers or heard 'em secondhand. That's fine, I don't need to know 'em. You want to tell me, I'm happy to listen. But I don't need the gory details to know you've got no reason to condemn yourself."

"How can you say that?"

"Because I've known you for thirty years, Jackson. I know what kind of man you are. And I know you wouldn't have killed those people if you had thought there was any other way to save Hillary."

"But that's just it. There were other ways."

"Like what?"

"Calling the cops, the FBI, the Air Force."

"And why didn't you?"

Jackson sighed. "I didn't know who I could trust—how far up the corruption went. And I didn't think I had time."

Leroy nodded.

"But once I started . . . once I started killing people, I should have stopped."

"And done what?"

"I don't know. I was in too deep and things were happening too fast."

"Like I said, kiddo. You did what you thought was best. And I don't question that for a second."

Jackson sat back. "I just wish I didn't."

Leroy got up and walked toward a framed photograph on the wall, showing the entire Douglas family—Leroy, Marsha, David, Hannah, Jackson, Grant—one Christmas. He stared at it for several moments. "You know, there isn't a day goes by I don't miss your grandmother. First her, then your parents and Grant, now this . . ." He turned around. "Reminds me of Elijah. Thought the whole world was against him. You remember what God told him?"

"That there were still seven thousand who hadn't bowed to Baal."

Leroy nodded. "You know what else He told him?"

Jackson shook his head.

"In simple terms, 'Get back to work.'" Leroy sat back down. "I don't mean that to be cold or unfeeling, and I don't think He did either. But when Elijah was down in the dumps, God's answer was to have him anoint a couple of kings and appoint Elisha as his successor."

"What exactly are you saying, Grandpa?"

"That sometimes the answer to trials and despair is to keep on doing what you're supposed to do. The Bible doesn't say that Elijah went down from the mountain suddenly feeling good about things. But it does say he obeyed and did what God told him."

"So what am I supposed to do?"

"You're sharp. You'll figure it out."

Jackson nodded.

"In the meantime, I was promised a steak."

"It's practically a hurricane," Jackson said, gesturing at his grill on the deck.

"As I recall, you'll dry."

Chapter Nine

JACKSON'S CELL PHONE shrieked from the stand beside his bed. He groaned, rolled over, winced at the light, and fought desperately to hold off the recollections of the previous night at Cameron's. When the founding fathers had come up with the idea of giving people the right to peaceably assemble, they should have made an exception for high school girls. The entire junior and senior female contingent of some nearby high school—Jackson couldn't remember which one—had descended upon Cameron's for some kind of feminist, freshman-bashing, Spirit Week dinner celebration. Jackson was considering quitting his role as whatever it was he did for Reggie.

After getting home at two-thirty in the morning, Jackson should have put his cell on vibrate. But now that he was awake, he reached for his phone in a mad effort to silence it. He succeeded only in knocking it off the nightstand, but not hard enough to break it. It shrieked again, and he reached down for it, nearly tumbling out of bed himself.

"Hello?"

"Mr. Douglas?"

"Yeah."

"This is Taylor Howell, Viggo Polansky's P.A."

Jackson had a sinking feeling in his gut that somehow he wasn't going to get paid.

"Yeah," he repeated.

Taylor cleared his throat. "Mr. Douglas, there's been an amendment to the script of your episode, and Mr. Polansky asks that you make time this morning to shoot one quick scene."

Jackson's initial thought on the request that had sounded less like a request than a demand was to tell Taylor to tell Viggo to forget it. It was also his second thought.

"Forget it."

"Excuse me?"

"No thanks," Jackson said. "I'm retired."

"Uh, Mr. Douglas, I was told to offer you fifty percent more than your original compensation."

Jackson sighed. It was easy money. And this nonsense at Cameron's couldn't go on forever. The more he stocked away now, the less work he'd actually have to do later.

"When and where?"

"The parking lot on the south side of the Venice Pier, and as soon as you can get there."

Jackson sighed again. It was a twenty-minute drive, and at present, he was still wearing yesterday's shirt and pants. "Give me forty-five minutes."

"Yes, sir."

Jackson closed his phone, growling instead of sighing, and went downstairs to make a pot of coffee. While it brewed, he showered and changed. He hoped it wasn't a problem that his beard had grown. He'd heard that the cast of *24* had had to cut their hair every five days.

At 8:20, carrying a travel mug of coffee and a couple of still-frozen, leftover waffles, Jackson headed for the car. It was another overcast morning, but as he headed down out of Pacific Palisades and cruised south through Santa Monica, the clouds began to thin, letting in filtered sunlight. He'd seen this type of morning hundreds of times. By noon, it would be sunny and warm.

Compared to the much more famous Santa Monica Pier, the Venice Pier was a joke. It had no restaurants, no rides, no attractions of any kind. It was just a concrete pier extending halfway to Okinawa. In 2005, a heavy northern swell had caused part of it to collapse into the ocean. Despite engineers' assurances that the pier was now safe, Jackson wasn't going out on it, no matter how much money Viggo offered him.

There were almost no visible signs of a television crew when Jackson arrived at the pier. A trailer sat in the corner of the parking lot, and two passenger vans were parked next to each other a few spots away. No camera crew, no actors and actresses standing around trying to look important, and no Craft Service tent with donuts and expensive bottled artisan water.

Jackson parked and headed for the trailer, scanning the beach as he walked. It was early, and with the sky still somewhat overcast, the beach and pier were largely vacant. That explained the lack of cars in the lot, only five or six scattered here and there.

The trailer door burst open and Maura stepped out. She spied Jackson, took a moment to recognize him, and then smiled. It vanished in a hurry. Hollywood types didn't have time for long smiles. "Jackson, you're here. Good."

"I'm here," he said.

"Step inside. Skeleton crew this morning. Andres and Sandra can get you in costume."

"Sure."

The trailer was a buzz of activity. Andres and an Asian woman were finishing up with a girl in leather at the makeup table, two other people Jackson didn't recognize—one of them might have been Broderick—were huddling over a script in the corner, and Taylor Howell was on a video conference at the far end of the trailer. And two others, a man and a woman, stood to the side of the door, tapping on their tablets, both thoroughly engrossed in whatever was on their tiny screens.

When Maura followed Jackson into the trailer, they both looked up.

"Kellen, Tara, this is Jackson Douglas, A.K.A. Grayson."

"Hi."

"Hello."

Jackson nodded.

"Andres, are you about ready?"

"*Un momento.*"

"Sandra, you have Grayson's jacket?"

The Asian woman stood up. "Right over here."

"Perfect," Maura said. She studied Jackson's white Dodgers tee. "Where's Grayson from?"

"Um . . ." Kellen said, consulting his tablet.

Tara found it first. "La Habra."

"That will work," Maura said.

"All set," Andres chimed, and Maura directed Jackson to take the chair recently vacated by Leather Girl. She had joined the duo looking over the script, and Jackson sat down for a few touchups from Andres.

"Here's the overview," Maura said, moving so Jackson could see her in the vanity mirror. "We're shooting a scene that occurs the day before your previous scene in the hotel. You're going to meet up with a girl named Roxie to discuss your presence in L.A."

"And this is an amendment to the script?"

"Yes. Viggo has full creative license with the show, and he likes to throw curveballs."

"Fair enough."

"We're still finalizing the script, so as soon as we've got something, you'll see it."

Jackson nodded, which caused Andres great consternation. From what Jackson knew of the guy, it was pretty much a permanent state of being.

When Andres finished, Sandra presented Jackson with the leather jacket he had worn for his previous scene. Jackson got up, and Tara slipped a script into his hand. He scanned it, getting the tone, trying to figure out his "motivation." He paused on the doorstep of the trailer, causing Tara to walk into him.

Jackson turned around. "I need to talk to Maura."

"Why?"

"I can't say this."

Tara didn't balk, but turned over her shoulder to Kellen. "Get Maura."

Jackson stepped down onto the pavement, reading the rest of his lines. Six in total. Not bad for several hundred dollars.

Maura arrived in less than a minute, swiping her bangs off her forehead. "What's the problem?"

Jackson pointed to the script. "I'm not saying that."

"Why not?"

"Because it's disrespectful."

Maura smiled. "Look, I had nine years of Catholic schooling, so I know where you're coming from. But I think God will understand if you say it one time as an actor."

"I'm sure He will, since He understands everything," Jackson replied. "But He won't approve, and I'm not saying it."

Maura's smile dissipated like the clouds overhead. "Jackson, I'll be frank with you. We're kind of crunched for time. This entire scene has been added at the last minute. My hands are tied, and it is just a line."

"I respect that, and I don't want to be difficult, but it's not happening. You can change it or you can find another Grayson, but I'm not saying it."

She sighed audibly. "Tara, I need Viggo."

"Right away."

Maura raked her eyes over Jackson and headed inside. He leaned against the trailer, sorry about having to pull the old "we play by my rules or I'm taking my ball and going home" routine, but not at all sorry for his reason for doing it.

Two minutes later, Maura exited the trailer with Tara, Broderick, and Broderick's companion. Their faces all displayed varying degrees of frustration and panic. "Viggo says the line stays as written."

Jackson nodded. "In that case, you all have a good one." He turned and started for the Granada, and was almost there before Maura shouted.

"Wait!"

He stopped, didn't turn.

"Just wait," she said, and he turned this time to see her already back on the phone. She paced away from everyone, talking in hushed tones. A minute later, she snapped her phone shut, then motioned for Jackson with a single finger. He joined her.

"Viggo said you don't have to say it."

"Good. What's my line instead?"

Maura flicked the script toward him, her pencil markings overwriting the objectionable material. Jackson scanned it quickly. "That I can do."

"Good. Five minutes?"

Jackson nodded and the crew dispersed. Moral high ground saved.

Four minutes later, Jackson was seated inside a gray '85 Camaro. Windows down, sunglasses on. His script was on his lap and the cameras were set up around the car. Everyone was waiting for Maura, who paced in front of the car as she talked on the phone. When she was ready, she ordered everyone into place. Knowing that Viggo's directive talents—and authority—flowed through her, they obeyed.

"Are you ready, Jackson?" she asked, peeking in through the window.

"Let's do this."

Maura double-checked to make sure everyone was set, and the scene began. The cameras, in Viggo Polansky style, looked over the hood of the Camaro and picked up Leather Girl as she approached from Ocean Front Walk. As she drew closer, the camera pulled back and panned to the side to include more of the car. Eventually, it swung all the way around so that it was looking in at Jackson as she approached his open window. A second camera, shooting in through the passenger window, recorded the other side of the conversation.

Leather Girl sauntered over and rested her elbows on the door. Her real name was Noelle St. Pierre, a fact Jackson had learned during an eight-second introduction and handshake before he got in the car. He'd been running lines in his head and wondering how close Maura was to firing him, and he had barely noticed her. Now, as she leaned her head into the car, he got his first real look at her.

She was tiny for one thing. That he had noticed before. Just over five feet, a hundred pounds, maybe. With the jacket and boots. The black was a contrast to the chin-length flaxen hair and bright blue eyes. A stud in her right nostril matched the five total in her ears, and the necklace dangling in front of her low, red V-neck was of a human skull. Despite the bad girl persona, Jackson realized she was quite attractive.

"Cut!"

Noelle stood, then stepped out of Maura's way. She stuck her head in the window. "You gonna say your lines or ogle her bust line?"

"I wasn't ogling."

"Did I mention we're behind schedule here?"

"Yeah. Consider me scolded. Let's roll."

Maura gave him a stern glare for a good three seconds, then backed away. "Let's take it from the top." She cast another look at Jackson as she stepped back, called for places, and let the P.A. announce the scene and take. She finally broke her gaze and called, "Action."

Noelle repeated her approach and leaned in on the door.

Jackson slowly turned his head her way, his posture a cross between absentminded and apathetic. "You're Roxie, I take it."

"That's right."

"About time. You got the money?"

Noelle reached into her jacket and pulled out an envelope. She handed it to Jackson, who looked at her for just a moment (pure artistic license on his part, as he figured it was how Grayson would respond to a cash payment from Roxie) and then thumbed through the envelope. He nodded. "Okay." He reached for the ignition.

"You do know where to draw the line, don't you?" Roxie asked.

"You want to supervise, it's going to cost you more."

"I don't want anyone getting hurt . . . too bad."

Jackson stared at her for a moment. She slowly cracked a grin. He didn't. "We done here?" he asked.

"Yeah, we're done."

He raised the envelope in a salute. "Pleasure doing business with you." He dropped it on the passenger seat, reached for the ignition to fake turning on the car, and then lowered his hand to the gearshift.

"Cut!" Maura ran in. "That was perfect! Noelle, great work. Jackson, you too. That was it. Two takes. Fabulous."

"You're not going to stiff me on my pay, are you, because if so, maybe I should have flubbed a line or two."

"You'll get paid in full."

"Then good. I can still make *Days of Our Lives.*"

Maura rolled her eyes and Jackson got out and returned to the trailer where he turned in his jacket. As he was leaving, Maura stopped him. "Viggo sends his thanks and congratulations. He just saw the take and said it was excellent."

"Good."

"He also instructed me to invite you to our episode wrap dinner tonight. Eight o'clock at Buca di Beppo, on 2nd." She offered a thin, perfunctory smile and headed inside. It wasn't the most sterling invitation ever, and as Jackson headed for his car, he decided to stay home and watch baseball playoffs instead.

Chapter Ten

7:54 p.m.

JACKSON PARKED ON a side street a few blocks away and enjoyed the walk through the heart of Santa Monica. It was his first time out in weeks. No dinners with Sam, no events with Maggie; only the occasional shift at Cameron's or pizza at Reggie's. And it felt good. The night air, balmy and breezy, was invigorating. And Santa Monica, cultural melting pot that it was, was a festive, happening place on a Friday night.

Reggie had called mid-afternoon. It was homecoming season, and one of the local high schools had rented the banquet room for an after-dinner party while another had made special plans to reserve the rest of the upstairs at Cameron's. Reggie could use the help with crowd control, and offered Jackson some hours. That's when Jackson conveniently remembered his dinner invitation from Viggo and declined.

A large Ficus tree stood in front of the restaurant, spotlights nested in the crook of the trunk illuminating its upper branches and casting a soft glow on several outdoor tables. And on Shawn Thomas, nursing a Heineken next to its trunk. He wore dark blue jeans and a plaid shirt, sleeves rolled to just beneath the elbows. Jackson had gone for a similar look, only his shirt was solid gray. He'd never been to a cast dinner, but he figured bit actors could wear what they wanted. And truth be told, he figured the invitation had been more obligatory than sincere, and doubted he'd be staying too long.

"Douglas," Shawn Thomas said with a smile as he lowered his bottle.

"Aaron."

"You're here. Jess owes me twenty bucks."

"Glad to stimulate the economy. What are you doing out here?"

"Waiting for Elisha."

"Isn't that a Victorian play?"

"My girlfriend."

Jackson nodded. Bauer's daughter on *24* had been played by a girl named Elisha. Could it be? Nah. Not with Shawn Thomas.

"I'm new to the Hollywood scene," he said, "but aren't you supposed to pick your girlfriend up for a date?"

"She's coming from work, dude," Shawn Thomas said with a smile, then tipped his bottle up again. He nodded toward the door. "We've got a private room. Just ask the hostess."

"Thanks," Jackson said, and headed inside. The hostess showed him to the banquet room, where he was greeted by the clamor of a dozen different conversations and by the crooning of Dean Martin. Maybe Perry Como. It wasn't Sinatra, at least, that much he knew. Leroy loved Sinatra.

Jackson recognized a handful of faces, most prominently Maura's when she flitted by. She offered a quick, "Nice job today," and was gone again. But it was an improvement from her death glare when he refused to take the Lord's name in vain on set.

"You came."

Jackson turned to see Jess. Knee-high boots, very-mini-skirt, low-cut blouse that could double as a negligee. Her hair had to have taken an hour, light and feathery, in stark contrast to her scowl.

"I came," he said.

"We never invite bit actors."

"I must have one of those personalities."

She shook her head and stalked off. Nobody was seated yet, so Jackson leaned back against a chair and scanned the room. The walls were lined with pictures of famous Italian people—actors and actresses, musicians, popes. And of course, murals of naked angels with cloaks floating around them to cover just enough of the right places.

"You're Grayson?"

Jackson looked up. Not too far up. The guy in front of him was a few inches shorter than he was, gelled black hair, a smooth face that was either cool or smug. He offered his hand, smiling wide to reveal elegant teeth. "Mario Bell. 'Ty.' Nice to meet you."

"Jackson Douglas. Nice to meet you too. Ty?"

"Ty Balducci, the Miami playboy."

Jackson nodded.

Mario glanced over his shoulder. "V must dig you, man. Usually they keep these things a little tight."

"So I've heard."

Mario tapped Jackson in the chest with the back of his hand. "That's good, man. Could be your 'in.'"

"Maybe."

"Hey, open bar. You want something?"

"No thanks."

"Come on, bro. You're here, that means you're one of the gang. V'll be insulted."

Jackson shrugged and followed Mario to the bar, where he asked for a Pepsi. Mario made a face, as if he'd ordered a spinach smoothie. Then again, in this world, spinach smoothies were probably big.

"I don't drink," Jackson said before Mario could ask the question.

"What, never? Why not?"

Jackson shrugged again. "A lot of reasons."

"Religious?"

"You could say that. Among other things."

"Yeah, Maura mentioned something about not swearing today. Man, V might be the wrong director for you."

Jackson frowned. "Isn't that more the writers?"

"Normally, yeah," Mario answered. He looked over his shoulder. "But this is V's baby. The script is really more of a suggestion until he gets it."

The things one learned about show business.

Jackson received his Pepsi and took a drink, and no sooner had he set it down than somebody clinked a glass. Jackson, along with Mario and the rest of the crowd, turned toward the far corner. Viggo Polansky, still in ponytail, now wearing a black suit coat over a blue dress shirt—unbuttoned a touch too far for his figure—held up his glass. The room grew silent.

"Welcome everyone. I'm happy to announce we have finished shooting for episode one-six, 'Past Sins.' On time!" he added with a grin, and everyone laughed and cheered. "As usual, great work by everybody, great job overcoming the challenges thrown at us, so let's celebrate tonight and keep the good times rolling!"

More cheering followed, and the group filtered toward the tables. Jackson lingered behind, making sure he didn't take anybody's seat. He ended up with Mario on his left and the late-arriving Shawn Thomas on his right. His Elisha was a brunette, too tall for Kim Bauer.

71

The food was served family style, in courses. First up, bruschetta and fried calamari, along with house bread. Jackson ate slowly, listening to Mario's stories and Shawn Thomas bragging to Elisha about his upcoming directorial debut. From the comments made from across the table by Jess and an unknown young woman sitting next to her, that debut wouldn't be on *Twenty Something* or upcoming all that soon.

Jackson also overheard the loud, wine-aided voice of Viggo Polansky from the next table over, regaling his dinner partners with stories from shoots around the world. Everyone was festive, as if they had just finished a season or even a series, not just the sixth episode.

The salad—Caesar, of course—was served next.

"So how long you been acting?" Mario asked.

Jackson swallowed a bite of the zingiest Caesar salad ever. "Mm, about four days."

"Four days?"

"Yeah, we hired him off the street, didn't you hear?" Shawn Thomas asked.

"Should have left him there," Jess mumbled.

"What are you talking about? He was great."

"Off the street?" Mario asked. He leaned forward. "What are you talking about Shawny?"

Shawny drained the rest of his Heineken before answering. "He bumped into Jess and me on the beach the other day."

"Bumped is right."

"We needed a Grayson, and tell me he doesn't look like him." He held up the bottle, looking for a refill.

"I never even met the first Grayson." Mario frowned. "So what do you do?"

Before Jackson could answer, Shawn Thomas raised his hand. "Noelle! You made it."

Jackson looked up to see his morning counterpart entering the room. He thought. The leather was gone (she now wore designer jeans and a teal tunic blouse) and so was the tough-girl-working-on-a-wad-of-gum countenance. Instead, Noelle's face bore an embarrassed smile and soft, subtle makeup. Gone was the stud in her noise and the excessive earrings, replaced by two small silver hoops. But the biggest difference was her hair, wavy—almost crinkled—instead of straight. And very cute.

He worked hard not to stare for real this time as she looked around for an open seat. He was about to offer his, when Mario stood up.

"Here, take mine."

Noelle smiled, again appearing embarrassed. "Are you sure?"

"Absolutely. I need to get some air anyhow." He reached for his wineglass. "Nice talking with you, man," he said to Jackson. "And no offense. You're getting an upgrade in dinner companion."

Noelle walked around the table and Jackson took a drink of Pepsi while marveling at the difference between Roxie and Noelle.

"You get lost in traffic?" Shawn Thomas asked over his shoulder as Noelle walked past.

"My brother dropped by out of the blue."

"Should have brought him."

"I don't think so. We're not his crowd." She offered Jackson a thin smile and sat down. Almost immediately, a waitress brought her a fresh salad plate and clean cutlery, taking Mario's used dishes back with her. Noelle took a moment to settle herself in, draping the napkin on her lap and telling the waitress that she was content with water for a beverage. Then she turned to her right.

"It's Jackson, right?"

He nodded. "Noelle-slash-Roxie."

She smiled. "They tell me you're not a professional actor."

"It wasn't obvious?" Jess asked.

"Jess, you getting enough fiber?" Shawn Thomas said. She stuck out her tongue.

"I thought you did really well," Noelle said. "Only two takes."

"Thanks," Jackson said, wanting to clear up that he really and truthfully hadn't been ogling her bust, as Maura had alleged. But it wasn't dinner conversation, and if he was getting the right vibe about Noelle, she didn't think it anyhow.

The third course was delivered before she could make much progress on her salad. There were two choices, both served in large, steamy bowls. Jackson helped himself to both the fettuccine alfredo and chicken rigatoni, and was rewarded on both counts. Shawn Thomas and Jess got into an argument over how the credits had appeared in the pilot episode and then Shawn Thomas had to explain what a pilot was to Elisha. Noelle, meanwhile, on Jackson's left, ate quietly, a fact observed by a balding guy across the table, introduced as Ricky. Jackson didn't know if that was his real name or his character's name, and frankly, didn't care.

"So, Noelle, how'd you like being the star?" Shawn Thomas asked.

"It was a long two weeks," she answered.

"You should be happy," Jess said. "At least you had something to do."

"It's just grinding, having this much of an episode focused on you," Noelle said. "It's pressure to keep a good thing going."

The rest of the table shifted to other conversations, and Jackson decided to satisfy a little curiosity. "So what was the episode about?" he asked.

And for the rest of the third course, and into the start of the veal or eggplant parmigiana, green beans, and garlic potatoes that constituted the entrée, Noelle gave Jackson the rundown of the series thus far. The pilot had introduced twenty different characters, all called to L.A. by the unknown benefactor, code name Mr. X. Most of them had taken the expenses-paid trip, but when Mr. X never showed, gone home. Four characters—Braylon, Cate, Roxie, and Ty—had remained in Los Angeles in an effort to determine who Mr. X was, why he had summoned them, and how he knew so much about them. That quest, Noelle explained, seemed to be driving the first season of *Twenty Something*. The individual episodes answered a few questions while raising a lot more, and also served to profile the main characters. It was the basic synopsis Shawn Thomas had given him over coffee at Cameron's, but her explanation was somehow more interesting.

"So who's Roxie?" Jackson asked.

"She's a brat," Noelle said with a thin smile. "A tough street kid from Milwaukee, an attitude, looking for a fight." She bit her lip for a moment. "I'm still learning all about her, actually. I know who she is, but not why."

"What's her relationship to Grayson?"

Noelle shrugged. "I don't know. I think it's supposed to look like she was paying him to attack Jess, but with Viggo's mind, you never know."

Jackson had questions about Viggo, about working for him, but he left them on the table. He was more interested in Noelle. "Have you ever worked with him before?"

"No, my first time. This is only my second 'big' role. Mostly just small stuff, bit parts."

Jackson nodded. "I don't know, bit parts seem to be the way to go. You work for an hour, get the free lunch, dinner parties."

Noelle grinned. "Viggo must like you. Except after the pilot episode, these episode wrap dinners have been pretty small and familial."

"It seems like the whole cast and crew are pretty close," Jackson said. He flicked his eyes at Jess. "Mostly."

Noelle giggled and reached for her water to cover. "Mostly," she agreed before taking a sip.

Jackson finished his veal and sat back, stuffed. It beat a Hot Pocket while watching American League baseball, that was for sure.

"So what's the after-dinner entertainment at these things?" Jackson asked. "Song and dance routines, karaoke?"

"No, mostly just a lot of drinking," Noelle said. Jackson glanced at Shawn Thomas, his arm draped around Elisha. Jackson had lost track at four Heinekens, and those were just the ones he had seen Shawn Thomas drinking. And the way wine bottles were being passed around the tables, he wondered how many people the Buca di Beppo cleaning crew would find passed out under the tables. And what the bill must be for this dinner.

Also finished with her meal, Noelle pushed her plate forward. She took a drink, then slipped her chair back. "The desserts here are terrific, but if I'm going to eat any more, I need to walk that off."

She excused herself, and Jackson nearly threw out an, "I'll join you." But instead, he waited for a minute to see if there were any conversation bones lying around. When there weren't, he drained his Pepsi and headed for the men's room. On the way back out, he ran into Viggo.

"Mr. Douglas."

"Mr. Polansky, thanks for the invite."

"Viggo, please. And you're quite welcome. The takes from your scene with Miss St. Pierre were excellent, and Maura hasn't stopped singing your praises."

"Really?"

"Indeed. She says you nailed the part, and even improvised a little."

Jackson wasn't sure what she'd meant by that, unless it had been the look he'd cast at Noelle/Roxie before taking the envelope of cash. That could hardly count as improv, could it?

"I just followed Shawn Thomas's advice and tried to be Grayson."

"Well done."

"Thank you."

"Now about the script change you forced."

Jackson swallowed. "Yes, sir."

"I generally do not appreciate having my entire production crew hijacked by an actor, especially a bit actor, especially a bit actor who isn't even an actor. I expect this sort of thing from the union folks, but you . . ."

"I'm sorry, really. But I'm afraid it was a non-negotiable for me."

"Non-negotiable? Are you sure you've never done this before?" Viggo stifled a grin. "At any rate, despite the frustration you caused Maura and the unintentional hijacking of the crew, I do respect a man who will stick to his guns."

"Really?"

"Quite a shock in this town, I know."

"I did—"

"And I like you, Mr. Douglas. You've got an attitude that resonates with me. And that's why I want to offer you a job."

"A job?"

"Yes. Not acting, although we may have need of Grayson before the season is over. But as my personal assistant."

"I thought Taylor was your personal assistant."

"He is, technically. I'm talking in a more private role. A personal gofer might be a better term. You run errands for me, on set and off. It would be on an ad hoc basis, fifty hours one week, twenty the next, doing whatever I find need of. The pay is terrible, but it's a foot in the door, Mr. Douglas, and in Hollywood, it's not so much about talent as it is connections. There are thousands of beautiful, buxom actresses in Los Angeles and just as many 'brilliant' screenwriters with the next *Seinfeld* rattling around in their brains. But the key is connections. Most of them fail because they don't know anyone. I'm offering you a connection, Mr. Douglas. Do what you will with it."

"I'm flattered, Mr.—Viggo. But why me?"

"I like you, Mr. Douglas, as I said. And my previous errand boy quit to follow his girlfriend to New York. The fool, she's on her way to stardom and he aspires to remember two sugars, one cream and not the other way around. But we're off track. I hate to be a stickler, but I'll give you twenty-four hours to decide, and then I need to pursue other options."

"Understood," Jackson said. "I'll call you in the morning."

"Fabulous. Just not too early."

They shook hands, Viggo went to look at the nudity on the walls in the bathroom, and Jackson returned to the table. He was just in time for dessert—homemade cheesecake or tiramisu. It was Viggo's dime, so he went for a slice of each. On his right, Shawn Thomas had the same idea. Noelle, her dinner walked off, had just the tiramisu.

Dessert conversation centered around where the show was going. None of the cast knew the ultimate end game, assuming *Twenty Something* didn't get canceled first. Most shows did. But they didn't even know where the season was heading. Who was Mr. X.? Would they find him? Who would end up sleeping with whom? That was Shawn Thomas's focus, and it got him in trouble with Jess and Elisha. No matter, beer me.

Jackson hung around long enough to have a cup of coffee and determine that Shawn Thomas was indeed drunk. Judging by the noise level and nature of conversation around the room, he wasn't the only one. Noelle had just gotten up to leave too, and it was the clincher for Jackson. He said goodbye to Shawn Thomas, Elisha, and even Jess. He passed Mario on the way out, paused to shake his hand, and literally followed Noelle out the door.

Out on the sidewalk, she looked over her shoulder. "Hey. They get a little suffocating, don't they?" she said.

"Inebriated, too."

Noelle nodded and reached for her hair. She twirled the end of a strand. "I meant what I said earlier, Jackson. You did good work today. I know what Jess says, but don't listen to her."

"Thanks, Noelle. I appreciate that."

She smiled, adjusting her purse on her shoulder. "So, will we be seeing you again?"

"I don't know. I talked with Viggo, and he said there was a chance Grayson might need to make another appearance yet this season." He didn't tell her about the job offer, because he didn't know what to make of it just yet. "So we'll see," he concluded.

"Well, in that case, it was nice working with you," she said, offering her hand. Jackson took it, amazed at how small it felt in his.

"You too, Noelle. It was nice to meet the real you."

She smiled at him, adjusted her purse again, and then turned down the sidewalk. He watched her go for a moment before heading for his own car. Funny, he thought as he walked, for two whole hours he hadn't thought about what he'd done in Nevada.

Chapter Eleven

JACKSON HAD PICKED up the phone to cancel three times. And yet here he was, refusing to look at the same old magazines while he waited for Alaina to tell him, "You can go in now."

Being in Nevada had caused Jackson to cancel his last session with Dr. Zachary, and what happened there had been the primary motivation in wanting to cancel this one. It was also the reason Jackson had forced himself to come. That was progress of a sort, wasn't it?

It had been a long weekend that concluded with back-to-back shifts at Cameron's Sunday and Monday. There hadn't been much do be done, and Jackson felt like Reggie was going out of his way to give him work. But at least it had been something to occupy his time. The rest of the weekend had been a snore, spent watching baseball, playing video games, or catching up on sleep lost Friday night. Jackson had been up late after dinner at Buca di Beppo, marveling at the lifestyle of people like Shawn Thomas, mulling the difference between Noelle and her character, and contemplating Viggo's job offer.

Noelle really surprised him. He knew it was called acting for a reason, and not everybody was the person they played on TV. But she seemed so quiet, unassuming, polite. And from what he knew of Roxie, the character was anything but. He chalked it up to show business.

The door opened and the same thin man who always left the office right before Jackson went in came out, smiling timidly as usual. "You can go in now," Alaina said to Jackson. He refrained from calling her Captain Obvious.

Dr. Furman T. Zachary—"Zach" to his patients—was tall and wiry. His black hair was pulled into a tight, short ponytail that made high cheekbones and a pointed nose even more pronounced. His goatee was meticulously groomed, in contrast to a dress shirt that was too short for his arms, a sweater vest that was a remnant from Cliff Huxtable's closet, and pants that didn't quite match the shirt and vest. That was okay, because the black sock on his right foot didn't match the navy blue one on his left. That, at least, Jackson assumed was a mistake.

Zachary carried a pad of legal paper in one hand and a pipe in the other. He sat in an old wooden glider in front of a window looking out at the Malibu Lagoon. Jackson took to the couch opposite the chair, and, as always, lay down.

Crossing his legs, Zachary began to rock. "How have you been?"

"You watch the news?"

"I do."

"There you go."

Jackson felt bad being snippy to his court-ordered therapist. Technically, the court's order had expired when Zachary concluded that Jackson didn't need to keep coming to him. But they both agreed it was in Jackson's best interest. Most days.

"I didn't ask what was new, Jackson. I asked how you had been."

"Crummy."

Zachary pursed his lips for a moment. Then he traced his eyebrow with his finger. "Let's explore crummy."

"You know what happened, Zach. I killed twenty people. I feel like crap."

"According to the news, those killings were in self-defense, to save an innocent girl from scoundrels."

Jackson hadn't heard the news reports, but he was surprised it had gotten reported as self-defense. And he was certain no newscaster this century had used the word "scoundrels."

"Yeah, but still . . ."

"That was, what, three weeks ago? How have you been coping?"

"Mostly with video games. I've won two Rose Bowls."

"Congratulations. I'm not sure video gaming is coping."

"More like avoiding?"

"Something like that."

"So tell me, Doc, how does one cope with taking the lives of twenty people—good or bad, justified or not?"

Zachary reached for his pipe. "I'm not sure there's an easy answer to that."

"There are never easy answers," Jackson mumbled.

"But I'll tell you, you aren't alone. The men and women in our armed forces, law enforcement officers—even doctors sometimes—have to deal with taking and losing lives. Sometimes innocent lives. I know it's not that simple, but they understand that it goes with the territory. And accepting that, accepting that people are going to die, is part of the coping process. It's unpleasant, and we certainly wish we could prevent it, but people do die."

"Well, I'm afraid I'm not in that territory anymore," Jackson said. "I've had my P.I. license revoked."

"Permanently?"

Jackson shrugged. "Indefinitely. But I'm wondering if it might not be for the best. I got into this business thinking I could do some good, and look what's happened since."

"Are you familiar with Dietrich Bonhoeffer?"

"I know the name."

"He was a Lutheran pastor in Nazi Germany who joined the *Abwehr*—German military intelligence, yet also the center of the anti-Hitler movement in Germany. Bonhoeffer was eventually arrested and hung for, among other things, plotting to assassinate Hitler."

"Is he the guy from that Tom Cruise movie?"

"A Tom Cruise movie?"

"Yeah, he played a one-eyed German general." He snapped his fingers. "*Valkyrie.*"

"No, I don't think so. But he, as a Christian, wrestled with the idea of taking the life of another man, even one so vile and despicable as Adolf Hitler."

"What'd he conclude?"

Zachary paused to light the pipe, then to smoke it for a moment. "He never finished his magnum opus. He was arrested before he had the chance. But in it he wrote, *'Before other men he is justified by dire necessity; before himself he is acquitted by his conscience, but before God he hopes only for grace.'*"

Jackson stared at the ceiling. "Meaning?"

"You're here today, not in prison. I take it that means that your actions were justified by men, or perhaps more accurately, The Man. And in your heart of hearts, you know the truth about what you did, why you did it, etcetera. And you already have the grace of God through Christ Jesus. Now there may be some things you need to address with Him, but if so, once you do, leave it to Him to take care of them."

Jackson thought for a moment. "You make it sound easy."

"Believe me, I know it isn't. But the crux of the matter is this, Jackson." Zachary leaned forward. "I don't mean to be glib, but what happened in Nevada, stays in Nevada. You can't change it. It's part of you, for better or worse, forever.

But if your conscience is clean, you need to rely on God's grace and seek His strength to bring you through the trials. And if your conscience isn't clean, then you need to go to Him as well."

Jackson closed his eyes. He wasn't convinced. Not that he disagreed with anything Zachary had said. But he'd done all that. He'd analyzed and agonized over every minute of his time in Las Vegas, out in the desert at the Air Force base, and on the houseboat on Lake Mead. He'd concluded that his actions had been justified. Most of them, anyhow. But could he have done something different, something smarter? And what about the fact that it had come so easily, almost naturally? Was that a byproduct of playing so many shooter-style video games with Mouse, or because he had skills for legit black ops? Or was it because his heart was dark and sinister? And even relying on the grace of God, how would he ever make this overwhelming black cloud above his head dissipate?

"So what are you going to do with your life?" Zachary asked.

"Huh?"

"If you're not a private eye anymore, what are you going to do?"

"Well, I owe Connie a million favors."

"Connie?"

"My neighbor. I was in debt to her already, and then I was kind of in a funk and blew off a promise to entertain her niece. Let me tell you, never make a large Italian woman angry."

"I'll make note of that."

"Anyhow, I'm back in her good graces now, but I owe her everything but the kitchen sink."

Zachary nodded.

"So that will keep me busy."

"What about employment? You have any line on work, since you're no longer a P.I.?"

"Yeah. Hollywood."

"I beg your pardon?"

Jackson explained how he had landed a guest role on *Twenty Something*, how it had parlayed into a second scene, and concluded with Viggo's invitation to be his personal gofer.

"Did you accept?"

"Yeah. I start next Monday, once they get back from shooting in San Francisco."

"San Francisco, huh? Cate's backstory?"

81

Jackson frowned. "Do you watch *Twenty Something?*"

"It's in a convenient timeslot."

"Trying to understand the younger generation's mindset, or do you just like the melodrama?"

"We're getting off topic."

"Which was?"

"Are you really going to make show business your calling?"

"No. This is just part-time anyhow. I haven't figured out what I'm going to do."

Zachary nodded. "How are things with Maggie and Sam?"

"Nonexistent."

"Let's explore nonexistent."

"Maggie and I had a falling out over the matter of me being a bigot and I haven't seen Sam since I got back."

"Why's that?"

"I don't want her to have to deal with all this, and I know, that's her call. But I've made it anyhow."

Zachary held up his hands.

"Sorry," Jackson said.

"It sounds like you miss her."

"Of course I do."

"I don't know Sam, but if I had to guess, I'd guess that she would understand."

"Can we talk about something else?"

Zachary nodded. "What's going on with Stephanie?"

"She's still living with Sam. Brady's getting therapy, which I'm monitoring."

Zachary nodded.

"Ironic, huh," Jackson said. "A guy who beats his wife has to make the grade of a guy who shot twenty people."

"You can't beat yourself up, Jackson. That's one thing I've learned. Even when you're in the wrong—and I'm not saying you are—you can't beat yourself up. The devil does enough of that."

"Funny, that's what my grandpa said."

"Smart man."

"Yeah. And everything you've told me is the same thing everyone keeps telling me."

"That's not great for my job security," Zachary said. "But don't you think that—pun not intended—tells you something?"

*   *   *

Tuesday, January 1
3:37 a.m.

SLEEPLESS NIGHTS weren't the worst. You could get up and play video games or watch old Westerns or find some means to occupy yourself. It was the nights where you kept waking up, hour after hour, unable to stay asleep. Those were the nights that really dragged on.

Jackson knew, because he was experiencing such a night. There was no clock that he could see, but somehow he knew he had a ways to go before morning.

He tried to sit up, letting his eyes adjust to the darkness. His throat was dry, and he thought about calling out for Reggie to ask for some more ice chips. But Reggie was immobile, likely asleep, and Jackson determined it was better to let a sleeping giant lie.

That one was funny, he was sure of it.

He closed his eyes. So he'd been shot. But by whom? Thing was, he was pretty sure he didn't have a clue, even if he wasn't still coming off the anesthesia and possible concussed from his fall. He had gone to the cemetery, but to meet whom? And why?

That one he knew, if he could only get his brain to function. The who was a mystery. One he wasn't in the mood for solving now.

Why hadn't a nurse come to talk to him yet, to tell him to press this or that button to summon a nurse? Or to tell him how to get pain medication? Or to see if he needed ice chips? Then again, he barely remembered talking to Reggie, didn't remember anything from before the surgery, or much of anything after the gunshot. Maybe he'd been visited multiple times by a nurse.

The gunshot.

The gun discharged, emitting a brilliant white flash and a deafening report. Jackson's mind processed both the sight and sound in the instant before he felt a bullet tear into his flesh, commanding all of his brain's attention.

He spun backwards from the blow, staggered once, and fell to the ground. His brain was pummeled by neurons that jostled for position to announce new and unheard of levels of physical pain.

The final moments in the cemetery were vivid in his mind, even in his drug-induced state. But try as he might, he couldn't peer far enough into his memory to see the face of the shooter.

Chapter Twelve

Monday, October 22
6:28 a.m.

JACKSON WHIPPED INTO the parking space nearest the Paradise Cove Pier, keeping one hand on the drinks in the passenger seat. Viggo had phoned him the night before, telling him to be there at six-thirty with an assortment of coffees. The line at Starbucks had been brutal, and Jackson had had to speed to make it on time. But it was bad form to be late for one's first day at work.

The pre-dawn air was crisp and cool, and Jackson wished he'd donned more than a T-shirt that morning. But for six-thirty a.m., he thought he was doing well to be dressed at all.

With four drinks in a tray in his right hand and two more paper cups balanced in his left, Jackson hurried onto the pier. Viggo, Maura, and a handful of others Jackson sort of recognized were huddled there, glancing back and forth between the eastern sky and their watches as if the two were playing tennis.

"Venti Caramel Macchiato," Jackson called out, holding up his left hand. Half of the group turned to acknowledge him, including Maura who raised her hand. "This one," Jackson said with a twist of his wrist.

"Thank you."

"Grande Pike Place?"

"Me," an unknown black man with a bag of gear over his shoulder said.

"And a Venti Mocha Valencia," he said, lifting Viggo's cup out of the drink carrier.

"Your math needs work," Viggo said, taking the cup from Jackson. Whereas everyone else in the group seemed subdued and sleepy, Viggo appeared to have been awake for hours.

"One for the gofer," Jackson said, removing the nearest cup, "and the other two are black coffees. For whoever." He passed the tray around and received several thanks. Brownie points on his first day.

84

"Six-thirty," Maura declared with a look at her watch. All eyes turned to the parking lot, then the eastern sky. It was glowing orange, a half hour or so away from actual sunrise. The view was pretty good, showing a dozen miles of dark ocean framed by the Santa Monica Mountains on the left, which were growing more and more distinct with each passing moment. Beyond the ocean, lights twinkled as Los Angeles came to life.

"Oh, thank goodness," a voice called as headlights swept over the pier. A car stopped, and everyone waited.

"What am I missing?" Jackson asked the black guy with the gear.

"The talent," he answered, blowing over the mouth of his cup.

A figure approached, and Jackson squinted through the darkness. He had no idea what scene was being shot. A slimmed down cast and crew had been in San Francisco for the last week, shooting on location as the characters followed a clue as to Mr. X's identity (and, if Dr. Zachary was to be believed, Cate's past). They had returned the day before, and why they were in Malibu before dawn, Jackson had no clue. He didn't even spot any actors or actresses, just some very stressed crew members.

"It's not her," Maura said.

The vehicle had belonged to a fisherman who strolled out to the end of the pier for an early start on his day.

"That's it, call her," Viggo said.

"She isn't going to like it."

"I don't give a rat's furry little biscuits if she likes it. We've got . . . thirty-five—no, thirty-four minutes before sunrise and rain in the forecast for three days. Call her."

Jackson frowned. Rain forecasts sure put a damper—pun intended—on Mondays.

Taylor, who Jackson just noticed was in the group, pulled out his phone. A moment later, he lowered it. "No answer."

Viggo swore and slurped his coffee. He checked his watch again. "Taylor—No, Jackson. Go wake the two laggards parked in the Jimmy by that palm tree. Bring them to me."

"Yes, sir."

With a chug of his coffee and a notation that Viggo now referred to him as Jackson instead of Mr. Douglas, Jackson headed for the vehicle in question. It was purple, old and rusty, and gave every appearance of having been left in place overnight. And he had a feeling in his gut that he knew at least one of the laggards. He took another drink, then rapped on the driver's side window with his knuckles.

He saw movement, then the window came down.

"Douglas, what are you doing here?" Shawn Thomas asked.

"Viggo wants you and whoever's in there with you."

Shawn Thomas blinked, then yawned. "Yeah, we're coming. Jess here?"

"Nope."

Shawn Thomas turned and whacked his passenger. "Dude, get up."

"Huh, what?"

The passenger sat up and Jackson recognized the smooth features of Mario Bell.

"V wants us," Shawn Thomas said. "Jess isn't here."

"What do you mean?"

"I don't know, ask Douglas."

"Is it that complex of a statement?" Jackson said.

"We hit it kind of hard Saturday night in Frisco," Shawn Thomas explained as he opened the door. "Then V springs this sunrise thing on us."

"Sounds like he springs a lot of stuff."

"Yeah."

"Tell me, does the cast of an actual, in-production TV show usually sleep in a '94 Jimmy?"

"Ninety-eight, and this old piece of crap kicks butt."

"Whatever you say, dude." Jackson swigged his coffee.

"You got one for me?"

Jackson handed it to him. "Kind of bitter anyhow."

"No spit-back?"

"No promises."

Shawn Thomas thought for a moment, then took the cup. Mario staggered out of his side of the SUV, and the trio headed toward the pier. "Don't tell V about last night, all right?" Shawn Thomas said.

"Last night?"

"We sort of partied last night too."

"After finding out you had an early wake-up call?"

"Guilty. Just don't tell V."

"I don't know what to tell him."

"I like this guy," Mario said.

Viggo turned as they arrived. "Gentlemen."

Mario nodded. "Mr. P."

"We're thirty minutes from sunrise, and Miss Leigh isn't here. Any ideas where she might be?"

"You call her?" Shawn Thomas asked.

"No. What a novel idea, Mr. Aaron. Someone, try calling her."

"We don't know," Mario said with a shrug. "I bunked at Shawny's place last night, and we came straight here."

"Anyone else 'bunk' with you?" Maura asked.

"No."

"Taylor?" Viggo asked, turning over his shoulder.

"Still no answer, sir."

Viggo's curse punctured the still sea air. "All right, set it up. If she does show, I don't want to miss our opportunity. Taylor, stay on the phone. Call Miss St. Pierre and see if she knows anything about Miss Leigh's whereabouts. Mr. Aaron, Mr. Bell, go with Andres and see if he can undo the hungover frat boy appearance. The rest of you, let's go."

Jackson was last in line, following Viggo off the pier and onto the beach. They walked past a restaurant and stopped at an open expanse of beach, the parking lot on the right, and cliffs blocking their path ahead. Viggo pointed to a thin strip of sand running between the cliffs and the ocean. "We're going to shoot with just one camera," he said. "Facing her, looking west, into the darkness. Once Braylon and Ty arrive, we'll slowly pan, clockwise, until we're behind them, facing the rising sun. The last shot is the three of them walking into the sun. It's symbolic of the change in the tone of the episode."

Several comments were made, questions about angles, lighting, footprints, number of takes before the moment was gone. Properly attired and made up, Shawn Thomas and Mario joined the group. Viggo checked his watch again, holding it up against the lightening sky. A cause and effect relationship had developed, and he swore again.

"Can't we just shoot at sunset instead?" Shawn Thomas asked.

"Mr. Aaron, in your experience, does the sun often set in the east?"

"No."

"Then I think it's safe to assume it won't this evening."

"What if we shoot at sunset but pretend it's a different beach, one that faces west. I mean, east. I mean—"

"Jackson?"

"Yeah."

"You live in Malibu, do you not?"

"Pacific Palisades."

"Close enough. How many north-facing beaches are there in the area?"

"None."

"In all of Southern California, in fact?"

"Uh, none that I know of."

Viggo glanced at Shawn Thomas. "Taylor?"

"Still no answer, sir."

Viggo paced, consulted with Maura, and swore at the sky, his watch, and Jess some more. Jackson approached Shawn Thomas, who if he was chafing from Viggo's remarks, didn't show it. "What is this scene, anyhow?" Jackson asked.

"We get back from Frisco all frustrated, relationships fraying and everything. And Jess is especially mad because of a quick rendezvous with her ex—not Grayson—that didn't go so well. She goes for a late night-turned-early morning drinking binge and walk on the beach, planning to quit. We console her and encourage her to keep at it. It's supposed to be a nice bonding thing," he added as he took a sip of Jackson's coffee.

"V stressed we had to have everything down pat," Mario said, "because we'll only have the one, maybe two takes."

"What about Noelle?" Jackson asked. "Isn't she part of your group of four or whatever?"

"Roxie and Cate are feuding," Shawn Thomas answered, "so she doesn't come with us."

"Meaning she gets to sleep in," Mario muttered. "Or at least did," he added as Viggo approached.

"Miss St. Pierre says the two of you invited her to a 'welcome back' party last night," he said, eyeing Shawn Thomas and Mario.

"Yeah, so?"

"So, did you invite anyone else?"

They looked at each other, then Shawn Thomas spoke. "Yeah. Dana, Kevin, Paulie, a few others."

"Miss Leigh?"

"Yeah, it was at her place."

Viggo exhaled. "The party was at Miss Leigh's apartment?"

"Yeah."

He turned. "Jackson, first assignment: Go to Miss Leigh's apartment and see if she is by any chance there in some inebriated, unconscious state."

"You got an address?"

"Check with Taylor. Call me when you find her, and I'll instruct you where to deliver her. We'll have to reconstruct our episode."

"I'm on it."

Jackson stopped to get Jess's address from Taylor—a condo in Calabasas. Then he trudged to his car, feeling very much like a private investigator again.

Calabasas was a small, affluent city situated in the hills overlooking the southwest corner of the San Fernando Valley. It was about a half-hour drive, mostly winding through the mountains, and Jackson used the time to clear his head. Here he was, less than a month removed from his awful, heinous, unforgiveable actions in Nevada. A month had added distance, little else. He'd gotten advice from Reggie, Leroy, Dr. Zachary, even Hillary—all telling him he did what he had to do, he was justified, it would get better, blah, blah, blah. Maybe they were right. But his life—just like it had after his parents and Grant died—had become a constant search for a distraction, for something to give him a few minutes when he wasn't tormented by the past. Oddly enough, his brief times with the cast and crew of *Twenty Something* had been some of the best distractions. And now, first thing on a Monday morning, he was headed to a hungover diva's house to wake her from her debauched sleep. Yes, his life was certainly on the upswing.

The shadows of Malibu Canyon gave way to bright sunshine and the Ventura Freeway, and with it, traffic. Jackson's frustrations with the infernal L.A. freeways took his mind off his other problems, and once he finally left the crowded 101, he was focused on trying to find Jess's building. It was opulent, perched on the side of a hill, with its own pool and tennis court and a pretty nice view of the valley. Jackson assumed Jess had had at least a decent career before *Twenty Something* came along.

According to Taylor, she lived in unit four, on the second story, accessible by an exterior walkway that wrapped around the building. Jackson rang the bell, and when nobody answered, he tried to peak in the massive picture window. The blinds were drawn. He walked around the side of the condo, where two smaller windows looked west. The blinds were drawn there too.

He returned and rang the bell again, then pounded on the door with his fist. He gave it another minute, then tried the knob, just so he could tell Viggo he'd given it his best shot. Thirty-five minutes here, thirty-five back, mileage reimbursement at almost sixty cents per mile . . .

The door opened.

"Hello? Jess?"

He stepped inside and almost puked. The sickly sweet smell of marijuana was almost as powerful as the odor of leftover pizzas on the living room table, spilled—likely by several methods—tequila on the floor, and he could only guess what else.

He covered his nose with his shirt. "Jess, you in here?" He took a few steps into the living room, careful not to step in anything unidentifiable. Then he stopped, having heard what sounded like a moan. He peered into the dining room, where a man—sans pants—sat at the table. One arm hung limp beside him, the other was flopped across the table, next to a tipped over and half empty tequila bottle. The man's face was smashed against the table and a paper plate of something gooey.

But he wasn't the moaner. That distinction belonged to a woman slouched on the kitchen floor beside an open dishwasher. Open, it appeared, so she had been able to vomit into it.

Despite moaning, she didn't appear to be conscious. Straggly light brown hair hung over her face and onto her shoulders, one of which was bare. The other was covered by a crooked—perhaps intentionally, though Jackson didn't think so—blouse. At least she wore pants, or rather, a very short skirt. One high-heel sandal was loosely strapped to her foot. The other was in the corner. Apparently she'd only had time to remove one shoe before unloading into the dishwasher.

Jackson left them alone and turned down the dark hallway. It led to a bathroom and two bedrooms. The far bedroom, the larger of two, was completely black thanks to drapes over the windows. The door was ajar only a few inches, and with dread in his heart and eyelid reflexes primed, he nudged it open.

Jess lay on top of her bed, clad in flannel pajamas. Her hair was pulled back to make room for a washcloth on her forehead. One knee was raised, one arm flopped flat on the bed. The other held the washcloth in place.

"Go away," she moaned.

"Rough night?" Jackson asked, speaking loudly to make sure she could hear him.

She groaned.

"I said rough night?" he asked, raising his voice.

She raised her groan.

Jackson walked over and pulled back the drapes, which caused another groan. This was too much fun. He pulled open the blinds, and Jess whimpered.

"Viggo sent me," Jackson said, still on the verge of hollering. "You missed roll call this morning."

Jess rolled over with another groan, burying her head under a pillow.

Jackson opened his phone and dialed Viggo's number. He got Taylor instead. "Hey," he said. "I'm at Jess's place. She's here, drunk as a skunk."

He waited while Taylor checked with Viggo, and was surprised when Viggo himself came on the line. "Jackson. She's there? In what condition?"

"You've heard the phrase 'death warmed over'?"

Viggo cursed. "Get her down here as fast as you can."

"At the pier?"

"We're rewriting the scene. Half the episode, in fact," he said.

"All right, but I'm not sure she's in acting shape."

"Won't be the first time. Just get her here, ASAP."

"Yes, sir."

Jackson closed the phone, then headed for the kitchen. He stepped over the woman on the floor and rummaged through Jess's drawers and cupboards until he found a butter knife and a glass. He took them back into the bedroom, and held the glass in his left hand and the knife in his right. He leaned over Jess's head, inserted the knife into the glass, and shook it for all he was worth.

"Aaagh!" Jess wailed, rolling over and clenching her head with both hands.

Jackson continued to clang the knife inside the glass. "Rise and shine, beautiful."

She groaned and sat up. "I'm going to kill you."

"You want to pick out your outfit or should I?" Jackson asked.

"I'm calling the police."

"Good luck remembering the number. Viggo wants you there posthaste. I'll give you ten minutes to shower, although it's fifty-fifty if you'll drown or not. You want coffee?"

"Go away!" she screamed, then held her head again on the verge of tears. Jackson almost felt sorry for her, until he remembered a hangover was not a migraine. It was avoidable.

Jess flopped back onto the bed, and Jackson almost reached down to pick her up. Then he thought of lawsuits and how in twenty-first century America a cross-eyed glance could be construed as sexual harassment. He stared down at

Jess for a moment, and realized she wouldn't remember anything in ten minutes. Besides, he could always threaten to take cell phone photos to the tabloids.

Regretting his decision to get into show business, Jackson picked Jess up and threw her over his shoulder in a fireman's carry. Leaving the drunkards in the dining room and kitchen, he carried her outside, downstairs, and to the passenger seat of his Granada. He thought briefly about going back to get clothes, but that would involve underwear, and there was no way he was picking through her bras and panties, potential sexual harassment charge or not. Not for what Viggo paid him. Let Wardrobe worry about it.

Jess moaned, grumbled, and made a few death threats. But by the time they reached the freeway, she was slumped against the window, and Jackson called Viggo to let him know his leading lady was on the way.

Chapter Thirteen

12:22 p.m.

"YOU JUST CARRIED her out of her apartment?" Taylor asked wide-eyed, forgetting for the moment his ham and cheese sandwich.

Jackson nodded.

"In her pajamas?"

"I wasn't going to change her."

"Shut up, Shawn Thomas," said a junior production assistant (or something like that, Jackson couldn't remember) before Shawn Thomas could make any comment.

"What'd she say, man?" Mario asked. "Anything?"

"Made a few death threats," Jackson said with a shrug. "That was about it."

All in all, Jackson concluded his retrieval mission had been a success. No terribly awkward moments, no mention of a sexual assault charge, and high praise on a job well done from Viggo. And the Granada had come through unscathed, although Jackson had to pull over once and jerk Jess out of the car so she could vomit on the side of the road instead of in his front seat.

"Man, you should have seen V light into her in the trailer," Shawn Thomas said. "I thought he was going to blow a vein."

"About time," the junior P.A.—Skip was his name—said. "After running Monique off the show, then that whole beach-shot debacle."

Jackson frowned. "Beach debacle? Monique?"

Mario waved it off. "Jess is always fussy about wardrobe. Particularly swimwear, camera angles . . ."

He nodded, guessing her fussing wasn't modest in nature.

"And Monique was supposed to be the fifth musketeer," Shawn Thomas said. "But Jess couldn't stand working with her and complained they had rotten chemistry and it was either Monique or her but not both. We were already shooting the pilot and had to scrap her at the last instant."

"So how does Jess not get canned?" Jackson asked. "She's clearly not here for her charming personality."

If he wasn't mistaken, Shawn Thomas and Mario exchanged glances.

"This is her show," Taylor said.

"I thought there were four leads?"

"Technically," Mario said. "But everybody knows Jess is the star."

"She had that castle vampire series," Shawn Thomas said, "What was it again?"

"*MidEvil*," Skip answered.

"Yeah. Very clever. It was her breakthrough, and rumor has it, Viggo couldn't land a home for *Twenty Something* until he cast her."

Jackson nodded.

"And, uh . . ." Shawn Thomas said with a clearing of the throat and a glance around him, "rumor also has it that Viggo and Jess have a little side-street romance going on."

"What?"

"It's just a rumor," Taylor said.

"Stemming from their time in France working on *MidEvil*," Mario said.

Jackson thought about Jess—primped, prissy, perhaps surgically altered— and then about Viggo and his white ponytail. Anywhere else but Hollywood, he'd never buy it. Even here, he was skeptical.

"So, to make a long story short," Shawn Thomas said, molding the last hunk of his sandwich into a bite-sized ball, "whether or not he's getting his Jess desserts, Viggo reams her and then it's back to business."

"Jess desserts?" Skip asked. "That's the worst pun I've ever heard."

Shawn Thomas grinned through his sandwich.

Skip rolled his eyes, then checked his watch. "Taylor, we've got a meeting in five."

"Right."

The two assistants got up, leaving Jackson alone with Shawn Thomas and Mario.

"So how bad was it?" Shawn Thomas asked.

"Bad," Jackson said. He told them about the man and woman passed out at the table and on the kitchen floor. "What'd you guys do last night anyhow?"

"Nothing, man. Just beer," Mario said.

"And tequila," Shawn Thomas said.

"Right. But we were out of there by midnight."

"One."

"Was it?"

"Quarter to."

Jackson described the other drunks, but neither Shawn Thomas nor Mario recognized them. "Then again, there were about twenty of us there," Mario said. "Most of them Jess's friends."

"And Kevin, Paulie . . . Dana."

"Who?" Jackson asked.

"Couple of guys on the crew." Shawn Thomas reached into a bag of chips. "What's V got you doing this afternoon?"

"I'm scouting some place in Marina del Rey with Maura and a location guy named Dusty. For the next episode."

"One day and he's got you scouting locations?"

Jackson grinned. "What can I say?"

Shawn Thomas shook his head, then raised a finger as a signal. "Hey, Noelle." He nodded, and Jackson turned to see Noelle headed their way.

Rather, Roxie. Black leather, low-cut blouse, hair straight instead of wavy. Ready to kick some butt, at least until she smiled and said hello to the three guys.

"I thought you had off today," Mario said.

"Viggo called me in," she said, taking the top bun off her sandwich and then removing the onions. "Everything got rearranged, apparently."

"Maybe you shouldn't pull your punches when you attack Jess," Mario said.

"What?" Shawn Thomas asked.

"You didn't hear?" Mario asked.

Shawn Thomas shook his dumbfounded face back and forth.

"I get in a fight with Jess on the beach," Noelle said.

"What? That wasn't in the script."

"Everything changed because of missing sunrise, apparently. Now you guys don't have your powwow right away at dawn, which means she's still in a funk when I get back, and we . . . get into a fight." Her shoulders slumped. "Which means now I need another session with Cole so I can fight like a street kid from Milwaukee."

"What are you and Jess-slash-Cate fighting about?" Jackson asked, still trying to figure out the plot of a series that made *Lost* look straightforward.

"Not relevant, Douglas," Shawn Thomas said, leaning forward. "Tell me about the fight. Slaps, punches, wrestling in the waves?"

"All of the above," Mario said with a smile.

Noelle winced. "You guys are pathetic."

"Please tell me I don't have to be somewhere else then," Shawn Thomas said, looking heavenward.

"I don't think God grants prayers allowing you to watch a catfight," Jackson said.

"Don't worry, you'll be there," Noelle said. "The two of you break it up."

"It leads to a four-way powwow," Mario added.

"I love my job," Shawn Thomas said, and she rolled her eyes.

"Is Jess up for an action scene?" Mario asked. "She had all she could do to pull off a walk-and-talk on the beach."

"I think Viggo's punishing her," Noelle answered. She paused before biting into her sandwich. "What kind of party did you guys have last night anyhow?"

"Not half the one she did," Shawn Thomas said.

"Let me guess, you were in bed by ten," Mario teased.

Noelle swallowed and flashed a thin smile. "Ten-thirty."

"What are you two going to be wearing for this fight?" Shawn Thomas asked.

Noelle ignored him with a grimace.

"Douglas, you gotta talk to Viggo—see if you can scout the harbor with Maura and Dusty later."

"You're scouting locations?" Noelle asked, happy for a change of conversation.

"Yeah. Viggo asked me."

"What's up with that anyhow?" Mario asked. "Why you? And what are we doing in Marina del Rey in episode one-eight?"

Viggo hadn't sworn Jackson to secrecy, so he shrugged and said, "Ty's going to hire a private eye, and he wants me to verify that the setting is authentic."

"A P.I.?" Mario asked. "What, does he live on a boat?"

Jackson shrugged.

"Why you?" Shawn Thomas asked.

"I was a private eye. And I know the area. My grandpa lives there."

"Your grandpa lives in Marina del Rey?" Noelle asked.

"You were a P.I.?" Mario asked.

Jackson nodded to answer both of them.

"Get out," Shawn Thomas said. "When?"

"Until about a month ago."

"You were a P.I.?" Mario asked again.

"Yeah."

"Does Viggo know?"

"Yeah, it came up before."

"That must be why he sent you to roust Jess this morning," Shawn Thomas said.

"What?" Noelle asked.

"You didn't hear? Douglas was the one that stormed into Jess's apartment at seven a.m. and dragged her down here."

"You did?"

"It was more of a fireman's carry."

"So are you the spying through keyholes kind of P.I. or the corporate espionage kind?" Mario asked.

"Somewhere in the middle," Jackson said. More like the blowing up phony Army Rangers kind, but there was no need to bring that up.

"I bet you have all kinds of stories," Shawn Thomas said. "Is it like on TV, where you get all the women?"

"You think I'd have had lunch with you two if I did?"

Maura appeared out of nowhere. "Jackson, five minutes?"

"Ready when you are."

She nodded and was gone.

"Hey, you have fun with that, Douglas," Shawn Thomas said. He looked to Mario and nodded. "Let's go dig up a script. I want to anticipate everything that's going to happen and figure out where to flub my lines so I can see the best parts over and over."

Mario grinned as he got up, and Shawn Thomas slapped Jackson on the back as he left. Noelle watched them leave, and as her eyes cut back to her sandwich, they crossed Jackson's. He made what he hoped was an empathetic face.

Noelle took a bite and washed it down with a sip from her bottle of water. "Can I ask you something?" she said, her hand still on the bottle.

"Sure."

"You're a guy. What is it about girls wrestling or making out or getting all wet and dirty that turns you on? I mean, I don't like watching guys fight, and to each his own, but I don't get a kick out of watching guys kiss. What is it with men?"

Jackson leaned back. "You want the long or short answer?"

"How about the truth."

"Guys are pigs," Jackson said.

"All of them?"

"Mmm, pretty much most."

"I can't help but notice you're not drooling."

"No, I'm not."

"Hmm. Well in my experience, that means one of three things."

"Oh?"

She nodded. "Either you're gay, you're religious, or you're just too polite to let your perversion play out on your face."

Jackson let his nod of consideration morph into a smile. "Care to guess which?"

"Not gay, because you don't dress the part and you wouldn't be quasi-flirting if you were. And not religious, because most religious guys I know don't flirt either, and they definitely wouldn't hang out with Shawn Thomas. That only leaves polite."

Jackson grinned. "Definitely not gay, not wild about the term religious, and I can't say many people accuse me of being polite."

"Not wild about the term religious," Noelle said. She rested her chin in her hand. "So either your beliefs about God don't fit in the typical religious box, or you don't like being associated with those who share your beliefs."

"Maybe a little of each," Jackson said. "Religions are based on works and methods, on something we do to get to God or heaven or wherever each religion claims its followers get."

"And you?"

"I believe God did all the work. I just have to trust Him."

Noelle nodded. "And that keeps you from being a pig?"

"Sort of. He gives me a chance to resist temptation."

"So you are tempted?"

"In more ways and more often than I care to admit."

"So we're back to my original question. What about pillow fights and mud-wrestling and girls kissing girls appeals to guys?"

Jackson exhaled. "You'd have to ask a psychologist. Probably something dark and unpleasant."

Noelle looked down. "I guess what bothers me is it seems so much like we're used as a display. I mean, I'm not a goody-goody or a moralist or anything—whatever you're into. And I get that sex sells and everything. I just think Jess and I wrestling on the beach seems a little . . . staged."

"Yeah, I'd agree."

Noelle shrugged. "I'll just have to channel Roxie. She probably mud-wrestles on the weekend back in Milwaukee."

"You could refuse to do the scene," Jackson said. "What are they going to do, kill off Roxie?"

"Knowing Viggo, they might. Besides, I don't have Jess's pull."

"Jackson!" Maura hollered.

"Coming," he called over his shoulder. "Back to the salt mines," he said to Noelle. "Good luck."

"Thanks. And for the record, I think you're quite polite."

Jackson winked. "Piece of advice?" he asked as he stood.

"Sure."

He raised loose fists in front of his face. "Keep your dukes up."

"I'll try to remember that."

Still grinning, Jackson turned and trudged toward an anxiously waiting Maura. A Hollywood actress who actually had reservations about exploiting her sex appeal. Maybe the earth was still on its axis after all.

Chapter Fourteen

Wednesday, October 24
8:00 p.m.

"WAIT, TURN THAT up," Jackson said.

Esteban adjusted the volume on the TV over the bar.

". . . was found dead in his Lake Bancroft, Virginia, home this morning," the attractive blond news anchor announced. "Authorities are still investigating the cause of death, but preliminary indications point to suicide."

"You don't have the game on?" Reggie asked, taking a seat at the bar beside Jackson. "Burgers will be—"

"Shh," Jackson said, holding up a palm toward his friend.

"A three-star general in the United States Army, Reynolds had served for forty-three years. Wow. He was sixty-one. More on this story as it happens." The news anchor moved on to other headlines, and Jackson waved at Esteban. He turned the TV to the National League Championship Series.

"What was that all about?" Reggie asked.

"Officially, I can't tell you."

Reggie raised an eyebrow.

Jackson reached for a couple of pretzels. "General Ernest Reynolds was one of the bigwigs behind the operations out at Blane Air Force Base. It was from his houseboat that I rescued Hillary. When Secretary Wittingham briefed me on the deal they gave me, he made no mention of Reynolds. I thought maybe he was too valuable to take the fall or they were giving him a Code Red behind the scenes or something. And now . . ."

"He's dead?" Reggie said, pointing at the screen, which now showed a Braves-Giants game.

Jackson nodded.

"You think they silenced him?"

"They say it looks like a suicide."

100

"You think they silenced him?"

Jackson crunched on a pretzel, unsure of his answer. "I don't know what to think, about any of this."

"You heard anything at all from this Secretary . . . what was it of?"

"Secretary of the Air Force, and no. Nothing." Jackson sighed, beginning to come to terms with not being a private investigator. He'd thought that it was his calling, but had started to question that of late anyhow. What kind of a calling led a guy to kill people and have them commit suicide on his watch?

Reggie opted for a change of subject. "How was work?"

Jackson grunted. It had been a long day of shooting, mostly on the soundstage. Everyone had been in bad moods. The actors kept flubbing lines, Wardrobe committed a major continuity error with Jess's outfit, lighting had been off for Viggo's taste, and something had happened to damage a roll of film already shot. They'd worked till seven, with Viggo finally calling it quits amid a slew of bad language that had even Shawn Thomas blushing.

While Jackson related events to Reggie, the kitchen finished their burgers, and they took them back to Reggie's office. The NLCS was on there too.

"So you going to quit this job too?" Reggie asked.

"I never quit," Jackson said.

"No, you just kept turning down assignments."

"Well now you make it sound like you're the CIA."

Reggie grinned and bit into his burger.

"No, I'll give it at least another day."

"Hoping for another cameo, right?"

"I actually like the people. The big cheese looks like a pro wrestler, he's foul and coarse and has a temper like the Hulk. The lead actor fits every stereotype of the sex-crazed, debauched male. Jess is a not-quite-so-cute, less well-known Lindsay Lohan. The bad girl is actually reserved and swee—"

"Wait a second," Reggie said. "You're calling Lindsay Lohan cute?"

"Well, when she's sober."

"When is that?"

"They're a strange bunch," Jackson said. "Except for Noelle, they're largely undesirable, and yet . . . I kind of like them."

"Noelle?"

"She's the quiet one, plays the bad girl from Milwaukee."

Reggie nodded. "You know, they say when you work in a restaurant, in the kitchen, you'll never eat at one again the same way."

"Thank you for that non sequitur."

"Is it the same with TV, now that you've been behind the scenes?"

"Yeah, I doubt I'll ever watch *Everwood* reruns quite the same."

"I see the experience has made you snarkier," Reggie mumbled.

"That possible?"

"So what's on your plate for the rest of the week?"

Jackson shrugged. "Coffee at dawn tomorrow, and from there, whatever Viggo wants. Next week I have to coach some actor on being a P.I."

"Couldn't you just have him watch *Psych* and *Rockford* reruns for a week?"

Jackson slapped his forehead. "Of course. *The Rockford Files*. I don't believe it."

"What?"

"We were shooting at Rockford's beach the other morning. I knew it looked familiar."

"Where's that?"

"Paradise Cove. How did I miss that?"

"Maybe you were enamored with all your new friends."

"Jealous?"

"We'll see. You work weekends too?"

"I don't," Jackson said. "My union won't allow it. Which reminds me. Any chance we can reserve the bistro for our episode-wrap Friday night?"

"Episode wrap?"

"Yeah," Jackson said, making a face. "Kind of schmaltzy, but they have a cast and crew dinner to wrap every episode, generally every other Friday. Since I'm V's assistant, I get to attend."

Reggie mused. "It's kind of late notice, but for a friend, I'll see what I can do."

"Great. I get the feeling I could use as many points as I can get with the new boss."

They finished eating while watching the Giants blow an early lead against the Braves. Reggie was ambivalent when it came to baseball, but Jackson never missed a chance to celebrate the Dodgers' rival's failure. When the game ended, Jackson announced he was headed home.

"Man, already? It's quarter to nine."

"Long day," Jackson said. "And I have a feeling another long one tomorrow."

"Yes, but you meet such interesting people."

Jackson nodded in lieu of laughing. "Call me about Friday."

"Will do."

"Hit me on my hip, as they say."

"I'm not sure they say that anymore, J. Or ever did, for that matter."

"Whatever. See ya, dude."

"So long."

As Jackson drove home, he found himself replaying the week thus far, wondering how long he could continue with the "Hollywood" life. Then he thought of an old Bible verse, how Mordecai had told Esther that maybe God had put her into her position as queen for "such a time as this." Working for Viggo hardly made Jackson royalty, and his testimony had been somewhat diminished by his multiple homicides.

It had indeed been a long day, but Jackson wasn't tired. He flipped open the laptop at the small desk in his bedroom/office and checked up on some of his coworkers. His Google search for Viggo generated a few interesting hits, mostly stuff Jackson already knew. Next he typed in "Tess Leigh rehab" but his search came up empty. Worth a try. Wikipedia told him the story of *MidEvil*, which in short was nonsense: A narcissistic vampire inadvertently turned the fortunes of several nations, largely by seducing various world leaders. Spawned in the Middle Ages, she had gained the ability to travel through time, thus impacting civilizations since the beginning of time up into the projected future. The whole thing felt lifted from *Forrest Gump* and *Back to the Future*, with a vampire thrown in to win the generation.

He checked up on Shawn Thomas and Mario, whose last name he learned was actually Giacobelli, shortened to Bell. And then he found himself on the Internet Movie Database, reading Noelle St. Pierre's bio.

Born on September 28, 1986, in Kansas City, Missouri, she had lived in Kansas City and Arvada, Colorado, before her family moved to Fullerton in the early '90s. She took up acting in the sixth grade, and was the star of a number of school plays at Sunny Hills High School. After three semesters at USC—Jackson knew there was something he liked about her—Noelle had gotten her break when several TV commercials parlayed into a bit part on *The West Wing*.

Jackson sat back, closing his eyes, trying to picture the episode in question. He thought he remembered it vaguely, but couldn't place Noelle in it. He shrugged and switched over to her filmography. After *The West Wing*, she had appeared in a handful of lesser-acclaimed TV shows and a few movies, all in minor roles.

In 2009, after several years of insignificant parts, she had landed a medium-sized gig on a short-lived CBS sitcom. She had appeared in three episodes, and that had been enough to earn what looked like a starring role in *Safe at Home*. It didn't ring any bells, and after scouring the remainder of her credits—mostly more small roles and bit parts until Viggo and *Twenty Something* had come along—Jackson read the plot synopsis on *Safe at Home*.

The movie centered around a washed up minor league baseball player who met a waitress—played by Noelle—who helped him see things in a different light, and ultimately turned his life around. A chick flick dressed up as a sports movie, Jackson thought. Maybe if he and Sam ever resumed their dinner-and-a-movie "date" nights.

He Googled Noelle and clicked on her official webpage. He was greeted by a head and shoulder shot, her against a slate gray backdrop. She looked nothing like Roxie. Her hair was wavy, almost curly, drawn from right to left across her forehead, contrary to the way her body was tipped slightly right. Her shoulders were raised, and her smile was placid and disarming. She was cute, and a little bit alluring, but mostly just cute. Kid sister meets girl next door. It matched what Jackson knew of her so far, which was anything but what he expected from a budding actress.

The website was simple and easy to navigate. It provided a lot of the same biographical info—with a few more details—that Jackson had already found elsewhere, as well as her film and television credits, signup for a newsletter, and a link to her Twitter account. Jackson didn't use social media, and decided he'd been online long enough.

Surfing the web had made him drowsy, and Jackson closed his computer and got ready for bed. As he laid down, shortly after ten o'clock, he pondered several things. Who had killed General Reynolds—himself or someone else—and why? What motivated people, assuming it wasn't a great personal tragedy, to drink until they puked in a dishwasher and passed out? Why did guys enjoy watching girls wrestle in mud, Jell-O, feathery pillows, or the Malibu surf? How close had Noelle, and a hundred other actors and actresses, come to quitting before getting their break?

And how long would he last in the world of television before losing his mind, his soul, or both?

*   *   *

Friday, October 26
9:14 p.m.

JACKSON WAS into his after-dinner coffee. Shawn Thomas, Viggo, and most of the rest of the cast and crew were into something much stronger. Their loud conversation and off-color jokes were carried away by a gentle ocean breeze blowing over the night air. Plans had changed when the weather had turned Thursday afternoon, and instead of reserving Cameron's upstairs, Jackson had bartered with Reggie to let the cast and crew occupy the outdoor seating on the beach. Reggie had been somewhat hesitant until Jackson mentioned their alcohol consumption and the potential bar tab.

They had arrived at eight, dined on casual fare, and celebrated another successful episode. "On the Rocks" had wrapped on time and on budget, cause for much celebration (and alcohol). It had been a successful finish to the week as far as Jackson was concerned too. No more rousing drunk starlets, no more lust-laden conversations with Shawn Thomas, and no major hiccups. He'd largely been a standard gofer—fetching coffee, delivering equipment or film or whatever Viggo needed delivered, and otherwise serving as the director's yes man. It beat a factory, at least.

"So," Reggie said, slipping into the chair next to Jackson. The rest of his dinner companions had started to mingle and he was temporarily alone. "How's it going?"

"Ask me after everyone's left, not broken anything, and not committed vehicular manslaughter on the way home," Jackson answered.

"You too low on the caste system to associate or something?"

"You should have been here ten minutes ago," Jackson said. Shawn Thomas and a handful of others had plied him for stories from his life as a private investigator. It turned out they were more interested in any potential sensual exploits that were an offshoot of his profession than they were in hearing tales from the Douglas Files. He'd spoiled their hopes and they'd lost interest.

An employee called for Reggie, and he excused himself, leaving Jackson alone with his coffee. But only for a moment. Noelle approached, hands in her pockets, a thin smile on her face. "Hi," she said softly.

"Hey, how's it going?" Jackson smiled back and nudged out a chair for her.

"Actually, I was wondering if you wouldn't mind taking a quick walk?" Noelle said, scrunching her face a little. "There's something I'd like to talk to you about."

"Sure," Jackson said. He pushed his coffee cup in and stood. "Lead the way."

They slipped away from the crowd and started down the beach, leaving the raucous cast and crew in their wake. The night was still balmy and, as Noelle walked on the ocean side, the sleeves on her purple blouse flapped in the breeze.

"This is kind of awkward," she said after a minute, "but I'm wondering if I could hire you."

"Hire me?"

She looked up at him. "Yeah. As a private investigator."

Jackson nodded and took a few steps. "I would say yes, but I'm not a private investigator anymore."

Noelle's shoulders fell. "Oh. I thought when you said the other day that you had been until a month ago you meant because of *Twenty Something*."

"A little before that, actually."

"Oh." She took a few steps in silence, her eyes cutting out to the ocean.

"Why. What's on your mind?"

She stopped and faced him. "I can't believe I'm saying this, but . . . I think I have a stalker."

"A stalker?"

Noelle nodded. "A handful of sensual tweets and a passionate e-mail." She smiled shyly as she added, "And he sent me roses."

"You're sure it's not a secret admirer?"

"I don't know," she said, running her fingers through her hair. "Maybe. I don't want to make a federal case out of it if it's nothing, but it's a little uncomfortable. When I heard that you were a P.I. the other day, I thought maybe you could check it out for me."

"I would, Noelle, honest. But I don't even have a license anymore."

"Why not?"

Had she not heard what happened in Nevada? Not connected his name to the events? Maybe she didn't go home at night and Google her coworkers.

"It's a long story," he answered. "But I can't legally investigate for profit."

Noelle started walking again, and Jackson followed.

"What about not for profit?" she asked.

"You mean a favor?"

"Something like that." She tilted her head to the side. "What if you did me a favor, as a friend? On the house, free of charge, completely legal. And then in response, I—as a friend—chose to do a favor for you out of gratitude—a favor that just happened to roughly correspond in value to your typical fee?"

Jackson grinned. "A favor for a friend?"

"Yeah." She reciprocated his grin, and it was not all that dissimilar from the smile on the picture on her website—sweet, a little carefree, and a touch beguiling.

"I suppose I could do that," Jackson said.

"I won't ask you to do anything that could get you in trouble. I just need someone with a little more expertise to poke around."

"I'll do what I can, as a friend."

Noelle's smile widened. "Thank you, Jackson. I'm running down to San Diego to see my dad tomorrow, but are you by any chance free Sunday? I have everything saved on my tablet, so I can show you all his messages, give you all the gory details."

"Sure."

"You care where or when?"

"Afternoon, you pick the spot."

"Santa Monica Pier, under the Route 66 sign? Say, one o'clock?"

"Sounds good."

"Great," she said, beaming. Then she looked back through tendrils of breeze-blown hair at the party. "Um, I'd appreciate it if you didn't mention this to anyone else. I don't want them making a big deal out of it."

"My lips are sealed."

"Thank you."

They returned to Cameron's and Noelle announced, first to Jackson, then to the rest of the group, that she was heading out. Everyone hollered goodbyes, and Noelle offered Jackson a small smile and wave as she headed for the parking lot.

Chapter Fifteen

Sunday, October 28
1:07 p.m.

JACKSON WAS CAUGHT in an aroma war between Bubba Gump and Pier Burger. On one side, fish and crab legs and shrimp—buttered, garlic, Cajun, and coconut. On the other, an assortment of burgers and sandwiches, hot dogs, fries, and ice cream treats. He found himself hoping for a long, hard-fought stalemate. And that Noelle hadn't eaten lunch yet.

The day had dawned warm and sunny, and the Santa Monica Pier was quickly getting busy. Playful shouts and screams from the beach mixed with the buzz of a dozen conversations that moved and flowed around Jackson. Human noise was joined by the chatter of circling gulls. A gentle western breeze carried the sibilant rush of the waves onshore, and with it, the clamor from Pacific Park. The people were thin and tan, decked in everything from beachwear to business casual. Some dressed for the sun, others for the warm but still autumnal air. And they were of every race and creed.

Jackson was toying with the idea of grabbing a churro or two when he saw Noelle walking up the pier toward him. She wore blue jeans and a brown, cap-sleeved shirt, with a large knit purse around her neck and over her right shoulder. Her hair was wavy, not straight the way Roxie wore it. Butterfly sunglasses covered her eyes until she arrived in front of Jackson and pushed them up on top of her head.

"Hi," she said with an embarrassed smile. "Sorry I'm late."

"Don't worry about it. You eat already?"

"Um-hmm. Grabbed something on the way out."

He nodded. "Okay, so take me through this, from the beginning. When did you first hear from this guy?"

"I didn't know until just recently, but he's actually been following me on Twitter for three years, since shortly after I joined. Looking back on them now, his tweets were pretty innocuous, just saying how much he liked my work in a movie, thought I was pretty, that sort of thing."

"Three years ago," Jackson said. "*Safe at Home?*"

Her mouth opened. "You know it?"

"I did some research," he said.

"Wow, you're thorough."

Never mind that his research had been conducted before she had "hired" him.

"It was my only real starring role until *Twenty Something*," she explained. "I didn't think I was all that spectacular, but he disagreed." She shrugged. "But tweets like that aren't uncommon on an actor's Twitter feed. We all get them, some from real fans, others from people looking to get a semi-famous person to reply to them."

"Do you remember exactly what he said in these tweets?" Jackson asked.

Noelle stopped and reached into her purse. She pulled out what Jackson at first thought was a journal. But when she opened it, he realized it was a tablet. She tapped the screen a few times and handed it to Jackson. He had to tip it just right to fight the glare, but he was able to read the words.

@Noelle_SP you were the perfect Annie. #Oscar-worthy performance. #SafeAtHome

Just watched #SafeAtHome. Stellar movie. @Noelle_SP steals the show. #MustWatch

@Noelle_SP are you on Facebook? Loved you in #SafeAtHome. Can't wait to see your other work.

Anybody know when @Noelle_SP will be appearing on TV or big screen? Let's get #NeedSomeNoelle trending!

"I was not that good," she said, peeking over his shoulder as he read.

"He started a hashtag for you."

"Trying to get noticed, I'm sure."

"Did you reply back to him at all?"

"I wrote him back once or twice," she said with a shrug. "I try to answer fans as often as I can. I'm still flattered and a little shocked that I have actual fans."

Jackson reread the messages, looking for any clues.

"@2EdgedPen," he said with a shrug as he read the stalker's Twitter handle. "He inventing a new pen, or is that a pen-mightier-than-the-sword reference?"

"Don't know. Anyhow, there were a few more here and there, corresponding with appearances on different shows, all more of the same. The first indication that he might have been anything more than a casual fan was this," she said, swiping down on the screen.

Jackson read the tweet aloud. "'*@Noelle_SP did you say Lindsay was from Pasadena? I go to school in Pasadena. Maybe we know each other, lol.*'"

"Still pretty innocuous," she said.

"Who's Lindsay?"

"My character in an episode of *Vegas or Bust*."

"Never heard of it."

"Nobody else has either."

"When was this?"

"About a year ago. He still wasn't on my radar." They passed the arcade, and for a moment the clamor coming from inside it drowned out any conversation.

"What changed?" Jackson asked.

"He seemed really hyped for my role on *Twenty Something*, and then tweeted this during the airing of the pilot." She had taken back the tablet and scrolled to another message. She tipped it so Jackson could see.

WOW, sweet @Noelle_SP has a dark side . . . and I like it!!! #TwentySomething

"In the next one, he called me 'super cute.' I remember seeing that one, and actually wrote him back."

"What'd you say?"

"He'd said I stole the show, and I thanked him. I was just being nice to a fan, still didn't think there was anything more to it than maybe some guy having a crush on me. But I remembered him, and the next day someone delivered a dozen red roses to me, on the set in San Francisco. There was a card."

They had reached the entrance to Pacific Park, the renowned theme park housed over the ocean. They turned away from it, however, and approached the railing at the edge of the pier. "What'd it say?" Jackson asked.

"'Noelle, I can give you so much more.' It was signed '2EP.'"

"Two-edged pen."

She nodded. "Even that might not have been so bad had it not been for the e-mail that came in later that night." She tapped on the tablet screen. "I only noticed it because of the subject, 'Roses are Red.'" She handed him the tablet. "It's kind of embarrassing. And illicit."

Jackson swallowed as he began reading. Not limited to a set number of characters, the e-mail was long, several paragraphs' worth. The first was about the roses. The writer said he hoped she liked them and said she deserved them and so much more—recognition, fame, probably more money. To be loved.

Jackson leaned against the railing as he continued reading. The second paragraph read like the Song of Solomon, only without the biblical virtue. Several sentences were dedicated to flowery and vivid descriptions of various parts of Noelle's anatomy, and only because Jackson was investigating did he read through all of it.

The third paragraph was worse, moving into the realm of fantasy. This guy, 2EdgedPen, and Noelle, engaged in a sexual encounter. Graphic, it was also ornate and fanciful, the type of stuff that would be lauded in some liberal school of arts.

But perhaps the scariest part of the message was the final line, set apart from the previous three paragraphs. *I love you, Noelle. I will be waiting.*

Jackson looked up. Noelle was blushing. To reduce the awkwardness, he started walking again. They were past the park now, to the point where the pier narrowed. They continued farther out to sea, toward Mariasol's Mexican restaurant and Santa Monica Pier Bait and Tackle. Here the crowds thinned a little, and Jackson turned to Noelle.

"Have you showed this to anybody else?"

"No. I was too embarrassed. I know the stereotype of Hollywood actresses, Jackson, but . . . that's not me."

He nodded.

"I did tell Janet, my PR gal, that I'd received the e-mail and gave her the general overview, but I didn't tell her all the details."

Jackson nodded again. "And you said this came while you were in Frisco?"

"On the seventeenth."

"What was the episode right before that?"

"We were shooting 'On the Rocks,' but the ep that aired Tuesday the sixteenth was 'Solve for X.'"

"Anything particularly sensual that might have set him off?"

"No. It was still pretty early on in the show, and I didn't even have that big of a role."

Jackson glanced down at the tablet again. "There's something about this," he said. "The way it's written."

"It's iambic heptameter," she replied. "He's a poet."

Jackson glossed over the e-mail again. He stretched a few of the rhymes, but at least made the effort. It was written in paragraphs instead of lines, but each of the sentences contained exactly fourteen syllables, or seven iambs. He'd learned

111

briefly about such things in school, but generally passed them off to guys who wore scarves and berets.

"What do you think?" she asked.

Jackson nodded at a bench set in a small extension of the pier. They sat, facing south, looking down at solid water. The waves crashing against the beach were well to their left.

"Is this it?"

"A few more tweets," she said, holding out her hand for the tablet. She quickly accessed them, and Jackson tipped it to ward off the sun. "This was sent while one-four was airing, about the time of Shawn Thomas and Jess's love scene."

Jackson flicked that mental image aside and read the tweet:

When do we get to see a @Noelle_SP love scene? Volunteering to play the lead! #NeedSomeNoelle

The next tweet, sent forty minutes later, basically described the finer points of Noelle's physique, containing the NeedSomeNoelle and TwentySomething hashtags, along with one more: #Clarity.

"What's Clarity?" Jackson asked.

"A movie I was in. I was an extra, no lines, just a girl in a crowd. A girl in a bikini."

Clarity. Of course. Jackson remembered it from when he had researched her filmography. He knew nothing about it other than the name.

"This the last one?"

"One more. I saw it Friday night when I got back."

He scrolled down to read. *Just watched "Not the Only Ones" again. Can't get enough @Noelle_SP! #TwentySomething.*

"I thought about blocking him," Noelle said, "but Janet suggested I didn't. This way I can still see his tweets. She said they could be evidence."

"Makes sense."

"So what do you think?" she asked, scrunching her shoulders together. "Am I overreacting?"

"No, I think you have legitimate reason to be concerned," he said. "He's clearly escalated from first contact where he was an enthusiastic fan to now, where he comes off like a Victorian predator."

"Do you think I'm in danger?"

Jackson looked Noelle in the eyes. "Probably not. Usually, these guys are all bark and no bite. But like I said, I would be concerned, and I would be careful."

She nodded. "So will you help me?"

"I wouldn't be much of a friend if I didn't."

Noelle beamed beatifically. "What do we do?"

"There's two parts to this," Jackson said. "First, we have to figure out who he is. He uses the same handle on Twitter, e-mail, and his note. It's a personal moniker for him, and it might be as simple as tracking that down. But once we find him, we have to determine how to handle it."

"How do you mean?"

"It depends on what level of a threat he is. He could be nine or ninety, and he may live in L.A. or he may live around the world. And he may just be all talk, or he may actually be one of the nutjobs who acts on his misguided emotions."

"Worst case scenario," she said. "What if he is serious and lives here in L.A.?"

"We can file a restraining order, for starters. And if there's reason to believe he's more than just a nuisance, we go to the police with whatever evidence we have and let them take it from there."

Noelle folded her hands in her lap. "How can I help?"

"Well, is there anything else you can think of?" Jackson asked. "Other ways he's communicated with you? Or have you noticed anyone lurking around the set, heard any comments about weird guys asking for you, anything like that?"

"No."

"Any idea how he found you in San Francisco?"

"No, but it wasn't a secret we were shooting there And the flowers came from a local florist. It wouldn't have been too hard for him to send them."

"So there's no reason to assume he's somehow involved with the cast or crew."

"No."

"Anything else suspicious Anything at all?"

She thought for a moment, then shook her head. "No."

"If you do think of anything, hear anything, let me know. And I'll be on set. I'll keep an eye out."

"So that's it?"

"Yeah, for now. Other than be careful. Lock your doors, don't go out alone if you can avoid it, especially at night—the obvious stuff."

"Fortunately I'm not a big socialite."

"No?"

"No. I'd rather go for a walk on the beach or curl up with a good romance novel or movie. I don't give stalkers much of a chance to stalk."

"That's good. And come tomorrow, he won't be able to get near you without somebody—hopefully me—noticing."

She nodded. "Okay, now let's talk fees."

"Friends don't charge friends," Jackson said.

"Right. But if I were to compensate you as a friend," Noelle said, "what would be considered an appropriate gift?"

Jackson nodded at a vendor cart a little ways back down the pier. "I usually bill my clients one soft pretzel."

She glared at him from the top of her eyes.

"Let's catch the guy, first," he said. "Then we'll worry about friendly remuneration."

"Okay, but you're not weaseling out."

"Oh no. I insist on the soft pretzel."

Noelle bought two, one for each of them, and they strolled back toward land.

"So how did you become a private investigator?" Noelle asked.

He popped a bite of pretzel in his mouth. Warm and salty—perfect. He swallowed. "I've always been pretty good at solving problems, observing people and things, picking up clues."

"You can read a person?"

"In a manner of speaking."

"What do you read about me?"

He glanced at her, then answered before stuffing the next bite of pretzel in his mouth. "You don't fit in Hollywood. I don't mean your acting, which is incredible, by the way."

"Incredible?"

"Um-hmm."

"You've seen what, two scenes?"

He swallowed. "I've seen you as Roxie, and I've seen you as Noelle, and the two couldn't be farther apart. Unless you're schizoid, you're an excellent actress."

"Maybe a little mistaken, but I appreciate the sentiment. What else?"

"Well, you don't seem anything like the typical Hollywood star. And I again mean that in a good way. You're down to earth, sensible, nice."

"How can you tell all that, just from a few conversations?"

"You blush when you're complimented. You're appalled by an obscene e-mail. And niceness is obvious, unless of course, you're acting now too," he said with a smile. He shrugged. "I don't know. I can't always quantify it. But you work in the business. You can tell when someone's acting genuine and when they're really truly genuine, can't you?"

"Yes, I can," she said, meeting his eyes for a moment. Then she tore a piece off her pretzel.

"What about you?" Jackson asked. "What interested you in acting?"

"You'll think it's silly."

"Try me."

"When I was a little girl, I always found myself wishing for something more. And I had a good childhood," she said, sweeping away hair blown into her face by a sudden gust. "I'm not the running-from-a-broken-home actress that seems to be the stereotype. We had it good, but, it was also kind of bland. Mom and Dad worked, Seth and I went to school. It just seemed so routine. So I started inventing fantasies to add some flavor to life."

Noelle looked down, fingering her pretzel. "I would play princess, write little plays I forced Seth to be in, spend hours at a time lost in my dream world." She looked up. "Silly, right?"

"Not really. When I was little, I played football in the backyard. Sometimes with Grant, sometimes without. I rewrote the NFL history book. The Rams won every Super Bowl from 1986 to 1992. Never lost a game, in fact."

She smiled. "Did you ever come to the dinner table in character as the star quarterback, though? Go to school as a different player every day until you were on the verge of suspension?"

"Can't say I did."

Noelle shrugged, as if shaking off an unwanted thought. "And I'm happy with who I am—always have been. But Noelle can only do so much, experience so much. My little dramatic dream world opened up all new realms of possibilities."

"So how'd you get from there to here?" Jackson asked. "I've got to think there are a lot of little girls like you who didn't end up in Hollywood."

"I started acting in school plays, church Christmas programs. I was Mary four years running. My parents divorced when I was fifteen, and I threw myself into acting as therapy. I worked hard, kept at it, and caught a break."

"And she lived happily ever after."

"We'll see about that."

He nodded and finished his pretzel. They had reached the end of the pier, and Jackson offered to walk her to her car, a blue Kia Cerato parked in the lot on the pier. They exchanged phone numbers, and he told her to call if anything came up. "I mean it. You notice something, even if you think you're paranoid, I'll check it out."

"Thank you, Jackson."

"Absolutely. And I know this sounds like double-talk, but try not to worry."

She forced a smile.

"I'll see you tomorrow," he said, then watched and waved as she drove away. As he headed for his car, he mulled over what ringtone he could assign to Noelle.

Chapter Sixteen

2:08 p.m.

FROM THE PIER, Jackson drove to Mouse's house in Culver City. It was actually a duplex, shared with his sister, Pam. They both worked unpredictable schedules, Mouse at Starbucks and Pam for a different employer every time Jackson inquired. The latest had been a Petsmart on Jefferson, but that had been months ago. To be safe, Jackson had called ahead. Mouse was home video gaming, and Pam was out with her on-off boyfriend, Clark.

The door was unlocked, since it was still daytime, so Jackson let himself in. He followed the sound of sub-woofed alien shrieks and Gardetto's being crunched back to Mouse's bedroom. Bedroom in that it contained a bed. Otherwise, it was a gaming hub. Multiple screens, multiple consoles, with controllers and clothes and half-eaten bags of snacks everywhere. Jackson pulled up an extra chair and waited until Mouse had a chance to pause his game. He reached for a handful of Gardetto's first, then acknowledged Jackson with his gray-brown eyes. "Hey, dude. What's up? Long time."

"Yeah. Hey, I need your web savvy, Mouse."

"How so?"

"Social media."

"You really need to get with the times, dude," he said, shaking his head to flick a mop of dark brown hair off his eyebrows. "Old grandmas have mastered Facebook."

"Old grandmas have nothing better to do "

"Can it wait five?" Mouse asked, reaching for a half-empty two-liter of Mountain Dew Code Red. "Almost to the end of the level."

"Knock yourself out."

Mouse turned his attention back to the screen. He began phasing bionic swamp creatures as he slogged through a dark jungle. Aside from rocking in place, a tic he had picked up in childhood, Mouse showed no signs of being stressed by the growling, attacking beings. He just shot them with ice-cold accuracy, all while collecting power crystals hidden in a bog and inside a hollow tree. He reached a river, was prompted to save his progress, and having done so, closed his game and spun to face Jackson. "What's going on?"

Jackson recapped the last few weeks for Mouse, who responded with a lot of "Dude, no way's" and "Get out of here's." When Jackson finally convinced him that he had been hired by Viggo Polansky and was working on the set of *Twenty Something*, Mouse sat back and actually stopped rocking. "So what do you need me for?"

"One of the actresses asked me to help her find a potential stalker."

"One of the actresses?"

"That's right. Noelle St. Pierre."

"Should I know her?"

"Maybe. She's been in a few things over the years."

"Okay, so why are you here?"

"He's sent her a lot of tweets. She showed them all to me, but I want to see what else he's been up to. I'm hoping to figure out who the guy really is."

"Sure. Where to first?"

They began with Twitter, where it had all started. Mouse spent five minutes creating a dummy Twitter account, then followed @2EdgedPen, and they began looking at his tweets. There were a lot, and while they sorted through relevant ones, Mouse grilled Jackson on life as an actor/gofer. He also took a break and Googled Noelle.

"Man, she's hot."

"She's not bad."

"Not bad? That's right, you like tall girls."

"I'm not choosy. She's cute. But she's a client."

"I thought you were retired."

"It's a favor."

"And you're just friends with this girl?"

"Yes. Can we get back to work?"

They looked through six months' worth of tweets, finding that @2EdgedPen had followed some other actresses and made similar comments to them as he had to Noelle. Then Jackson had Mouse try to find @2EdgedPen's real name. He came up empty.

"Can't you hack something?"

"Twitter doesn't require you to give a real name anyhow. Just an e-mail address." Mouse pointed to it on the screen. It was the same one @2EdgedPen had used to e-mail Noelle.

"Can you get this guy's name?"

"Whatever name he signed up for the account with," Mouse replied. "Gimme a few."

Jackson sat back and Mouse swigged some Dew. He continued to peck away at his keyboard, tap on his mouse, and chomp on Gardetto's. Finally, he spun in the chair again. "William Blake."

Jackson repeated the name. "Is there any way to print off all the tweets he's ever sent?"

"All of them?"

"Yeah."

"On paper?"

"Papyrus if you got it."

"Pap-what?"

"Yes, Mouse, paper. And if you can, highlight anytime her handle comes up or the hashtag 'Twenty Something.'"

"Seriously?"

"Come on, man."

"All right, all right. Give me a few minutes."

While Mouse worked, Jackson paced, rehashing what Noelle had told him and the tweets and e-mail he had read. Without knowing if @2EdgedPen—A.K.A. William Blake—had sent smutty e-mails and roses to other actresses he followed on Twitter, there was no way to know if he was just an internet creep or had developed a more sinister attraction to Noelle.

Mouse's laser printer whirred and began shooting out sheets of paper. Mouse reached a hand up, waited until it had finished, and presented the sheaf to Jackson. The stack was at least a quarter inch thick and the print was so tiny he needed to squint to read it.

"You are the man," Jackson said.

"Any other mediums you'd like me to check?"

"Yeah," Jackson answered. "Facebook, Instagram, whatever else is hot this week." He gave him Noelle's website. "Check the message boards, e-mail sign-ups, etcetera."

Mouse started with her website. "I don't see any message board posts," he said after a few minutes, "but it looks like he signed up for her newsletter with the same address as above."

"What'd you just do?"

"Signed you up," Mouse answered.

"Great."

"Relax, it'll look investigative. She have a hulking boyfriend or something?"

"Not that I know of."

"And the two of you are just friends. You sure you're feeling all right?"

"Fine."

"How much is this girl paying you?" Mouse asked.

"So far, one soft pretzel."

Mouse shook his head, sighed, and faced the screen again. While he looked into William Blake's online presence, Jackson scanned the tweets Mouse had printed, looking for the light gray highlighting that indicated they were about Noelle. As she'd said, most of them were harmless, praising her work, complimenting her, making corny jokes. There were large gaps in time between them, corresponding to lulls in her acting career, Jackson guessed. Aside from one inquiry into when she would be appearing on TV or in the movies again, they were all in response to an appearance on some show or role in a movie. It was all a little dorky, a little obsessive, but in the way a loser with no life could become infatuated with a celebrity they put too much stock in. There was nothing to suggest Blake was stalking her.

Until recently. Then his messages started to focus on Noelle the attractive woman more than Noelle the beautiful, talented actress. The transformation culminated in the erotic e-mail he had sent her on the seventeenth and the more sensual tweets thereabouts. Noelle had promised to forward the e-mail to Jackson, and he was toying with the idea of asking Mouse to hack Blake's e-mail. But not just yet.

"Okay, his Facebook page is sterile. No personal information, no giveaways on his profile page, nothing."

"What about his friends. Who are they?"

"He doesn't have many. Nobody that stands out."

"Can you check a few, see if you notice a pattern. Are they in L.A., California, the U.S.?"

"You know he could have a thousand friends all from L.A. and still live in New York, right?"

"Yeah," Jackson nodded. "But it's unlikely."

Mouse continued searching, and Jackson reread the list in his hand. One of the first tweets Noelle had showed him caught his attention. "Hey, Mouse, listen to this. '*@Noelle_SP did you say Lindsay was from Pasadena? I go to school in Pasadena. Maybe we know each other. lol.*'"

"If only there was a database of complete losers."

"You seen anything about a school in Pasadena?" Jackson asked.

"Nope."

"Can you find a list? There can't be that many."

"School schools or colleges?"

"Both."

Mouse sighed. And searched. "Um, wanna bet? There's like a hundred."

"Can you cross-reference those with his name?"

"Dude, Google doesn't have a cross-reference feature."

"Come on, Mouse. She's as sweet as she is pretty. If this guy is really stalking her, I want to bag him."

"You sound protective."

"I'm developing Big Brother Syndrome. So shoot me."

"Hey, man, easy does it. I'll check. Just give me a minute."

Jackson strummed his fingers. Mouse rocked in place. Five minutes elapsed. "I don't see anything, man."

"Okay, stupid question here, Mouse. I need to be on Facebook to view a Facebook page, right?"

"Depends on their settings. Unless you're me, of course." Mouse shrugged. "We're on now. Have a look."

"Yeah, but you have swamp aliens to kill."

Mouse shrugged again.

"All right, I'll take a brief look," Jackson said, sitting down to peer at the screen. Mouse turned it his way, and Jackson quickly browsed Blake's page, checking out his list of friends, likes, and statuses. It was thoroughly uninteresting and uninformative, and he was about to give up when he spotted a status from several months back, referring to a "stirring" poetry reading. The comment was made on Blake's wall by a guy named Wally Perron. Jackson wouldn't have thought anything of it except he had already seen another post by Blake that referred to a poetry reading. It took him five minutes to locate the post. Both tagged a restaurant in Alhambra called The Black Bull.

He quickly checked the dates of the posts. Wednesday, August 15, and Thursday, October 25, but in reference to the previous night. It wasn't exactly a smoking gun, but Jackson considered checking out The Black Bull's poetry café. Maybe someone there would recognize Blake.

He clicked off Facebook and sat back, turning his eyes down to the papers in his hands one more time, willing himself to find something that would give him a clue to who William Blake was.

"Wow."

Jackson looked up. Half a dozen thumbnail images of Noelle filled the screen. Her with black hair and a black eye. Her in a red sundress looking wistfully over her shoulder. Her in a silver evening gown. Her in a pink top, probably a swimsuit, seeing as how her hair was wet. A pair of headshots.

"Sweet as she is cute?" Mouse said. "She must be really sweet."

"She is."

"Anything else?" Mouse asked.

"You going to be around later, if I need help?"

"I work at four."

Jackson checked the clock. 3:12. "Thanks, Mouse."

"Anytime."

Wishing him luck in his gaming, Jackson headed home. He stopped at a local movie rental store on the way and checked out everything of Noelle's he could: *Clarity*, *Safe at Home*, *Catch and Release*, and the 2010 season of *The Big Bang Theory*. He left the store tapped and with his Sunday evening mapped out.

Chapter Seventeen

4:01 p.m.

SAM THREW JACKSON'S plans a curveball. A big, Clayton Kershaw, twelve-to-six stinker of a curveball. Her blue Ford Fusion was parked in his driveway when he returned from Mouse's, and he parked behind it with a frown. As he got out, the Fusion's door opened and Sam emerged. She wore distressed jeans and a fitted pink T-shirt that made her look very pretty. The look on her face, however, did not.

"Sam? What are you doing here?"

"How dare you!" she said, her voice loud and on the verge of cracking.

"Dare I what? What are you talking about?"

"I'm talking about you cutting me out of your life, Jackson. You call me and tell me you're in Vegas on a case, then tell me Hillary is missing, and the next thing I know, I'm seeing on the news that you're wanted for murder and domestic terrorism. Then your phone dies and I don't hear from you . . ." She shook her head and bit down on her lip. "Do you know how worried I was?"

"I'm sorry, Sam. What can I tell you, they arrested me? I spent two days in various forms of jail."

"And you've been out for a month, Jackson! I had to find out from Reggie that you were even alive." She was breathing hard, fire about to shoot out of her eyes or nostrils. Or both.

She took a step closer. "I accepted that, considering the circumstances. And I gave you time, I gave you space, because I understood you had been through a lot. But you never called. You never returned my calls. You haven't been to church in weeks. I had to pry the truth of what actually happened out of Reggie. So yes, I repeat my original question, Jackson. How dare you?"

He let her stare at him for several seconds before answering. "I was protecting you, Sam."

"From what?"

He hesitated.

"From what?"

"From me!"

Her anger was replaced by incredulity. "From you? From you how?"

Jackson sighed. "Sam, you know what I did in Nevada."

"No, I don't know," she said, shaking her head. "All I know is what the news told me, and what Reggie told me, which is still just the bare bones. I'm still in the dark."

"It's better that way," he said, looking away.

Sam turned his head back with both hands. "Why won't you tell me? I'm not being curious or nosy. I care about you, Jackson, and I don't like being shut out."

He lowered his head.

"Jackson, why won't you talk to me?"

"Because I can't bear the thought of you knowing what I did!"

They locked eyes for several seconds, hers welling with tears.

Jackson gently took hold of her wrists and lowered her hands. "Sam, I care about you too. That's why I've been avoiding you. I think it's better for your sake if someone like me isn't part of your life."

Sam's face displayed disbelief, then disappointment, then a flash of anger. Then she slapped him.

"How dare you, Jackson!"

"Sam, I'm sor—"

Sam turned her back and paced toward the bumper of her car. Slowly, she turned around. "Do you have any idea how much that hurts?"

"Hurts? I'm trying not to hurt you."

Sam shook her head. "You're telling me that you're withdrawing from my life for my protection. What do you think that says about me? That I'm too pretentious to want to be around you anymore, or that I'm too fragile to take it? Is that what you think?

"No. I think that the last month has been agonizing. And I didn't want you to have to go through that. And it wasn't just Nevada. It's Ryan and Stephanie. It's Ashley and the Grays and the Silvaz. My life is a mess. I was just trying to keep you from having to be a part of the chaos."

She pursed her lips as more tears flowed. She walked over and again cupped Jackson's face in her hands. "Jackson, don't you see . . . I want to be part of the chaos."

"Why?"

"Because you're part of it. You're in the middle of a storm, and so I want to be there too. Jackson, I want to be there for you." She slid her hands down his cheeks, her fingers under his ears, thumbs on his cheeks in front of them. "And let me tell you, there is nothing you could do that would make me stop caring."

"I believe you, Sam. Really. That's why I wanted to shelter you."

"I appreciate that. But I'm a big girl. I can take it. And if you want proof, try me. I'm not running for the door when it gets hairy." She dropped her hands, found his, and clenched them tight. "I'm here."

Jackson looked into her eyes, deep as ever, still moist from the tears. Slowly, he nodded. "Fine. I'll tell you everything. You wanna come in?"

She nodded and he led her inside. They sat down, side by side on the couch, and for the next half hour, Jackson explained in thorough detail everything that had taken place in Nevada—Hillary hiring him, going undercover, Hillary's disappearance, the horrible mind-control experiments that had been conducted at Blane Air Force Base in the Nevada desert, and the lengths Jackson had gone to in rescuing Hillary. He recounted kidnapping and torturing the crooked sheriff, shooting his way onto and through the base, forcing information from Senator Moore at gunpoint, and finding Hillary on the houseboat. He told her about his arrest, his talks with various law enforcement agents, and the deal that had been struck to keep him a free man. And lastly, he divulged what life had been like since coming back, how he had been trying to cope with what he had done.

Sam held his hand throughout, squeezing tighter as the story grew more tragic. When he was finally finished, she engulfed him in a long, warm hug. Eventually, it became wet as well, and he realized she was crying. And holding him as tightly as he'd ever been held.

When she finally let go, she sniffed and wiped her eyes. Then she cradled his hand in hers. "I'm so sorry you had to go through that."

"I didn't so much go through it as do it, Sam."

More tears streamed down her face. "You were saving Hillary."

"Yeah."

Sam lowered her head, sniffed a few more times. Jackson put his hand on her back, now consoling her.

"I wish you would have come to me," she said.

"This is why I didn't, Sam."

"I could have helped you through this. You didn't have to be alone."

Jackson stood. "Sam, what happens the next time I get in too deep, and you get hurt because you're close to me?"

She sniffed one more time and nodded. "Yeah, that's possible." She stood too. "But what happens to Ashley if you don't go in to save her? Or to Stephanie if you just drive by? Or Hillary if . . . if you didn't do what you did?"

Jackson didn't say anything, and Sam walked over to him and again clutched his hands. "Jackson, you don't need to be alone. I get where you're coming from, I really do. But that's not what I want. I don't think it's what Reggie wants, or your grandpa. We all love you, Jackson. And we are here for you, no matter what."

He nodded, unable to speak.

"And God is here too, Jackson. I don't want to sound trite, but we are told to cast our cares on Jesus."

"I know."

"I know I'm not your church monitor, but you haven't been there in a long time."

"I felt a little guilty going with blood on my hands."

"Well there's no point running from the One who can see everywhere. And remember, His blood trumps all the rest."

"I know. But everyone keeps telling me it's not my fault, that I did what I had to do, that I was justified in killing all those people."

She nodded.

"Well if I was guilty, it would explain this weight on my shoulders, and if I confessed it, I could get rid of it. But if the weight isn't sin, what is it?"

"Life," Sam said.

He looked down at her.

"Sometimes life is heavy. Life is a burden, unbearably so in some cases. But you don't have to carry it alone. Let us in. Let God in."

Jackson swallowed.

"I'm not taking no for an answer," she said. "I know what's between you and God is between you and God, but I'm not letting you slide away into the Slough of Despond. I'm picking you up for church next Sunday, and if I have to physically drag you out of bed, I will."

"I'd like to see you try."

Her eyes flashed playfully in response.

Jackson actually smiled.

"Jackson, promise me that you won't shut me out again. If you want to end our friendship and get rid of me for good, then do it. But as long as you and I are friends, I want in. Got it?"

"I got it. And for what it's worth, I'm sorry, Sam. I didn't mean to hurt you."

"I know."

"But I did. And I'm sorry."

"I forgive you," she said, and reached her arms around him for another tight hug. Jackson hugged her back, relaxing against her and leaning his head on hers. He had missed Sam, and truth be told, had maybe been shutting her out for his own sake too—a pity party of sorts. But that was over now.

At last, they separated. "You want to stay for dinner?" he asked. "There's leftover sloppy joes with your name on them."

"Mm, tempting but I can't. I have to get home to Stephanie."

"I haven't forgotten about her."

"No?"

"No. I haven't just been playing video games. I checked in on Brady last week."

"And?"

"And it's been three months. He needs a little more time."

Sam nodded. "I should get going."

"Thanks for coming, Sam. And I really am sorry."

"I know. It's in the past." She stepped forward and pecked him on the jaw. "Goodbye, Jackson."

"Bye, Sam."

*   *   *

Monday, October 29
1:47 p.m.

THE AIR was still warm, but the skies had clouded overnight and not broken throughout the day. Rain wasn't in the forecast, just gray, hazy, mountain-obscuring clouds. It took the joy out of the trip northeast to Pasadena. At least the freeways weren't clogged early on a Monday afternoon.

The first day of shooting of episode 1.8, "All We've Got" had begun without fanfare. When Jackson had explained to Viggo that he was working to find Noelle's stalker—it had been news to Viggo that she even had one—the *Twenty Something* director had let Jackson leave early. Various things—the weather forecast, a guest star's union paperwork, miscommunication with Craft Service— had delayed shooting on several scenes anyhow.

Jackson, distracted for a while by his talk with Sam, had stayed up until two a.m. Sunday watching Noelle's greatest hits. Parts of three movies, three episodes of television (on DVD and streaming online), and one commercial on YouTube—Noelle enjoying yogurt in sweats on the couch while a female voiceover tried to make the idea sexy and fun. He'd learned something though. William Blake was right about two things—Noelle was indeed attractive, and she was a very good actress. How she had missed out on a major role as long as she had was a mystery, but then again, L.A. was teeming with pretty faces, and everybody in California was an actor of some caliber.

He had also reread every single tweet William Blake/@2EdgedPen had ever sent. He'd made several suggestive comments about other actresses, but nothing as forward as offering to star in a love scene with any of them. Mostly it had been pathetic hero worship with way too many LOLs and smiley faces for a real man. At quarter till two, still fighting sleep, while finishing *Catch and Release* (Noelle's two short scenes were long over, but the overall plot was mildly interesting) Jackson had stumbled upon a handful of tweets referring to a Pasadena City College. Combining them with the tweet where Blake had told Noelle he went to school in Pasadena, Jackson figured it was worth investigating.

Pasadena City College didn't look like a typical city college. The administrative offices off Colorado Boulevard were separated from the street by a long, tree-lined reflecting pool. The lawns were immaculate, striped with walkways that connected the various buildings. Right, left, and ahead, the structures were imposing, several stories tall, all white. Jackson felt as if he were on the campus of a major university, not a city college.

His first stop was the administrative building. He talked with a woman there who was less than helpful when Jackson asked if she could direct him to his friend, William Blake. She didn't know anyone by that name and was not legally permitted to access school records to find him without justification (and Jackson didn't have any in her eyes). She did offer that it probably didn't matter. Pasadena City College had no housing on campus, so without Blake's class schedule, finding him would be almost impossible anyway.

Before leaving, Jackson ventured to the library, the bookstore, the gym—he had to try everywhere—and the cafeteria. He talked to seven people, six students and a janitor, none of whom knew a William Blake. He asked the last of them how big the campus was. Almost forty-thousand students. Oh-for-eight wasn't so bad then.

Jackson loitered for another twenty minutes, long enough to speak with two more students and a police cadet. None of them knew William Blake and the cadet suggested Jackson leave the campus. He obliged.

It was only early afternoon, and Jackson thought about swinging down to Alhambra to check out The Black Bull. But unless Blake was tight with the owner like Jackson was with the owner of Cameron's, it was unlikely he'd get a hit. Plus Reggie wouldn't roll on him, so why should he expect the owner of The Black Bull to roll on Blake . . . if he even knew him? He headed for home instead.

Lamenting a wasted trip, Jackson pulled out his cell phone and dialed Noelle's number. She had been shooting on the soundstage in the Valley that morning, so Jackson hadn't spoken with her. He wasn't sure on her afternoon schedule, and was happy when she answered with a quiet, "Hello?"

"Noelle, it's Jackson."

"Hey. You find anything?"

"A name. William Blake."

"Doesn't ring any bells."

"Afraid that's all I have right now, but I'm still investigating."

"Oh."

"I wanted to ask you, do you by any chance have access to your old work? I was able to rent the movies and catch most of the TV shows online, but I'm still missing a few pieces."

"Why are you watching my work?"

"Blake watched it all," Jackson answered. "And somewhere along the line he switched from an overly enthusiastic fan to an obscene fanatic."

"And you think something in one of my roles triggered it?"

"It's possible. I figure it's the best way to get in his head."

"This is embarrassing," Noelle said, "but I actually have a copy of everything on DVD. My commercials, uncredited roles—even my audition tapes. It's so vain."

"Not at all."

"Which ones do you need?"

Jackson replayed the list in his head, and recited the titles he hadn't been able to find at the rental store or online. "Any chance you're at home. I could swing by and pick them up?"

"I'm actually just on my way out," Noelle said. "Dentist appointment."

"Trouble?"

"No, just found a time they could squeeze me in. I'm due in twenty minutes, but I can drop them off after."

"Sure." He gave her his address, wished her the best at the dentist, and settled in for the long drive back across town.

Chapter Eighteen

JACKSON STARTLED AWAKE instead of fading in. The room was still dark, although not as dark as it had been. That quickly changed as a door closed, and Jackson figured out what had startled him. A nurse exiting, checking vitals or something.

He wished he had awakened earlier, in time to ask for some morphine. His shoulder was starting to hurt again. It was just a dull ache, but he had a feeling it was going to get stronger.

The nurse had left the door a few inches ajar, allowing enough light into the room to illuminate the couch by the wall. Jackson couldn't help but smile.

Curled up at the far end, still in her pastel blue hospital scrubs, was Sam. The light from the open door played across her face, tranquil as she slept, using her hands for a pillow. Her golden hair had largely come out of a makeshift ponytail, and traced her cheeks in a way that made Jackson's hands jealous.

He sighed and closed his eyes again. Just having her there seemed to make the pain in his shoulder and the reality of having been shot seem a little less traumatic.

He slept fitfully, dreaming of the shooting again and again. Every time it started with him in the cemetery, and every time it morphed into something else: Sam chasing him through his house and her apartment with a gun, Reggie and Leroy shooting it out on a dusty Old West street, doctors and nurses having a free-for-all in the emergency room. Several times, he found himself half awake, able to marvel at the absurdity of his dreams but unable to escape them.

The last dream had him as the shooter, taking potshots at an indoor range. But instead of shapeless black cutouts, the targets were various women he knew—Sam, Maggie, Ashley, Stephanie, Noelle Consciousness slowly pulled him from the horror, and as he opened his eyes, he hoped against hope to see daylight. He'd settle for predawn light streaming through the blinds.

Even better. Sam was standing by the side of his bed.

"Hi," she said softly.

"Hey."

"You okay?"

"Dreams," he said, blinking a few times to shed any reminder of them. He glanced at the rolling table beside his bed. His eyes settled on the cup of ice chips, or more likely by now, just water. "Would you mind?"

Sam reached for the cup, her hands half covered by the sleeves under her hospital scrubs. The Styrofoam squeaked as she picked it up and leaned over the bed. Jackson caught the faint smell of citrus—perfume, lotion?—as she extended a spoon of ice chips to his mouth. He slipped the ice off the spoon with his tongue and concentrated on Sam. Little if any makeup, hair wavy from having been in the ponytail, and a yawn as she placed the cup back on the table. She'd never been more beautiful, and Jackson was pretty sure she exceeded any fantasy about a tender, loving nurse any guy had ever had.

"Sorry I missed our date," he said.

"Date?"

"You know what I meant."

Sam smiled. "I'm sorry too."

"Rain check?"

"Count on it."

He settled back into his pillow. "So you're a nurse. How bad is this?"

"The doctor says you'll make a full recovery."

"I mean, how long am I going to be stuck here?"

"You just got out of surgery a few hours ago."

"Which reminds me, I assume I had a catheter. I'm still hooked up, right, because else I . . . Sam, what's wrong?"

She had bitten down on her lip, her eyes fixated on his bandage.

"Sam?"

"You were shot, Jackson."

"Ah-ha. So that explains the hole in my shoulder."

"I'm serious. Somebody did this to you."

"I know. And I'll find them."

"You'll find them? What about letting the police find them?"

"I, we. They'll get found. But after I sleep, okay?"

"Of course. I'm sorry."

He reached for her hand. "Thanks for being here, Sam. Sorry to ruin your night."

She responded by tucking her hair behind her ear and leaning down to kiss his forehead.

"You missed by a few inches," he said.

"Go to sleep."

*   *   *

Tuesday, October 30
6:15 a.m.

VIGGO CALLED at quarter after six. They were shooting on the soundstage that morning, and he didn't need Jackson to come in. He did, however, need him to run to Rancho Palos Verdes and pick up a contract from a homeowner there. They would be shooting several scenes at the house next week, and this was typical paperwork. Could he pick it up and meet them at one at Marina del Rey?

Groggily, Jackson agreed and took down the address. Then he slept for two more hours.

By nine a.m., he was on the road. Rancho Palos Verdes was at the southwestern tip of Los Angeles. From its location at the end of the Palos Verdes Peninsula, the coast ran north past all the beach communities, the airport, and ultimately Santa Monica before curving west. The coastline ran almost due east in the other direction, past the port and Long Beach before curving south again. Nestled in the hills, Rancho Palos Verdes was an escape from flat, gridlocked L.A. The only downside to living there was the lack of beaches, more than made up for by the spectacular cliff-side views.

The drive would take about an hour, plus traffic delays. Ten o'clock. An hour back. Eleven o'clock. Jackson decided he had time to swing by the Airport Courthouse on La Cienega, one of seven buildings to house Los Angeles' public records. Searching through all of the William Blakes in Los Angeles would be almost impossible, but Jackson had two potential sources to help him.

Brandon, an old friend of Grant's, was manning the front desk. Jackson had sort of been hoping for the other source, but this one was definitely cheaper. They made two minutes of small talk, and then Jackson asked for help finding William Blake.

133

"Is that all you know about him?"

"He might go to Pasadena City College, but yeah."

"So we're looking younger than older?"

"Probably, but not for sure."

"Have a seat, I'll see what I can find."

"Actually, I've got to run an errand in RPV. Can I swing by on the way back?"

Brandon shrugged. "Whatever works for you, man."

Jackson thanked him and left. Back in the car, he called Connie. She worked part-time at the DMV. Her second of three husbands had left her more than enough money to live on, but Connie had fine tastes—at least she claimed they were fine—and worked to stay busy and to finance her extravagance. He knew she was working Tuesday morning, and when she didn't answer, he left her a voicemail.

She called back as he was turning onto Palos Verdes Drive, causing his cell phone to explode with "Shout it Out Loud" by Kiss. He scooped it off the seat. "Hey, Connie."

"Jackson. You called?"

"I need a favor."

"Goodness, child, you're going to owe me your soul pretty soon."

Perish the thought.

"Name your price, Connie."

"I don't know. Last time I did you a favor you reneged on our deal."

"I know, and I'm terribly sorry. And I made that up to you, remember?"

She was quiet for a second.

"Connie?"

"Fluffy needs to go to the vet Thursday morning, and I have to work. Schedule mix-up."

Jackson winced. Fluffy was Connie's Pomeranian. He loathed the little varmint, a feeling reciprocated by Fluffy. But he wasn't in a position to say no.

"What time?"

"Ten a.m."

"I'll have to clear it with my boss."

"That television producer?"

"That's right."

She thought for a moment. "What do you need?"

"Information on a William Blake."

"What kind of information?"

"Age, address, photos."

"Jackson, you know I can't give you that information. I thought you weren't working anymore anyhow."

"It's a favor for a friend, Connie. Please."

"You'll take Fluffy?"

"I will make sure she's at the vet at ten."

More silence. "What's the name again?"

"William Blake."

"Probably more than one, honey. It's a big city."

"And I'm not sure which one it is that I'm after.' He winced even as he asked, "Can you get me info on all of them?"

Connie's sigh was like an airplane taking off. "I'll do what I can. Give me some time."

"Thanks, Connie."

He closed his phone before she could make any more demands.

The day was cool and clear, and the views were splendid. Catalina had never looked so close, despite being twenty miles away. The house was on Sea Cove Drive, just past Terranea Resort. It was a classic mission-style home, with adobe walls, orange clay shingles on the roof, and palms dotting the yard and lining the street. Jackson was sure his Granada was way out of place, but then again, so were his blue jeans and long-sleeved tee.

A butler opened the door, and Jackson announced that he was Mr. Polansky's courier.

"Please come in," the butler said, inviting Jackson into an expansive marble entryway that looked through the length of the house, out and down to a patio and pool overlooking the ocean. "One moment, sir."

Jackson waited. Three minutes, and then the butler returned. He carried a manila envelope, sealed. "Here you are, sir."

"Thank you."

"My pleasure, sir. Good day."

Jackson returned to his car, wondering how much money you had to have so that you didn't even have to deal with the person you were dealing with so you didn't have to deal with another person. Probably more than he had.

He circled around Rancho Palos Verdes on the way back, taking in as many views of the ocean as he could. It was one sight that never grew old.

As he headed for the Airport Courthouse again, his thoughts turned back to the case of William Blake. Last night, he had watched the remainder of Noelle's professional acting work, which she had dropped off late afternoon. Prior to *Twenty Something* there had been eight different TV shows—eleven episodes total—three feature films, one made for TV movie, a live spot on *Ellen* to promote *Safe at Home*, and five commercials. Her roles had included a waitress, a corpse, another waitress, a political lobbyist, a star-struck groupie, a flirty neighbor, a witness to a crime, a psychic, a loser's girlfriend, and a girl in the crowd. That and Girl in Bikini #2 in *Clarity*, the role that apparently had turned William Blake into a stalker.

At least, that was the best Jackson could figure it. There was nothing in any of her roles that screamed "stalk me." She was fun and flirty in her three episodes of a short-lived sitcom called *The Champs*. Her character on *The West Wing* was a buttoned-down professional. She had attitude as the loser's girlfriend, and was perfectly annoying as the groupie. Aside from her leading role as Annie the waitress in *Safe at Home*, she wouldn't have stood out in any of the other works had Jackson not been looking for her.

He'd also reread Blake's more recent tweets, trying to detect a shift in them that corresponded with his piqued interest in Noelle. But nothing in the rest of his behavior was the least bit unsettling, and none of his tweets hinted at his true identity. Ironic, the impersonality of social media that was supposed to protect people from sexual predators was having the reverse affect for Noelle.

Jackson checked in with Brandon, who reported there were seventeen William Blakes in the system. He provided Jackson with basic demographic info for each of them, and Jackson thanked him and took the info to Leroy's houseboat in Marina del Rey. He still had over an hour before he was supposed to meet the rest of the cast, so he bummed a roast beef sandwich off his grandpa while scouring the info from Brandon. He was able to discount six of the seventeen due to age demographics. Two were under the age of ten, and four were over the age of seventy. Geezers running around with canes didn't scare him.

"Thought you weren't supposed to be working, bud," Leroy said.

"I'm not. This is a favor."

"A rose by any other name . . ."

"Funny you should mention roses," Jackson said, and gave Leroy the basics of the case, sparing him the graphic details.

Leroy frowned. "Sounds like a nut."

"And I don't get it. I watched everything she's ever been in, and I matched up the release and air dates of her work with the comments Blake made on Twitter."

"Are we still speaking English?"

"Messages on the internet."

"I'm with you."

"The pattern was always the same. Noelle put out a twe—posted a message, something to let her fans know that she was going to be on a show that was about to air or a movie that was due to come out, and each time, he would respond, excited and praising her work, making dorky jokes. He was a little goofy, but not dangerous."

"So what changed?"

"I don't know. He was fine until a few weeks ago, right after the first episode of *Twenty Something* aired. Then his comments turned creepy. In fact . . ."

"I hear wheels turning."

Jackson nodded. "That's when his comments about *Clarity* came, just last week in fact."

"*Clarity?*"

"A movie she was in back in '08, just a bit part. She was in a bikini, it was rather flattering. But he didn't say anything about it at the time because he wasn't following her then."

"He's followed her?"

"Metaphorically, Grandpa. Online. He wasn't aware of her until *Safe at Home* came out. That's when he first became a fan of hers. Watched everything . . ." He closed his eyes and pictured the list. "A month ago, September 29, he said he was watching everything she'd been in. But he wasn't creepy then either. Not overly, at least, and no mention of *Clarity*. Not until after seeing *Twenty Something*."

"So what happened in *Twenty Something?*" Leroy asked.

Jackson slouched back. "I don't know."

"Ain't that your show, kiddo?"

"Yeah, but it was before my time."

"Maybe that's where you should look."

Jackson furrowed his brow. "I'm sure I can get a copy from somebody. Maybe that's where the trigger is. Why didn't I see this earlier?"

Leroy shrugged. "You want another sandwich?"

"No, I'm—"

Kiss started playing again, and Jackson reached for his phone. "Hey, Connie."

"Twenty-three William Blakes with California driver's licenses."

"How many in L.A.?"

She counted quietly. "Twelve."

"Any live in Pasadena?"

"No."

"What's the closest?"

"Must I get out a map?"

"Ballpark."

Connie sighed. "West Covina."

That wasn't that close. "Any way you can e-mail me what you've found?"

"Already done. Fluffy likes to get to the doctor a little early, at least ten minutes. Helps her calm down."

Jackson gritted his teeth. So would a kick in the snoot. "I promise, Connie."

"Let me know if you need anything more," she said. Her voice sounded tired and upset, but Jackson could hear the alligator grin as she mentally compiled more chores for him to do.

"Never get into debt, Grandpa," he said as he returned the phone to his pocket. "I gotta go."

"Don't be a stranger."

"I won't."

Leroy waved as Jackson headed for the door. From Leroy's boat, perpetually situated off Bora Bora Way, Jackson had to circle to the far edge of the harbor, to Mindanao Way. He parked and went on foot into the Burton W. Chace Park at the end of the manmade peninsula. The park had been commandeered by the crew of *Twenty Something* for the afternoon, and already their activity was obvious, clearing areas, rigging lighting, checking angles. Jackson looked for a familiar face, and found one in the line producer Linda.

"Hey, do you know where I can find a computer around here?"

She looked up from hers, a tiny laptop resting on a couple of crates of equipment. "For what?"

"Check e-mail."

"Use your phone."

He swallowed. "Uh, it doesn't do e-mail."

Linda stared at him as if he had landed in a spaceship and walked to her on three legs. Then she sighed. "Here, you can use mine."

"You sure?"

"I have to call Maura anyway."

"Thanks."

"Sure. No porn. I don't need a virus."

"Just e-mail."

Linda stepped away and Jackson quickly logged into his e-mail account. He brought up the message from Connie and scanned her information on the twelve William Blakes in Los Angeles. Names, addresses, dates of birth, height, weight, hair and eye color. No pictures, which prompted a frown. If he was going to take Fluffy to the vet and not the pound, he deserved photos.

Jackson sighed. Twelve descriptions, two of whom he crossed off because they were on the over-seventy list. That left ten William Blakes with driver's licenses in L.A., plus an eleventh Brandon had info on but Connie didn't because he apparently didn't own a driver's license. Then there were another eleven in California, and countless others roaming the country, any of whom could be Noelle's online stalker.

"You done?" Linda asked.

Jackson logged out of his e-mail. "Yeah, thanks."

She scooted back over and took control of the computer.

"Um, who do I see about getting copies of previous episodes?" he asked.

"What for?"

He shrugged. "Curiosity."

"They're on the show website."

"Of course."

"Anything else? I'm kind of busy."

"No, thanks again."

Jackson left Linda and found a bench under an all-white pergola. His phone indicated he had nine minutes before one. He called Mouse.

"Hey."

"Hey, man. Can you do me another favor?"

"Name it."

Jackson looked around to make sure he wasn't being overheard. "William Blake's online handle. There any more you can do with it to find out who he is?"

Mouse hesitated. "Depends how far I'm authorized to go."

"I have no authority, Mouse."

"Then I'm pretty much at the end of the line."

Jackson sighed. "I tell you what. Do whatever you're comfortable with. And don't tell me what you do."

"I'll call you back in a few."

"Thanks."

Jackson clapped his phone shut with another sigh, then turned over his shoulder as he heard Viggo's voice booming across the park. It was time to go to work.

Chapter Nineteen

6:04 p.m.

AFTER WORK, JACKSON drove home and put a frozen pizza in the oven. While it was cooking, he went upstairs and printed off everything Connie had sent him. Taking his computer downstairs with him, he collapsed on the couch and waited for the oven timer to ding.

Due to something having to do with permits and stretched camera crews, Viggo had been adamant about getting the Chace Park scenes filmed Tuesday. It had made for a chaotic afternoon, especially when there was a problem with the main camera and Mario couldn't remember his lines and the stiff playing the private investigator that Mario's character was hiring was all wrong. Jackson had made the mistake of making a comment to Viggo between scenes, saying the guy seemed too much like a caricature, and for the rest of the afternoon, Viggo had asked Jackson to critique every word and gesture the actor made. By the end of the day, the actor hated Viggo and Jackson equally, and Jackson—through Viggo's directing—had molded the guy into a carbon copy of himself, complete with two wardrobe changes, a new accent, and a squint instead of sunglasses. That brought up a whole new set of problems as the sun began to set and the actor looked as if he was blind. Finally they had completed the scenes, and Viggo had left fuming that he might have to rewrite the end of the episode because he wasn't sure the actor would ever work for him again.

"Don't worry about it," Mario had said after filming. Jackson, among others, had just taken a verbal beating from Viggo. "He's not mad at you."

"I'd believe that if my face wasn't blistered."

"He asked for your opinion, man. He followed it. His call."

"Yeah, thanks."

"Besides, I'm the dope who couldn't remember my lines."

"I hear it happens to the best of them."

"I wouldn't know. Hey, Shawny and I are hitting the town tonight. You interested?"

"Thanks, but I got stuff I've got to take care of at home."

"All right. Don't worry about it, man. He's like this when things get hectic."

"Great."

Jackson had left without talking to anyone and toyed with the idea of calling Noelle on the way home. She hadn't been at the park, since she wasn't in the scene, so they hadn't spoken yet that day. But he had nothing new to report. Just a call from Mouse to tell him that he had traced something to something, and IP address this and that, and the majority of the tweets had originated from an apartment building in San Marino. None of the William Blakes lived anywhere close to San Marino, a small community east of downtown, halfway between the 10 and the 210. But San Marino was close to Pasadena and Alhambra, so that was something.

"How sure are we that his name is really William Blake?" Jackson had asked Mouse.

"Not. Dudes use fake names all the time online."

And with that, the idea that William Blake wasn't really William Blake had taken hold. Jackson had been preoccupied the rest of the afternoon, trying to run the facts that he remembered in his head. But he'd only glanced at the information from Connie and Brandon. So when they had finally wrapped for the day, he'd been anxious to get home and get to work.

If only he wasn't so mentally exhausted.

The oven beeped, and Jackson snapped back to the present. He sliced the pizza into fourths and brought half of it back to the living room. After some quick channel flipping, he settled on a MAC football game. He had no interest in a matchup between Bowling Green and Toledo, and judging by the stands at the game, neither did anyone else. He muted the TV and studied his printouts as he ate.

Connie and Brandon had provided him with info on eleven William Blakes in a potentially dangerous age demographic. Two in Anaheim and two in Compton, and one each in Florence, Huntington Beach, Lakewood, Rowland Heights, Van Nuys, West Covina, and Yorba Linda. Ages from seventeen to sixty-four. Two military veterans dropped to the bottom of the list. Same with one of the two in Anaheim, because he was the one without a driver's license, and thus would have to take the bus or drop a fortune on taxi fare to get to the coast and cause Noelle any real harm. Neither was ideal for such purposes. William Blake in Lakewood was a tenured professor at USC, which didn't make him a saint, but lessened the chance he was an internet stalker. That left seven, none with any apparent ties to Pasadena City College.

Next, Jackson again pored over all the messages Blake had sent Noelle, looking for anything in them that linked to any of the William Blakes on his list. It would have been a reach to connect anything.

His mind was at the point of shutting down, so he quit the research for a while. He found the *Twenty Something* website and quickly located the four episodes that had already aired. Grabbing another slice of pizza, he watched the show from the beginning.

Jackson found himself losing interest by the middle of the third episode. The idea of Mr. X was intriguing, but *Twenty Something* seemed to be slipping into the mold of too many serial dramas—plenty of intrigue, but way too drawn out and way too much extra stuff going on. Serial dramas were designed to span multiple seasons, dozens and dozens of hours of television. Most only had the plot to carry a six-part miniseries, maybe a half season at best.

Leaving the episodes streaming to catch Noelle's voice, Jackson began rereading everything—the tweets Blake had sent to her, the information from Connie and Brandon, the erotic e-mail—one more time. It was mind-numbing, going through it all again, and a glance at the clock told him he really should get to bed. Viggo, in one of his moments of relative calm, had instructed Jackson to be at the Hotel Oceana at eight. The entire group was going to be there, including Noelle, and Jackson wanted to have something to tell her, other than he found her new hit show to be ho-hum. So he kept working.

As the fourth episode, "Not the Only Ones," wound down with the "shocking" revelation that Braylon, Cate, Roxie, and Ty weren't the only ones trying to find Mr. X, Jackson completed another read through of everything. He tossed the papers down in disgust and rubbed his bleary eyes.

There was nothing there besides what he had already picked up. And nothing from the first four episodes seemed to be a trigger for Blake's sexual obsession with Noelle, unless he had a thing for straight hair or leather. She didn't dress overly immodest, didn't flaunt her sexuality, and didn't do anything that struck Jackson as inflammatory. Then again, he wasn't a stalker.

The MAC football game on TV was long over, and the screen aired a blond-haired, bright-eyed female reporter as she stood in front of the New England

Patriots' stadium. Oblivious to the on-screen text that would explain what she was talking about, Jackson's eyes glazed over as he stared at her. Something in his brain made a connection, and he snapped to and sat up.

Setting his laptop on the coffee table, Jackson got up and fetched a pencil and a pad of paper. Normally he could do this sort of thing in his head, but his brain was fried. He flipped on the light, sat back down, and sketched a rough graph, numbering it from one to eleven. Going over the descriptions of the William Blakes from Connie and Brandon, he marked down hair and eye color.

Hair: four blond, three brown, two black, one red, one bald.

Eyes: five brown, three green, three blue.

He scanned the combos: blond-blue, blond-blue, blond-brown, blond-brown; brown-blue, brown-brown, brown-green; black-brown, black-green; red-green; bald-brown.

Bells were ringing in Jackson's head. He opened the e-mail from Blake and forced himself to read it a third time. When he reached the third paragraph, words seemed to leap off the screen.

It was a graphic description of Blake and Noelle caught up in a rapturous sexual interlude. He described everything, including them staring into each other's eyes, the azure and apple combining to form a turquoise the color of a "sultry Caribbean lagoon." Noelle's eyes were sky blue, meaning—if Jackson was reading the poetry properly—that Blake's were apple. Green.

He read on. "*Your flaxen tresses drape a wanton but angelic face. Dappled with sweat my hair is yours but darker by a trace.*" Blake had blond hair too. Jackson turned to his list again, mumbling the words as he searched. "Blond-green, blond-green, blond-green." None of the eleven William Blakes had blond hair and green eyes.

It was a smutty poem. Somewhat poorly written, if Jackson dared be a critic of such things. And "yours but darker by a trace" was ambiguous at best. But if he was interpreting the information properly, then none of the eligible eleven William Blakes registered in Los Angeles with the DMV or the department of records were the William Blake who was stalking Noelle.

The name was an alias.

*　　　　　*　　　　　*

Wednesday, October 31
7:53 a.m.

VIGGO HAD called at quarter after six again, putting in the morning coffee order. It was always a standing order, and any changes were usually made the day before. Jackson concluded Viggo was punishing him, and when he was unable to sleep any longer, he got up, growled at the drizzle, and went to stock up on caffeine.

The drizzle was steady by the time Jackson arrived at the Hotel Oceana. Everyone was there, scurrying around, trying to keep equipment and themselves dry. As Jackson passed out coffees to barking directors and producers and camera dudes, he gathered that the plan had been to shoot a scene around the pool, with the four main characters hashing out their plans now that the search for Mr. X had fizzled. But people didn't sit around a pool in the rain.

"Let's just move it into the room."

"We're not set for a room shot."

"Let's get set."

"Anybody seen a radar?"

"Is this decaf?"

"Radar's never right anyhow."

"Whose room should we use?"

"They're all the same."

"What do you mean it's never right? It's radar."

"We need Props if we're shooting in the room."

"Do we still have access to the rooms?"

"I didn't hear any answer on the radar."

"Our actors are in a room right now."

"Can we postpone?"

"We don't have any rain scenes scheduled."

"Yeah, and we're already tight."

"Looks steady all morning, afternoon's iffy."

Viggo's curse ended the free-for-all. The group dispersed slightly, each preparing to pout or contemplate on their own or in small huddles. Viggo turned to Jackson. "Any bright ideas?"

"Are you serious?"

"Nominally. One never knows where one might get inspiration."

"This is right after the empty warehouse from yesterday, right?"

Viggo sipped his Mocha Valencia. "The next morning, after they've slept on their find, or lack thereof."

"Can I see a script?"

Viggo turned and waved Taylor over. He carried an umbrella, the runoff causing him to stand several feet away. Neither Viggo nor Jackson were concerned about the falling rain. "Get Jackson a script."

Taylor reached into a file folder and pulled out a dozen sheets of paper. Jackson took the script, scanned it quickly. He looked up at Viggo, who was having a brief discussion with another assistant. The assistant moved on, and Jackson said, "Have it in the courtyard, in the rain."

Viggo didn't reply, just looked at him.

"Amp up the emotion, the intensity. Ask the folks at *Lost*—you want a climactic scene, make it rain."

"And why would they be out in the rain?"

Jackson shrugged. "Cate throws in the towel and is going to leave, and the others rush out to stop her. I don't know."

Viggo sipped his drink again. Then lifted his head and yelled. "Maura!"

Jackson wasn't sure if he was going to run the idea past her or have her call security to throw him out. She scampered over, a rain jacket with hood keeping her dry. "What's up?"

"We do the scene here, now, in the rain."

"What?"

Viggo explained Jackson's idea in his own words.

"It could work." She tilted her head. "It could work. We'll need to revise the script somewhat, get Props over here with some luggage. It could work."

"Get me Props," Viggo said. "Broderick!" He turned to Maura again. "And I want to see a radar for myself. Two of them."

"Anything I can do?" Jackson asked.

"Yes. Find my stars. They're in room 214. Tell them we're shooting in ten! We'll go out of order until Props can get me a suitcase."

Jackson nodded and departed, taking the steps to the second floor corridor. He rapped on the door of room 214 and a moment later Shawn Thomas opened it. "Hey, Douglas. What's up?"

Jackson stepped into the room. Mario was lying on a bed, watching one of the morning shows. Noelle sat on the other bed, reading a magazine. Jess was fussing in the mirror. One big happy family.

"Jack, what's the word?" Mario asked.

146

"If we're not shooting, I'm going back to bed," Shawn Thomas declared.

"We're shooting," Jackson said.

"Where?"

"Courtyard."

"It's raining."

"We're shooting in the rain," Jackson said.

Jess cursed into the mirror and spun around. "What?"

"Why?" Mario asked.

"What idiot had that idea?" Jess practically screamed.

"When?" Shawn Thomas asked.

"V said ten minutes."

"Fabulous," Jess huffed.

"Don't worry," Shawn Thomas said. "Wet is sexy."

"Shut up."

"Shooting in the rain's fun," Mario said.

"For you, maybe," Jess said. "Do you know how hard it is to look this good?"

Jackson looked from Shawn Thomas to Mario, expecting one of them to take the opening. Neither did, and he bit his tongue himself. Then he made eye contact with Noelle. "Can I talk with you a second?" he asked, nodding toward the door.

Mario frowned and Shawn Thomas smirked as she followed him outside onto the covered walkway. "What's up?" she asked.

"Good news and bad news," he said. "I think William Blake is an alias."

She studied him. "Is that the good or bad?"

"Both. Good that we're making progress, but bad in that it takes us back to square one."

Her shoulders dropped slightly, and he explained his reasoning about the stalker's hair and eye color to her.

"So what's next?" she asked.

"I also found a couple references on Fake Blake's Facebook page to poetry readings at a restaurant in Alhambra. I did some checking online and it looks like they have one every Wednesday night, including tonight. I figured I'd swing by and ask around. Blond hair and green eyes is pretty uncommon, so maybe somebody knows who he is."

"Worth a shot I guess."

"And I also wanted to watch *Safe at Home* again."

"Why's that?"

"Its release seems to coordinate with the time he first took notice of you. Could be he just sat down in front of a movie and was captivated by you. But it could be something else that triggered it, something that has made him obsessive."

"But he hasn't been obsessive until just recently."

"I know, and that still bugs me." He shrugged. "But it's worth a shot."

"So have you watched everything I've been in?"

He nodded.

Noelle winced. "This is embarrassing, being scrutinized like this."

"Nothing to be embarrassed about. You're good."

"You're just saying that."

Jackson shook his head. "I don't just say stuff. I mean it."

The door opened and Shawn Thomas poked his head out. "You two kids doing all right?"

"Mind your own business, Shawn Thomas."

"Oooh, snarky," he said, smiling at Jackson. Then he stuck his tongue out, wide-eyed, a "go get 'em" look.

"Jackson!" Viggo's voice echoed through the courtyard.

"Duty calls," Jackson said. "I'll talk to you later."

Noelle nodded, and he hurried down to the courtyard to do Viggo's bidding.

Chapter Twenty

THE BLACK BULL was located a block west of Garfield on Main, among half a dozen other eateries in Alhambra's commercial district. Jackson parked in a lot around back and shuffled in.

Rain had fallen all morning, making for a dramatic scene around the pool. It had taken nearly twenty-five takes, leaving everyone drenched and cranky. None more so than Jess, who had somehow learned that the idea to shoot in the rain had originated with Jackson. The rain had continued throughout the afternoon, messing with Viggo's vision of the script and causing numerous delays. He'd gotten crankier, as had the cast and crew, and there had been no small amount of relief when Viggo finally called an end to the day's shooting.

Tired, damp, and a little cranky himself, Jackson had gone home to change before heading across town to The Black Bull. Traffic had been brutal, and a drive that should have taken thirty-five minutes tops had taken over an hour and a quarter. By the time he arrived, he was seriously considering moving to rural Wyoming.

The place was half full, and Jackson took a seat around a horseshoe-shaped bar. He ignored the TVs and ordered a burger and fries. The bartender was a woman, middle-aged, moderately attractive, and when she had a break, Jackson signaled her.

"Yeah?"

"I hear there's a poetry reading deal here on Wednesdays?"

The woman studied him. "You don't look like the poetry type."

"New hobby."

She nodded to the right. "In there. Starts at eight."

Jackson followed the nod toward a pair of double doors, one open, leading to a separate seating section. "Great."

149

The bartender nodded toward a blond girl bussing a table. "That's Mallory. She can tell you more."

"Mallory? Thanks."

She nodded, and Jackson waited until the aforementioned girl carried her load of dishes into the kitchen and returned. Then he slid off his stool and approached her as she started collecting items from another table.

"Mallory?"

"Hmm?" She looked up. "Yeah, I'm Mallory."

"Lady at the bar said I should talk to you about the poetry group that meets back there."

"Yeah, eight o'clock. You're welcome to join us."

"How many of you are there?"

"Varies. Some nights only a dozen. Some we pack the room. Tonight it's Halloween, so hard to tell."

He nodded. Here came the tricky part. "Any of the regulars happen to be a guy named William Blake?"

She shook her head. "William Blake?"

"Yeah."

"No. Are you sure that's not a penname or something?"

"Why?"

"William Blake was a Romantic poet in the late seventeen and early eighteen hundreds."

"Hmm. Never heard of him."

"This guy a friend of yours?"

"More like a loose acquaintance."

"Well, you're welcome to join us, like I said . . . See if he shows up."

"Uh, I've never actually met him in person yet," Jackson said. "All I have is the name William Blake and a general description."

"What's he look like."

"Blond hair, light green eyes. Shorter . . ." he added on a whim.

"Shorter? Sounds like Rod."

"Rod?"

"Yeah. I don't remember his last name. He comes now and again."

"You know anything else about him?"

Mallory frowned a little, but if she was suspicious, it didn't hold her back. "Not really. I think he's a student around here, but so are most of the people who come."

"Thanks," Jackson said.

"If I see him, I'll point him out to you."

"I'd appreciate that."

Jackson left her and returned to the bar, where his burger and fries were already up. "Quick, thanks."

The lady bartender nodded as Jackson took his plate into the poetry room. He found himself a corner, lit only by candlelight, and tried to eat. But the incense made it hard to taste his delicious beef smothered with mushrooms and Swiss. Mallory was next into the room. She smiled and checked the candles before taking a seat. Gradually, the room filled up, about fifteen people by the time a guy in a sweater, beret, and scarf (it was possible he was dressed up for Halloween, but Jackson didn't think so) announced they were beginning. So far, no sign of William Blake/2EdgedPen/Rod. Or anyone dressed up for the holiday, at least that Jackson could tell.

The lights, if possible, got lower, and the guy in the scarf—Jeremy—read something brief and airy to set the mood. Then he invited a college-aged girl to the front. She had long blond hair, streaming over her shoulders almost to her waist. With an ashen face, she recited some long, flowing ode to the inexorable link between true love and death. The author sounded familiar, but it wasn't Tennyson or Frost or somebody everyone knew.

She finished and composed herself, and then Jeremy invited anyone who had some of their own poetry they would like to read to come forward. A black guy named Arlis edged to the front of the room and, accompanied by his pal on the bongos, read a diatribe against The Man. Nothing rhymed, and Jackson was pretty sure there was no meter being followed. But everyone snapped (poetry applause) when Arlis was done. Jackson gave Rod fifteen more minutes.

Rapunzel recited another tearjerker, and then some Goth took the stage. Jackson was ready to bow out and try his luck at Pasadena City College when his cell vibrated in his pocket. He slipped from the room, grateful for the legitimate excuse.

"Hello?"

"Jackson!"

It was Noelle. Panicky.

"What's up?"

"I just got another e-mail. He says our time is drawing near."

Jackson immediately recalled the end of Rod's first e-mail: *I will be waiting.* Now, it sounded as if he was growing tired of waiting.

"Where are you?" he asked.

"At home. Would you mind . . . I can forward it to you, but could you maybe come over? I'm nervous about being alone right now."

"Sure. I'm leaving Alhambra now. I'll be there as soon as I can."

She gave him her address and thanked him. He quickly paid for his dinner and hit the road.

Traffic had improved, and he made the drive to Palms in just over half an hour. Noelle lived on the third floor of a modern apartment complex. Jackson knocked, heard footsteps, and then heard deadbolts being turned. Noelle opened the door. She wore black lounge pants and a pink hoodie. Her hair was damp and crinkly, and she cradled a mug of something steamy in her hand. She managed a nervous smile as she let him in.

"You all right?" Jackson asked as she re-barred the door.

"I think so. This one wasn't graphic, but it had implications."

She led him to a glass coffee table in her living room. It was adjoined to the dinette and kitchen, with a single hallway leading off to the right. The apartment was small, but cozy, and Noelle had decorated it warmly.

"It's up on the computer," she said, nodding at a white sofa. Jackson sat down. "You want something to drink?" she asked.

"No, thanks."

She eased down beside him as he leaned in to read the e-mail.

My dear Noelle,

The time has almost come,

Our love to make complete;

We'll be alone at last,

Our flesh and souls shall meet.

Jackson looked at her. "Implications all right."

"Read the next part."

The day and hour unknown,

But soon we shall be one;

Alas we'll share true love,

Beneath a setting sun.

"That sounds specific," she said.

Jackson only nodded and reread the poem. "When did this come?" he asked.

"He sent it last night, but I just checked my e-mails and saw it right before I called you."

"I'm going to send it to Mouse, see if he can get a trace."

152

"Mouse?"

"Uh, a friend of mine. A computer whiz. He tracked the tweets to an apartment in San Marino."

"San Marino," she repeated.

"Next door to Pasadena and Alhambra."

"Were you at the poetry reading tonight?"

He nodded. "I talked to a waitress there, who told me that William Blake was an eighteenth century Romantic poet. She thinks it's an alias too, and said the description matches a guy named Rod."

"Rod?"

"Ring any bells?"

Noelle shook her head.

"She thought he was a student, so I'll check him out at Pasadena City College, now that I have the right name."

Noelle stood up and paced. She placed a hand on her hip. "Jackson, should I be worried?"

He stood too. "Maybe. According to this, he sounds like a guy with a plan."

"What do we do?"

"Unfortunately, he hasn't threatened you—not overtly—so I'm not sure we have anything to take to the police. But as soon as we find out who he is, we can get a restraining order."

"Will that help?"

"When he gets served a copy of it, hopefully. If he makes any further contact with you after that, he goes to jail."

She ran her hand through her hair. "I can't believe this is happening."

"We'll get him, Noelle. We know where he lives, likely where he goes to school, where he hangs out. I'll go back to PCC tomorrow, and if I don't find him there, I'll stake out the apartment until I find him. Or better yet, I can probably get Mouse to hack in and find him, now that we have a name."

"Is that legal?"

"No."

"I told you I don't want you doing anything that will get you in trouble."

"Not me so much as Mouse."

She grinned.

"It's a last resort," Jackson said, returning to the computer. "But we'll make sure nothing happens." He quickly forwarded the e-mail to Mouse, with a note asking for help tracing the sender.

"So," she said, playing with the carpet with her foot, "have you watched *Safe at Home* again?"

"That was my after-dinner plan," Jackson said.

"Do you want to watch it here? I have the theatrical version, and I'd kind of like a little company."

The way she asked, tentatively, was cute. It reminded him a little of Sam. He nodded. "Sure."

Noelle smiled. "Popcorn?"

"Why not."

She entered the kitchen, climbed a small stepstool to retrieve a bag of microwaveable popcorn from the cupboard, and directed Jackson to her collection of DVDs, in the console beneath the TV. He read the description on the back of the case before inserting the *Safe at Home* DVD into the player. With Noelle's instruction from the kitchen, he figured out the remotes and cued the movie to start.

"Now you want something to drink?" Noelle asked as she removed the popcorn from the microwave.

"Sure, just some water."

She handed the bag to him, filled a glass with water, and then joined him on the couch.

"Go ahead and put your feet up on the table," Noelle said. "My brother always does."

Jackson smiled and at least removed his shoes first. Noelle popped up to flip off the lights, then rejoined him and they started the movie.

Safe at Home opened with Dale, a minor league baseball player, who for some reason or other—mostly knee injuries—never made it to the Majors. By his early thirties, he was depressed, jaded, generally pessimistic about life. Over time, he struck up a friendship with Annie—played by Noelle—a young woman still trying to find her direction in life, who meanwhile worked as a waitress at a cozy little diner Dale frequented.

Their friendship evolved over the first thirty minutes of the movie—they went on several casual dates, talked over coffee and pie late nights at the diner, and shared bits and pieces of their life stories. Everything was going along smoothly until Dale had a try-out for the Arizona Diamondbacks. After a promising couple of days, he got the call from his buddy in the team office. "Sorry, Hot Rod. They opted for another righty."

Jackson paused the movie and turned to Noelle. "Why Hot Rod?"

154

She shrugged. "Dale's last name is Rodney."

The wheels in Jackson's head spun so fast they smoked. "So Rod sees the movie, sees you, sees a character nicknamed Hot Rod . . ."

"You think he latched onto me because of that, some sort of transference?"

"I wonder."

They resumed the movie, which brought plenty of laughs and tears—at least for the female viewers—before ending relatively happily. Noelle wiped a tear from her eye as the credits rolled.

"What'd you think?" she asked.

"I think you were great."

She smiled as she got up and flipped on the lights. "I loved this role because I felt Annie was so much like Noelle."

"Maybe that's what Rod saw too," Jackson said.

Noelle sat back down on the couch, facing him, legs tucked under her. "I'm scared, Jackson."

He nodded. "I understand. One way or the other, we'll ID this guy soon. If everything goes well, we can file the restraining order yet this week."

"That would be great."

"Before you know it, this will just be a bad memory."

Noelle fidgeted with the cuff of her pants. "So . . . do you think I'm safe here by myself at night?"

Jackson's phone vibrated. He checked the ID. "It's Mouse." He excused himself and took the call. "Yeah?"

"Hey, I traced that e-mail. Same apartment building in San Marino."

"Can you get any closer than that?"

"Afraid not. I tried everything I can think of, but there's no way to pinpoint it. I can tell you there are sixteen units in the building."

"What if I gave you a name?"

"Might help."

"Rod."

"Rod what?"

"That I don't know."

Mouse sighed. "I'll see what I can do. No promises."

"Call me when you get something."

"Will do."

Jackson closed his phone and returned to the couch.

"Anything?" she asked.

"Same apartment as the tweets. He's checking the name."

Noelle nodded, picked at her cuff some more.

"In answer to your question," Jackson said, "I think you—"

Someone knocked on the door.

Noelle frowned as she glanced at the clock, closing in on eleven. She walked to the door, peeked through the peephole, and turned back to Jackson with a frown. "Nobody there."

He frowned too and stood. He approached the door and nodded for her to step back. She did and he put his eye to the peephole. Nothing.

He slid back the chain and turned the deadbolts. The he opened the door.

A small glass vase sat by the threshold. It contained two roses, one orange, one red, the stems wrapped around each other several times. Jackson poked his head out and glanced up and down the hall. There was no sign of anyone.

He stooped down and picked up the vase, holding it at the lip, just between his thumb and forefinger. Closing the door behind him, he carried it into the living room. "Get the lights," he said.

"What?"

"Get the lights."

Noelle flipped off the living room lights, and Jackson hurried to the window. He peered down toward the street, looking for signs of movement. He saw nothing. Maybe the guy was already gone. Maybe he was still in the building. Maybe he was a neighbor.

"Jackson?"

"It's okay," he said.

"He was here."

"It's okay," he repeated. He pulled Noelle into a hug. "He's not going to hurt you, I promise."

"He was here, Jackson."

"And he didn't make any effort to harm you."

"This time." She pulled back and wiped her eyes.

"The next time he does anything, he'll be in violation of a restraining order. We'll make sure of that."

She swallowed hard. "Can you stay here?"

Big Brother Syndrome kicked in, hard. Jackson nodded. "Yeah. Sure."

Noelle blinked away tears, then slipped back into his hug.

Chapter Twenty-One

Thursday, November 1
8:41 a.m.

"YOU'RE SURE SHE'LL go for this?" Noelle asked.

"Let's hope so. Underneath the crust and the Revlon, she's got a soft heart." He knocked on the door. "You're sure you don't mind?"

"If it brings an end to all of this, no."

A moment later, Connie, in a tiger print blouse and black pants—along with cat ears and a painted nose—opened the door to unleash the smell of gourmet coffee and fresh-baked treats. "Jackson, you're early."

"Connie, you're a Bengal tiger."

"Oh, this. I completely forgot," she said, swiping the ears off her head. "We're all dressing up for work. Happy Halloween!"

He frowned. "Halloween was yesterday."

Connie waved her hand. "Two ladies in the office have birthdays today, so we combined our celebrations."

"I see," he said, although he didn't really. "Connie, this is Noelle. Noelle, Tigger."

"Please, come in," Connie said, ignoring Jackson's comment.

Noelle seemed unaffected by Connie's garb. "Thank you," she said as Jackson stepped aside to let her pass, as did Connie.

She caught Jackson and whispered, "Girlfriend?"

"Just friend."

Connie pointed at her watch, but Jackson let the unspoken comment pass.

"To what do I owe the pleasure?" Connie asked.

Before Jackson could answer, a shrill yelp sounded, followed by scratching. Then an orange ball of fur tumbled around the corner.

"Noelle, meet Fluffy."

"Oh, she's so cute," Noelle said, bending down to cuddle the pooch into her hands.

"If it's okay with you," Jackson said, "Noelle will take Fluffy to the vet. I'm doing her a favor that requires me to be somewhere this morning, so she's doing me a favor by doing my favor for you."

Connie pondered this for a moment. "I don't know."

"You trust me," Jackson said. "And I trust her."

"It's not a matter of trust," Connie said, looking down at Noelle. "If he says you're good, honey, then that's good enough for me." She looked back to Jackson. "I just don't like the idea of this poor woman doing you favors."

Funny, Connie had no problem with him endlessly doing her favors. Jackson bit his tongue.

"Believe me," Noelle said, "it's the other way around."

"Well, all right. I have to be going." Connie shuffled into the kitchen and returned with several containers of baked goods in her hands, her purse dangling from one of them. "Jackson, make sure you tell her that Fluffy likes to get there early."

"I think you just did, Connie." He shooed her out the door, made sure Noelle had everything she needed, and hit the road himself.

It had taken some doing, but after delivering coffee, Jackson had managed to clear his Thursday with Viggo. He played upon the director's desire for one of his star's wellbeing, and promised no more rigmarole after this week. And fortunately, Noelle hadn't needed to be on set until after lunch.

Jackson had spent the night at Noelle's, sleeping on her couch. Mostly he had thought and mulled. He'd also used her computer to make sure he was fully acquainted with taking out a restraining order in Los Angeles—what was required, how the procedure was done, length of time it took, penalty for violation. There were no surprises. He'd slept fitfully, woken up by thunder, vehicles without mufflers, and dreams of a baseball player chasing Noelle across a diamond, continually hitting ground balls at her while quoting bad poetry louder and louder.

He'd taken the vase that the roses had been in, hoping to implore Detective Ashley Larson—a source he'd acquired back when she, working undercover, had sought out his services back in May—to pull prints off it. He was also considering the possibility of calling or visiting local florists, envisioning distracting them so he could peek over the counter at their registers like the '80s TV detectives he loved would do. But those were both failsafe plans if he couldn't find Rod at Pasadena City College.

Parking off campus, Jackson started at the Shatford Library. He asked around, did anyone know a guy named Rod with blond hair, green eyes, and an affinity for poetry? No, it was not some sort of a gag. He still struck out.

Jackson moved on to the cafeteria, and found it closed. A lounge contained a dozen students, none of whom were any help. He tried the administrative building, hoping not to catch the same lady as he had on Monday. He didn't, but it didn't matter; he was given the same no as an answer. Almost to the point of trying to find random people roaming the campus, he saw a flyer posted on a wall, something called the *Campus Crier*. It was two pages, advertising upcoming student events and clubs. Including the Poetry Club. Jackson headed to the *Campus Crier* office, which happened to be next door to *The Courier*—the college newspaper—office.

He came to *The Courier* office first, and got the same standard reply. Nobody knew Rod.

He tried *The Crier* next and spoke with a scowling redhead. He trotted out the same question: You know a guy named Rod, blond hair, green eyes, a poet?

"A poet?" she asked.

"Yeah."

She shrugged. "I know a Rod with blond hair, never checked the eyes. But I don't know that he's a poet."

"You know his last name?"

"Finley. Why?"

"It's kind of complicated, but he sent flowers to a friend of mine, and she wants me to find out who he is."

"Oh, that's sweet," she said, the scowl removed.

It was not sweet, but Jackson didn't bother to correct her. "Any idea where I can find him?"

"Uh, it's Thursday, so he's in an art history class right now."

"You know where?"

"Robbins. Other side of the quad."

"You know the room number?"

"Sorry, no."

"All right. Thanks."

"Don't mention it. I hope it works out for him and your friend."

Jackson forced a smile as he left, then hurried across the quad to the Catherine J. Robbins building. Checking the time, he headed inside and asked the first person he saw if they knew where the current art history class was being held. No idea. Second person said R122 or R124 and gave Jackson directions. He thanked them and hurried down the hall.

He found the room and waited, leaning against the wall, fiddling with his phone. He was old fashioned, and so was his phone. It flipped open, didn't have apps, was designed to talk on. If it texted, he didn't know it, nor did he know how to take a photo, if his phone even had a camera. But he considered himself at least moderately clever and tech savvy, and just as the door opened and students started streaming out, Jackson figured it out.

Pretending he was texting, he kept an eye out over his phone for blond guys. He wasn't close enough to tell eye color, so he stopped the first girl who came his way. "Hey, can you point me to Rod?"

"Which Rod?"

"Uh, Finley."

She turned around. "First one out, over there."

Great, heading the other way. Jackson thanked her and pushed through the crowd. Rod had a red backpack with "PCC" stamped on it. Jackson hung a few dozen paces back and followed him out a side entrance. Rod struck out across a commons, heading toward the football stadium, or maybe a parking garage.

Jackson was parked on the other side of campus, and if Rod reached a car, it was over. So Jackson started jogging. He passed Rod, continued to the end of the sidewalk, then stopped and reached for his phone. Panting for effect, he put the phone to his ear. "Hello?"

Rod was ten steps away.

"Yeah," Jackson said, then lowered the phone and pretended to check something on the screen. He was just in time to snap two quick pictures of Rod as he passed. He covered by putting the phone back to his ear. "It sent, but I don't see what . . ."

Rod was gone, and Jackson headed for his car. On the way, he called Connie. "Hello?"

"Connie, it's Jackson." He sighed. "I need another favor. Very quick, very easy."

"What is it?"

"I need the address of a Rod Finley. Twenties, blond hair, green eyes. I think he lives in San Marino."

"I've got a customer. I'll call you back."

"Thanks, Connie."

Jackson jogged to his car, then drove to Alhambra, to the Black Bull. The net was closing, and now he just needed confirmation. Mallory had just arrived for her shift, and when he showed her the photo of Rod on his phone, she frowned. But she studied it carefully and nodded. "Yeah, it's him."

"You're sure?"

"Yeah. That's him."

Jackson thanked her and headed for the car. He was about to call Noelle when Connie called him.

"Hey, Connie."

"I have the address."

"Shoot."

"Rod Finley lives at 3-1-3 Culpepper Way, Apartment 2A in San Marino."

"Thanks. Tack on whatever you want."

"Now, Jackson, that hurts a little."

"You mean it's on the house?"

"We'll just say it's included for the price already paid."

"Thanks."

Jackson hung up with a smirk. They had him.

*   *   *

Friday, November 2
4:40 p.m.

AS SOON as Viggo released him for the day, Jackson drove east to San Marino, traveling the familiar I-10.

The day before, Noelle had finished her last scene at three. Jackson had been waiting for her, and they had quickly filled out the necessary forms—printed off the internet—and driven to the West Los Angeles Courthouse, arriving shortly before closing time. Noelle had officially filed for a restraining order, and been told to check back the next day sometime after noon. Friday morning when she had explained things to Viggo, he had granted her and Jackson a long lunch break. They had returned to the courthouse to find the judge had issued a temporary restraining order and set a court date for the following Friday. They'd returned to work, after which Noelle had gone home relieved while Jackson had undertaken one final mission.

He arrived at Finley's apartment, knocked, and got no answer. So he waited, tried again, waited some more. Eventually he camped out in the parking lot with a view of Finley's door until just after seven when he returned home.

Jackson watched him enter and then climbed the stairs to apartment 2A. Finley answered the door almost immediately after Jackson knocked. Blond hair a little mussed from the wind and rain, green eyes vacant.

"You Rod Finley?" Jackson asked.

The eyes locked in. "Yeah. I saw you after class yesterday, at PCC, didn't I?"

"Yeah." Jackson handed him a manila envelope. "This is a restraining order. You're not allowed within one hundred feet of Noelle St. Pierre. You can't call her, write her, text her, tweet her, Facebook her, or otherwise have any contact with her. That includes the sending of roses. It's all in there," he said, pointing at the envelope. "I suggest you read it carefully, along with the potential penalty if you violate the order. The court date is also there. The only thing not listed is the additional penalty if you harm or harass her in any way. You'll pay that to me and you'll pay it in blood. Any questions?"

Finley's eyes were vacant again, and Jackson nodded. "Good. See you in court."

Jackson turned before Finley could reply and strode to his car. He glanced one more time at the apartment and then drove to Noelle's. Before the door was closed behind him, she asked, "You serve him?"

"I did."

"What'd he say?"

"Nothing. He looked stunned. Maybe scared."

"So it's over?"

"All depends on the judge, but I don't see how it could not be."

Noelle's shoulders sagged with relief. She opened her eyes and smiled. "Thank you."

"My pleasure."

"Hardly," she said. "You've worked night and day for the last week, crisscrossed town how many times? Slept on my couch."

"All part of the job."

"You mean favor," she said. "Which I guess means it's time to discuss a matching favor."

"I'm sick of favors, and honestly, your 'thank you' is all the repayment I need."

She dipped her shoulder, hand on her hip.

"I'm serious, Noelle. No need to repay me or do me an equal amount of favors. You asked as a friend, and I did it as a friend. In my book, we're even."

"You are serious, aren't you?"

He nodded.

Noelle shook her head. "You're something else, you know that?"

"So I've been told."

She sighed. "Well, have you eaten yet?"

"I was going to grab something on the way back, but I wanted to let you know right away."

"Then let me at least buy you dinner," she said. "I need to express my gratitude somehow."

"Rumors will fly. Paparazzi, Shawn Thomas . . ."

"Let them fly."

Jackson slowly smiled. "Then you've got a deal. Just so long as it's not a pub in Alhambra."

Chapter Twenty-Two

Friday, November 9
8:41 p.m.

NOELLE STIRRED HER cappuccino. "So what will you do then?"

Episode 1.8, "All We've Got," had wrapped shooting just before sunset, and a few hours later, the cast and crew had met at Ocean & Vine for dinner. Jackson and Noelle had cut out early to grab dessert.

It had been a frantic week of shooting, including a few scenes from episode 1.9, which would be filmed on a short schedule to accommodate for Thanksgiving. That morning, the judge had approved Noelle's restraining order against Rod Finley and instituted a permanent one. Finley had been stoic in court and had made no contact with Noelle since Jackson had served him the temporary restraining order the previous Friday.

Viggo had announced to everyone at dinner that filming was moving to Vancouver in a few weeks as the search for Mr. X led Braylon, Cate, Roxie, and Ty to the Great Northwest. He had not offered Jackson a job on the Vancouver crew, and Jackson hadn't asked. He wasn't moving for *Twenty Something*.

Jackson shrugged as Noelle blew over her cup. "I have some money saved up. My work the last month more than paid the bills. I'll be all right."

She finally took a drink. "So . . . you never did tell me why you stopped being a private investigator. Am I prying to ask?"

"No, you're not prying." He reached for his coffee. "It's better that you hear it from me than on the internet."

Noelle put down her cup. "Is it bad?"

Jackson sighed. "I'll let you decide." He then walked through the events of September, from Hillary to Vegas to the massacre at the decommissioned military base to his probation. He told her the most sanitized, least gruesome version he could, but felt he still came out looking like a rogue.

When he was finished, Noelle reached out and put her hand on his arm. "I had no idea."

"It's not exactly something I brag about."

"Have you talked to somebody about it?"

"Lots of people. The thing is, it's not really something you can talk away."

"I'm sorry," she said. There was no condemnation in her eyes, no fear of sitting across from a monster. Just compassion. Same as he'd gotten from everyone.

They sat quietly for a few moments. Jackson exhaled. "Change of subject?"

"Sure."

"What do you think happens in Vancouver?"

"Who knows?" Noelle said.

"Viggo?"

"Maybe." She giggled. "But I wouldn't bet on it."

"How long will you be there, any idea?" Viggo hadn't gone into details during his dinner announcement, but Jackson had caught snatches of personal conversations between the director and cast or crew members revolving around the switch of venues.

"Mario said we're shooting two episodes there before the Christmas break, and then a couple after. Then it depends if we get picked up for a second season."

"What do you think?"

She shrugged. "I haven't paid any attention to ratings, but from what I hear, it sounds like we're on the bubble."

Jackson nodded.

The waitress returned with the check, and Noelle displayed lightning reflexes to snag it before Jackson could. "I still say we're not quite even," she said.

They headed outside and to their respective cars. The wind had died down after sunset, but there was still a chill in the air. Noelle's car was closest, and she played with her keys for a moment.

She looked up. "Thanks again, Jackson. For everything."

"You're welcome. After all, what are friends for?"

*   *   *

Tuesday, January 1
7:48 a.m.

HIS SHOULDER was throbbing, and Jackson reached for his nurse call button. He couldn't locate it—wasn't there some sort of remote control, or was it on the bed itself?—but his fumbling did have a result.

"Morning, kiddo."

Jackson turned his head. Leroy sat on the couch, in blue jeans and a worn San Diego Chargers sweatshirt. His hair was a little unruly, but that wasn't all that unusual. He was reading a newspaper, presumably the *Los Angeles Times*.

"Grandpa."

Leroy folded the newspaper carefully, keeping the sections in order, and stood with a grunt. "How are you feeling?" he asked as he walked over and leaned on the edge of the bed. Something, probably the bed, creaked.

"Swell. I do have this slight ache in my shoulder though."

Leroy grinned. "You had us a little worried."

"Had myself a little worried."

A nurse entered the room. Bustled into it, was more like it, swiping some hand sanitizer on her way over to the bed to check on Jackson. She asked him the usual questions about how he felt, what his pain scale was, and nodded to every answer as if she was merely inquiring out of curiosity. She gave no indication that she could or would do anything to alleviate the pain.

"What's my status?" Jackson asked.

"The doctor will be around before long," the nurse replied.

"I'll go to the horse's mouth then."

She frowned, and left the way she had come, bustling and sanitizing her hands.

Jackson turned back to Leroy. "What time is it?"

"Mmm, a little before eight."

"I thought doctors made their rounds at the crack of dawn."

"It's New Year's. He was probably out late last night."

"Wonderful." Jackson sighed. "Anybody else here?"

"We convinced Sam to go home and get a few hours' sleep, and Reggie's getting us some breakfast."

"Hey, that sounds like an idea. I'm starved."

"Want some ice chips?"

"What a treat."

"That a no?"

Jackson sighed and Leroy reached for the cup. It was pure water, and he went to get some actual ice. While he was gone, Jackson tried to remember his night. The shooting itself was crystal clear, but the rest was just a collection of images: in the ambulance, white walls and a blond-haired nurse, repeatedly waking up to see that it was still night and Reggie or Sam or nobody was on the couch. Sam . . . hadn't she kissed him? Oh yeah, just on the forehead. And what had he been doing in the cemetery anyhow?

Leroy returned with the ice chips. He was followed a few seconds later by a different nurse, a prettier one, who brought Jackson some pills and asked if he preferred a hot or cold breakfast.

"Hot."

"Okay. We'll get that sent up for you."

She disappeared, and no sooner had she left than Reggie returned, carrying a McDonald's bag and a pair of coffee cups. "Hey, J, what's up?"

"Oh, nothing much, homes. Just chillin'."

"Funny." He reached into the bag. "Here you go, man." He handed Leroy two sandwiches and a hash brown, then sat down beside him on the couch and retrieved two sandwiches of his own from the bag. They began to eat.

"Don't mind me," Jackson said, smelling their sandwiches with relish.

"Yours is coming," Leroy mumbled, not pausing to swallow first.

They were almost finished by the time Jackson's breakfast arrived, in the form of a bowl of cream of wheat and a small carton of milk.

"Really?" he asked the nurse.

"Keep that down and you can have something more substantial."

Jackson nodded and stirred a packet of sugar into his mush, waiting for the nurse to leave. When she was gone, he nodded at Reggie. "Dude, break me off a McGriddle."

"Sorry, man, doctor's orders."

"The doctor hasn't come yet."

"Oh. Right. Well, better safe than sorry."

"Some friends you are."

"Eat your oatmeal."

"Cream of wheat."

"Whatever, man. Besides, don't you think it's time we discuss the elephant in the room?"

Jackson held up a spoonful of his breakfast, staring at it. He turned the spoon upside down, and nothing happened. His appetite was gone. "What's that?" he asked.

"Somebody shot you, man. Any idea who?"

Leroy looked up, his sandwich halfway to his mouth.

Jackson bit down on his lip and slowly shook his head. "Not a clue."

*   *   *

Wednesday, November 21
2:44 p.m.

"IT'S FROM scratch, Sam."

"Scratch?"

Jackson switched the phone to his other ear. "You know, mix up the ingredients, pour them into the crust."

"Using what, the recipe off the back of the can?"

"Well unfortunately my pumpkin crop was a little thin this year, so . . ."

"Cherry too?"

"Pitted them myself."

"Um-hmm."

"What, you wanted pies, you're getting pies. I figured the recipe off the can and a pair of pre-made crusts are better than bringing a couple of frozen Sara Lee's."

"I suppose so," she said.

"How's your turkey coming?"

"Thawing as we speak."

"You figured out all your oven settings and times?"

"You getting even by questioning my cooking skills, is that it?"

"Something like that. You sure you don't need me to bring anything else?"

"Your grandpa is bringing a couple of sides, so don't forget to bring him."

"I won't."

"And when you stop to buy your pies, get some Cool Whip too."

"If I bring over the empty cans of filling will that convince you?"

"Maybe."

"Look, I'd love to keep bantering," Jackson said, squatting to peer into his oven, "but I have to stick a knife in my pie to see if it's done. The fact I know that should tell you something."

"I'll see you tomorrow."

"Right."

He closed his phone, set it on the counter, and reached for a butter knife. He opened his oven and inserted the tip of the knife into the center of the pie. It came out with a little pumpkin filling clinging to the sides, so Jackson decided to give the pie another five minutes. While he waited, he went out to get the mail.

It was unseasonably cool for Los Angeles, even in late November. But it was sunny and crisp, perfect autumn weather. The cast and crew of *Twenty Something* had finished shooting episode 1.9, "All Roads . . .," that morning, thus ending Jackson's brief Hollywood career. As much as he'd learned and—frankly—enjoyed his time working on the show, he was glad to be free of it. He didn't know what that meant for his near employment future, but for the time being, he was happy to breathe in the fresh air and enjoy an afternoon off.

His phone was ringing as he returned inside. Dropping an electricity bill and a credit card application on the table, he scooped it up and checked the Caller ID. Unknown. With a shrug, he flipped it open.

"Jackson Douglas."

"Mr. Douglas, it's Bill Braxton with the *L.A. Times*," he said in a voice like a road grader.

"Bill, what can I do for you?"

"If you're free this afternoon, I was hoping I could buy you a beer."

Jackson frowned. "Not a beer drinker, Bill, but thanks." He eased into a dining room chair. "What's on your mind?"

"I'd rather not discuss it on the phone. Can I make it a coffee? Burger? You name it."

"I'm actually pretty well set, and I've got two pies about to come out of the oven. Want to swing by my place instead?"

"That's probably not a great idea," Bill said. "I'm sorry to be so secretive, but I can explain in person."

Jackson hesitated.

"Please, Mr. Douglas. It's very important."

"All right. How about Starbucks at 25th and Santa Monica. Say, four o'clock?"

"Four would be great. Thank you, Mr. Douglas."

"Jackson. And I should inform you, I'm not currently licensed as a private eye."

"That won't matter. Thanks."

Jackson closed the phone against his chin, musing. Maggie had spoken of a Bill at the *L.A. Times*—said they'd dated once or twice. And this voice matched a mystery guy who had unexpectedly answered her phone a few times. Was it the same Bill? Did his urgent meeting have anything to do with her? Jackson hadn't seen Maggie in almost three months, since their Labor Day fight at Dodger Stadium. When she hadn't made any effort to contact him after he got back from Nevada—knowing that as a reporter she had to have heard what happened—he'd concluded she wanted nothing more to do with him and had given up on her.

He remembered his pies and stood to check on them. They were perfect, and he took them out to cool, then called Mouse. He worked at the Starbucks in question, and just in case, Jackson wanted a "man on the inside." Not that Mouse would offer much assistance, unless of course Bill was luring Jackson somewhere so he could hack into his phone or skim his credit card. It didn't matter; Mouse's shift had ended at two.

Jackson had a few minutes, so he browsed to the *Times'* website. He confirmed that Bill Braxton worked in Arts and Entertainment, and if memory served, Maggie had said Bill was in Entertainment. So what did he want? And what was with all the cloak-and-dagger, not-over-the-phone business?

Pre-Thanksgiving traffic was a mess in L.A., and despite intending to arrive a few minutes early, Jackson walked into Starbucks exactly at four. He had no idea what Bill looked like (he pictured a young Johnny Cash to match the voice—no, actually more of Joaquin Phoenix in *Walk the Line*) so he didn't bother scanning the room. As work was letting out, the place was busy, and he absentmindedly studied the menu boards while inhaling the aromas. He wasn't a coffee guy. He drank it, but not as much for the taste as for having something to drink. He especially didn't go in for five-dollar mixed drinks with convoluted names.

"Jackson?" a voice asked at the same time someone brushed against his elbow. He turned to see a "tall, dark, and handsome." Long sideburns, a day or two of shadow on his square jaw, eyes just a little lighter than that ageless guy from *Lost*. Jackson was immediately jealous, even though he and Maggie were clearly on the outs.

"Bill?"

He nodded and extended a hand. His grip was firm. "Thanks for meeting me."

Jackson returned the nod.

"What's your poison?" Bill asked.

"Black coffee."

Bill didn't bat an eye, instead edging into the line. A few minutes later and eight bucks poorer, he carried two tall (technically venti) cups of coffee toward a corner bistro table. "Black coffee," he said, scooting one of the cups toward Jackson as they sat down.

"I'm not sure if she mentioned me or not, but Maggie and I dated a couple of times," Bill said as Jackson pried the lid off his cup, letting the air cool the brew. "Very casual, more like hanging out than dating. Anyhow, from what I hear, the two of you have a similar sort of relationship."

Jackson wasn't particularly in the mood to categorize his relationship with Maggie to Bill or anyone else. So he merely nodded his acceptance of the statement while making a mental note that Bill had said "have" instead of "had."

"When was the last time you saw Maggie?" Bill asked.

Jackson leaned back so his chair creaked. "I don't like the sound of that."

Bill said nothing, his dark, deep-set eyes probing Jackson.

"Early September," he answered. "We went to a Dodgers game."

"She say anything to you?"

"Anything like what?"

"You'd know if you knew."

"Bill, I don't mean to be rude, but I'm not really in the mood for games today. The last time I saw Maggie, she accused me of being a religious bigot and more or less implied we had no future as friends or anything else. I haven't talked to her since. What's going on?"

Bill nodded. "The long and short of it is she's in Mexico, she's in trouble, and I need you to come with me to bring her back."

Chapter Twenty-Three

Thursday, November 22
12:17 p.m. (CST)

THE BROWN, BARREN countryside below had been swallowed up by hazy, high-level clouds. That was okay, it was Mexican terrain, nothing really to look at. Jackson and Bill had departed LAX at 6:00 a.m. for Acapulco, Mexico, by way of the capital of Mexico City.

Bill's details the previous afternoon had been sketchy at best. Over coffee, he'd told Jackson that Maggie had flown to Mexico in early September, armed with the knowledge that three U.S. politicians with ties to Big Oil had died under mysterious circumstances in the last four years. They were not alone according to Maggie's colleague from Dallas who had given her the tip. One of the politicians, Texas Congressman Booker Dade, had been good friends with Mexican Minister of Justice Ferdinand Sanchez, who had been kidnapped in 2010 and never found.

"Why Maggie?" Jackson had asked as they sipped coffees at Starbucks.

"Excuse me?"

"Why didn't this colleague chase down the story? You said he worked for the *Morning-News*?"

Bill nodded. "Said he didn't have time. Family and an addiction to Cowboys football, according to Maggie. And his editor didn't think there was anything there."

"But Maggie's did?

"Yep. Sanchez was just the tip of the iceberg. Her preliminary research uncovered a total of six murdered politicians and government officials—three American, three Mexican—since 2008. Two were outright assassinated, but the other four were made to look like accidents. Another Mexican Minister of Justice, Diana Quintana, was kidnapped way back in 2008, and Maggie found multiple instances of Mexican politicians being bribed."

Bill spoke from memory, pausing only to inhale coffee.

"What's a Minister of Justice?" Jackson asked.

"A state judge."

Jackson nodded. "Aren't bribery and kidnappings par for the course down there?"

"Somewhat. But when Maggie arrived in Mexico, she discovered that all of the murdered, kidnapped, and bribed officials had either opposed the sale of a huge piece of government land outside Veracruz to a company named GR Limited or had stood against the privatization of Mexican oil production. Until 2011, Pemex—owned by the state—served as the only petroleum company in Mexico. But in July of 2011, a company named Mexól was granted operating rights and opened a huge facility in Veracruz."

"What did the U.S. politicians have to do with that?"

"Directly, nothing, but they all had ties to Big Oil in a way that would have hindered Mexól's potential profits." Bill took a drink. "Maggie uncovered all this, reported back to her editor, and got permission from him to keep going. She got a job at Mexól and worked there for about a month. She linked them conclusively to GR Limited and a huge crude reserve under a four-hundred-foot-deep *cenote*."

"A what?"

"A *cenote*. A natural sinkhole, usually filled with water. They're common in Central America. Only this one wasn't just water, but crude oil. Barrels and barrels and barrels of it."

"So Mexól bribed and killed its way to legitimacy and a huge windfall?"

"Yes."

"And Maggie's going to expose them?"

"That's right."

"Of course she is," Jackson sighed.

"About four weeks ago, she began working for a man named Rafael Vasquez. He's the VP of an international investment consortium owned by his father, Leonardo, named LOVE."

"Love?" Jackson asked.

"Leonardo Oscar Vasquez Enterprises. L-O-V-E for short. According to Maggie, they're closely linked to Mexól and, she believes, may have been pulling the strings all along."

"Okay."

"She knew she was sniffing around at some pretty dangerous stuff, and whereas working in a low-level admin position for Mexól was one thing, now she was walking into the wolf's den. So she set up a failsafe."

"A failsafe?"

Bill nodded and took a long pull on his coffee. "Every forty-eight hours, she would check in with me. If she missed, I was supposed to call a contact of hers named Ali. If I couldn't reach him within twenty-four hours or if he couldn't verify her safety, I was supposed to call you."

"Why me?"

"She said you would know what to do if something went wrong."

"And it did?"

"She called me Sunday night, said everything was okay. That meant she was due to check in last night, and didn't. I called Ali last night and this morning but couldn't reach him either time. Then this afternoon, Maggie called. I knew something was off right away."

"Why?" Jackson had lost interest in his coffee.

"She didn't make any sense based on anything she'd told me previously. And she dropped the code word, 'Trojan.'"

"What's that mean?"

"It means something went wrong. So here I am."

The plane jolted and Jackson looked back from the haze. Beside him, Bill had stirred awake. He wore the same pullover as the night before, now with durable khakis and tennis shoes. He hadn't shaved, and his face had taken on a darker complexion. He had the rugged handsome look, and it bugged Jackson. But he refused to succumb to petty jealousy at a moment like this.

After explaining everything at Starbucks, Bill had gone home to book flights and Jackson to pack. He'd also dropped his pies off at Sam's, offering a pitiful explanation for why he wouldn't be coming to dinner on Thanksgiving. She hadn't pressed him, but had clearly been suspicious, and maybe hurt. Leroy, when Jackson had called a few minutes later, had been more curious than anything else.

The earliest arrival in Acapulco was 4:00 p.m., Central Time—2:00 in L.A.—which had meant a short night of restless sleep before Bill had picked Jackson up at four to make it to LAX in time for a six o'clock departure.

"So why me?" Jackson asked again as Bill looked around the plane to get his bearings. His eyes settled back on Jackson, squinting at the sun coming in through the airplane window.

"How's that?"

"Why me? Why isn't Maggie's failsafe to have you call the American embassy?"

"Probably because she doesn't think they'd do a dang thing. Shoot, we had a Marine in Mexican custody for a year and neither side did jack to get him out. How much less a reporter snooping around where she didn't belong?"

"So what exactly are we supposed to do?"

"I think that's your call," Bill said.

Jackson nodded. They had no weapons, no authority to use them if they did, and no idea where Maggie was. According to Bill, she was working as Rafael Vasquez's secretary at LOVE's office in Acapulco. But he had no idea where she was living, where she had called from, or what danger she was in.

"What did she say on this call again?" Jackson asked.

"She said, 'It's me. I need you to bring the Trojan package to Acapulco. You've got a week.'"

"Trojan," Jackson mused.

"She said you were a Southern Cal fan. I assume that's why she picked the word."

"Give me the message again."

Bill quoted it a second time, verbatim. Jackson repeated it a few more times, looking for meaning.

"She didn't use either of your names?"

"No. I'm pretty sure somebody else was listening in."

"And nothing she'd said in any previous calls clued you in to where she is or what's wrong?"

Bill shook his head.

"Then I guess we'd better hope this guy Ali comes through for us."

"Assuming we can find him."

Jackson rolled his head to the side to look back out the window. At every free moment, his mind had flashed back to his and Maggie's day in Monterey. He'd assumed it would be the last good memory of her, given the way their Labor Day had fallen apart. Bill had confirmed that Maggie had been made aware of the potential story in late August and had already talked with her editor about pursuing it in Mexico by Labor Day. Had that been on her mind during their fight? And if so, why hadn't she said something?

"I knew this would happen someday," Bill said.

Jackson looked back. "What?"

"Maggie getting into trouble. She's a real . . ."

"Bulldog."

"Yes. I tried to talk her out of it, you know, going to work for Vasquez. I said it was too dangerous. But she said she was too close to quit, that she needed to do so to get the proof and finish her story."

"That's what they always say."

"Who?"

"The good-looking brunette reporters who get in trouble in South America. It's a common TV trope. But look who I'm telling."

Bill studied him quizzically.

"So what happens in a week?" Jackson asked.

Bill shook his head.

"Yeah. Well, let's not find out, huh?"

*   *   *

3:48 p.m.

AFTER A brief layover at Benito Juarez International Airport in Mexico City, Jackson and Bill had boarded an eggbeater with wings for the flight over the mountains to the coast. Bill slept for most of the flight, to Jackson's amazement. The plane shook and rattled the whole way, and he took his mind off the probability of a crash landing by reflecting on his half hour of online research the night before.

Discovered in the 1520s—arguably by famed conquistador Hernán Cortés—Acapulco was situated around the *Bahia De Acapulco*, a body of water in the shape of a mushroom. The top of the mushroom was covered in sand, a crescent-shaped beach of postcard fame. The north half of the bay comprised "*tradicional*" Acapulco, popularized by the rich and famous in the 1950s. The south side housed the newer developments, the high-rises and upscale resorts. *Tradicional* catered more to the middle classes who were drawn to its clubs, restaurants, and authentic Mexican hotels, as well as to the boardwalk and main square.

In addition to spring breakers, cliff divers, and millionaire vacationers, Acapulco had become flush with drug cartels. Then again, where south of the Rio Grande hadn't? Other resort cities were surpassing Acapulco, whose streets were flooded with prostitutes and peddlers and garbage. And dirty cops, which apparently were also quite common south of the border. Jackson didn't get the fascination. Malibu or South Beach would do any day.

Out of nowhere, the Pacific Ocean appeared on the horizon, a welcome beacon, a familiar friend. Jackson sat up, eager to be on solid ground again. Compared to the descent into Mexico City, they nose-dived into Acapulco, landing seemingly in minutes. Soon they were at the gate, or rather, parked on the apron. Jackson and Bill were near the front of the line, and as they stepped onto the stairs leading down to the pavement, they were blasted by hot, tropical air.

Jackson looked around, taking in the scenery. The airport was on a flat strip of land between the ocean and a small lake, well south of Acapulco itself, and Jackson felt as if he were in another world. This was really a vacation hotspot? Then again, flights into LAX landed over an oil refinery, not the Hollywood Sign or downtown.

They'd gone through customs in Mexico City, so the duo proceeded to the "air-conditioned" terminal to collect their luggage. Giving the fatigued guards with Uzis a wide berth as they exited, they proceeded to a taxi stand. Bill, who spoke Spanish better than Jackson, procured a cab and gave the driver a destination. Fifteen minutes after landing, they were zipping north on the multilane *Boulevard de las Naciones*. Their driver was engrossed on a conversation in *muy rápido* Spanish with someone on his Bluetooth, so Jackson considered it safe to talk.

"I take it you know where we're going?"

Bill nodded. "Maggie told me in passing that Ali hangs out at a hookah bar in *Tradicional* Acapulco. I figure we ask around or wait for him to show up."

"A hookah bar?"

Bill nodded.

"In Mexico?"

"I think they call them *tietras* here."

"And who exactly is this guy Ali?"

"Her contact."

"Right, but who is he? What's he do?"

Bill shrugged. "His real name is Alejandro Alfonseca, and Maggie said he was invaluable to her. Other than that, I don't know much."

"Except that he hangs out at a hookah bar."

"Right."

Jackson sat, massaging his temples. How did he get into these sorts of situations? Right now, he could be sitting down to a delicious Thanksgiving dinner with Sam, his grandpa, and Stephanie. Instead, he was riding through a dirty Mexican city with Maggie's sort-of boyfriend.

They climbed and wound through the hills south of town before descending into Acapulco proper. As they circled the bay, Jackson drank in the panorama. Cruise ships in the bay. Discothèques that weren't even open yet. People everywhere. What was it about other countries that made people stand on top of each other? Los Angeles was crowded, but nothing like this.

As the buildings grew older and shabbier, Jackson's nerves tightened. "You know what this Ali looks like?" he asked Bill.

He turned from gazing out his window and shrugged. "Mexican?"

"You know how it always goes on TV, when the detectives burst into a bar looking for somebody? They usually are directed out back to an alley where a former NFL linebacker-turned-actor with a mustache is waiting."

"Don't worry. These guys are just blowing smoke."

"Funny. Really. I'll laugh later though."

The cab left the main street and drove along several side streets, crossing a river beneath a concrete embankment. On a smaller, dingier scale, it was the L.A. River through the heart of the city. The cab stopped in front of a single-story building with dirty white paint. Windows on either side of a glass door were adorned with colorful curtains, pulled back to reveal strings of beads instead of blinds. A small sign on the door tabbed the place *Ricardo's*.

Bill, who'd had time to get to the bank before leaving, paid the driver as Jackson got out. The sidewalk was cracked and infested with weeds, which distinguished it from the grimy but weedless street. Up and down the narrow thoroughfare, the neighboring properties were a mix of residential and commercial, none of them fit for the ghettos of South Central. And yet, just a few blocks away, a reasonably modern hospital towered over the neighborhood.

"How good's your Spanish?" Bill asked, joining Jackson on the sidewalk as the cab sped away with a cloud of smoke.

"As good as the average Mexican's English."

"I see. Come on."

Bill led the way, and as soon as Jackson entered the bar, his senses were assaulted. A heavy cloud of smoke hit his eyes and nose, causing the latter to sting. A minty grape scent also reached his taste buds. His eyes blinked away the smoke and tried to see through the darkness, but the lighting was minimal, coming from hanging stained-glass lamps. Even his ears suffered, as the dull lilt of what Jackson's musically-challenged brain deemed a flute repeated like a broken record.

The bar was packed, with only men. Most of them were sharing communal hookah bowls that sat on tables surrounded by low couches with more pillows than a woman's bed. A few of the men smoked cigarettes, drank herbal teas or Turkish coffees, or snacked on what Jackson imagined were the Arabic-Mexican version of Doritos. They were all dark-skinned, but Jackson couldn't tell if they were Indian, Arabic, or Mexican with a taste for the Middle East. Their dress didn't give it away either. They wore everything from cheap business suits to clothes fit for yardwork.

Bill approached a counter on the right side and leaned against it. *"Hola,"* he said to a middle-aged man with a mustache. His slick black hair was pulled into a tight ponytail, and his smile revealed two missing teeth in the front.

"Gringos, welcome," he said in English.

"Thanks. We're looking for Alejandro Alfonseca. Is he here?"

Ponytail pointed to the front corner, where a rotund man with scraggly hair, a bushy mustache, and an unshaven face sat at a table by himself. He wore a loose dress shirt, untucked, over dark pants with sandals. His eyes were open, but barely, as he nursed some shisha through a hose connected to a hookah bowl at one end and a mouthpiece at the other.

"Gracias," Bill said, and led Jackson to the table where Ali sat. There were three vacant chairs, and he nodded at two of them. *"¿Podemos sentarnos?"*

Ali nodded almost imperceptibly and took another hit.

"¿Eres Alejandro Alfonseca?" Bill asked when he and Jackson were both seated.

"Sí, y yo hablo Inglés." He set down his mouthpiece. "What do you want?"

"We're friends of Maggie's. She said you might be able to help us."

The big man's eyes rotated from one man to the other, then flitted over them to the rest of the lounge. *"Sí,* I can help you. But not here." He reached into a pocket and withdrew a business card and a pen. He scratched something quickly and slid it to Bill. "Meet me there in one hour."

"Thank you," Bill said.

Ali nodded. He inserted the mouthpiece into his mouth and closed his eyes.

Jackson didn't need an invitation. He stood and exited the lounge, breathing in fresh air, such as it was. He turned back to Bill. "Where are we meeting him in an hour, a Bolivian cupcake bar?"

"Palmeras. Cantina on the main drive. Walking distance."

"You know Acapulco?"

"Did some research of the area. Supposedly Palmeras has great fajitas. Come on."

Bill set out across the street and Jackson followed, pondering how this "source" could help them rescue Maggie.

Chapter Twenty-Four

6:23 p.m.

THE SUN HAD set over the peninsula that closed in *Bahia De Acapulco*, but the air was still warm as the breeze carried it into the outdoor seating at Palmeras. Ali was tardy and had done nothing to alter his somewhat slovenly appearance. He joined Jackson and Bill at a table that was isolated from a handful of tourists and even less locals. He ordered *fajitas de carne y dos cervezas* from a waitress who had already taken Jackson and Bill's orders (also for fajitas), then tipped the table his way by leaning an elbow on it.

"Why are friends of Maggie's here in Acapulco?"

"Yesterday, she called and said she was in trouble," Bill answered. "We've come to rescue her."

Ali laughed a laugh that was far too high-pitched for a man of his girth. "Americans. They always think they can ride in on a white horse and save the day. You have no idea what you are dealing with."

Bill's eyes narrowed. "No, we don't. That's why we've come to you. Maggie said if there was trouble, we should call you."

"Why didn't you? Why did you come all the way to Mexico?"

"Because you didn't answer my calls."

"I have been busy."

"Sure looked like it this afternoon," Jackson said.

Ali stared at him through slits.

"Please, anything you can tell us is more than we have," Bill said.

Ali sat back, crossed one leg onto the other knee, and reached for a bottle of beer as the waitress set two on the table. "*Gracias*," he said to her. "Maggie arrived at my door five, maybe six weeks ago, asking for information about Leonardo Vasquez and LOVE. You know it?"

"We do," Bill said.

"Why your door?" Jackson asked.

"Because it is well known in this city that if you need something that is not readily available, Ali Alfonseca is the man to contact."

"What did you tell her?" Bill asked.

"The basics. LOVE is a global investment group, made up of a combination of businessmen and subsidiaries. Leo Vasquez is the head, at least of their Central and South American operations."

"Mexico's in North America," Jackson said.

Ali shot him another glare. "Technically, perhaps. Specifically, she asked about LOVE's relationship with Mexól and GR Limited. I did a little digging. GR Limited is a Mexico City-based shell company for LOVE. Its primary shareholder is a man named Geraldo Ruiz. His brother, Franco, is the president of Mexól."

Jackson and Bill had both ordered bottled waters, not trusting Mexican tap water or, in Bill's case, his mind on alcohol. They both took drinks as Ali continued.

"The vice president of LOVE is Vasquez's son, Rafael. He is a good-for-nothing, promoted to keep him out of trouble. Maggie was looking for a way to get close to Vasquez, and I suggested Rafael might be that way."

"Why?" Bill asked.

"He likes beautiful women," Ali said with a leering smile, "and Maggie is a beautiful woman."

"You're telling us that Maggie seduced her way into a position with LOVE?" Jackson asked.

"I do not know what she did." Ali took a swig. "I recommended it. And now she is working for Rafael."

"Doing what?"

"She is his assistant."

"Where does she work?" Bill asked.

"They have an office here. Downtown."

"You know where she's been living?"

"Until Monday, no."

"What happened Monday?"

"She and Rafael went to Vasquez's hacienda in the hills. She has been there ever since."

"How do you know?" Bill just beat Jackson in asking.

"My cousin, Rodrigo, works for Vasquez at his hacienda. He is a cook. Maggie sent word through him that she was there."

"Why?"

"I imagine in case you came looking for her."

Bill looked at Jackson. "So her call yesterday was indeed under duress."

The fajitas arrived quickly and were delicious. While the trio ate, Ali gave them more details about LOVE. He gossiped—with a few facts thrown in—about Rafael Vasquez, and told them where Leonardo Vasquez's hacienda was located, approximately twenty miles north and east of Acapulco.

"But if you are thinking of going there, you are *muy loco*."

"Why's that?" Bill asked, wiping his mouth after inhaling his dinner.

"Because it is a fortress. You will never get in."

"You're sure Maggie's there?" Bill asked.

"I have not heard from her or Rodrigo since yesterday. Yes, I am sure."

"Then we'll get in," Jackson said.

Ali gave them a few more tips, including "colleagues" of his they could speak with, who might know more about the Vasquez family or LOVE. It wasn't likely he said. He also recommended someone who could "set them up" with any "supplies" they might need. Then he drained the remainder of his second beer and stood.

"You will get the check, no?"

"We will," Bill said.

"A pleasure," Ali said, shaking both of their hands. Then he shuffled off into the night.

*   *   *

7:25 p.m.

BILL CALLED for a cab, then used his phone to reserve a hotel room at a Holiday Inn on the beach. He and Jackson had hung around at Palmeras for another five minutes, agreeing that they wanted to storm Leonardo Vasquez's hacienda with guns blazing. But they simply weren't prepared enough. And they had no guns. So they had agreed to use the rest of the night and the following morning to do some research.

As they waited for their ride, they plotted. Acapulco was a city of almost seven hundred thousand, so "asking around" about Maggie was pointless. So too was trying to locate which apartment she had rented or hotel room she had occupied since arriving roughly six weeks ago. Bill surmised that she had likely stayed with Rafael Vasquez anyhow. As much as Jackson didn't want to admit it, he agreed.

They debated trying to find his place and going there, or attempting to gain access to LOVE's downtown office. But both were dangerous, and the potential rewards were minimal. They knew where Maggie was, in all likelihood. Why specifically she was there didn't matter all that much. What did was knowing what was happening to her there and figuring out a way to free her.

The cab came and they settled into the backseat, this time listening to loud Latino hip-hop instead of a cabbie's phone conversation.

Unable to easily converse, Jackson mulled what Maggie had said to Bill on the phone. They now knew she had called after being taken to the hacienda, saying, "It's me. I need you to bring the Trojan package to Acapulco. You've got a week." The most likely probability was that Vasquez was on to Maggie's investigation and her plans to expose LOVE and Mexól.

So why was she still alive? Why had they let her make the phone call? Had she convinced them that someone else had some valuable information, something of which "the Trojan package" would seem like a description? Had her coded message to Bill also served to placate her captors for a week?

It was all speculation, and there was nothing in the message to tell Jackson and Bill where on the hacienda she was being held, in what status, or how to free her. They had their work cut out for them.

The room at the Holiday Inn was simple—two double beds, a small writing desk, and a balcony looking out at the bay. The two men quickly set up their laptops, connected to the hotel's Wi-Fi, and got to work.

Ali had given them three names—sources—and Bill, the Spanish speaker, found contact numbers and gave them calls. Meanwhile, Jackson resorted to the most basic of detective methods and poked around on the internet. Leonardo Vasquez didn't warrant a Wikipedia page, nor had he turned up in any American newspapers, blogs, or trade journals. The same was true for LOVE. Jackson used a built-in translator option on several Mexican web pages to glean that Leonardo Vasquez was somewhat reclusive, seldom leaving his hacienda. He conducted a brief search on Rafael and confirmed what Ali had said—the younger Vasquez was a playboy. It was far from comforting.

Bill ended his third call and tossed his phone on the bed. He leaned against the wall beside Jackson. "We may have an in."

"What's that?"

"Tomorrow is Leonardo Vasquez's fiftieth birthday. He's having a little soirée."

"I think you mean fiesta."

"Touché."

"How little?"

"Not all that."

"As in a couple of bachelors could sneak in unnoticed?"

"Maybe. I'm going to track down the Society and Entertainment people with the local papers and see if any of them have any buzz."

"Guess we're lucky you're here."

"I don't know about that. I review movies and sitcoms for a living. You want to know if *Modern Family* will keep winning its timeslot or if *Argo* is going to break any box office records, I'm your guy. Balls and birthday fiestas for the rich and famous are a little out of my league."

"Well, play up."

Bill nodded and sat down at his laptop.

"You get any lead on potential weapons?" Jackson asked.

"Didn't even ask. Truth is, I've never fired a gun in my life. I think that's why Maggie had me call you."

Jackson nodded and leaned back. "Why'd she call you?"

"Excuse me."

"Why were you her contact, instead of her editor or anybody else at the paper?"

If Bill took offense at the question, he didn't show it. "We've been friends a while, and I was bugging her about going to a movie when she got the call from her colleague in Dallas, so I was sort of in on the ground floor."

Jackson nodded.

"Plus, she said that since we sort of have history, if someone happened to discover our communications, they might think it was her calling up an old friend instead of a coworker. Contacting an editor at the *L.A. Times* would look suspicious. A stiff covering Hollywood news, not so much."

Jackson nodded again.

"She said no, by the way."

"What?"

"To the movie."

Jackson shook his head, looking for the connection.

"She told me that you and her were, I don't know, 'sort of dating.'"

"She kind of told me the same thing about you."

"Not really," Bill said. "We've gone out a few times, but it was just as friends. And not in a while."

"Why are you telling me this, Bill?"

"You seem like a cool dude, not the kind to get all sensitive. But if this does get hairy trying to rescue Maggie, I wanted to clear the air ahead of time."

Jackson nodded, then a second time. "Consider it clear. My only concern is getting Maggie back onto U.S. soil safe and sound."

"Mine too."

"Good. Now, see if you can't get us invited to a party."

Chapter Twenty-Five

Friday, November 23
7:04 p.m.

"WHAT IN THE Sam Hill are you doing in Mexico?" Leroy asked.

"I can't tell you. And you never got this phone call," Jackson added.

Leroy harrumphed. "You missed quite a meal yesterday," he said, reminding Jackson that it was the day after Thanksgiving. "Samantha puts out a good spread."

Jackson had been triply sad to have to cancel. One, it looked bad after recently promising to be more open with Sam to have to tell her he couldn't explain why he was canceling. Two, he would miss out on a delicious, traditional Thanksgiving meal. Three, he didn't trust Leroy around Sam without him being there to mitigate anything Leroy said.

"I'm sure she does, Grandpa." He looked up as Bill exited the bathroom. "Look, I'll call you when I can, okay?"

"Be careful, bud. I don't like the tone in your voice."

"I will be."

He clapped his phone shut and dropped it in his pocket.

"Everything good?" Bill asked.

"So to speak."

"You ready?"

Jackson nodded, and the duo took the elevator down to the lobby. It had been a busy morning and afternoon. Jackson and Bill had called every source, friend, friend's source, and friend of a source—all somehow connected to Ali—to learn what they could about the Vasquez hacienda and the fiesta for Leonardo that evening. Ultimately, Bill had pulled several strings and used his position at the *L.A. Times* to persuade a colleague to call in a favor that opened a door that enabled him to coax a local journalist to user her pull to get Bill and Jackson's names on the list of invitees. They'd also scoured the city's public records—both online and in person—in an effort to find blueprints, satellite images, and various other intel on the hacienda. Then they had rented tuxes and a red Peugeot convertible, and placed a few inquiries about attaining weapons. Not wanting to raise any red flags, they had to be discreet, and as a result, got nowhere.

"I feel like James Bond," Bill said as he tipped the valet and slid behind the wheel of the Peugeot.

"Except I'd be a smoking brunette and wouldn't be carrying our bags," Jackson said, having stowed them in the trunk. Their room at the Holiday Inn was reserved for another night, but they also knew they might leave the hacienda hot. So they had packed up their few possessions before leaving.

Darkness had fallen over Acapulco, and the city had come alive with partiers, revelers, diners, and drinkers. Bill navigated like a pro, and soon, he and Jackson were traversing the mountainous terrain north of the city. Jackson found his heart racing, partially out of fear for Maggie's safety, partially out of dread at suddenly recurring memories from two months ago in Nevada, and partially because he and Bill had no plan. They had a rough layout of the hacienda, a basic overview of the party, and little else. No idea where Maggie was (assuming she was still there). No idea what condition Maggie was in. No idea, for that matter, if Maggie was still alive. Bill was quiet, and Jackson wondered if he shared the same concerns.

They turned off the main highway and wound through the hills on a narrow, two-lane road. It crested a tall hill, offering splendid views of the desolate canyon as the Peugeot's headlights swept over it. The sky had clouded, blocking any celestial lights, and leaving those areas not pierced by headlights in total darkness. That changed when Bill rounded the next corner and dropped into a valley. Up ahead, several red dots identified other vehicles on the same serpentine road. Their headlights illuminated a large, wrought-iron gate flanked by stucco guardhouses.

"I think we're here," Bill said.

"You sure our names are on the list?"

"For all the work to get them there, they'd better be."

It took them a minute to wind farther into the valley and come to the checkpoint. Satellite photos had shown that the Vasquez hacienda was nestled in a long, wide valley, on either side of which, scrub-covered hills provided security. So did an eight-foot-tall iron fence, bound with coils of barbed wire, that bordered the hacienda complex. And complex was the word for it. Along with a sprawling, two-story main building that was roughly shaped like a U around an east-facing courtyard, were two free-standing structures southeast of the main building, a pool cabana, a third free-standing building north of the main building, and then a four-stall garage. All were surrounded by acres of pristine green grass, a sharp contrast to the surrounding terrain.

"*Bienvenidos a la Casa Vazquez. ¿Sus nombres, por favor?*"

"*Giancarlo Rivera y Jorge Castañeda,*" Bill said, using aliases he had contrived.

The guard studied a tablet while Jackson prayed no ID would be requested.

None was, and they were waved through with a smile.

"So far, so good," Bill said, accelerating on the paved driveway. It ran for the length of a football field before circling around a fountain in front of the hacienda's main entrance. All around the circle, as well as along an offshoot of the driveway that led to the garage, were an array of cars befitting a Motor City auto show. Bill braked to a stop and he and Jackson got out, and a valet provided Bill with a small device similar to a beeper at a restaurant.

The front walk formed a figure 8, in the middle of which were two more fountains, each topped with a nude marble figurine. On either side of the path, an array of flowers rivaled that at any botanical garden, and short, perfectly sculpted hedges formed a barrier between the lawn and the house. Its white stucco walls were bathed in the soft light of dozens of hidden spotlights. Tall, lazy palm trees caught the beams and cast long, eerie shadows on the walls.

"I think we've outkicked our coverage, Bill," Jackson said as the duo passed through the dual front doors, held for them by a small Latino man in a tuxedo just as immaculate as theirs.

"Uh-huh."

They were in a main entry hall as big as Jackson's house. To the right, a coatroom fit for an opera house was tended by another tux-clad servant. Jackson wasn't sure why, seeing as how it was seventy-five degrees outside and nobody would have worn a coat. Two gently curved staircases climbed to a balcony on the second level, beneath which the entry hall extended to an open courtyard. The din of voices and the festive tune of a mariachi band flowed through the opening, along with the aroma of Mexican food.

"So how do we play this?" Bill asked.

"First thing, get the lay of the land. See how much of the house is open, see where people are and aren't. Then, figure out how to search for Maggie without looking like we're searching."

Bill nodded. "Lead on."

Jackson's rental shoes clicked on the marble floor as he and Bill passed under the balcony and stepped onto the courtyard. It was ringed on three sides by a covered portico that served as the support for a second-floor walkway. A variety of doorways on both levels opened to other rooms, with people flowing out of them. They also congregated around a rectangular pool beyond and several steps below the courtyard. Rows of palm trees provided a canopy over the pool, which was lit from beneath by built-in lights and from above by tiki torches that also spanned the courtyard.

Jackson estimated fifty people filled the courtyard, the men dressed in tuxedos (and in a few cases, military uniforms) and the women in colorful, elegant evening gowns. Most of them were Latino, but a handful of the partygoers were white, black, or Asian. They stood in small circles conversing, ate food abundantly provided at more than a dozen small bistro tables interspersed throughout the courtyard, and danced to the lively mariachi music.

"You know something?" Jackson said out the side of his mouth.

"Mm, what's that?"

"Our rescue mission is basically lifted from ¡Three Amigos!"

"That worked, right?"

"Yeah, like a charm."

The current song concluded with a crescendo, and Jackson and Bill joined in applauding those who had been dancing.

"You see Vasquez?"

"Maybe. Wouldn't know him if I did," Bill said.

"He in the military?" Jackson asked, paying close attention to several men with ribbons of medals on their chest. Judging by the uniforms, several different branches or even nationalities were represented.

"Not that I know of, but that doesn't mean no."

Jackson nodded as the band began playing another lively number. He was about to suggest they split up when a woman on the far side of the courtyard caught his eye. She wore a long, flared red gown that accentuated every inch of every curve as she glided merrily around the courtyard with a dashing man in a tuxedo. He had flowing brown hair, very feisty revolutionary, and seemed to be enjoying his view of her almost as much as she enjoyed twirling around the floor with him. Jackson stood mesmerized at the dance until it concluded, inciting more applause. He didn't participate, hands in his pockets, watching the couple.

Laughing, the woman patted the man's lapel, then turned and picked a flute of champagne off a passing waiter's tray. She took a refined swallow before weaving her way across the makeshift dance floor, right to Jackson and Bill. She studied them through narrowed eyes, biting down on her bottom lip. Then her mouth formed a provocative smile.

"So, which of you two studs wants the first dance?" Maggie asked.

*   *   *

Tuesday, January 1
8:26 a.m.

THE DOCTOR who checked on Jackson was not the dainty, stern-faced Dr. Nelson. It was the slightly rotund Dr. McCarthy. He studied Jackson and Jackson's e-chart equally, smiling good-naturedly all the while. Then he turned his attention fully to Jackson. "How are you feeling?"

Jackson wasn't sure how his response might influence Dr. McCarthy, but it was worth a try. "Good."

"Is that the truth?"

"A reasonable facsimile thereof."

Dr. McCarthy turned to Reggie, who was scanning Leroy's newspaper while Leroy was in the restroom. "He always a smart aleck like this?"

"Usually, yeah."

"Seriously, Doc, you think I can get out of here this morning?"

"This morning?" McCarthy took a step back. "Why the rush?"

"Because the Rose Bowl kicks off at two."

"Ah yes, it is New Year's Day, isn't it? You have tickets?"

"I wish. I do have a package of cheese-filled smokeys in the refrigerator though."

"Well, I can't match the smokeys, but we have a television right here."

"No offense, but this isn't quite the same as watching from the comfort of your living room."

"No, I don't suppose so," McCarthy said, forcing a grin onto his face.

Jackson wasn't done lobbying. "I mean, if I'm in danger of bleeding out or my heart's going to stop or something, I get it. But otherwise, what's the holdup? Either the bag on the floor or the bed sheet should tell you I'm clearly able to pee, and if you guys would give me some real food, I could knock out number two."

McCarthy's smile morphed into a grimace. "Well, I'm not crazy about you going home just yet, especially without any supervision. You were shot less than twelve hours ago."

As if on cue, Sam walked in, changed from her scrubs to jeans and a purple knit top, sleeves pushed up to the elbows. "Hi," she said while the doctor checked some more statistics and measurements on the computer. "How are you doing?"

"Not so hot," Jackson said. "Dr. No here doesn't want me going home unsupervised."

"Look out, Sam," Reggie muttered.

"Read your paper."

"The doctor's right, Jackson," Sam said, patting his hand. "You were shot last night."

McCarthy smiled superciliously.

"What happened to emptying the beds to get new patients in here?" Jackson asked.

"You must have good insurance," Leroy said as he shuffled past the end of the bed and back to his seat beside Reggie.

Jackson frowned. He hadn't even thought about his thin, cheap insurance. He turned back to McCarthy. "You said unsupervised. What if I had supervision?"

"Look out," Reggie muttered again.

"From a qualified healthcare professional?" Jackson continued, turning his eyes to Sam.

She smiled through closed lips. "I have to work today."

"Of course you do."

Sam straightened her posture. "I might be able to switch with somebody."

"Make sure they aren't a football fan," Reggie said.

"Would that work, Doc?"

McCarthy turned his head. "I'll tell you what. I'll talk to the nurse about getting you some solid food so we can see about 'number two,'" he said with a sideways glance at Sam. "And then I'll check back in a couple of hours, and we'll see how you're feeling then. How's that sound?"

"That sounds like a no."

"We'll see in a couple of hours."

Jackson sighed as he left the room. "Reggie?"

"DVR's already set."

"You're the man."

"How are you really feeling?" Sam asked. "Football aside?"

"Like I got hit in the shoulder with a shovel. And I'm starved. Do you have some gum in your purse or something?"

She rolled her eyes. "I'll go make a few calls, just in case."

He grabbed her hand before she could go. "Thanks, Sam."

"Thank me if I can find a sub. Then thank them. And then thank Dr. McCarthy if he capitulates and lets you go."

"Did you hear that, Reg? Run down to the gift shop for me, will you? Flowers all around."

Chapter Twenty-Six

Friday, November 23
8:11 p.m.

JACKSON AND BILL looked at each other. The shock on Bill's face matched what Jackson knew was on his own. Never mind that he'd never seen Maggie even close to decked out like she was. Never mind that her normally long hair had been chopped to just past chin-length. Never mind the alluring, carefree smirk on her face. Had they completely misinterpreted her message? Had the status quo changed? Was this some odd version of *The Game*, with Jackson as Michael Douglas, Maggie as Deborah Kara Unger, and Bill as Sean Penn?

Maggie didn't wait for them to figure it out. She stuck out her hand and tugged Jackson's from his pocket. She simultaneously thrust her champagne flute at Bill and pulled Jackson onto the dance floor.

"Are we in character or are you drunk?" Jackson asked.

"A little of both," she said as she wrapped her arms around him. "You should probably lead."

Jackson was not a dancer, but the band was beginning again, a slow song this time, albeit with a little fiesta flair. So he did his best to follow the beat. He quickly figured out a basic shuffle that would keep him from kicking Maggie's shins or stepping on her dress. He focused his attention on her.

She looked really good. Maggie always looked good, a naturally beautiful woman whose lack of effort seemed only to enhance her appearance. He'd only seen her "dressed up" once or twice, never in an evening gown. He wanted to tell her how good she looked, wanted to make an effort to repair the bridge he thought had been burned on Labor Day, and wanted her to explain why they were slow-dancing in the open-air courtyard of a Mexican business mogul's secluded hacienda. But before he could figure out where to start, she spoke.

"We don't have much time, so listen very carefully."

He nodded.

"Vasquez is holding me here until I provide him all the evidence I have on him and his operations. Once I do, he'll have no need to hold me. He'll kill me."

Jackson frowned.

"He's also got dignitaries and military attachés from several NATO countries visiting, so a bloodbath would look bad. But they'll be gone by Monday and so will I if you don't do something."

"Any bright ideas?"

Another couple drew close, and Maggie bit her tongue until she and Jackson had sashayed away from them. "I saw the news, about what you did in Nevada, rescuing the lawyer."

He nodded.

"I need you to do it again. I need you to play the hero and save the girl."

Jackson said nothing, fighting the flood of emotions coursing through him. He was willing to do whatever was necessary to rescue Maggie, yet appalled at the thought that he might have to take more lives.

"Spin me," Maggie said.

On autopilot, Jackson performed a rudimentary twirl. Then Maggie was back in his arms, her blue-gray eyes intensely tracking his.

"I know what I'm asking," she said as they continued to dance across the courtyard-turned-dance floor. "I feel terrible dragging you down here into this mess, especially after how things . . . ended between us. But, I didn't know what else to do. And truthfully, there's no one else I trust more than you."

The word "ended" stuck in Jackson's brain, driving a finality to what he had assumed for months—that whatever it was he and Maggie shared in terms of a relationship really was over. And that was hardly relevant at the moment, but it sure wanted to be. He forced himself to become robotic, unemotional. It was the only way he stood any chance of going to the places he would need to mentally if he was going to break Maggie out, and it was the only way he could possibly concentrate on what needed to be done instead of the range of feelings inside him.

"What do you need to take with you?"

"Nothing," she said. "The clothes on my back. Everything else is in the cloud."

"Stunning as you look, Mags, you may want to consider something more practical for a breakout."

She grinned. "Even now, you crack funnies."

"It is my nature. You have any allies here?"

The grin faded. "I did. His name was Rodrigo. They killed him, Jack. In front of me. They . . . they shot him."

"I'm sorry."

"His cousin . . ."

"Ali. We talked to him."

"I don't think he knows. He . . ."

"Don't think about that now, Maggie. You have to shut down all emotions. Ignore everything that isn't tactical and essential to getting you out."

"Then I'm alone. I have nobody but you."

The song ended and Maggie stepped back, clapping. Jackson just watched her. He wanted desperately to reach out and hug her, to hold her, to assure her that everything would be okay. But the crowd was moving, and Maggie was already being courted by another young bachelor. Their eyes lingered on each other as their bodies drifted farther apart in the crowd. Then Jackson turned his head and found Bill.

"What's up?" Bill asked.

"You need to dance with her," Jackson said. "Find out where she's staying, is there a guard, what's security like. Get as many details as you can."

"Okay?"

"Skip the intros and good to see yous and how are you and get right down to business."

Bill nodded.

"We'll compare notes later. Right now, I'm going to circulate and act the part of a bachelor who just danced with the best-looking girl here."

"Where should I find you?"

"Two guys, no dates . . . probably by the booze."

For the next twenty minutes, Jackson wandered, memorized faces, ate a few delicious appetizers, and did his best to get the lay of the land. Vasquez's hacienda was a maze of interconnected rooms, all focused around the courtyard or the covered portico that lined it and then ran north and south from the ends of the "U" it formed around the courtyard. There were several drawing rooms or parlors, a two-story library, an art gallery, a music room, a billiard room, a cigar lounge, and a home theater—all open to guests. Jackson gleaned that the dining and kitchen facilities were north of the courtyard, along with a spa and gym. South of the main courtyard, and separated from the main building by its own spacious patio, was a free-standing structure that appeared to contain half a dozen guestrooms. There was also a pool house that could be occupied by guests, and Jackson had yet to visit the second floor. He guessed it contained Vasquez's quarters, and likely his office. Servants' quarters were in a separate building north of the main house. It was, in short, a palace.

Jackson wandered around, trying to listen in to conversations and gather some semblance of intel. But the majority of conversations were in Spanish, which limited his chances of learning much.

When the band took a break, Jackson found his way to one of several tended bars, where Bill joined him a moment later. *"Dos whiskys, por favor,"* Bill said, holding a pair of fingers up for the bartender. He poured their drinks, and they took them and sauntered away to a lounge off the courtyard, then to a hallway and ultimately the cigar lounge, where an old man in a Mexican military uniform was finishing a cigar by the window. He ignored them as they stood in the opposite corner.

"She's staying in the north guestroom, second floor," Bill said. "In the detached guesthouse."

"Guards?" Jackson asked, flitting his eyes to the uniformed man. His eyes were focused on a trio of ponds just outside the window. His ears were another matter.

"There's a guard who patrols the courtyards each night. Shift changes around midnight." Bill took a drink of his whiskey. "According to Maggie, there are sensors in the lawn that detect anything larger than a field mouse, set off alarms if you stray from the patio. The fence that circles the property is electrified and topped with barbed wire, and just to be careful, a pair of armed guards with Dobermans patrol it all night. Also a guard at the front door and front gate all night"

"Who is this guy, *El Chapo?*"

"Vasquez sleeps in the north wing of the main house, probably has his own guard, although she doesn't know. Rafael's been sleeping in the mother-in-law suite in the southwest corner of the house for the last few days, and there's a few other guests in the guesthouse with her. Throw in the kitchen staff, maids, butlers, who knows how many people are prowling around here at night. Her words."

"She have any good news?"

"They haven't hurt her. Questioned her pretty intensely, and killed Ali's cousin in front of her."

"Yeah, she told me that. She have any ideas? Any tunnels from the wine cellar to the cliffs over yonder or something?" Jackson asked.

Bill shook his head and took another drink.

The man in uniform suddenly dropped the stub of his cigar in an ashtray and, without so much as glancing at Jackson and Bill, exited the room.

Bill swirled the whiskey and took another gulp. "Don't worry," he said. "I can hold it."

Jackson pitched the contents of his glass in a nearby plant.

"You got a plan?" Bill asked.

"My first impulse is to try to sneak her out now, while the party's in full swing. But I'm guessing, for all the appearances that she's just another guest enjoying the party, the guys at the front gate won't let her pass."

"Oh, that's the other thing," Bill said. "You notice her dress?"

"Hard not to."

"Floor-length. Covers the ankle bracelet she's wearing. She somehow manages to get through the front gate, it goes off. She disables it—"

"It goes off." He sighed. "We get through the front gate, we're halfway home."

"You thinking a basic smash and grab?"

"I don't know. We've got nothing to smash with. I don't even know if the Peugeot could crash that gate. Before we try that, I want to think."

Motion drew his attention to the doorway, where two men entered. One was handsome and smooth, his tuxedo a perfect fit. His raven black hair was wavy and shiny, and the lopsided smirk on his face capable of charming a brick wall. Jackson immediately deduced he was Rafael Vasquez, and felt a sudden urge to split his lip. The other man kept him from doing so. He was built like a Mack truck, straining every fiber of his tuxedo jacket. More importantly, he held a small, black pistol in his right hand.

"*Señores*, welcome to my father's party," Rafael said in accented but perfect English. "Please, won't you come with me?"

Jackson looked at Bill as they both set their glasses down, then followed Rafael from the room, the tank bringing up the rear. Rafael led them back to the entry hall, then up to the second floor. As they walked, Jackson searched for Maggie in the crowd below. He failed to spot her.

Rafael led them around to the north side of the courtyard, then through a double set of doors into a warm, plushly carpeted hallway. A pair of doors directly ahead of them were closed, as was a duel set on their right. But double doors midway along the hall on their left were open, and Rafael stopped and gestured through them like the maître d' at a five-star restaurant.

Jackson and Bill entered a magnificent office. The ornate desk was huge, its mahogany surface polished to a shine. The chairs in front of it were equally lavish, their seats padded better than Jackson's recliner. Bookshelves on the back wall framed a mirror befitting an Old West saloon. Every piece of furniture was beautifully crafted. The paintings on the walls were probably originals of some famous artist. Jackson could almost smell the wealth.

Seated behind the desk was a man who was just as impressive as his surroundings. Immaculately tailored, not a hair out of place, he had the same features as his son, only the hair was shorter and tinged with gray, and his beard was full—albeit well-groomed—instead of a dark shadow. His presence in the room was powerful, not just because he was impeccable or because he was so big that he practically looked down on Jackson and Bill despite being seated. There was an aura about him, and it made Jackson, normally cool and at ease, uncomfortable.

Swallowing the fear he felt, Jackson forced his persona. "Guess we should have been drinking Dos Equis," he said to Bill.

"That's funny," Leonardo Vasquez said without smiling. His voice made Bill's sound falsetto by comparison, and when he rose from his seat, he towered over them both like Goliath. "You can continue to make wisecracks to mask your fears and insecurities and I could bluster and bloviate and impress you with the incredible power I wield, but that would just waste time, and, to be perfectly candid with you, I am enjoying this wonderful celebration. So let's cut to the chase, as you Americans are fond of saying." He paused only long enough to eye them both. "Where is it?"

Jackson quickly recalled what Maggie had said, that Vasquez wanted the evidence she had gathered against him, and replayed in his mind her coded message to Bill, asking him to bring the "Trojan package." How Vasquez knew who Jackson and Bill were was a good question, but irrelevant for the moment. Instead, he had to find a way to stall.

"We didn't bring it."

"Then we have a very large problem."

"To the party," Jackson said.

"We're not stupid," Bill added. "We show up with our only leverage, with you and your goons running around . . ."

"Goons. Another tasteful Americanism."

Bill shrugged.

"You have one day," Vasquez said with something akin to a sneer. "Bring me everything. All copies. All evidence." He looked at his watch. "You're late by one minute, and she dies."

Jackson pursed his lips to keep from falling into the cliché of calling Vasquez names or threatening vengeance if he "so much as touched one hair on her head." Instead, he concentrated on finding a way out of this mess. He also gave some thought, as Vasquez paced around to the front of his desk, to how, in the magnate's mind, they were ever supposed to prove they didn't have copies of the evidence stashed elsewhere. After all, that was his concern, keeping Maggie from releasing whatever dirt she had gathered.

Vasquez stood in front of his desk, just inches from Jackson and Bill. Instead of delivering a threat, he leaned back on the edge of his desk and plucked a business card off a small stand. He then scribbled something on it and handed it to Jackson. "You give me a call on that number by noon tomorrow and I will give you instructions on where to bring the evidence."

"Noon isn't one day," Jackson said.

"I have business in Veracruz tomorrow evening. I'm leaving at noon. You have until then. Now, if you'll excuse me, I have guests to entertain." He smiled. "By all means, stay a while, enjoy the party."

He stood and brushed between them, subtly letting his size send another message. Rafael followed him out the door, and the heavy with the gun motioned for Jackson and Bill to follow. By the time they reached the walkway above the courtyard, Leonardo and Rafael were gone. The man with the gun motioned to the stairs, and Jackson and Bill wasted no time.

"Now what?" Bill asked quietly as they descended to the ground level.

"I have no idea."

Chapter Twenty-Seven

10:15 p.m.

MAGGIE HAD DISAPPEARED. Either she was capable of blending into the crowd or Vasquez had told her to leave the party. Jackson guessed the latter, but the party flowed over so much of the hacienda, it was hard to be sure.

He and Bill had continued to circulate, committing the layout of the house to memory, searching for security cameras, contemplating options. Jackson visited the bar three times and began to act as if he was impaired. Bill, meanwhile, had found a voluptuous *señorita* to accompany him. Jackson had no doubt Vasquez's people would be watching them, and since they couldn't afford to leave, they had to construct plausible reasons for remaining at the party. Jackson hoped drunken despondence and devil-may-care flirting would be construed as such.

At ten-thirty, Jackson and Bill met at a snack table. The party was still in full swing, as was Bill's lady friend who clung to his arm. "She doesn't speak a word of English," he said, then uttered something to her in Spanish that caused her to giggle and wriggle on his arm.

"Camera panning the courtyard from your six o'clock," Bill said as Jackson faced east, toward the pool. "Also one over both doors of the gallery. I haven't seen any others."

"Maggie's in the north bedroom, you said?"

"Yeah, second story."

"On the other side of the theater is a two-story lounge with a door onto the portico that runs to the guest quarters. That's our entry back into the main house."

"Where Leonardo, Rafael, and their entire staff will be."

"Right."

"So what's our getaway?"

"Still working on it."

Bill's date whispered something into his ear and slinked off.

"What'd she say?"

"Powder room."

"You think Vasquez has the entire staff on the lookout for us?"

Bill shrugged. "This is your game more than mine."

"Off the cuff, you think the valet knows to watch when we leave?"

"Fifty-fifty."

"Yeah."

"Why, what are you thinking?"

"Before we can work an exit strategy, we need an entrance strategy. The party will go on for hours, but eventually it will wind down and we become conspicuous. Somehow we have to stay here without Vasquez knowing we did."

"Any thoughts?" Bill asked, reaching for a snack. Like Jackson, danger apparently didn't diminish his appetite.

"Maybe. Who's the girl, any idea?"

"I'm pretty sure she works for Vasquez."

"How so?"

"As an escort. He stocks his party with a bunch of tall, long-legged women to make sure his stag guests go home happy."

"That could work. She like you?"

"She digs *tipos blancos*," Bill said.

"Enough to go home with you tonight?"

"I only have to ask, Jack."

"Good. If Vasquez has the valet or guards at the gate checking faces, we're in trouble. But if not, we've got a chance."

"You going to read me in?"

"In due time. For now, just keep the lady happy."

*   *   *

11:51 p.m.

JACKSON SPENT the better part of the next hour acting drunk, tie loosened, half-empty glass dangled from his hand, looking bullish at anyone who passed by. Unlike when he'd stormed a decommissioned military base to rescue Hillary from a private militia and rogue CIA agents in September, he wasn't armed to the teeth. He and Bill had no weapons. He also wasn't alone, for what Bill was worth.

And while he didn't have CIA-worthy intel, he wasn't going in completely blind. He had some framework of the territory.

Just like then, he didn't have much of a plan. In September, he'd gone in hot, shooting his way to Hillary and *Die Harding* her out. The toll those actions had taken was still heavy upon him, and the thought of impersonating Rambo again made him physically ill. Almost as much as not getting Maggie out alive. So while he played the sullen drunk, he forced his brain to mull and ponder ideas and scenarios, pros and cons. His brain didn't like it. It preferred to ruminate at its own pace, often subconsciously, and usually productively. But there wasn't time for rumination.

If the party was dying down, it wasn't doing so discernably. The dancing, drinking and eating, and pomp and pageantry continued oblivious to Jackson or his plight. Leonardo and Rafael made one appearance, to thank the guests and blather about their business. Neither so much as cast a glance at Jackson. He thought that was a good sign. Maggie was absent, which was not a good sign. He thought about trying to get to her room now, but concluded it wasn't wise with so many people milling about. So he waited and thought some more.

Bill caught his eye from across the pool as Jackson was wondering if there was any possible way to beat the sensors in the lawn. He'd given up, realizing if so, the electric fence, barbed wire, and Dobermans were a sufficient deterrent.

They met in the courtyard.

"Where's the girl?" Jackson asked.

"Getting something to drink. You have a plan?"

"We need to find a place where we can talk. You, me, and her."

A minute later, she sashayed over, and Bill said something in Spanish to her. Jackson caught the word *privacidad*.

She smiled and reached a hand to trace Bill's tuxedo lapel.

"Tremos todos," he said, and she immediately frowned. Then she motioned for them to follow. She led them to the northwest corner of the courtyard, from which a doorway opened to a small anteroom. Beyond it, accessible by double doors, was an elaborate dining room. The woman led them through it, into the kitchen, and out the other side to a small breakfast nook. Small relatively. It contained seating for eight at a table, four more at an elevated bar that looked at a bank of flat screen TVs, and four more in a loveseat and dual armchairs by a fireplace. A row of windows looked out to the west. With no lights on in the room, Jackson was able to see a stone wall straight ahead, the garage to the right, and, if he craned his neck, the servants' quarters. The garage and servants'

quarters were connected by a sidewalk beside an arched, concrete wall. If his memory of the satellite images he and Bill had viewed was accurate, a similar walkway connected the servants' quarters to the main house.

The woman rattled off some rapid Spanish, and Bill turned to Jackson. "She wants to know what's going on."

"Tell her you'd like nothing more than to get out of here with her, but you're worried about me because I'm clearly drunk."

Bill turned to the woman and relayed the message.

"Dejenlo, pues."

"She said to leave you."

"What's her name?"

"Isabella."

"Ask her if she can drive."

Bill spoke, and her response was a terse, *"Claro que si."*

"Yes."

"Ask if she's ever driven a Peugeot convertible."

Isabella said nothing in reply to Bill's translation, but her eyes widened.

"Tell her you'll give her the keys to your car, which she can take back to our hotel and wait for you. You and I just have to take care of one small business transaction first, and then you can ditch me and romance the night away with her."

"You're serious?" Bill asked.

"Very."

He turned to Isabella again and unleashed another torrent.

"¿En serio?"

Bill grinned. "She says, 'Seriously?'"

"Jingle the keys in front of her."

"I don't have the keys. Valet, remember?"

"Oh, right. Well, convince her."

Bill spoke some more Spanish, to which Isabella merely nodded.

"Deal?" Jackson asked.

"Deal."

"Okay, now comes the hard part." Bill looked skeptically at Jackson, who reached out a hand. "Give me the beeper."

*　　　　　*　　　　　*

Saturday, November 24

12:02 a.m.

TIMING WAS everything. Jackson, Bill, and Isabella lingered near the front entrance until they saw another couple—a man in a Mexican military uniform and another of Vasquez's "employees" by the look of things—prepping to leave. Then they headed outside and presented the beeper to the valet. He returned in a minute with the Peugeot, leaving it idling as he hurried to bring the other couple's vehicle.

"Okay, quick," Jackson said.

Bill helped Isabella into the car, repeating instructions to her in Spanish. He leaned down to give her a quick kiss, then closed the door—with its tinted window—on her. With a vroom, she was off, and Jackson and Bill quickly ducked back into the shadows of several palms, reaching them before the valet returned with the other couple's car. Fortunately, the couple was quite enamored with each other and didn't pay attention to two guys shipping off a girl by herself and then hiding in the foliage. As long as the guards at the gate weren't checking passengers and comparing them with the guest list to make sure everyone left and as long as Vasquez didn't question the guards to make sure they had seen him and Bill leaving, Jackson's plan should work.

The valet turned his attention to a smartphone when the couple was gone, and Jackson and Bill sneaked along the western edge of the hacienda, doing their best to stay out of the light and, to a lesser degree, out of the flowers. They had spotted a security camera over the front door, looking at the entry hall, meaning they couldn't re-enter the building without being spotted by it. Jackson's plan was to enter via the cigar lounge, which opened to a small patio that overlooked a flower garden. He surmised that the lawn sensors weren't yet engaged, and as they came around to the southwest corner of the building, that belief was proven accurate. Walking between two of the three reflecting pools in the small garden was a man in a tux and a woman with a long, navy blue dress and equally long, luxurious dark hair.

Jackson and Bill quickly dropped to the ground and hid behind a hedge. The man was talking quietly, in Spanish, and the woman giggled at almost every phrase as they slowly meandered toward the south side of the hacienda. They were almost out of sight when they stopped and he pulled the woman toward him. He kissed her, then began working his lips toward her ear. Suddenly she shrieked, then stepped back and slapped his chest playfully. Taking his hand, she pulled him around the corner of the building.

"Was that . . ."

"Raf-a-el," Jackson muttered. "Yeah."

"Guess he's not worried about estate security."

"Come on."

Jackson and Bill hurried through the garden to the patio, risking being spotted by anyone inside the cigar lounge. Unless it was Vasquez or one of his henchmen, it wouldn't be all that suspicious for two men to walk into a cigar lounge. But it was empty, and Jackson searched inside and outside to make sure they hadn't missed a camera before. Unless it was hidden behind an air vent, they hadn't.

"I assume we find a hiding place now," Bill said.

"There's a closet off the billiard room," Jackson said. "Looks like odd storage."

There was a rather heated billiard game being waged, with two slender women in resplendent gowns watching. Jackson and Bill waited for "next," hoping Vasquez or one of his people didn't wander in and spot them. The game turned to a best two-of-three, which went three, and then the victor played a quick "game" with the two women, both of whom were with him. Eventually, they ran out of booze, and turned the table over to Jackson and Bill. They racked up another game as the trio filed out. When they were gone, they headed for the closet.

"So what do you think the odds are they need to stash a bunch of party supplies in this closet?" Bill asked as Jackson opened the door.

With a small smirk, Jackson answered, "Fifty-fifty."

Chapter Twenty-Eight

3:17 a.m.

"FOR THE RECORD, this was a dumb plan," Bill said as he and Jackson emerged from the closet.

They had been in the smaller-than-thought space for close to three hours, enduring two more games of pool and a heated, rapid conversation in Spanish that Bill said sounded like a business negotiation between a Mexican colonel and a man with cartel connections. Virtually every muscle had fallen asleep, and they had quickly realized they had no way of knowing when the party was over. But it had been at least an hour since the last visitor to the room, and the distant sounds of music had long since died out. Jackson had concluded it was safe to at least send out an exploratory committee, and neither man opted to remain behind in the closet a second longer.

"Let's just hope they bought our little ruse," Jackson said.

"I'm on your six," Bill said.

"Here, grab some ammo," Jackson said, pocketing a couple of billiard balls. Bill did likewise, then followed Jackson.

The maze of rooms connected in an odd assortment of ways, such that the only way to get to the free-standing guesthouse off the southeast corner of the main building was via the lawn (in the footsteps of Rafael and his lady friend); via the main courtyard, past the pool house, and to the patio between the main building and the guesthouse; or via the second story. But to get to the second story, they would need to pass through the courtyard (guarded) and main entry hall (monitored by a camera). So they resorted to a combination of options. Across the hall from the billiard room was a lounge, consisting of several rich, deep sofas and armchairs. It connected to a drawing room, a less formal version of the lounge, which in turn connected to the two-story library. Jackson and Bill sneaked their way through the house, keeping a watchful eye out for guards, passed out partiers, or security cameras. They saw none, and reached the library unseen.

"Man, this is bigger than some small-town libraries," Bill whispered, eyeing fully stocked shelves all around the perimeter of the room. Three aisles cut through shelves in the middle of the room. The middle row of bookshelves was interrupted by a spiral, wrought-iron staircase that led to the second floor. Climbing carefully to minimize the clack of dress shoes on the grated iron steps, Jackson and Bill ascended to the second level, which was half open to the first floor. Catwalks ran right and left from the top of the stairs, connecting to a balcony that circled all four walls. Three of them were lined with more bookshelves, while the fourth opened to a large, east-facing window.

"I'm surprised the guy can read," Jackson mumbled.

"Maybe on the way out, we can drop a match in here and torch his precious collection."

"Nazi."

Bill grinned.

The only exit from the second floor of the library was to a conjoined sitting room. Or a lounge. Or a parlor. Or a drawing room. Jackson had no idea what constituted one or the other, but the hacienda seemed made up of dozens of such little alcoves. This one looked collegial, with a mixture of comfortable-looking chairs and couches and desks with little green-shaded lamps, perfect for cozying up with or studying a good book. Bill had understated the library. It was bigger than that in many small cities.

From the sitting room, Jackson and Bill had access to the guest lounge, a two-story facility that housed a standard living room with a full entertainment center and a trio of TV screens, a small kitchenette, a powder room, and a another private sitting room. There was nothing unique to this lounge that wasn't duplicated multiple times elsewhere in the hacienda, but this lounge was exclusively for guests residing in the guesthouse. One of them apparently had insomnia.

From their position in the shadows of the doorway, Jackson and Bill observed a man on the couch of the second-floor living room as he watched a soccer match on one of the TVs. At first Jackson thought he was looking at Rafael, but he realized quickly that it wasn't him. The man wore dress pants, a collared white shirt, no jacket or tie. He loosely held a bottle in his hand, which he swigged from every few minutes.

"Great," Bill whispered.

"Bond would have a dart gun and would just put him to sleep," Jackson said.

"Magic eight ball to the head?"

"What if you miss?"

"I was a pitcher in college. I won't miss."

"What college?"

"Cal State-Fullerton. Almost made the College World Series senior year."

Jackson nodded. "Let's give it a little while."

They waited fifteen minutes, after which, fortunately, the bottle ran out and the guy got up, flipped off the TV, and headed toward the guestrooms. Jackson and Bill waited five more minutes, then followed.

From the living room, they had a view of the courtyard, bound on three and a half sides by buildings—the library on the north, the guest lounge on the west, and the actual guestrooms on the south and east. The portico that ran along the guestrooms extended to form the southern edge of the lounge, while the walkway beneath it at ground level opened to the garden. And the courtyard opened on its northeast corner to the patio that ran past the pool house to the main courtyard. Otherwise, it was enclosed.

"Didn't Maggie say there was a guard?" Jackson asked.

"Yeah," Bill said.

A moment later, a man in all black stepped from under the portico and paced across the courtyard. He wore a machine gun over his shoulder, and swept his eyes back and forth as he patrolled.

"Great," Bill said.

Jackson observed and timed the patrol. Three times, the guard exited the guest courtyard and headed toward the main courtyard. Each time, he returned in approximately two minutes, give or take ten seconds. Jackson reported as much to Bill.

"So we have two minutes to get to her door."

"Yeah. Actually, we take it in chunks. We make it to the support column in the corner," Jackson said, pointing to where two arches converged in a column. "He hasn't come upstairs yet. We get there, hide, wait till he leaves again, then go for Maggie's room."

"Let's hope she's awake."

"And doesn't have a guard in the room tonight, since Vasquez knows we're here."

Bill exhaled. "On your mark."

Jackson waited until the guard returned, then he and Bill exited the lounge to the bridge, shielded from sight in the doorway. They crept to the corner and waited. It was maybe forty feet to the corner, with two doors on the right, out of which soccer-loving guests who couldn't sleep could emerge at any moment.

The guard circled the courtyard, gave a quick glance to the spiral staircase at the northern end of the guesthouse, then started along the east edge of the main house. Jackson held up a hand, waiting twenty seconds, before nodding at Bill. "Go."

They walked quickly but quietly under the portico, which was lit only by soft, recessed lights in the ceiling. Sweeping arches connected a trio of support columns, the last of which was in the corner. The arches were low enough to cast plenty of shadow from the scant ambient light. As Jackson reached the corner shortly after Bill, he had no problem blending into the shadows.

They caught their breath and waited for the faint scuffle of leather on stone indicating the guard had returned. He shuffled around for a while, and Jackson, unable to see his movements, could only imagine what he was up to. When the sound dissipated, Jackson chanced a peek. The guard was moving north.

Jackson held up a hand with all five fingers extended. He lowered them one at a time, then nodded at Bill. They again walked quickly to the only door on the east side of the courtyard. As quietly as possible, Jackson rapped on the door with his knuckles. He waited through an interminable silence, refusing to let his eyes drift to where the guard would soon be returning. He knocked again, slightly louder this time.

He heard a chain sliding, then a deadbolt, then the door drew back.

A blond woman stood behind the half-open door. She wore a men's button-down shirt and no pants. She blinked twice, clearly having just woken up. Her eyes darted between Jackson and Bill.

"Who are you?" she asked.

*   *   *

Tuesday, January 1
9:19 a.m.

THE SOLID food wasn't a great improvement over the cream of wheat. It certainly wasn't as warm. But Jackson was thankful for anything of substance and plowed into it with relish. Reggie, Leroy, and Sam all huddled in the hospital room, dissecting every last word in the paper and watching an early bowl game on TV.

Gradually, talk turned back to who might have shot Jackson. "You really have no idea?" Reggie asked.

Jackson shook his head.

"What were you doing at the cemetery?"

Jackson stared a hole in the wall. "I can't remember."

"Doc said the trauma could erase the memory of what happened."

"I remember what happened. Just not why."

"You working any cases?" Leroy asked.

"No license, remember?"

Leroy huffed.

"I'm not being coy," Jackson said. "I don't kno—"

Sam's phone interrupted him. She checked it quickly, then excused herself out into the hallway.

"Aren't cell phones illegal in hospitals?" Jackson asked.

"That's at gas pumps, and don't change the subject," Reggie replied.

"Reg, believe me, I wish I knew. I mean, I've got suspects, people from past cases, but no reason to suspect one of them over the other."

"Couldn't you get a look at the guy?" Leroy asked.

"Not much of one."

"And you're a private investigator?"

Jackson held out his hands.

"What about Maggie?" Reggie asked.

"What about her?"

"A month ago you went down to Mexico to rescue her from a bunch of gangsters."

"They weren't gangsters," Jackson said, "and I honestly don't think this was about Maggie or Mexico."

"What about Mexico?" Sam asked as she returned to the room.

"Nothing," Jackson answered quickly. Too quickly.

Sam's eyes went from him to Reggie to Leroy with his head in the newspaper and back to Jackson. "What aren't you telling me?" she asked.

He sighed. "You remember Thanksgiving, when I couldn't come?"

"That seems to ring a bell."

"A friend of mine got into some trouble in Mexico, and I helped out a little."

Reggie huffed.

"I helped out a lot."

"What kind of trouble and what kind of help?"

"It's a long story, and it has nothing to do with my getting shot." He nodded at the phone in her hand. "Who was that?"

"Tianna. She's agreed to cover my shift. She said she had nothing better to do than watch football with her boyfriend."

Jackson perked up. "Does this mean you can do it?"

She nodded.

"Maybe you should use the word 'will' instead of 'can,'" Leroy said from behind his newspaper.

Jackson turned to Sam. Her blue eyes were wide as a smile threatened to break out.

"Sam, will you sacrifice your New Year's Day to come watch the Rose Bowl with me and my cheese-filled barbecue smokies and make sure I don't start hemorrhaging puss or bleeding internally?"

The smile crept out. "Yes."

"You are the best."

"Assuming Dr. McCarthy okays your release, which is doubtful, I have to tell you."

"I'll be persuasive."

"I don't think he's susceptible to your 'boyish charm.'"

"You think he'd take a bribe?"

"I'm going to call my supervisor and let her know of the change. When I get back," she said, placing her hand on Jackson's wrist, "I want to know what happened in Mexico."

"Since when did you get nosy?"

"Since you got shot."

"Is it really necessary?"

"Unless you want to watch the Rose Bowl on that TV with hospital chicken tenders it is."

Jackson sighed.

Sam patted his hand. "I'll be back in a few minutes."

"Could you bring back a contraband candy bar or something?"

"You just ate."

"Technically."

"I'll see what I can find."

"This should be good," Reggie said when she was gone.

"Tell me about it."

From behind his newspaper, Leroy just chuckled.

Chapter Twenty-Nine

Saturday, November 24
4:07 a.m.

A DOZEN THOUGHTS flashed through Jackson's brain. Who was the girl? She wasn't Mexican. Had he seen any blondes at the party? Why was she in Maggie's room? Had Bill misunderstood where Maggie was? Had Maggie deceived them for some reason? Was something else going on they didn't know about? Had Vasquez double-crossed them and harmed Maggie already? How long until the guard came back? Had he heard the door open or heard the girl? She was just a girl, no more than twenty or twenty-one. What was she doing here?

Jackson forced all but the immediately pertinent from his head. "Are you alone?" he asked.

"What? Who are you?"

"We work for Leonardo. There's been an incident. May we come in?"

"Um." She switched her weight to the other foot. Hesitation still on her face, she drew the door back a few more inches, and Jackson used the opening to step into the room. The girl moved back, revealing a bed behind her, in which slept—slumbered, more like—a heavyset Latino man.

Bill quietly closed the door behind him and stood beside Jackson. The room was huge, like a very nice hotel suite, with a king bed in its own "chamber," a seating area, office space, and a full kitchenette. The only light came from a small lamp by the bed, which did nothing to diminish the *siesta* of the man in the bed. It did cast a small pall on a green military jacket draped over a nearby armchair.

"You want to tell me what's going on?" the girl asked in perfect English. She stood with arms folded across her chest, the dress shirt big enough and long enough that it functioned more like a dress.

"Have you been in this room all night?" Jackson asked, whispering.

"Since about one a.m. Why?"

"Anyone else with you, besides him?"

"No. What is going on?" she asked, raising her voice so that her whisper was a squeak. "Why did Leonardo send you?"

"He thinks a guest may have escaped."

"What do you mean escaped?"

"With several valuables from the gallery."

"What does that have to do with me?"

"We're searching room by room, at his request," Jackson said. "We're very sorry for the intrusion."

Bill had kept an eye out the window beside the door, peeking through sheer drapes and drawn blinds. He lightly tapped Jackson's elbow. "Guard's in the courtyard," he whispered into his ear.

"I didn't steal anything," the girl said.

"What about him?" Jackson asked, nodding at the man in bed to continue the ruse.

"General Hugo? Are you kidding? He's one of Leonardo's closest friends. You accuse him—you even wake him—you'll face a firing squad at dawn."

"Wouldn't think of it," Jackson said. "In fact, we think the perp may be an American woman, about five-nine, chin-length brown hair."

The girl shrugged.

"We had reason to believe she was staying in this room."

"Not since one a.m. she isn't."

He frowned at the girl, sensing more than just hostility in her eyes. He softened his tone. "What are you doing here?"

"My father does business with Leonardo. I'm here to help close the deal," she said.

"Is your father here now?"

"Just down the hall. Wouldn't recommend interrupting him, by the way."

"Thanks for the tip." Jackson looked at Bill, who nodded subtly. "We'll be going now. We're sorry to intrude."

"I've been here several times, and I've never seen you before. How long have you worked for Leonardo."

"Eight years," Jackson said. "Mostly overseas stuff. He brought us in tonight for . . . special security."

"Whatever."

"Thank you, ma'am. We'll see ourselves out."

They quickly and quietly slipped from the room.

"Now what?" Bill whispered.

Jackson turned his eyes north. The guard had disappeared. "I don't . . ."

"What is it?"

Jackson pointed over the edge of the pool, to a small balcony extending from the north wing of the main house. Fluttering in the very gentle breeze, was a piece of red cloth.

"What?"

"Look familiar?"

Bill squinted. "No. Wait . . ."

Jackson nodded. It was the dress Maggie had worn that night, knotted around the railing of the balcony and hanging in such a way that it was likely hidden from anyone at ground level—say, a patrolling guard—by a cluster of small palm trees. At the very least it would be far less evident.

"I don't get it," Bill said.

"Come on," Jackson said, tugging on his elbow and leading him back to the safety of the lounge before the guard returned.

"You want to tell me what's going on?" Bill asked as they walked back through the lounge and into the sitting room.

"You much of a religious guy, Bill? Go to Sunday school as a kid?"

"Try to make it to church on Christmas Eve."

"Yeah, well, Rahab doesn't usually make an appearance on Christmas Eve."

"Who is Rahab?"

"She was a prostitute in the city of Jericho."

"The one where the walls fell down?"

"Yeah. She made a deal with Hebrew spies, and they agreed to spare her when they took the city. But only if she hung a red cord out the window."

"You think Maggie's telling us where she is?"

"I do," Jackson said, pausing at a door in the siting room that opened to a hallway. It connected to the second-floor portico that surrounded the main courtyard. It also provided access to the mother-in-law suite where Rafael was allegedly residing.

"How?"

"How what?" Jackson asked.

"How would she know that? Know to send you that signal?"

"She may not believe it, but Maggie's read the Bible."

"Okay, so where is that? Off Vasquez's office?"

"That hall they brought us in to get to his office had doors opening to the other side. I'm guessing it's a den or a study or something. His bedroom was at the end of the hall."

"You sure on that?"

"Nope."

"It's possible that's his bedroom, that she's . . ."

"Let's not go there."

"Okay. So what's the plan?"

"We have to time the guard again. Avoid the camera over the front door. Then probably a guard in the hallway."

"You think so?"

"Vasquez had Maggie moved, expecting we might try something. Yeah, there'll be a guard. Plus, it's where he sleeps. Eighty-twenty there's a guard."

"I didn't know I'd be staging this rescue mission with Harrah's. So what's your plan to neutralize him?"

Jackson smiled and tapped his right forearm. "Get the righty up in the bullpen."

*   *   *

4:19 a.m.

JACKSON AND Bill again crouched in the shadow of a support column. They had timed the guard and belly-crawled along the west portico around the courtyard, hoping to avoid detection from the camera over the front door. It looked down, but still peripherally could see some of the open portico. They huddled in place for one full guard rotation, then advanced to the column directly in front of the double doors opening to the carpeted hallway and Vasquez's office. When the guard headed toward the guesthouse again, Jackson stood and approached the double doors.

They were made of glass panes and covered on the inside by shear curtains. But there was enough light behind them for him to make out the movement of a single guard. He stepped back into the shadows beside Bill, waiting for the guard again.

"With a guard, I'm hoping they're not locked," he whispered. "I'll crouch down and open the right door. You're going to have one shot, so make sure you drill him in the head. Don't paint the corner. Right down Main Street."

Bill nodded.

"I'll jump up and finish him off if you don't kayo him. Wait out here in case he yells or makes a lot of noise. If so, hide. I'll need a rescue mission of my own."

Bill nodded again.

"I'll give you the all clear and we'll advance."

"Okay."

"You ready for this?"

"I could use a rosin bag about now."

"Just out of curiosity, you didn't miss out on Omaha because you got shelled in a Super Regional or something, did you?"

"Three hits over six innings. No hitting."

Jackson winked. "Ain't gonna be your problem tonight, Bill."

They waited for the guard again, and as soon as he disappeared around the corner of the building, Jackson crept to the door. Bill stood back, in the stretch position, ready to shake off a catcher before delivering the money pitch. Jackson held out one hand with which to signal a countdown to Bill, while with the other he grasped the door handle. It felt loose in his hand, unlocked. He waited until the guard, who was pacing slowly, had reached the door and turned back the other way.

Signaling with his hand, Jackson twisted the door handle and pushed the door open.

The guard heard the noise and spun.

Bill's fastball from a dozen feet away cracked against the guard's skull, and he dropped like the proverbial sack of potatoes. The machine gun over his shoulder made a muffled thump on the carpet, as did the billiard ball, which then rolled against the baseboard with a soft thunk.

Jackson rushed into the hall, ready to deliver a knockout punch that wasn't needed. He quickly motioned for Bill to join him, and twenty seconds after they had opened the door, it was closed behind them again. All was quiet, aside from the thudding of Jackson's heart in his chest. He had pocketed a dishtowel from the guest lounge, which he handed to Bill, motioning for him to gag the guard with it. He removed the gun—some model he'd never seen before—from the guard, frisking him for any other weapons and finding a utility knife attached to a sheath on his belt. He also removed the belt, which he used to bind the guard's hands behind his back. Then he and Bill stood, breathing deeply, listening for nearly a minute. If their intrusion had been detected, there was no indicator.

"What if there's a guard in the room?" Bill asked as Jackson approached the double doors.

"Don't throw the changeup."

Instead of trying the door, Jackson very softly tapped on the glass pane in the left of two doors that were identical to those that had led to the hallway. A moment later, the shear pulled back for just a moment, then the door opened.

"Jack!" Maggie hissed. She pulled him into the room—a study or a den, by the look of things—and enveloped him in a quick, tight embrace. She let go and reached for Bill, tugging him into the room as well, and giving him a similar hug while Jackson closed the door.

"What took you guys so long?" Maggie asked, hands on her hips. She had changed into jeans and a black tank top. Aside from dim moonlight shining through translucent shear drapes, the only other light was from a small lamp in the corner. It was still enough for him to see bloodshot eyes. Maggie hadn't slept.

"We had to march around the hacienda seven times," Jackson said.

Bill frowned but Maggie grinned. "I was hoping you'd pick up on that."

"Slow kid in the room, but that's okay," Bill said. "What's the plan?"

"You ready to go, now?" Jackson asked.

Maggie nodded. "Vasquez had his people stash me in here just after we danced. They must have suspected you."

"They did."

"He let me pack a change of clothes, at least, but this is all I have."

"Where's the rest of your stuff?"

"My old room?"

Jackson shook his head. "*Ocupado.*"

Maggie shrugged. "I don't need it. It's all replaceable."

"You have shoes?" Jackson asked, looking down at her socked feet.

She nodded.

"Put them on."

"Where are we going?"

"That depends. What's at the end of the hallway?"

"Leonardo's quarters. Bedroom, private office, master bath, a private kitchen."

"Have you seen it all?"

"Not the bedroom or bathroom, but I've been to his private office. It's where they questioned me. Where they . . ."

Jackson put a hand on her shoulder. "We saw satellite photos that showed a walkway between the servants' quarters and the main building. Do you know what it connects to?"

"There's a servants' lounge off a hallway that connects to the kitchen."

"What's above the servants' lounge?"

"Um, Leonardo's office."

"Window?"

"Better. A balcony."

"Okay. That's our exit."

"Exit. To where?"

"It's best if I don't tell you."

"Why?"

"You'll lose your nerve."

She bit her lip and looked at Bill.

"We made it this far," he said with a shrug.

Maggie sighed. "Okay, let's go."

*   *   *

4:34 a.m.

"YOU'RE RIGHT," Maggie said. "I've lost my nerve."

They stood in Leonardo Vasquez's private office. The door had been locked, and after thinking for several minutes, Jackson had returned to the den where Maggie had been staying. He'd crushed the lamp's lightbulb between two sofa cushions, removed the filaments, and, after checking on the guard—finding him still unconscious in the hallway—returned to Bill and Maggie. He'd then wowed them by picking the lock with the filaments, gaining them admittance to Vasquez's private office. Now they stood looking out the balcony doors. Approximately four feet over from the balcony was the eight-foot-high, arched wall that ran beside the walkway connecting the main building to the single-story servants' quarters. Another such wall and walkway connected it to the garage, a hundred feet away as the crow flies.

"That's a long jump," Bill said.

"I figure we can stand on top of the balcony railing," Jackson said. "That makes it a longer way down, but we should have no problem getting there."

"Sticking the landing might be another problem."

"Yeah."

"This is really your best plan?" Maggie asked.

"We've got one gun," Jackson said. "Even with the element of surprise, we'd be sitting ducks. If we can get to the garage undetected, we've got a chance."

218

"What about the guards? They make a routine patrol. Won't they see us? Even in the dark, there's enough ambient light to spot three people walking across a ledge."

"We'll have to time it right. Once we get to the roof, we can shimmy around to the opposite side and stay hidden. I think."

"Great."

"I know it's less than ideal, but we're an hour from daybreak."

"Only plan's the best plan," Bill said. "Who's first?"

"My plan, so I'll go first." He winked at Maggie. "You ready, Mary Lou?"

Chapter Thirty

4:56 a.m.

LOOKING LIKE AN old Roman aqueduct with its graceful arches, the wall was about nine inches thick. That was plenty wide if not for the multiple cracks and fissures and the vines that grew primarily on the west side, but in some cases climbed to the top and draped over the wall. To make matters worse, it had started to rain, very lightly, but enough to make the "balance beam" wet. If Jackson, Bill, and Maggie could even get there. The chasm was looming large as Jackson climbed onto the balcony railing.

They had watched the perimeter guards for a painstaking quarter of an hour. There were two sets, each with a Doberman, making an orderly circuit around the property. Approximately twelve minutes separated the patrols, but the trio would be visible by guards on both the east and west perimeters. That narrowed their window to only a few minutes after one set of guards disappeared beyond the corner of the house before the next set appeared from around the other side of the house.

Observing their pattern, Jackson had formulated a few additions to the plan. Their goal was to use the first window of time to jump to the ledge. If they stood tight against the building, a trio of palm trees would block them from the view of guards circling from the northwest corner, and the protuberance of Leonardo Vasquez's master bedroom would likely shield them from the guards rounding the northeast corner. Then, once both sets of guards' line of sight was blocked by the house, the trio could dash to the roof of the servants' quarters. It would be close, but they should make it.

As soon as the first patrol was out of sight behind the house, Jackson jumped. He was not a gymnast, and instead of sticking a perfect landing, he flopped his entire body onto the top of the wall. It was far from graceful. He cracked his jaw, bit his lip, scraped his shoulder, banged his knee, and suffered reduced manhood, all while nearly flying too far and tipping over the far side of the wall. But he managed to right himself, ignore the pain, and get to his feet.

Maggie was next, and stood for a moment on the wobbling balcony railing.

"Come on, Mags," Jackson hissed.

She bent her knees and jumped, aiming to land on top of the wall. She judged it perfectly, and used the wall at her side to steady her as she landed, along with a hand from Jackson.

He grinned. "A regular Gabby Douglas."

"Only twice the size."

"No comment."

"Smart."

They shimmied along the wall to leave Bill room, and he performed his jump like the former college athlete he was. With all three of them safely on the ledge, they pressed themselves against the wall and waited. The rain began to fall harder, which would perhaps mask line of sight but would also make their balancing act that much more challenging.

When the next guards disappeared around the side of the main house, Jackson started out. Arms extended like a tightrope walker, he kept his eyes on his wingtips. They gave him no traction, but he crossed the twenty-five-foot span without incident. The roof of the servants' quarters was approximately two feet above him, with no gutter. But the wet clay shingles had Jackson nervous as he remembered the raptor scene from *The Lost World: Jurassic Park*.

He clambered up on his side, and took his first look back. Maggie was right behind him, and he pulled her up. As Bill was reaching up, Jackson saw movement out the corner of his eye. It was the next guard rotation, already appearing around the east side of the house.

Bill flitted his eyes in the same direction, and immediately turned back to Jackson. "Get down," Bill hissed, withdrawing his hand. He then dropped to his knees and slid off the wall, hanging on the west side by just his fingers. Jackson flattened himself on the slope of the roof and waited.

The servants' quarters was built like three stacked squares, each overlapping one-fourth of the previous one. As a result, the roof had numerous peaks and valleys, and hiding as they were on the west side of a north-south ridge, Jackson and Maggie were hidden from the guards to the east, and would remain hidden by an east-west roofline as they came around to the north side. And the main house blocked any potential view from the south. It was only when the patrol came around to the northwest and west that they would be in danger.

Bill, similarly, would be exposed at the same time, if he could hang on that long. If he couldn't, he would fall and set off the ground sensors. In the movies, characters could grip almost anything with a few fingers and hang on interminably. This was not the movies, and as soon as the guards and their Doberman were out of sight behind the servants' quarters, Jackson scrambled to the edge of the roof.

His face strained, Bill hung onto the ledge, his arms shaking. Jackson quickly dropped to the ledge and helped Bill up. He panted deeply, shaking out his arms.

"We're sitting ducks," Jackson said. "Can you get up on the roof?"

"Yeah."

Their window was short. The original plan had been to use the time period while the guards were circling the northeast corner of the property to cross the roof, then drop down to the wall connecting the servants' quarters to the garage while the guards were behind the garage. Another cluster of palms would shelter them until those guards were out of sight, then giving the trio enough time— maybe—to dash across the wall and to the garage. But now they were behind schedule, and the rain was coming down harder than ever.

"New plan," Jackson whispered. "We get to the ledge while they're behind the garage."

"Then?" Maggie asked.

"One step at a time."

Nearly a dozen palm trees were clustered behind the garage, giving them a little more time once the guards were out of sight. They hurried as much as they could across the roof of the servant's quarters, hoping the sound didn't alert anyone below. The clay shingles were more slippery than a standard asphalt-shingled roof, but not to the point of being treacherous. They dropped down onto the ledge without incident, although Maggie nearly lost her balance and toppled over the side. Jackson righted her as Bill dropped down, and the trio huddled again.

An instant later, the guards appeared on the west side of the property.

"At least they don't have bloodhounds," Bill said.

"Now what?" Maggie asked.

"By the time they're out of sight, the other group will be coming around the house. We wait until they're behind the building, then make a dash to the garage."

"Can we make it in time?" Bill asked.

"We'll see."

"You know, your smart-aleck aloofness is wearing thin," Maggie said.

"Better question is how we get into the garage."

"Door's probably locked," Bill said, eyeing the door at the end of walkway.

"I'll get it open," Jackson said.

Maggie raised her eyebrows.

"Be ready. We're only halfway home once we get there."

Keeping an eye on the guards, Jackson nudged both Bill and Maggie to make sure they were ready. When the time was right, they took off, walking as fast as they safely could atop the ledge. It was twice as long as the previous one, and Jackson knew they were running out of time. So when he reached the garage, he crouched down, then launched himself down and at the door. He hit with his shoulder and drove all his weight into the door, just above the doorknob. It crashed open and Jackson somersaulted into a Porsche.

He was on his feet instantly, despite the throbbing in his shoulder. He motioned for Maggie to jump, standing by the side to pull her in if her momentum didn't carry her. Bill was next, and made it easily. That quickly, Jackson closed the door behind him.

"That was your idea?" Bill said. "Wreck your shoulder on the door?"

"I pictured myself as The Rock in *The Rundown*."

"You think they heard the door break?" Maggie asked.

"Get to the window, see if you can tell. Bill, barricade this door with something."

It was pitch black in the garage, and they tripped and stumbled about their tasks. Maggie monitored one of two windows in the back of the garage, and Bill found a workbench he and Jackson were able to drag in front of the door when Maggie gave them the all clear. Then, while she and Bill kept a lookout, Jackson, his eyes adjusting to the darkness, took stock of the situation.

Along with the Porsche, there were three other vehicles—a Land Rover, an Audi luxury sedan, and a motorcycle—lined up in that order from east to west. Each had its own garage door, facing south. It took Jackson two minutes to find the wiring that connected all the doors to a panel on the east wall, and he ripped it loose.

"Um, why'd you do that?" Bill asked.

"I want control of who opens them. I need you to find a gas can, preferably with gas in it, and something we can use as a fuse—a rag, paper towels, anything—and a lighter."

"You're the boss."

"Maggie, what's it look like?"

"No change. I don't think they know we're here."

"Good, see if you can find keys."

"Can't you hotwire them?"

"A skill that's eluded me. Bill?"

"Nope."

"Keys," Jackson reiterated.

"For which car?" Maggie asked.

"Um, all but the cycle."

While they worked, Jackson scoured the garage for a few more items, which he brought over to the Land Rover.

"What am I doing with the gas?" Bill asked, holding a two-gallon tank in his hand.

"Put the tank in the back of the Land Rover. Stuff the fuse into the gas and leave it hanging out a few inches. Don't light it yet."

"Keys," Maggie said, holding several sets in her hand.

"Okay. Put the keys in the ignition of all three vehicles, but don't start them. Then keep an eye out for company."

Jackson opened the driver's door of the Land Rover and set two cinderblocks on the floor beside the gas pedal. Then he weaved together two lengths of baling twine to make it twice as strong. He was in the process of tying the steering wheel to the door pull handles when Maggie's voice sounded an alarm.

"Guys," she said from her position at a standard door at the far end of the garage, beyond the four overhead doors. "I think I was wrong. We've got two guards from the front gate and two more from the house all coming this way."

"Bill, help her block the door and stay down."

Bill hurried across the garage, while Jackson finished his task.

"They're surrounding us," Maggie said.

"The door blocked?"

"Locked and bolted," Bill answered.

"Okay, get back h—"

A volley of gunfire interrupted Jackson, and they all dropped to the ground. The gunfire ceased, and Jackson got back up. "No penetration. Just warning shots over the roof."

"How comforting," Maggie said.

"Bill, you said you never fired a gun, ever?"

"BB gun at camp. When I was ten."

"Okay. You and Maggie get in the Porsche. Start it on my signal, but don't go anywhere."

"Not a problem with the doors disabled."

"I'll take care of that."

Maggie grabbed his arm. "Tell me you have an actual plan other than you being bait to let us get away."

"I have a plan," Jackson said. He quickly explained it, then dropped to the ground as bullets spat into the doors and walls of the garage.

"Anybody hit?" Jackson asked when the quick barrage ended.

"No," Bill and Maggie echoed.

"Okay, let's do this."

He turned the ignition in the Land Rover and it jumped to life. He walked around to the back and used a butane lighter to ignite Bill's fuse in the gas can. Sure that it had caught and would stay lit, he returned and reached through the open window of the Land Rover to nudge the gearshift into drive. The next part was tricky.

First, he signaled for Bill to start the much quieter Porsche. Then he pulled a string of baling twine attached to one cinderblock on the floor of the Land Rover, yanking it off the brake pedal. That caused a second cinderblock, balanced ever so precariously against the corner of the first, to fall directly onto the gas pedal. With a squeal of tires, the Land Rover shot forward. A small web of baling twine attached to the steering wheel and the door pull handles took away any play in the steering wheel, keeping the vehicle on a straight path as it barreled through the garage door.

Immediately, a volley of bullets tore into the Land Rover, which continued with pedal to the metal across the driveway and toward the open lawn. Jackson didn't watch it, instead getting behind the wheel of the Audi and starting its engine. With his left foot on the brake pedal, he shifted into drive, waiting.

Suddenly a bright orange glow infiltrated the garage, followed by a muffled whoomp-WHOOMP! That was Jackson's cue. He stomped on the gas pedal at the same time as he let up on the brake pedal. The Audi lurched forward, plowing through the garage door. For a moment, it hung over the windshield, blinding Jackson. He swerved slightly and the door flew off.

Fifty yards ahead, the Land Rover had come to a stop, engulfed in a ball of flames. Jackson saw several guards on the ground or running away from the fire. A quick flit of his eyes to his rearview mirror showed Bill and Maggie in the

Porsche, Bill having navigated the small car through the Land Rover's blown-open garage door, and now on his tail.

Jackson pressed the accelerator, at the same time jerking the steering wheel hard right. He took dead aim at the front gate, driving with his right hand while the left extended the barrel of the machine gun he'd taken off the guard outside Vasquez's den. He squeezed off a few quick shots out his window, then ducked down as he crashed into the gate.

He felt the brunt of the wrought-iron gate, but the Audi easily plowed through. Jackson accelerated again, watching in his mirror to see the Porsche right behind him. He didn't hear any gunfire, but he was sure it was coming, and didn't stop until they had rounded a couple curves and begun to climb the hill out of the valley. Then he braked, allowing the Porsche to pass him. When it did, he turned the Audi to block both lanes of the road and killed the engine. He quickly got out, heaved the keys into the desert, and cast one last glance down toward the valley, where the flames of the burning Land Rover lit the pre-dawn sky.

Maggie opened the passenger door of the Porsche for him, pulling her seat forward, allowing him to dive into the backseat.

"Go!" he said to Bill, and they shot forward.

Chapter Thirty-One

5:29 a.m.

THE ADRENALINE WAS draining from Jackson's body, and he didn't like it. Maybe it was a product of watching too many action movies, where whenever the good guys had seemingly won, somebody always popped up from the ashes or turned traitor or somehow extended the plot.

They'd gone at least five miles, and Jackson had spotted no signs of pursuit. And none was likely coming, what with a boat on wheels blocking the road. But with Leonardo Vasquez's apparent connections, not to mention all the military personnel who had been at the party, Jackson wasn't ruling out an Apache or Black Hawk or whatever the Mexican Air Force flew sweeping down on them at any minute.

"Where to now?" Bill asked. "I have a feeling we can't just show up at the airport and drink espresso until our flight leaves."

"No, Leonardo will have the military at his disposal," Maggie said. She had spun around in her seat, leaning against the dash as she extended her leg back to Jackson. Using tools he'd pocketed from the garage, he was doing his best to disable the ankle bracelet that would, potentially, enable Vasquez to track them.

"How powerful is this guy?" Jackson asked.

"Very."

"Then we lay low, figure out a plan. Surely there's a dive motel or two in Acapulco."

"I hate to say it, but we—ow—look kind of conspicuous," Maggie said. "You two in penguin suits, driving a—ow—Jack, what are you doing?"

"Sorry," he said, reaching for a hammer.

Maggie's eyes looked dubiously at him. She turned to Bill. "You guys have some other clothes?"

"With Isabella," Bill said.

"Who is Isabella?"

"You don't want to know," Jackson said, checking over his shoulder. They had turned back onto the four-lane highway, which was empty at this hour. He focused on using his screwdriver as a chisel, and on hammering the device, not Maggie's tibia.

"She has our luggage," Bill said.

"Where is she?"

"Holiday Inn on the beach."

"Fat chance," Jackson said. "You stood her up, Big John. She has the Peugeot and this is a party city. I doubt she's waiting for you to come back."

"I really don't want to know, do I?" Maggie asked.

"No. Bill, how much cash you got on you?"

"Couple hundred. Why?"

"We need to ditch this car, find a taxi, and then find a hotel. There!" he said as the clasp on the bracelet gave way and he pried it off. "The skin will grow back," he said. He lowered his window and heaved the bracelet out into the desert. "Maggie, is there anybody in this spittoon of a country you trust who might be able to help?"

"Ali," she said, examining her ankle. She lowered her pant leg and swung back around.

"You think his considerably long arm can get us out of here?"

"If not, he'll know who can."

"Okay. We'll give him a call once we settle in."

"I can't thank you guys enough. Jack, after everything . . . And Bill, I didn't think you'd come down here too."

"No way I wouldn't," Bill said. "Jack, I won't say I never doubted you, but you're the real deal."

"I think we might want to adjourn this meeting of the Mutual Admiration Society until we're back in L.A.," he said with another glance over his shoulder.

"Was he this grumpy the whole time?" Maggie said while eyeing Jackson.

"Pretty much," Bill said, winking in the mirror.

Jackson hugged his machine gun, relieved he hadn't had to actually shoot anyone with it.

*   *   *

8:47 a.m.

THE PHONE rang. It was an old, rotary phone, in the crudest dive of a motel in the world. The walls were made of cardboard, and if the bedspreads had been washed or carpets cleaned, it hadn't been this century. But it was a place to hole up for a while. Bill had gone out and found breakfast, in the form of questionable coffee and even more questionable chorizo and egg burritos from a hole-in-the-wall convenience store. They'd eaten and let their nerves relax, and Maggie had left a message for Ali. That had been forty minutes ago.

"Hello? . . . Ali, it's me. . . . I'm safe, in Acapulco. . . . Safe too." She quickly explained their predicament and asked Ali if he had any knowledge of Vasquez's attempts to chase them down. Bill had tuned into a local news station, but so far nothing had come across the wire.

"That's bad," Maggie said. "Very bad. . . . As soon as possible. . . . He can do that? . . . You're sure, Ali?" She raised her eyebrows and nodded at Jackson and Bill. "Okay. One hour."

She set the phone down. "Ali said Vasquez has mobilized the military."

"Can he do that?"

"His pals can. We're hot."

"So what's the plan? What's in an hour?"

"Ali said he thought he could help, but he had to make some calls. I'm supposed to call him back in an hour."

"Discreet calls, I hope," Jackson said.

"Of course."

"So we wait."

"Will you stop being so glum? Ali will come through for us."

"Bill, how old are you?"

"Thirty-two. Why?"

"You're a movie guy, right? Probably seen all the classics?"

"Yeah."

Maggie narrowed her eyes.

"We've got some time. Tell her about *The Great Escape* and how none of them actually escaped. It's something of a misnomer."

"I've seen *The Great Escape*," Maggie said. "And some of them did make it."

"Not McQueen, not Rockford, Ducky, that white-haired guy from *Jurassic Park*." He shook his head. "Until Mexico's in the rearview mirror, I'm going to hold off on celebrating."

*   *   *

11:30 a.m.

JACKSON, BILL, and Maggie stood at a bus stop on a grimy corner of Acapulco's most rundown "commercial" neighborhood. Mid-morning sun had burned off the remnants of the weak disturbance that had moved through overnight, leaving heat and humidity in its wake. Bill had draped his tuxedo jacket over his shoulder. Jackson just wore his. With Maggie between them in jeans and a tank top, they looked terribly out of place. Or like they were shooting an album cover as a band where Maggie was both the drummer and lead singer. Either way, in this part of the world, it wasn't likely to get them noticed.

When Maggie had called Ali back, he'd told her that a friend owed a friend a favor, and he had arranged for a Mexican businessman named Salvador Delgado to fly them to Los Angeles. Delgado, according to Ali, was headed there anyway. He was also, according to Ali, someone who wasn't overly fond of the Mexican authorities and thus not reluctant to flout their authority. He also had the chops to do so.

Ali had given them the time and place where Delgado would pick them up, and the trio had arrived ten minutes early. Short of a beat cop spotting them and recognizing their description, which Ali said was circulating, they would be home free. Almost.

At 11:32, a black SUV turned the corner and approached the bus stop. It slowed and the tinted passenger window lowered. "Maggie?" the driver asked with a heavy accent.

"*Sí.*"

He nodded at the backseat. *"Entre adentro, por favor."*

Jackson opened the door and Maggie and Bill entered before him. There were two captain's chairs and a bench behind them. The far captain's chair was occupied by a man in a loose cotton shirt, white chinos, and loafers without socks. His hair was jet black, wavy. A thin, short goatee traced his mouth and chin. He could have been a younger Dean Cain.

"My name is Salvador Delgado," he said with a rich accent. "You must be Ali's friend Maggie."

She shook his hand as she sat on the bench. Bill joined her, and Jackson took the other captain's chair, across from Delgado. As soon as he was seated, the SUV began moving.

"Thank you so much for your help," she said.

"No es nada," he said with a wave. "Ali says you wish to go to Los Angeles?"

"Yes."

"I am flying to San Francisco on business, but I have directed my pilot César to file an amended flight plan to L.A. You will be home in time for dinner."

"Thank you." She introduced Bill and Jackson, first names only, and they shook Delgado's hand as well.

"The three of you look as if you've had a rough night."

"That would be an understatement," Bill said.

"It is none of my business, of course. When we arrive at the airport, we will proceed straightaway onto the tarmac to my jet. It is well equipped with a snack bar, an actual bar," he said with a smile, "and a spacious lavatory. You can refresh yourselves there."

"Thank you," Maggie said again.

"Do you all have your passports?"

Jackson nodded. He and Bill had fortunately kept their wallets and important documents on their person instead of in their bags which were now with Isabella or who knew where, and Maggie had had the foresight to grab hers before Vasquez had moved her to his den.

"Good. Then I foresee no problems with U.S. Customs upon our arrival. Try to relax. This will all be over soon."

Jackson watched the scenery, if it could be called that, out the window. Bill and Maggie seemed content to sit in a comfortable, clean environment and decompress, and Delgado accommodated, making only a few comments and asking a couple of questions. When they arrived at General Juan N. Álvarez International Airport, the SUV drove through a security checkpoint and right up to the base of a short flight of stairs belonging to a Learjet, its twin engines already whining. Delgado led the way, and his driver, Reynaldo, who was much bigger than he looked behind the wheel, brought up the rear. Five minutes later, they were taxiing to the runway.

"This is incredible," Maggie marveled, looking around the cabin. Plush leather, polished oak, salmon walls, and sand-colored carpet—all gave the jet a warmth and coziness with a decided Mexican flare. The soft music in the background didn't hurt the effect.

"I have worked very hard and also been very fortunate," Delgado said as he joined Jackson, Bill, and Maggie. "A very dynamic combination." They were seated in captain's chairs facing forward. Delgado's swiveled to face them. Reynaldo was seated near the back with his computer. The only other two persons on board were César the pilot, and Jerome the co-pilot. They had met them briefly before takeoff, and found César to be all business, and Jerome—a self-professed African-Hispanic—to be jovial and inviting. And to Jackson, anyone who wasn't fully Hispanic was a relief at present. He wanted nothing but to be out of Mexico, and when the plane lifted off and soared out of the reach of RPGs, he sighed with relief.

"Well, we have almost four hours in the air," Delgado stated. "Help yourself to drinks or snacks in the minibar, there are DVD players fore and aft, and as I mentioned, you're welcome to refresh in the lavatory. Sadly, I cannot offer you a change of clothes."

"You've done more than enough," Maggie said as he headed for the cockpit.

"If you'll excuse me, I have a few calls I must make. A businessman is always busy."

Maggie thanked him again, then, when Jackson and Bill gave the okay, went to use the lavatory first.

"I don't know about you, but I'm beat," Bill said. "Wake me when we cross the Rio Grande."

Jackson didn't bother to correct him on their flight path. He watched the blue of the ocean out his window to the left. Gradually, it was replaced by more and more land, as their path took them just east of the coastline. As they flew farther and farther north, clouds and haze began to obscure the view. By the time Maggie returned with her hair in a stub of a ponytail, the view had lost its appeal.

They had a lot to talk about, from details of her time in Mexico to the status of their relationship, but it could all wait. Jackson took his turn in the lavatory. He splashed water on his face before taking the moment of solace to say a brief prayer, thanking God for a safe exit from Mexico. Even as he did so, he couldn't quite shake the feeling that they weren't home free just yet—not until his feet touched down on American soil. This was too much of a whirlwind—the mysterious hookah-smoking Ali, his unlimited and far-reaching sources, a wealthy businessman with a Learjet willing to fly them home. So he prayed for continued safety.

Then he got out of the bathroom. Airplanes had never been his favorite place in the world, much less airplane lavatories, even one as posh as Salvador Delgado's.

Jackson passed Reynaldo, now buried in a paperback, and made his way to Maggie. She sat on the right side of the plane, beside Bill, who was already out cold. Jackson sat across the aisle from her and looked out the window. There was nothing but clouds to the right, but skies had cleared to the left, revealing jutting, barren landscape.

"You okay?" he asked.

"Yeah."

"Did, um, did Vasquez hurt you?"

"No," she said with a thin smile. "His thugs weren't exactly gentlemen, but I'm fine."

He nodded.

"Thanks again for coming, Jack. When I told Bill to call you . . . I never imagined it would actually happen."

"You must have known there was some danger in going undercover."

"I did, but I always figured I'd be able to skate my way out of it, you know?"

He looked down for a minute. "Look, I know we've got a lot to talk about, and it can wait till later, but there is one thing I've been wondering."

"What's that?"

"Why me?"

"Huh?"

"You said it last night, after the way things 'ended,' why was I the guy you told Bill to call if things went south?"

"Because you have an uncanny ability to turn into a superhero when need be. Like in Nevada, or when that lady cop was kidnapped by the Silvaz gang."

He nodded. He'd heard it from Bill, but wanted to hear it from her as well.

"And because there's nobody on this earth I trust more."

He snapped his head up.

"I mean that, Jack. I've got a lot of friends, but not many people I'm close to, that I know I can count on. I knew there was no way you'd let me down."

Jackson didn't know what to say, so he kept quiet.

"And true to form, you saved the day. Again."

"Day's not over," he said.

"You can can the modesty, Jack. A little chest-puffing is deserved right now."

He grinned and glanced back out the window.

"What is it?" Maggie asked.

"Huh?"

"You're frowning."

Jackson peeked back at Reynaldo again. He was paying them no attention.

"Look out your window," he said to Maggie.

"What?"

"Just look."

Maggie sat up straight and leaned toward the window. After several seconds, she sat back. "I don't see anything. Just clouds and occasional desert."

"Come look this way."

Eyes skeptical, she got up and stood in front of Jackson, peering out his window. "More of the same," she said. "Only less clouds."

"Anything strike you as odd about that?"

"Should it?"

"Where's the water?"

Maggie frowned.

"Or the sun, for that matter. It's after noon, past the middle of the day. If we're headed northwest, sun should be streaming in through these windows. Instead, it's off to our right."

"What are you saying, Jack?"

"I don't think we're going to L.A."

Chapter Thirty-Two

Tuesday, January 1
10:09 a.m.

SAM SAT ON the edge of Jackson's bed. Leaned against the edge, perhaps, was more accurate. There was room, and besides, he hadn't been shot in the leg.

She looked adorable in that position, her hair hanging on her shoulders, framing a smiling, teasing face. In her delicate hands, she held a package of Rolos, which she offered to Jackson one at a time—provided he agree to her terms. Dr. McCarthy had yet to agree to his discharge, but Jackson was bound and determined to make it home by kickoff. Sam, meanwhile, was bound and determined to make sure Jackson didn't put miniature hot dogs and pregame festivities ahead of his health and wellbeing.

"How many of these are there anyhow?" Jackson asked.

"Agree or not?" Sam asked, holding up an individually wrapped, caramel-filled piece of chocolate. The two of them were alone. Reggie had taken Leroy home and was stopping at Cameron's to make sure everything was running smoothly. It was a good thing, because this chocolate-bribery-from-the-edge-of-the-bed bit would have made them both sick.

"Yes," Jackson sighed, "you're the boss. Whatever you say goes. But doesn't that make any further rules unnecessary?"

Sam handed him a piece of candy. "Jesus said that all the law and the prophets hang on the two commandments, '*Love the Lord your God with all your heart and with all your soul and with all your mind,*' and '*Love your neighbor as yourself.*'"

He unwrapped the piece of candy and plopped it into his mouth. "So?"

"So, that didn't stop Paul from listing a lot of other commandments throughout the New Testament."

Jackson sighed again. "Okay, what's next?"

"Number two," Sam said, pulling out another Rolo and preparing to give it to Jackson, "the Rose Bowl does not interfere with any medical attention you may need."

"You mean if my wound suddenly starts gushing blood?"

She narrowed her eyes.

"Fine. Can we try to wait till commercials though? Reggie didn't come through with that Tivo for Christmas."

"We'll try," she said, "but if the game's on the line and I deem it necessary to treat you on the spot, it happens on the spot."

"Agreed."

"And no tough guy stuff. If you're in pain, you tell me. If something doesn't feel right, you tell me, not wait until halftime."

"Is that term number three or a codicil to number two?"

"That's part of two."

"Then where's my candy?"

She handed him the Rolo.

"Three?"

"We're nurse and patient."

"Meaning?"

"Meaning you're not using me to weasel out of getting the proper medical care. I'm going to treat you the same way I would treat any other patient."

"I think you get the candy on this one."

"I just want to make sure you understand the roles."

"I understand," Jackson said.

Sam handed him his third piece of candy.

"Just for the record," he said, "what happens to your normal patients when they get fresh with you?"

"I let Doreen handle them."

Jackson made a face. "Doreen look like she sounds?"

"Um-hmm."

"Well, it's good thing the two of you aren't a package deal."

"Look, Jackson . . ."

"Yeah?"

"Never mind."

"You sure?"

"Yeah, it can wait."

"Okay. Any more rules?"

"No. But you were going to tell me what happened in Mexico."

"Was I?"

Before he could say anything, someone knocked on the door. Sam looked over her shoulder, then stood as a man and a woman entered the room. He was short, decked in a cheap, rumpled suit. It matched his haircut. She was a few inches taller, her slacks pressed, her burgundy blouse attractive yet professional. She flashed a badge. "Mr. Douglas? I'm Detective Loyola, this is Detective Cavanaugh. We'd like to ask you a few questions."

He nodded.

"Is this your wife?" Cavanaugh asked.

"No," Jackson said, cutting himself off before tacking on a "just a friend."

"Family?"

"I'll be in the lobby," Sam said, taking her cue.

"Go work on Dr. McCarthy," Jackson said.

She patted his hand and smiled. On second thought, she grabbed the remaining roll of candy, winking at Jackson before departing.

"How can I help?" Jackson asked.

Loyola flipped open a small notebook. Good to see they were still using notebooks. "What can you tell us about the person that shot you?"

"Unfortunately, not much. It was dark, he was wearing baggy clothes . . ."

"Yes?"

"I'm not even sure it was a he. I never got a good look at his—or her—face."

"Did the two of you speak at all before he shot you?"

"No. Well, I spoke, but he never said anything."

"What did you say?"

"'You don't have to do this,' 'We can talk about it,' stuff like that. I don't remember word for word."

"What was he wearing?"

"A big black hoodie."

"That it?"

"Pants. Jeans, maybe."

"Height, weight?"

"About my height, maybe a little shorter. Weight hard to tell because of the clothes."

Loyola made a few notes. "Did you see anything distinctive? A tattoo, a piece of jewelry, something unusual about the clothing."

"Afraid not."

"Nothing stands out? Nothing at all?"

"No, sorry. Did you try getting prints off my gun?"

"We did," Loyola said. "But seeing as how you and the shooter both handled it, and given the rain, we weren't able to get any useful prints other than yours."

"Great."

Cavanaugh took over the questioning. "Do you have any idea who might want to shoot you?"

"Drawing a blank there too."

"You're a private investigator, is that right?"

"My license has been suspended for the last three months."

"Because of Nevada?"

Jackson nodded.

"You don't think that maybe gives somebody a motive?" Cavanaugh asked.

"Only if this is an episode of *The Walking Dead*."

"Senator Moore isn't dead. Isaac Cutler survived. All the family members of people you killed are still alive."

"It's possible, but I've got no reason to suspect any of them."

"We understand you also had an interesting few days over Thanksgiving," Loyola said. "You want to tell us about that?"

*   *   *

Saturday, November 24
1:14 p.m.

MAGGIE FLITTED her eyes back toward Reynaldo, then directed them straight at Jackson. "There must be some mistake. We should tell Delgado."

"No," he said, grabbing her arm. "Sit back down."

"What?"

"Sit down," he said. He let go of her and glanced back at Reynaldo. If the big man had noticed any movement, he didn't care. His face was still in the paperback.

"I don't understand," Maggie said, speaking in hushed tones across the aisle. "Where would he be taking us?"

"You said Vasquez killed Rodrigo, Ali's cousin?"

"Yes, right in front of me."

"Did you actually see him die?"

"What?"

"Did you see him die?"

"I saw Vasquez fire the gun, from six feet away. I saw Rodrigo crumble into a heap."

"Did you see blood?"

"What?"

"Did you see blood?"

"I don't—I . . . It happened fast, Jack. Then they took him away and started threatening me. Why, what are you getting at?"

"I think Ali set you up."

"No."

"Think about it. Why is a business mogul with a Lear doing favors for a hookah-smoking alley rat like Ali? I should have known something was off."

Maggie shook her head. "So we're flying east? Maybe we're diverting around a storm or other air traffic."

"Know what's east of Acapulco, Maggie?"

"What?"

"Veracruz."

The frown on her face intensified. "Why would we be going to Veracruz?"

"When we met with Vasquez last night, he said he had business there. It's where the oil reserve was discovered, where Mexól is based."

Maggie ran her hand through her hair, pulling most of it out of the ponytail. "I can't believe this. There must be another explanation."

"Look at the facts, Maggie. We took off north, and the way I figure it, we're going pretty much due east. We never made any sharp banks like you usually do in a plane, which means they're trying to make sure we don't notice we're going east. And Delgado just hides up front with the pilots while leaving the Hulk here to guard us."

"I still can't believe it." She looked up at the cockpit. "Can't we talk with Delgado? If he really is devious, what's the harm in trying?"

"The harm is the element of surprise."

"Surprise? What, are you thinking of doing, hijacking the plane or something?"

"Maggie, would you mind keeping your oice-vay down around the uard-gay?"

"Well then what is the plan?" she whispered.

"We talk to Delgado all right, but from a position of power."

"And how do we get in such a position?"

Jackson glanced at Reynaldo again. "Lean over the aisle," he said.

"What?"

"Pretend we're having a romantic little talk and are about to kiss."

Maggie slowly leaned toward him, their faces just inches apart. "Jackson, if this is all some complicated ruse so you can put the moves on me . . ."

"Maggie, putting the moves on you wouldn't require a complicated ruse, just me saying 'Sure.'"

"If I slapped you upside the head right now, would that blow our cover?"

"No, but wasting time will. Here's the deal. The pilots are busy flying the plane, so that makes it three against two. If we can take out Reynaldo, we can surprise Delgado when he comes out of the cockpit."

"Assuming they don't have a camera in there."

He shrugged. "Risk we'll have to take."

"Okay, how do we take out Reynaldo?"

"First, wake up Sleeping Beauty. But don't make it obvious that you're waking him up."

"How do I do that?"

Jackson shrugged.

Maggie hesitated for a few seconds, then reached out a hand and took hold of Bill's. He stirred. She squeezed. He opened his eyes. Maggie said something to him that Jackson couldn't hear, and Bill sat up a little. She laid her head on his shoulder, and Jackson looked back out the window while they conversed in low tones.

Just not seeing the ocean wasn't the end of the world. Maggie was right, they could be taking something of an alternate flight path that veered inland. But the sun didn't lie. They were going east. Due east. And that didn't wash.

After several minutes, Maggie sat up and turned back to Jackson. Bill looked over her shoulder. "Are you serious?" he mouthed.

Jackson nodded.

"What's the plan?" Maggie asked.

"Go back to use the restroom," Jackson said. "Tell him the light's broken. He'll come investigate, and I'll sneak up behind him."

"And then what? He's huge."

"Give me a lever and a place to stand, and I'll bash him over the head."

"You got a lever?"

"His laptop."

"And what am I for?" Bill asked.

"Backup."

"Are you sure about this?" Maggie asked.

"Not really."

"Jackson?"

"Maggie, if we do nothing, we end up in Veracruz. We do something and it fails, we end up in Veracruz. We have no choice."

She bit her lip.

"He's right," Bill said.

Maggie closed her eyes in resignation. Bill squeezed her hand. Jackson said, "You can do this," then nodded at Bill. "You awake?"

"Butch and Sundance ride again."

"Oh brother," Maggie said, pushing up from the chair. A moment later, Jackson heard her talking to Reynaldo and turned over his shoulder. The big man put down his paperback and stood. Jackson nodded at Bill, and they both rose and crept to the back of the plane. Reynaldo's laptop was nowhere to be seen, and Bill shot Jackson a wide-eyed glance. Jackson clenched his fists in reply.

Reynaldo tried the lavatory switch, and when it came on, he turned to look at Maggie quizzically. At the same time, Jackson swung, throwing everything he had in a right hook aimed for Reynaldo's jaw. The blow caught him flush, and he stumbled backwards, lost his balance, and fell. His shoulder hit the counter, which spun him sideways, and he cracked his head against the toilet. He was out cold.

Maggie stared at Jackson incredulously.

Ignoring the pain shooting from his knuckles up his arm, Jackson shrugged. "Hmm. Sorry to have to wake you, Bill."

"I have always wanted to do that."

"Key is actually punching from your legs. That's where all the power lies."

"Will you two quit it?" Maggie asked. "What are we going to do with him?"

"Get him back in his chair," Jackson said.

Reynaldo weighed at least two-fifty, and Jackson and Bill had to grunt and strain to place him back in his chair, tipped toward the window, as if sleeping. They quickly wiped up the blood on the lavatory floor, then returned to their seats to plot.

"Well, Delgado must not have a camera in the cockpit, at least," Jackson said, flexing the fingers in his right hand.

"Hurts, doesn't it?" Bill asked.

"Like you wouldn't believe."

"How do we get just him out here?" Maggie said.

"Tamper with the lavatory smoke detector?"

"I could really use less of your smartness right now."

"Really, because my smartness seems to be saving our butts."

"Jackson," she practically growled.

He smiled. "Levity alleviates tension."

"How do we get Delgado?"

"We can wait until he comes out on his own, or we can knock and ask to talk to him. Either way, I'll wait behind the door. When he closes it behind him, I strike. Or Bill can, if you don't mind ruining your pitching arm."

"I can't believe this. How can you be making jokes about everything?"

He shrugged. "Adrenaline leads to the jazz."

"The jazz?"

"Yeah. Watch *The A-Team*."

She shook her head. "Wait or knock?"

"We're getting closer to Veracruz by the second. Knock."

"What, me?"

"You're the girl with well-tanned arms."

"You're seriously admiring my tan at a time like this?"

"Just knock."

"What do I say?"

"Tell him you have some questions and does he have a few minutes."

She stood. "And what happens when we kayo him and Reynaldo and we're still locked out of the cockpit?"

"One bridge before the next."

Instead of going forward, Maggie turned toward the minibar.

"Mags, what are you doing?" Bill asked.

Jackson's subconscious intruded into the moment to note that Bill also called her "Mags."

"Getting some liquid courage," she said, turning around with a small bottle of tequila. She twisted off the lid and downed half of it. She set the rest on the bar. "Okay."

She turned toward the cockpit. Bill, then Jackson, followed her to the door. Jackson stood so that he would be behind it when it opened, and Bill stood flat against the wall on the other side, out of sight. Bill nodded at Jackson, who nodded at Maggie, who rapped on the door.

242

"*Señor* Delgado, do you have a minute? I've got a couple questions for you."

The door clicked and opened, and Maggie stepped back as Delgado stepped through. "Of course, Maggie. What is—"

As soon as the door closed behind him, Bill struck, launching with a right fist that caught Delgado flush in the jaw. He tumbled backwards into the side of the cabin, and Jackson pounced. Bill's punch had sent the Mexican businessman reeling, but it hadn't exactly knocked him senseless. And Delgado had quickly recovered. He kicked, knocking Jackson off balance before he could land a punch of his own. Just that quickly, Delgado regained his balance and attacked.

The three men grappled, their struggle resembling a hockey fight—a lot of grabbing and swinging, but not a whole lot of connecting. Finally, Jackson got control, slamming Delgado back into the cabin wall with enough force to knock the wind out of him. As Bill held Delgado in place, Jackson coiled his fist, ready to strike the knockout blow.

A shout stopped him.

Reynaldo, uttering his first words. While holding Maggie's head in a vice grip, leaving no doubt he could snap her neck if he so chose.

Jackson stepped back, followed by Bill, their eyes drawn to the panic in Maggie's.

Out of nowhere, Delgado slugged Jackson, a spit-bubbling punch that cracked his jaw, spun his head, and sent him to the floor. He had only enough time to observe Delgado drilling Bill similarly before he lost consciousness.

Chapter Thirty-Three

1:32 p.m.

JACKSON AWOKE TO throbbing in his head and jaw. And momentary blurred vision. It cleared, and he realized he had been transferred to a captain's chair, facing Salvador Delgado. He held a small bag of ice to his jaw, but lowered it as he realized Jackson was conscious.

"I take it you determined our actual destination," he said.

Jackson only stared at him.

Delgado set the ice bag on a small stand beside his chair. "You will notice you are not restrained. However, I think when you survey the situation, you will agree that another act of violence would be unwise."

Jackson glanced to his right. Across the aisle from Delgado, facing the same way as the businessman, was Maggie. She too was unrestrained, because sitting opposite her was Reynaldo. His face was bruised and discolored, but he seemed perfectly capable of holding the small pistol aimed at Maggie's chest. On Jackson's left, Bill was similarly unrestrained, but unconscious still.

"If you try anything," Delgado stated calmly, "Reynaldo will shoot Maggie in the stomach. She will suffer great pain, but should live long enough to tell *Señor* Vasquez everything he wishes to know."

"You're working for him," Jackson said.

"Not at all. We are simply businessmen who found it convenient to perform favors for one another. In exchange for my assistance in keeping various illicit activities out of the public eye and deflecting attention from deaths and disappearances, *Señor* Vasquez has agreed to sell me some very cheap shares of stock in Mexól. Shares that will erupt in value as soon as production takes off."

"How did you know who we were?" Jackson asked.

"*Señor* Vasquez called me and told me to expect a call from an associate of his, *Señor* Alfonseca."

"Ali was working for him?" Maggie asked.

"Not initially, but he was . . . persuaded to do so."

"Rodrigo?"

Delgado smiled.

"So why are you taking us to Veracruz? Surely you can torture information out of us in Acapulco."

"That is quite true. But *Señor* Vasquez has asked to meet with you personally. It is imperative that he knows what you know, who else knows it, and that he can retrieve all evidence you have against him."

Jackson figured he had nothing to lose in a little bluff and bravado. "Vasquez is really dumb enough to think Maggie has all her info on one little flash drive hidden in a safe somewhere? She's disseminated it to half a dozen media outlets by now."

"I don't believe you."

"Your loss," Jackson said.

"No. This is all my gain. Substantial gain, actually."

"Why?" Bill asked. Jackson and Maggie both looked his way. He was rubbing his head, eyes only half-open.

"Why what?" Delgado asked.

"Mexól and LOVE own the *cenote* and the oil reserve," Bill said. "Production has already started. Vasquez has what he wants. What's the harm in letting us go?"

"*Señor* Vasquez would prefer some of his more . . . distasteful activities not be brought to light."

"And what's to ensure that we tell you everything? That we give you everything?"

"*Señor* Vasquez can be very persuasive."

Maggie cursed him. Delgado merely licked his lips.

"So what if we cut a deal?" Jackson asked. "We hand over all the evidence and you let us go? We'll just be kooks without any proof, and your and Vasquez's word will carry a lot more clout than ours."

Delgado had smiled as soon as Jackson began talking, and when he was finished, he broke out into a laugh. "You are not even as brave as I thought," he said. "Merely the insinuation of torture has caused you to beg for your life."

"You've got your thug pointing a gun at a woman and you're lecturing me on bravery," Jackson said. "You Mexicans familiar with the concept of irony at all?"

"If you think you can goad me into another fight, you are mistaken, *Señor* Douglas. And it would all be for naught, since the first punch you throw will coincide with Reynaldo's firing of his pistol. Is your American pride really worth the pain it will cause her?"

Maggie swore again, calling Delgado names that normally would have made Jackson blush. Under the circumstances, he felt like making a few choice comments himself. But he refrained, knowing he needed to keep a level head if there was any chance of escape. First thing first, he needed to get the gun from Reynaldo's hand. But that wasn't happening without some change in the status quo. As they were, Reynaldo would sit with his finger on the trigger until they landed.

Maggie turned her head. "I'm sorry, guys."

"For what?" Bill asked.

"Dragging you down here. I never—"

"We chose to get on the plane, Maggie. Don't blame yourself."

Jackson nodded.

"This is very sweet, really," Delgado said. "And I suggest you take the time to say whatever you need to say to one other. Or perhaps to say your prayers. We will be on the ground in Veracruz in thirty minutes, and then life will get very unpleasant for you very fast."

"Say your prayers," Jackson said. "Really?"

"You should say yours," Maggie said, and then went on to make several comments about the eternal resting place of persons such as Delgado. He merely chuckled and crossed his leg in his chair.

Jackson, meanwhile, took the man's advice and prayed. A miracle would be great. Else wisdom to see some way out of the situation. Or at least some way to save Maggie's life. Jackson knew where his soul was going, albeit not the method it was leaving the body. But Bill and Maggie were a different story, and if they only had minutes or hours to live . . .

The plane jumped slightly, minor turbulence over the mountains. It shook again, then was calm. Delgado got up to get himself something from the minibar. He sat back down and took a sip of the golden liquid.

Jackson considered options. He could rush Reynaldo in an attempt to disarm him. Even if he got a shot off and hit Maggie in the stomach, it wouldn't kill her right away. Jackson would have time to save her, if he could take out Reynaldo and Delgado and arrange for emergency transportation to a hospital when they landed in Veracruz. But he didn't like an option where the best-case scenario involved Maggie getting shot. And what if rushing Reynaldo caused him to shoot high and hit Maggie in the heart or the neck or the head?

He could wait until they landed. Reynaldo could only train the gun on one of them at a time, and it might give Jackson an opening. But with Delgado and Vasquez working together, he had little doubt that half the Mexican Army would be waiting on the apron to escort them to the refinery or warehouse where the torture was to take place. That left him trying to fashion an escape en route to said torture venue, or else once they arrived. And neither of those options—

Suddenly the plane dropped, plummeting through the air and jerking to a stop. Jackson and Delgado were thrown from their seats and nearly collided. To his right, Jackson saw Reynaldo fumbling for the gun while Maggie clung to her armrests, trying not to be thrown through the cabin.

Jackson thrust an elbow at Delgado's chin and dove for the gun, at the same time glimpsing Bill making a move as well. Reynaldo was out of his seat and shouldered Jackson into the side of a chair. Recovering quickly again, Delgado drilled Jackson with a punch to the solar plexus. His reflexes forced him to cringe, and Delgado shoved him away from the gun, which had fallen into the aisle.

Reynaldo had shoved Bill aside and was almost to the gun. Desperately, Jackson kicked out, hoping to connect with either the gun or Reynaldo. He hit the gun, sending it flying toward the back of the plane at the same that Maggie lunged from her seat and into Reynaldo. She had the same effect as a cornerback trying to tackle a lumbering fullback, but she at least knocked him off balance.

Meanwhile, Jackson continued to grapple with Delgado, taking another punch in the stomach but landing one to the chin that stunned the Mexican. Jackson squirmed from his grasp, tripped Reynaldo, and sent an elbow to Delgado's ribcage as he attempted to grab him from behind. Jackson wasn't sure if it had been Delgado's ribs or his own elbow that he had heard crack, but he felt the grip loosen.

Jackson looked up, just in time to see Reynaldo palm the gun. Such moments were supposed to take place in slow motion, but he turned, aimed, and fired at Maggie stunningly fast. Jackson scrambled forward in a rage, charging into Reynaldo as he squeezed off a second shot. His weight drove the big man to the ground, and Jackson pummeled his face with punches. Reynaldo shoved him off and Jackson got to his feet just before the big man. The gun was on the floor at Reynaldo's feet, and Jackson did not feel like diving into the fray again. Instead, he jammed his elbow back into the glass encapsulating a small fire extinguisher. He retrieved it and swung at Reynaldo as he charged at him.

Reynaldo deflected the blow with his arm and Jackson fell off to the side and into the arm of a chair. Reynaldo turned, reaching toward Jackson's neck. Off balance, Jackson could do little but swing the fire extinguisher up with his right hand. It again glanced off the underside of Reynaldo's arm, but still caught him in the chin. His teeth clacked and he stopped in place. Jackson steadied himself and took the opportunity to grasp the fire extinguisher with both hands. Having just seen Reynaldo shoot at Maggie, he was filled with fury, and swung the fire extinguisher up with as much force as possible. It caught Reynaldo flush in the chin, cracking it with a sickening clong. He fell back and bashed his head on the minibar.

Jackson scurried after the gun, picking it up and turning. Delgado had recovered from the elbow to the ribs and grabbed Maggie by the hair, pulling her in front of him. Jackson saw no signs of blood on her skin or clothing and wondered if somehow Reynaldo had missed. He didn't take the time to think about it, and didn't give Delgado the chance to make Maggie a human shield. He fired two quick rounds into his left shoulder. Delgado fell, half releasing Maggie, half pulling her on top of him.

At the same time, the cockpit door opened and Jerome burst through. He immediately reached for a gun in a shoulder holster.

"Don't!" Jackson yelled, but the pilot went to a crouch and continued to draw. Jackson fired three bullets into the center of his mass and he fell back.

"Jackson!"

"Stay down, Maggie!"

He looked back and forth, making sure that Reynaldo, Delgado, and Jerome were all indeed down. None of them moved, and Jackson saw blood pouring from Delgado's shoulder and neck. One of the bullets must have hit an artery.

"Stay down!" he yelled again, taking cover behind a chair. No sooner than he did, the cockpit door opened several inches. A gun peeked out, all but the hand holding it shielded behind the door.

"*Señor* Delgado?"

"He's dead. Drop the gun, César."

"You drop yours."

"Maggie, stay down. No chance."

"Only one of us can fly this plane."

248

"Not with a bullet in his head. Either we both live and I tell you where to fly, or we both die. Your choice."

Several seconds passed. Minor turbulence caused the plane to creak.

"I am coming out."

"I want to see two empty han—"

The door flew open and a blur somersaulted through it and behind a captain's chair. Not bad for a pilot. Jackson crouched as two bullets flew his way. Maggie shrieked. The fire extinguisher rolled across the floor, waiting to be a bomb for a stray bullet. For that matter, one misplaced shot could cause unknown damage to the plane.

Jackson fired around his chair, aiming for the middle of the chair César was hiding behind. He then jumped to the other side of the plane and waited as two bullets came his way, one shattering the minibar and one lodging in the paneling at the back of the plane. He stood, over the chair, and fired four quick shots. He heard a sickening groan and a thud. When no bullets returned his way, he peeked out. César was sprawled near the front of the plane, his eyes rolled back in his head.

"Maggie!"

"Jack!" she said, her voice torn by tears.

He rushed forward as she tore herself free from Delgado. His hand was still around her hair, but he was not holding it. Like César, he was dead, blood pouring out of his neck.

"Maggie, are you okay?"

Instead of answering, she crawled across the aisle on hands and knees. It was then that Jackson realized Bill had been absent during the fight and gun battle.

"Bill!" Maggie shrieked, and Jackson hurried to her. Bill lay on the floor, blood bubbling through his white shirt, his skin pale. He coughed and blood spurted from his mouth.

"Bill, no!"

Jackson released the gun and dropped to his knees, immediately pressing both hands into Bill's wounds.

"Jack, do something!"

"See if there's a first-aid kit."

Maggie pushed herself up.

"Hang in there, man," Jackson said.

Bill tried to speak, but all that came out was a gurgle. His eyes rolled back in his head, then closed.

"Come on, Bill. Stay with me."

Blood was pooling over Jackson's hands, and he removed them just long enough to remove his tuxedo jacket, which he pressed back into the wound.

"Jack, I can't find one!" Maggie shouted.

"Forget it."

"What?" She joined him over Bill again. "What?"

Bill's eyes had closed, and his head had rolled to the side.

"He's gone, Maggie. Bullet must have hit him in the heart."

"No." She knelt down, cupping Bill's face in her hands. "Bill, come on. Don't give up. . . . Bill!"

"Maggie," Jackson said, reaching for her arm.

"No!"

"Maggie, he's gone," Jackson said, pulling her away.

She turned and buried her head in his shoulder, sobbing.

Jackson held her as she cried and shook.

And the unmanned plane continued to cut through the air toward Veracruz.

Chapter Thirty-Four

THE ACRID SMOKE of gunfire still filled the cabin. Five were dead, including Reynaldo, who hadn't taken any bullets. But he'd suffered multiple blunt force traumas to his head, and a check of his pulse indicated he was gone too.

Maggie sat in a captain's chair, looking down at Bill. Her hands and arms were smeared with his blood. Jackson's were stained with it. As much as he wanted to mourn Bill's passing, as much as he wanted to hold Maggie in a failing effort to console her, and as much as he wanted to mentally and emotionally process the four lives he had taken, he didn't have time for any of that. The Learjet was streaking through the sky, and he had to act.

"What do we do?" Maggie asked, her voice flat.

"We're on autopilot right now."

"How do you know?"

"Because we're level. No way César abandoned controls in turbulence without setting us on autopilot."

She shrugged. "We can't land without a pilot "

He reached out his hand. "Come here."

She took his hand and stood, and he led her into the cockpit. They each sat in one of two chairs, facing each other. Elbows on his knees, Jackson held Maggie's hands and waited until she looked at him.

"Maggie, we're going to get out of this."

"How?"

"I don't know yet, okay? But we will think of something."

"Tell me you know how to land a plane."

"I know what I've seen on TV: throttle back, adjust the trim and flaps, don't forget the landing gear."

"We're going to die."

"No we're not. Now listen to me. Listen to me," he said again, and she directed her eyes back to him. "I know you're torn apart right now, and so what I'm going to tell you is going to sound horrible. But you need to forget Bill right now. You need to wall off the emotion."

"He's dead, Jackson! He took—" She scrunched her face. "He dove in front of the bullet." Tears streamed down her face.

"I know." He released her hands and cupped her head in his hands, smearing her cheeks with smudges of blood. "I know. And I know you need to grieve, I know you need to process emotionally. But the cold, hard fact of the matter is, we don't have time for that right now. Right now, we need all of our focus and attention on surviving. Then we grieve."

He leaned forward and kissed her forehead.

"I don't know . . . I don't know if I can."

"You can. But you've got to mentally build a wall. Trust me, I've done it."

She swallowed.

He nodded. "First thing, we've got to turn the plane around. Head for L.A. Once we get within radio contact, we can call for help."

"How do we do that?"

"I'm figuring that out." He let go of her and spun his chair to face the console. The first thing he looked for was the fuel gauge. When he found it, he realized it was pointless since he didn't know how quickly a Lear burned fuel or how full it had been at takeoff.

The plane slowed and began dropping.

"Jack?"

"I know."

"Jack!"

"Look, we're just on auto approach. We need to disengage the autopilot."

"How?"

"Scan your half of the plane."

They looked for several minutes, reading gauges and knobs and screens. All the while, the Lear continued to descend. Jackson's ears began to pop, and he was getting nervous when Maggie shrieked. "Here!"

Jackson quickly reached for the autopilot control and disengaged it.

"We're still dropping."

He got back into the pilot's chair and took control of the yoke. He pulled back slightly and the craft began to level. Then tip left. Then farther left.

"Jackson!"

"It's okay, Maggie, I'm banking."

"Are you sure about this?"

"Yes. Check the compass. I'm guessing from just west of Veracruz we want about due northwest."

"Compass? This thing doesn't have GPS?"

"Maybe, but I trust magnets more than circuits right now."

"Okay, where's the compass?"

"So far I've found the yoke, fuel gauge, and autopilot."

Maggie stifled a scream. A moment later, she announced, "You're at three-fifty."

He continued to bank.

"Do you really think that LAX is just going to talk you down? You could take out half the city."

"Well, on *The A-Team* they actually discussed that and planned to give them a fake heading, drop them into the ocean. Said it was SOP."

"What? *The A-Team* again? Are you serious?"

"Relax, Maggie. We were on autopilot to Veracruz. This thing isn't brand new, but it's not a dinosaur either. It can probably land itself. If not, I'm sure this has happened before. They'll talk us down. What's my heading?"

"Three-three-five."

"Closer."

"So what if the autopilot won't land at LAX? It was programmed to Veracruz, apparently. Or what if the tower can't talk you down? Or won't?"

"If they won't, I threaten to aim for downtown L.A. They'll play ball then."

"Great, now we're terrorists."

"Maggie, don't worry. It won't do any good."

"I'm not worrying for its benefit."

"Heading?"

"Three-one-four."

"Close enough," he said, leveling off the plane. "What's my altitude?"

"Where's that?"

"I don't have a clue. Keep looking."

"Um . . ." Maggie looked all around the cockpit. "Seventeen-five."

"That's got to be higher than any Mexican mountains. Works for me."

With the plane level, Jackson spun away from the controls for a moment. He smiled. "You did good. We're going to make it, Maggie. I promise."

She shook her head. "Don't make promises you can't keep."

He shrugged. "No promise is certain. But the intent, that is."

She tried to force a smile, but it wouldn't come.

"We should search the cabin," he said.

"For what?"

He bit his lip. "Parachutes."

"Why do we need parachutes?" she asked through gritted teeth.

"Backup plan, Maggie."

She closed her eyes and shook her head. "Fine. I'll look. You stay here and keep . . . doing whatever it is you claim to be doing."

He took her hand and stopped her. "Maggie, we're going to be all right. I really do believe that."

Her smile was far from sincere. "Funny, you once told me it doesn't matter what you believe; it matters what's true."

"Then, Maggie, do what I'm going to do."

"What's that?"

"Pray real hard."

*   *   *

1:51 p.m. (PST)

FOR TWO hours Jackson manned the pilot's chair, taking them in the general direction of Los Angeles. He also prayed a lot. He didn't believe God was a magic "get out of jail free" card to be used whenever in trouble. But Scripture did tell him that the Almighty was "an ever-present help in trouble." And flying an un-piloted plane definitely counted as trouble.

Maggie, when not using the plane's Wi-Fi to scour the internet on Reynaldo's computer for tips on landing planes, searched the cabin and found one parachute. As far as she could tell, it was in working order, but she was not a rigger. She checked several times, in case there was a second chute hidden elsewhere, returning at last to announce it was just the one.

Jackson nodded absent-mindedly.

"What's that look?" she asked.

"We just seem a little south," he replied. He handed her a map. "Compare that to what you see below."

"I thought we had headings to follow."

"We do. I just don't know what they are, precisely. Check the map, there are a couple of notches on the east side of the Gulf of California. I'd think we should be going northeast of them, if we're on line to L.A."

She studied the map for a moment. "Yeah, so?"

"So, look out the right window."

She did. "That them?"

"The north one, I think."

"So adjust your course."

"Going to. Just wanted to check with—"

The roar of the engines suddenly quieted, and the plane felt as if it were floating instead of flying. Only for a moment, then it resumed with a small lurch.

"What just happened?" Maggie asked.

"I think we might be running out of fuel."

"Running out of fuel?"

Jackson leaned to check the gauge. "Yeah, we're on E."

"Haven't you been watching the gauge?"

"Not really. It's not like we can stop at a refueling station or switch to solar power."

"I don't believe this."

"Maggie, we have a parachute."

"One."

"And we're still running. We might make—"

The engine stalled again, leaving them floating.

"Jackson!"

"Look, we're not dropping too fast. I'm guessing it will kick in a few more times before it gives out completely." He turned the yoke to the right. "We'll get as far north as we can, then jump."

The engines kicked in again.

"With one chute?" Maggie asked.

"It should support us both."

"Jack, this is all desert. Or water. Where are we going to parachute to?"

"Terra firma. We'll take it from there," he said, pushing out of the chair and exiting the cockpit.

"What about Bill?" she asked.

Jackson slowly shook his head.

"We can't just leave him here to crash and burn."

"That's not Bill anymore, Maggie. His soul—"

"Save it. I do not want to hear any of your eternal life crap right now."

"It's a pretty good time for it."

"I thought we were going to be fine."

"No guarantees, in parachuting or life."

"And I'm supposed to repent now, is that it?"

"Never too late." He took her hands again. "Maggie, I'm sorry, but there's nothing we can do for Bill anymore. He's gone. And if we don't get out of this plane soon, we will be too."

"I cannot just leave him, Jack. He has a sister."

He placed a hand on her cheek. "We don't have a choice, Maggie."

She looked down at Bill's corpse, and Jackson gently turned her elbow. "Maggie. I'm sorry. I really am. But I need you with me right now."

She didn't speak or even nod, but her eyes did focus on his.

"I need your belt," he said.

"What?"

"Your belt. Also, see if there are any extra clothes or blankets. And raid the minibar and grab all the food, bottles of water, anything."

While she did, Jackson returned to the cockpit and checked the altitude as the engines gave out again. Sixteen-five and dropping. He looked out the windows, checked the map, looked again. The engines were still out. He thought about adjusting flaps to reduce drag, but they were probably already set to do so. He didn't know enough to make any other changes, and the engines were still out either way. Concluding there was nothing more he could do, he veered slightly left to make sure the plane didn't crash over land. Then he took the map and headed for the cabin. Maggie had compiled food and bottles of water. "Where do I put all this? My pockets are full."

Jackson knelt down and gently removed Bill's tuxedo jacket, since his was balled up in clotted blood. "Here," he said softly. "Stuff the pockets."

"This is so wrong."

He helped her, and when the jacket was full, he pulled it over his shoulders. It was tight, but that was fine. "Let's get you into the parachute."

"Me?"

"Yeah."

"You are coming, aren't you?"

"Yeah," he said, undoing his belt and setting it on a chair beside Maggie's.

"Can you give me a moment, with Bill?"

"A quick one. We're dropping fast."

256

Maggie knelt down by Bill's body, and Jackson looked out the window, watching the ground grow more distinct. He also counted, giving Maggie two minutes before they needed to bail. When he turned to announce it was time to go, she was standing in front of him, tears welling in her eyes. She sniffed once and nodded. "Okay. Let's go."

He helped her into the parachute, locating the rip cord and the emergency cord for her. They approached the aircraft door. The plane was dropping fast now, no longer feeling like a floating aircraft but like an eight-ton rock.

Jackson looped Maggie's belt around her right leg and his left, binding them at the thigh. He did the same with his belt on their other legs, pulling the belts as tight as he could without cutting circulation. He stood. "You ready?"

"As I'll ever be."

"We dive, get clear of the plane, and then pull the cord."

"You ever done this before?"

"No. I thought I heard something about ten-thousand feet once, but we're two people, so pull as soon as we're clear."

"How do I steer?"

"We'll figure that out."

"Great."

They shuffled up against the door. "Maggie?"

"Yeah."

"You have the chute, so do me a favor and hang on tight."

She wrapped both arms around him.

"On my count," Jackson said.

Maggie nodded.

He twisted open the door, and the rush of wind threatened to suck them out of the plane. Buffeted by the sudden draft, Jackson reached his hand for Maggie's head. He pressed his cheek against hers and held on tight, his other arm looping around her waist. "Ready?" he shouted.

"Ready!"

"On three. One! Two! Three!"

They leapt sideways and plummeted through open air, the jet continuing to glide while they fell. Jackson lost his grip on Maggie, but she held tight, and he buried his head into the side of her shoulder until he regained his hold. They fell sideways, then headfirst, tumbling and twirling in the air. Beneath them, the ground was a combination of different shades of tan and navy blue, alternating as they spun. Jackson wanted to shout for Maggie to pull the cord, but couldn't find his breath.

She said something, something that was snatched by the wind and disappeared for good. Then Jackson felt one of her hands release him, and for a second he thought they were separating. But the belts and his arms held, and Jackson squeezed tighter.

They continued to plunge, the terrain beneath them starting to take shape. Then, without warning, Jackson felt himself jerked upward. Maggie's arm caught under his arm, threatening to tear his arm loose, and one of the belts felt as if it gave way. Jackson slipped downward, but he managed to wrap both arms around her waist, his head buried in her stomach as they began to float downward, still far more rapidly than he had expected.

"Jack, you okay?" Maggie asked, shouting to be heard.

"Yeah. You?"

"Yeah."

She repositioned her arms under his, and Jackson reached for her shoulder, pulling himself up. The movement caused them to flutter to the side a little, then the parachute reconciled their fall. They continued to float.

"We made it!" Maggie said.

"We haven't landed yet."

"What if we splash down?"

Jackson, now a little more secure in his and Maggie's holds on one another, chanced a look down. The Baja Peninsula looked close enough to touch, and was coming quick. There was blue off to the left, but beneath them, all was brown, a mixture of desert and mountain.

"There's a road!" Maggie said.

"Where?" Jackson whipped his head to the other side and spotted a thin ribbon of gray zig-zagging through the desert. But there were no signs of civilization. And they were drifting toward the coast.

"Any idea how I steer?"

"Pull on the ropes."

For several moments, Maggie tried to adjust their direction. But the wind had other ideas, and being an amateur, her efforts were minimal at best.

"Jack?"

"Yeah."

"How do we land?"

"Try to run. Like the guys bringing the footballs in via glider."

"Those guys are Marines."

"Yeah, and they run."

"What about you?"

"I'll just hold on."

"Well hold on, Marine, because we're getting close."

Jackson could now make out individual scrub brushes on the desert floor. He spotted a burro, oblivious to their fall from the sky. They crossed a dry river gulley and then there was nothing beneath them but sand.

"Jack! Hang on!"

He strained against the belts holding their legs together, in an effort to slide his outside hers. "Run!" he shouted as they drew near the sand. He saw a wave, then another, then water. Then they splashed.

Maggie tried to run, but her legs hit water, and with Jackson wrapped around her, she lost her balance. Their momentum collided with the force of the water and they tumbled end over end, parachute cords entangling them and the canvas of the chute floating gently over them.

Jackson got a mouthful of water and came up sputtering, still bound by belt to one of Maggie's legs. He was sitting in about a foot of water, his entire world turning white as the parachute floated down on top of them.

He spat several times. "Maggie?"

She was on all fours beside him, trying to stand up. Still bound to Jackson, she fell backwards with a splash. The canvas covered them, and Jackson began clawing with his hands, swiping it aside until bright sunlight hit him. Then he reached for his leg and worked to undo the belt. Detached from Maggie, he helped her out of the parachute, untangling several cords wrapped around her leg.

"You okay?" he asked.

She nodded as he helped her to her feet. The parachute was half floating on the surface of the water, half being submerged beneath the waves that swirled around them.

Jackson coughed some more water and started for dry ground, removing the jacket as he trudged through the waves. Maggie stumbled once, then crawled up beyond the reach of the waves. Jackson dropped the jacket in the sand and fell to the ground beside her. He panted for breath, watching as the chute became waterlogged and rode the waves into the beach. Then he searched the sky, looking for a falling Learjet. He saw nothing but radiant blue.

Jackson turned to the side and spat, getting the last of the saltwater from his lungs. Then he turned to Maggie. "What'd I tell you?"

Maggie was on her knees, hands on her hips, breathing heavily. Her panting turned to a smile, and then she surged forward, knocking Jackson onto his back. She kissed him firmly on the lips, then began punching him in the shoulder.

"I can't believe it!" she said, and at first he thought she was mad. "We made it! We actually did it! You saved us!" She punched him again. "How—I can't believe it!" She planted another kiss on him, then rolled to the side, lying splayed in the sand beside him. "I don't believe it," she said again. She turned her head. "I am sorry I ever doubted you. Never again. You're like James Bond and Indiana Jones and Jason Bourne all rolled into one. Will you marry me?"

"I take it that's the adrenaline talking?"

She exhaled heavily, her eyes closing to a squint. "Did you see the plane?" she asked, suddenly mellow.

"No. It could have floated for quite a while."

Her breathing gradually slowed. The exhilaration ebbed, and soon tears began to form in her eyes. "I never should have come down here."

"Don't say that."

"Bill's dead because of me."

"No. Bill's dead because of Vasquez and Delgado. And your story is going to expose that in very exacting detail."

"It won't bring him back."

"No, but nothing will. I'm slowly learning, you can't change the past, Maggie. But you can honor it. Honor him."

She sniffed, nodded. "It will just be my word."

"Our word. And I thought you had proof."

"Oh, I do, of all Vasquez's corruption and killings and whatnot. But as for his ties to Delgado, it'll be hearsay."

"Well, not exactly."

She frowned as Jackson reached into his pocket and pulled out his cell phone. "You know how you always make fun of me for my old-fashioned phone?"

Her frown intensified.

"Well, it doesn't have all the bells and whistles, but it does have a few. Like a voice recorder."

She sat up.

"And before we knocked on the cockpit door, I set it to record." He shrugged. "I thought it might come in handy." He flipped open the phone and navigated to a saved recording. His battery light was blinking, so he hurried, while Maggie looked on in disbelief.

"Señor *Delgado, do you have a minute? I've got a couple questions for you.*"

Click.

"*Of course, Maggie. What is—*"

The sounds of a scuffle were muted and muffled, and Jackson tossed the phone to Maggie.

"How long did this record?" she asked, looking up skeptically.

"I stopped it once we got the plane turned around."

Her eyes widened and a smile overtook her face. She dropped the phone and lunged, knocking him sideways into the sand. Then she kissed him again.

Chapter Thirty-Five

3:34 p.m.

EVENTUALLY, MAGGIE'S EXCESSIVE praise and kissing came to an end, and she and Jackson got down to business. They had the clothes on their backs, a small assortment of nuts, pretzels, and a few energy bars, and two bottles each of orange and cranberry juice, one of tonic water, and one of tequila. Also a map, their passports, wallets, money, Jackson's dead phone, and a gold lighter engraved with a calligraphy S. Plus Bill's personal items, none of which would prove helpful.

"I searched the bodies," Maggie explained as Jackson held up the lighter, glistening in the sun.

"Good work."

"I figured it was the least I could do, after being so high-maintenance for a while."

"You weren't high-maintenance, Maggie."

"Agree to disagree. What do we do now?"

Jackson dropped the lighter beside the rest of the items. "Well, the beach is deserted as far as I can see. And I didn't see any buildings as we were coming down."

"There was the road."

"Yeah, connecting two ends of a desert." He nodded at the small rise above them. "I want to climb that while we still have daylight, see if I can spot anything. You up for a climb?"

Maggie had been limping slightly, a twisted ankle from their landing, one she hadn't noticed until the adrenaline wore off. But she nodded anyhow.

Making sure the supplies were far enough up the beach to survive high tide, they crossed the fifty yards of beach and scrub and began climbing the small ridge. The terrain was still sandy, and thus slippery, as well as jagged thanks to rocks that poked here and there. Clumps of scrub and wisps of grass also dotted the hillside, which Jackson estimated to be maybe one hundred feet above sea level.

"What if we don't spot anything?" Maggie asked.

"Then we collect anything that will burn. It'll be dark in a few hours, and we should probably camp for the night. Tomorrow, we strike out for the road and hope for a friendly motorist."

"Wouldn't you rather walk at night?"

He shrugged. "It'll be cooler, but I don't know what's out there in this desert. I'd rather be able to see."

"Do you always have a plan?"

He shrugged again.

"I really am sorry for being so panicky on the plane."

He stopped. "Maggie, you were not panicky. We were kidnapped, threatened with torture and death, involved in a shootout four miles above the earth, and then parachuted from a sinking airplane, on top of which you lost a good friend. You have nothing to apologize for."

She looked down but resumed walking. He followed, not knowing what to say about Bill. It was hard enough when there wasn't a we-kinda-sorta-date-now-and-again triangle involved.

It was hot, and the sun was unrelenting. Jackson's already damp clothes were soaked with sweat by the time they crested the hill, which tapered and rounded near the top, making their trek even longer. As he feared, all they could see was more of the same, with more mountainous terrain in the distance. Back behind them, the ocean stretched out forever, and they couldn't even see the beach because of the curvature of the hill. To their right, south, the terrain continued interminably. North it was about the same, only with a dry river gulch cutting through the desert.

Maggie wiped the sweat off her brow. "Great."

"The road, I'm guessing, is a few miles east. I don't think it was a main highway though. Looking at the map, I think we're probably ten to fifteen miles west of Highway 1."

"The Highway 1?"

He nodded. "Of course, I can't really tell exactly where we are. But we should be able to make it before our food gives out." He brushed a sweaty clump of hair off his forehead. "Back to the beach?"

"Whatever you say."

The climb down was just as tricky, and Jackson wasn't looking forward to tackling the terrain again in the morning. Their descent was made worse by their hunt for firewood, which in the absence of trees, was in short supply. Without a knife or a blade, there was no easy way to uproot any of the scrub, and Jackson's hands were raw and bleeding by the time they made it back to the beach. And he doubted they had enough to burn anywhere near through the night.

The sun had set in Acapulco a little after six, but they were farther north and farther west. Back in L.A., it had also been setting around six—Pacific Time—and Jackson guessed that would be the case here. Of course, he had no idea what local time was, so it didn't really matter. What did matter was that the sun was low in the sky, and Jackson had a feeling it would cool off quickly once it went down. So he busied himself arranging pieces of scrub into a very crude teepee. The Boy Scouts would not have approved.

Finished, Jackson wandered into the surf and washed his hands, letting the saltwater cleanse the wounds. And sting like nobody's business. He had to grit his teeth and growl against the pain.

"Superman has a kryptonite," Maggie said, sloshing out beside him.

"You should stay out of the water," he said. "Stay dry."

"It's ninety degrees."

"And it will be sixty soon. Being wet will make you cold."

"Now you're Bear Grylls too? Besides, you're wet. And I have no doubt you can summon fire from the earth if need be."

"Going to be quite a thud when your view of me crashes back to earth."

She came around behind him, looped her arms around his stomach and chest, and squeezed. "Jack, you saved us. That was borderline miraculous."

"We're still stranded."

"In Baja, not the Sahara. We may have to wander a little ways, may get a little tired and thirsty, but we'll find a friendly farmer or a little cantina. We'll make it."

He turned over his shoulder, into her wide, gray-blue eyes. "Now you're the optimistic one?"

"And you're in a funk? Where's the 'I believe' spirit?"

"Still there, Mags. I'm just trying to keep a level head."

"Says the guy who decided to turn the Learjet around and then parachute out before it crashed."

Jackson shrugged.

She released him and stepped in front of him. "What's the matter?"

"I killed four more people, Maggie."

"In self-defense. To save my life."

"I know. But the kill total's still rising. Plus Bill. And I'm not the detached, dispassionate, Daniel Craig James Bond. It bothers me."

"Good."

He frowned.

"If it didn't bother you, I'd be worried. It shows you're human. But when things were bleakest, you acted heroically. Like you did in Nevada. That's you, Jack, your DNA. I meant what I said before—you are James Bond and Jason Bourne and fill in the blank."

"John McClane."

Maggie smiled. "Him too. You're a hero, Jackson. And heroes . . ." She stepped forward and loosely wrapped her arms around his waist. ". . . get the girl."

She kissed him one more time, short and sweet. Then she pulled back, as if she knew a long, soft kiss at sunset with the waves lapping around their ankles might be too much for him to resist.

*   *   *

6:44 p.m.

JACKSON AND Maggie sat on the beach and watched the sunset, then watched every last hint of daylight fade from the western sky. Darkness revealed just how far away they were from anything. The stars had never been brighter, closer, more abundant. It wasn't just the big ones, the obvious ones. It was the tiny, microscopic dots that gave the sky a grainy look, as compared to the inky blackness it normally resembled. Twice they spotted ships out at sea, and Jackson remarked how it was just like Tom Hanks in *Cast Away*. Maggie asked which of them was Wilson.

They shared a can of mixed nuts for dinner, nursing a bottle of cranberry juice between them. Neither cared for cashews, so they picked them out and set them aside. In an emergency, they could eat them. Stomachs still aching for more, they saved the rest of the food. Jackson hoped they would find rescue before dark the following day, but there was no way to know for sure.

When Maggie shivered, Jackson lit the fire. The dry scrub burned quickly, and Jackson knew they would never have enough.

"Maybe we should break out the tequila," Maggie said. "Alcohol warms."

"We should save it."

"You, saving liquor?"

"It's a disinfectant. Could burn it as a signal, even make a crude bomb."

"Bomb? You think Vasquez will come after us?"

Jackson shrugged. "By now they know the plane went down, or at least didn't reach Veracruz. He still has the same objective, to keep you from publishing your story."

"And he has the full resources of the Mexican military at his disposal," she said.

"That bad?"

"From what I hear, he can pull almost any string he wants."

"Well, one tequila bomb probably won't matter too much then."

"No."

They were quiet for a while, listening to the fire crack and the waves lap against the shore.

"Can I ask you a question?" Maggie asked.

Jackson had almost fallen into a trance. He looked up. "Sure."

"When you were shooting in the plane, did you think about stray bullets ripping the plane apart?"

"No."

"No? Heroes don't take time to worry?"

"No, I think I saw a *MythBusters* once that disproved that whole deal."

Maggie smiled and shook her head. She sat with her arms resting on her knees. She still wore just a tank top, and when the night air caused her to shiver, Jackson emptied the pockets of the tuxedo jacket, shook the sand out of it, and draped it over her shoulders. He sat beside her, and she leaned her head on his shoulder.

"Can I ask you another question?" she said after a while. The shivering had largely stopped, but her body still shook every once in a while. Jackson wasn't overly warm himself.

"Anything," he said.

"Do you ever feel survivor's guilt, because of your family?"

He looked down at the sand. "No. I'm not sure the situation's right for it anyhow. But I'm too busy feeling all sorts of other pain."

"I just keep thinking that Bill took my bullet. Not even thinking that if he hadn't, I'd probably be dead." She sat up and looked at him. "It just doesn't seem right, that he's gone now because of that. I feel . . . I feel like I need to pay him back somehow, but I can't."

"I didn't know him very well," Jackson said. "But I could tell he cared about you. And I know it's going to be a cliché, but the fact that he didn't hesitate to get between you and the gun tells me that he wouldn't want you paying him back, even if you could. Coworkers pay each other back. Friends don't."

She lowered her head onto his shoulder again. "Bill was one of the good ones. An actual gentleman."

"I'm sorry, Maggie. I really am."

"We dated a few times."

"I know."

"Just casual. He never pushed for anything more. Never pushed to . . ."

"A gentleman."

"Yeah."

Jackson shifted his arm to wrap it around her, and they sat like that for a long time.

*   *   *

Tuesday, January 1
10:24 a.m.

DETECTIVE LOYOLA stood at the end of Jackson's bed, listening intently as he relayed Bill's call, their trip to Mexico, and their "extraction" of Maggie from Vasquez's hacienda. Meanwhile, Detective Cavanaugh paced and puttered and tried to drive Jackson nuts.

"So let me get this straight," Loyola said. "Out of the blue, a guy named Bill calls you and tells you your friend Maggie, who you haven't seen in months, needs to be rescued from Mexico. And at the drop of a hat, you fly down there with him, track her to some corrupt businessman's country estate, and stage a scene from *Mission: Impossible* to get her out and make your escape?"

"I think the IMF team would have pulled off something a little more elaborate, definitely worked in some disguises, but yeah."

Someone knocked on the door and Loyola hollered a, "Come in." Immediately, she returned her focus to Jackson. "So how'd you get Maggie back to the U.S.?"

The knocker had been Sam, and she stood hesitantly by the door. "I can come back?"

"It's fine," Loyola said. "Mr. Douglas?"

He was about to speak when another knock sounded and an unfamiliar nurse burst into the room, introducing herself as Renee. "Need to check your vitals," she said.

"Can we take five, Detectives?" Jackson asked.

"Sure," Loyola said without conviction. She paced to the corner and consulted her notes. Cavanaugh shuffled a few feet to the side and resumed smirking.

"Any word?" Jackson asked Sam.

"I didn't see Dr. McCarthy." She took a step closer, giving Renee plenty of room to work. "Who's Maggie?"

"His girlfriend," Cavanaugh said.

"She's not my girlfriend." He looked back to Sam. "She's a source, technically, who works at the *Times*."

Renee interrupted to have him breathe several times into an incentive spirometer, a device not unlike the high striker at the carnival. Its purpose was to force Jackson to breathe deeply—deeply enough to raise the plunger inside of the spirometer to an appropriate level—in an effort to prevent fluid buildup in his lungs.

"Maggie was in Mexico writing a major exposé and got into trouble with a guy named Vasquez," Jackson explained to Sam when his breathing had satisfied Renee. "Long story short, her contact back here in the States asked me to help rescue her when things went south."

Loyola sighed. "Mr. Douglas, if you don't mind, can we get back to it?"

"I'm through," Renee said. "You need anything?"

"No, thanks."

She smiled, patted his arm, and exited.

Jackson looked at Sam, studying her eyes. He couldn't tell if she was suspicious or simply concerned because he had once again found himself in harm's way.

Loyola checked her notes. "I believe you were about to tell us how you all made it back to the States."

With three sets of eyes on him, and being careful how he described things, Jackson began to explain.

Chapter Thirty-Six

Sunday, November 25
12:27 a.m.

JACKSON OPENED HIS eyes to see Maggie hunched over her knees, poking at a dwindling fire with a stick. He sat up, looking across the haze from the flames at her.

"I can't sleep," she said.

"Bill?"

"Everything."

"You want somebody to talk to, or you want to brood?"

"I'm not brooding," she said with a mock evil glare. "And heroes need their rest."

"Not sure I'd categorize lying in a wet tuxedo on sand as rest anyhow," he said, sitting all the way up. "If you want to talk, my therapist tells me it's cathartic."

"Maybe, but right now, I'm sick of thinking about it . . . about him."

"Wanna talk about something else?"

"Like what?"

"Bill gave me the basic details of your exposé, but want to fill in the gaps for me?"

She shrugged. "Sure. Where should I start?"

"From the top."

Maggie crossed her legs and leaned over them. "Reed, my friend from Dallas, was doing a puff piece on the transition that takes place when a politician dies in office. In the process, he discovered that North Dakota Senator Ted Simpson, Texas Congressman Booker Dade, and Mississippi Congresswoman-Elect Dominique Jolie had all died under rather unique circumstances. He dug a little deeper and concluded they had all actually been murdered. Both his editor and the FBI turned him down, said there was nothing there."

"Nothing to murders?"

"It was just Reed's conclusion. He didn't have the proof. But he was convinced, so he called me."

"Why you?"

"We were friends. I spent a summer in Texas during college and got to know him."

"What were you doing in Texas?"

Maggie smiled coyly. "Mostly getting to know a future reporter with the *Dallas Morning-News.*"

"I see."

"The story piqued my curiosity so I spent a few weeks doing research on my own time. I was about to give up, because, although I agreed that the deaths looked suspicious, I couldn't link them up. That's when I discovered that Dade, the Texas congressman, had a friendly relationship with Ferdinand Sanchez."

"The Mexican Minister of Something or Rather."

"Minister of Justice. They had worked on legislation to expedite Mexican oil imports to the U.S., which was the first link I found to Big Oil. When I discovered that Sanchez had been kidnapped in 2010, I broadened my search. Reed had checked out every other U.S. senator and representative who had died since the turn of the century and turned up nothing of interest. But I started looking at Mexican officials and found three more politicians and judges who had died under sketchy circumstances or been kidnapped."

"Bill said something about that, and bribes?"

Maggie nodded. "I took what I had to my editor, Walter, and he let me run with it. This was in late September. I spent a week poring over voting records and judicial decisions and found a common thread. Each of the U.S. politicians had worked in some shape or form to improve and enhance American oil interests— either by working with the Mexican government, introducing legislation promoting a major oil pipeline, or campaigning on behalf of renewed offshore drilling in the Gulf. In short, their efforts—if successful—would have reduced any potential need for the U.S., the world's largest consumer, to purchase oil from a private company in Mexico."

She poked for a moment at a log, turning it over and igniting the blaze again.

"I also found that the kidnapped or dead politicians and judges had all been involved in one of two disputes, either the highly controversial sale of land to a shell corporation or the battle to privatize the Mexican oil business."

"Bill mentioned that. So somebody was pulling the strings to make a boatload of money off this crude reservoir under a sinkhole."

"Right. And that somebody was LOVE, which has ties to both Mexól and GR Limited, the shell company run by the brother of Mexól's president."

"How'd you discover that?"

"Working undercover as an administrative assistant at Mexól's brand new Veracruz plant before negotiating a similar position at LOVE."

"How'd you pull that off?"

"Rafael Vasquez, the VP of LOVE. He's a rich kid; Leo Vasquez has been letting him ride his coattails and keeping him out of trouble."

"Trouble?"

"Rafael likes fast cars and fast women. He's wrecked two Lamborghinis and at least as many marriages. He also likes to imbibe, and in 2003 was nearly killed in a nightclub brawl in Porta Vallerta after hitting on the wrong person's wife. That's when Leo brought him into the company so he could keep an eye on him. He promoted him several times, eventually to VP, basically putting him where he couldn't do much damage. He was my in."

"How so?" Jackson asked although he already knew.

She looked his way "Well, I don't drive a fast car."

Jackson said nothing.

"Between my time at Mexól and working for Leo, I was able to uncover money trails showing conclusively that Leo, through LOVE, was not only responsible for the killings and kidnappings, but also for bribing almost a dozen other politicians, all of whom ruled in favor of the land acquisition or the legalization of Mexól. I also met Ali. He told me, on the record, that LOVE had a division—*Sigilo*—that handled such matters."

"*Sigilo?*"

"Stealth. At its core, LOVE is a global investment company, but I found evidence it has connections to a host of disreputable activities. According to Ali, this isn't the first time Leo has used such methods to get his way."

"Sounds like a Bond villain."

"I also talked to a former employee who had been fired when she tried to bring a sexual harassment charge against one of Leo's assistants. She confirmed some of what Ali had to say, and I also found the secret to loosening Rafael's tongue and got him to brag about some of the corporation's exploits. Altogether, I've got more than enough to blow the lid off what they've done."

"So how'd it all go wrong?"

Maggie pushed her stick into the fire and sat back. "I don't know. Monday night, when I got home from work, two guys were waiting in my apartment. They put a bag over my head, stuck something in my arm, and the next thing I know, I'm at Leo's hacienda. They interrogated me, browbeat me, killed—I thought—Rodrigo in front of me, all to find out what I knew and where my evidence was. I convinced them I'd been uploading it to a remote drive back in L.A. and that only I and one other person could access it. They let me make a phone call, and that's when I gave the coded message to Bill."

"Pretty clever."

"Not so much," she said. "But it worked. The rest, as they say . . ."

"And they didn't hurt you?"

"No. I may have mentioned earlier some bigwigs were at the estate, so they didn't want anything unseemly to happen."

"Is that why you were stealing the show on the dance floor instead of chained up in the wine cellar?"

"I guess. Plus, if they had killed me, they'd have lost their bargaining chip. I told them my contact knew to go public with what he had if he didn't hear from me every so often."

"Smart. Saved your life."

"Yeah, and cost Bill his."

*   *   *

5:11 a.m.

DAWN WAS nothing more than a dimming of the stars when Jackson woke up. He was cold, achy, and starving. And not looking forward to a day of hiking through the desert. But he was alive, not in a Mexican prison (yet), and not bitten by a snake, scorpion, or some unknown species of wild Mexican spider.

He roused Maggie, who took a few moments to come to. They shared an orange juice and the crumbs from an energy bar before packing everything else into their pockets. Still shivering from the cold, Jackson immersed himself in the water anyhow. Soon enough, it would be baking.

Then, navigating by flashlight, they carefully picked their way through the old, dry river gulch. There was no hint of it on the map, or of a river, or of the minor road they had seen while parachuting to the beach. By Jackson's estimate, they had at least a dozen miles to go before reaching the main road—Highway 1.

Give or take a few miles based on their exact location, the lay of the land, and Jackson's ability to lead them in a straight line.

They followed the riverbed until the sun peeked over the horizon, immediately raising the temperature. Jackson's sore back, which had been largely masked by adrenaline and inactivity the night before, hurt with every step. Maggie trudged behind him gamely, her ankle either improved or being ignored. Neither of them said much until Jackson stopped and observed they were veering too much north.

"How can you tell?"

He shrugged. "I just can."

Maggie shrugged too. "No reason to start questioning you now. What do we do?"

"Climb."

It took them longer than it should have to climb the bank of the river and to the top of a small ridge. Panting, they stopped and surveyed the terrain. The ocean was still visible to the west. East, there was nothing but desert. And the sun was rising fast.

Jackson pointed to a ridge on the horizon, he guessed several miles away. "See that?" he asked. "We get there, we can have another energy bar."

"Oh goody."

Because there was nothing else to do, Maggie talked about her story—how she was going to write it as an "according to this reporter" sort of piece. Very Howard Cosell, Jackson said. Mostly, he let her talk. He kept his eye out for rattlers and jackals and cougars and whatever else inhabited the barren Baja Peninsula. He also kept his eyes on the sky, just in case.

They reached the ridge, had some crumbs, and set their sights on the next ridge. The ocean was no longer visible behind them, thanks to the previous ridge, and it was unsettling. But they had no choice but to go on. One more ridge, Jackson said, and they could each have a sip of orange juice.

The road appeared out of nowhere, a curling ribbon of dust winding through a valley. Jackson stopped. "What do you think?" he asked.

"You're the Eagle Scout."

"Grant was the Eagle Scout; I made fun of his badges. And I think there's maybe a car a day that drives past here."

"We could follow it," Maggie said. "It'll lead somewhere eventually."

Jackson stretched out his hand. "That's east. Ish. This goes northeast. It'll hit the highway, but not nearly as soon as if we keep going east. Ish."

"Whatever you say, Pythagoras."

Three and a half hours, half a can of nuts, and most of a bottle of orange juice later, they stood atop another ridge. The sun was at its zenith, and Jackson was sweating so much he was almost cold. Maggie was glistening, hair tied behind her, complaining about sand in her shoe.

"You know," Jackson said, hands on his knees, "you'd make a good Israelite."

"Yeah? How's that?"

"Grumbling in the desert."

"So that makes you Moses then in your Old Testament fantasy?"

"No, I'd be grumbling too."

"Would be?"

Jackson nodded and stood. "If it wasn't for that."

Maggie turned to follow his outstretched hand. "I don't see anything."

He stood beside her so she could look down his arm. "Way off there in the distance, see that?"

Something reflected the sun, just briefly, then stopped. A moment later, it reflected again, longer and brighter.

Maggie turned her head. "A car?"

"The highway."

"If we didn't smell like gym socks, I'd kiss you right now."

"Don't bother. I'm out of saliva."

She smiled. "What are we waiting for?"

It took almost two hours to reach the highway, and Jackson rewarded Maggie by letting her drain the orange juice. "We may have another problem," he said as they crossed to the far side of the road.

"What's that?"

"If you were driving through the Mojave and saw a couple of Mexicans that looked like us, would you pick them up?"

"Maybe I should stuff a pillow under my shirt."

"Else we can just flap our cash."

"How much do we have?"

"About a hundred bucks."

"So what do we do when we get picked up?" Maggie asked.

"I've been thinking about that," Jackson said.

"And?"

"We need to find out how seriously we're wanted. Has Vasquez let this go because he doesn't want to draw attention to his illegalities, or has he called in every favor with the military, making us domestic terrorists with a shoot-on-sight directive?"

"Knowing Vasquez, I'd say the latter." Maggie sighed. "Remember, Ali said—"

"I'm not particularly inclined to base any more decisions off of 'Ali said.'"

"If you don't trust him, I can call Anapaula."

"Who is Anapaula?"

"She was one of my initial sources at *El Universal* in Mexico City. The newspaper. Her sister's husband is a police detective in Acapulco."

"He trustworthy?"

"I think so."

"Worth a try. We'll worry about it when we get a phone," he said, looking around. "Which by the looks of things could be a while."

Chapter Thirty-Seven

3:17 p.m.

THE FIRST CAR didn't even slow down. Maggie threatened to lie down in the road when they saw the next one approaching. She didn't because it slowed almost immediately. It was a pickup truck, old and rusty, with wooden slats forming a crude cargo bay in the flatbed. The tires were bowed in, and the windshield cracked and streaked with dirt. Not much different than the old man driving it. He wore a flimsy straw hat and leaned through the window and mumbled something unintelligible in Spanish.

Jackson turned to Maggie. *"Sí,"* she answered *"¿A donde vas?"*

The man mumbled again. Jackson didn't see any signs of teeth.

"¿Podemos ir contigo?"

"Sí." He jerked his thumb at the back of the truck.

"Ah, thank you. Uh, *muchas gracias!*" Maggie said. She and Jackson climbed into the flatbed, joining a goat and several bales of hay. The old truck shifted into gear and rumbled along the road.

"What happened?" Jackson asked. "You didn't pledge me to his daughter or something, did you?"

"He's giving us a ride into the next town, about twenty kilometers north of here."

"He said all that?"

She nodded.

"What do we owe him?"

"Nothing."

Jackson nodded. "He say what sort of services this town might have?"

Maggie shook her head, then reclined it against a hay bale and closed her eyes. She opened them when the goat bleated.

"You think this thing gives milk?" Jackson asked. He leaned back, trying to relax and let the tension out of his body. The constant rumble of the truck's

276

engine and the jolt of its suspension made it difficult. So too did the very real possibility that he might open his eyes to a goat licking his face.

"You look tired," Maggie said.

"I am tired."

"In fact, you've looked tired ever since I saw you on the dance floor."

"Jetlag."

"I mean more than physically."

"Yeah." He lifted a loose piece of hay and picked it apart. "Nevada took its toll."

She nodded. "And then I asked you to do it again. I'm sorry."

"Don't be."

Maggie was silent for several minutes. "I only saw what was in the news. Was it accurate?"

"*You* asking if the news is accurate?"

She grinned slightly.

"The news sanitized it pretty good," he said. "They didn't mention bullet-riddled bodies, blood splattered everywhere, how I mowed down people, tortured people . . ."

"In self-defense."

"So to speak. They're still dead."

"They had it coming," Maggie said. "They kidnapped Hillary, other men and women. They conducted all sorts of experiments, practically committed treas—"

"They're still dead."

The silence was deafening. Silence aside from the rattle of the truck and the chewing of the goat.

"If you don't want to talk about it, I get it, but . . ."

"Talking's cathartic?"

"It is." She shifted to come sit beside him. "I know I need to talk about Bill, and I will when it isn't quite so fresh. And I know you, Jackson. Not as well as other people, but I know you. It isn't good to keep it all in."

"I've let it out."

"Have you?"

"Bawled on Reggie's shoulder. Not pretty. Not terribly masculine."

"But it still eats at you?"

"Shouldn't it?"

She tilted her head. "I thought you were a 'why' guy."

"A 'why' guy?"

"You know. Why you do it is more important than what you do. Looking is lusting, hating is killing, that sort of a thing."

"Yeah, well, I skipped the hating and went right to the killing."

"But what about the why? Like on the plane, you killed to save my life, to avoid being killed and tortured yourself."

"Brings me up to about thirty this year. Might be a P.I. record."

She sighed. "What if I was being attacked, if some guy was raping me? What would you do?"

"Before or after I force-fed him his knee?"

"See, that's my point. The why behind your actions would be justified."

"I don't know that it's that simple."

"So what, you'd just let him attack me?"

"No," Jackson said.

"You'd ask him kindly to stop?"

"Of course not."

"Well then?"

Jackson sighed. He finally looked her in the eye. "I get that it was quote-unquote justified, that I did what I had to do and all that."

"So what then?"

"It came easy, Maggie. I just . . . It was like I was playing *Call of Duty* with Mouse. No repercussions, no consequences. I just killed and moved on to the next level where I killed some more, like it was natural, like I'm some kind of monster or something."

"Or a hero."

Jackson looked at her. "What is this, product placement for Skillet?"

"Quit deflecting. If you heard on the news that some Navy SEAL or Marine had done what you did, you'd be first in line to give that guy a medal."

"That's different."

"How? Because he's trained for it? Because it's his job?"

"No, because . . ."

"Because what, Jackson?"

"I'm supposed to be different."

"Because you're a Christian?"

He sighed again. "I know that sounds pious, but—"

"You think there aren't Christian SEALs, Christian cops?"

"Sure."

"Well?"

"I'm not saying I shouldn't have done what I did. But the how . . . It shouldn't have been so easy."

"It doesn't sound like it has been."

He slowly looked down, then away.

"Let me ask you something," she said. "What would Jesus have done?"

"Maggie."

"I mean it. If Jesus had been in your shoes, what would He have done?"

"Had more wisdom."

"I'm serious."

"So am I."

"Look, you once told me that Jesus isn't just a 'love and peace hippie' like people make Him out to be. So tell me, what would He have done?"

Jackson looked back. "Honestly, I don't know. But I doubt He would have channeled Steven Seagal."

"Okay, what about the Old Testament? Didn't God tell the Israelites to totally demolish cities, kill everybody, women and children too?"

"That was different."

"How so?"

"Those cities, those people, were e—"

"Evil," she finished for him. "The kind of people who might kidnap and abuse young women or manipulate genetics or something."

He studied her blue-gray eyes. They were the epitome of intensity. She didn't blink, and he finally sighed. "Since when did you become an expert on the Old Testament?"

Maggie cracked a smile. "I know this guy, a real Bible-thumper."

"Look, you're right, okay? Everything you're saying. Same with Grandpa and Reggie and—" He stopped himself just before saying "Sam." He looked down for cover. "Even my therapist. But that doesn't make it any easier."

"I know. Just so long as you're not making it harder."

"I'm trying not to Maggie. But at the end of the day, I still killed twenty people. I have to live with that."

*   *   *

3:39 p.m.

THE HIGHWAY sign labeled the town as San Diego, oddly enough. It was a dot on Jackson's map, and little more in the real world. The farmer dropped them off in the center of town, a small square half a block east of the highway. Jackson could see the edge of town in every direction. He could also see telephone poles running north along Highway 1, which gave him hope.

They glanced around, observing little activity in the sleepy town. Then Maggie nodded at a building on the corner, advertising *cervesas frias*. "I don't know about you," she said, "but I could use a beer."

"Yeah, let's spend our survival money on booze."

"How about this?" she asked, raking her hand through sweaty, clumpy hair. "If there's a phone inside, I get one beer."

"Deal."

The small bar did indeed have an old payphone in a dark hallway, but it was broken and didn't accept quarters. It was, however, operable by a calling card, said the gold-toothed proprietor of the bar. And he had such a card, with available minutes, for a fee. Maggie negotiated, and was given a rate of five minutes for five dollars. Her beer cost three, and she made a deal for ten minutes and the beer for ten dollars. Gold Teeth led her to the phone and showed her how to use the card, then returned to man his bar.

"Imagine the deal you could have struck if you had showered recently," Jackson said as Maggie dialed Anapaula's number from memory. She grinned, then perked up when someone answered.

She spoke in Spanish, and all Jackson caught was "Anapaula," "*federales*," and "Los Angeles." Figuring it was pointless to eavesdrop on one half of a conversation in a language he couldn't understand, he tapped her shoulder and nodded at the bathroom. He took care of business and returned to find Maggie dialing again. "Who now?" he asked.

"Julio."

"Who's Julio?"

"Anapaula's sister's husband."

"The detective?"

"She was going to call to give him a heads up that I'd be calling."

She raised the phone to her mouth and spoke again in Spanish. Jackson caught a few words, but waited patiently until Maggie finished. She hung up the phone and swiped the card off the top of the box. They returned it to Gold Teeth, who provided Maggie with a cold beer.

"What's the word?" Jackson asked as Maggie relished her liquor.

"Anapaula and Julio both said we're hot."

"How hot?"

She looked around, making sure Gold Teeth wasn't listening. He didn't appear to be. "Wanted in Acapulco for burglary, terrorism, and the murder of four people, including Salvador Delgado, a famous businessman."

"Great. Probably have just enough evidence planted and witnesses bribed to convince a Mexican jury the *Americanos* did it."

"Any bright ideas?"

"Well, we're probably as far off the grid as we can get," Jackson said. "Ask your friend if there's a hotel in this town."

Maggie hollered for Gold Teeth's attention, then spoke to him in Spanish. "No hotel," she translated.

"Where is the nearest hotel?" Jackson asked. *"Norte."*

More back and forth. Jackson understood the answer clear enough. *"San Quintin."*

"Great. That's poetic. How far to San Quintin?"

"Over three hundred kilometers," Maggie replied.

"Let's go back into the desert."

Gold Teeth said something else, and Jackson recognized the word *autobús*.

"¿Cuándo llega?"

"Mismo despues de la puesta del sol."

"Just after sunset," Maggie said.

"Let's hope it's less than . . . whatever this is," Jackson said, dumping the rest of their crumpled up money on the table.

"I guess that means *no mas cervezas.*"

"Sí, señorita."

*   *   *

Monday, November 26
1:09 a.m.

THE BUS had arrived at quarter after five, with no cops or *federales* aboard. It had taken them north along Highway 1, through some of the most barren country Jackson had ever seen. It had arrived in San Quintin a little after midnight, where Jackson and his "pregnant" wife had gotten a discounted motel room. They had $24 American left and were almost at the point of collapsing from fatigue. After checking in, Jackson raided a vending machine, another five dollars' worth, to buy them sustenance.

"How do we get to the border on nineteen dollars?" Maggie asked. She sat on one of two twin beds, eating M&M's.

Jackson sighed. "I think I may have an idea on that. But you're not going to like it."

"If it gets us home, I'll like it."

"I don't even like it."

"Let's hear it."

Jackson sighed again. "I know a guy who used to smuggle people in and out of Mexico."

"Not Brower?" she asked. "The guy you busted with that drug dealer?"

"His dad actually."

"Are you serious?"

"I told you you wouldn't like it."

"And you think he'd come down here for twenty bucks?"

"No, we'd have to figure out another way to finance him."

"Forget that, you think he'd do it for the guy who put his son away?"

"His son was consorting with drug dealers and human smugglers, struck a deal with the D.A., and got off with probation and community service."

"Still."

"If the money's right, he'd not only come down here but leave his mother behind as ransom."

"So where do we get the money?"

"I've got that covered."

"What, you got some trick where you keep folding money and it multiplies, fish and loaves-style?"

"It'd be questionable legally," he said.

"Questionable? Seems pretty black and white to me."

"I'm thinking U.S. legally. I don't care what the corrupt Mexican cops think. We're American citizens, and I'm not aware of any rule that says we have to come through their specified checkpoints to get home."

"Actually, I'm pretty sure there is such a rule, and I think our border authorities might talk with Mexico's. It's why they give us those nifty little books with our picture in them."

He waved. "Which we have, and we'll go to ICE or the NSA or port authority or whoever once things cool down."

"They want us for murder, Jack. I'm not sure things will cool down."

"You forget my clever recording of Delgado's confession. With your testimony and the backing of the *Times*, we should be okay."

Maggie eyed him skeptically, then drained the M&M's.

"Unless you have a better idea," he said, extending his hands.

"Brower. I think I'd almost rather try a coyote-style desert border crossing," she said.

He pointed. "That's when the authorities get cranky."

Maggie sighed. "I've ridden this pony so far . . ." She tore open a package of cheese-filled crackers. "Back to the having the finances covered bit . . ."

"In Vegas, before I went on my killing spree, Hillary and I were undercover at the Oasis, and in order to find out what Richard Holloway knew about everything that was going on, I broke into his safe while Hillary played poker with him and his pals."

Maggie stopped mid-chew.

"She cleared forty grand."

Maggie nearly choked on a cracker. "Forty grand?"

"We split it, and after expenses, I netted sixteen and change."

"Sixteen thousand dollars?"

"And change."

"And you're just mentioning this now?"

"I didn't want you to want me just for my money."

She flung the package of crackers at him.

"Besides, it's sort of blood money."

"It's a nest egg, Jack. And I don't see how it's relevant."

"I know it's late, Maggie, but we need money, and I have—"

"You're not using that money to bail us out."

"Well, unless you want to go back to Gold Teeth and see if he needs a waitress on the weekends . . ."

"Jack."

"It isn't doing me much good sitting in a safe while I sit here and rot."

"I'm going to pay you back."

"Sure. When CBS gets the rights to this story, you can break me off a few."

"I'm serious."

"I believe you. But we can worry about that when we get home."

Maggie shook her head. "I don't believe it." She looked up. "Okay, how do we broker this deal?"

"I call Reggie, see if he can spot me the money. Then I call Brower, arrange payment, haggle a little, and apologize for busting his son."

Maggie glanced at the clock. "What time's Reggie usually get up?"

Jackson grinned. "When his phone rings."

Chapter Thirty-Eight

SEVERAL MILES SOUTH of San Quintin was a small, southern-facing inlet. The brackish water was surrounded by rocky coastline and plenty of desert, but it contained the nearest boat dock to Jackson and Maggie's hotel. Larry Brower had arranged to meet them there at approximately four p.m. with his thirty-two-foot cruiser.

He was late.

It had taken five phone calls. Reggie had been grumpy until Jackson explained the gravity of the situation. Larry Brower had been grumpy until Jackson identified himself, at which point he had hung up. Jackson had immediately called back, his first words being, "Two thousand dollars." Larry had returned to just grumpy and upped the price to four grand. They had settled on three.

Reggie had delivered Brower fifteen hundred in cash—to be reimbursed by Jackson from Hillary's poker winnings—and would pay him the other half when Brower brought Jackson and Maggie to Marina del Rey. Brower had said he would leave immediately, per the deal, and estimated a fourteen to sixteen-hour trip.

Jackson and Maggie had slept till check-out time, then spent the rest of their cash on non-perishable food items. A friendly local had driven them to the dock, where they had eaten lunch and waited under the shade of a small metal shed at the end of the otherwise vacant dock. They'd been waiting for going on three hours.

"You think he'll show?" Maggie asked.

"Probably."

"I'm not bowled over by your confidence."

Jackson shrugged. "There's a chance he just wants to hose me for what I did to Landon. In which case, he might take the fifteen hundred and thank you very much."

"Super."

Maggie picked at a blade of grass, her hundredth of the afternoon. "So assume he shows."

"And is sober?"

"Oh, terrific."

"Says the lady who wanted to spend the rest of our money on cold *cervezas*."

She flung a dirt clod at him. "Assume he shows," she said. "Are we sure there won't be police waiting at the pier for us."

"Only if he called them. It's Vasquez I'm more concerned with."

"I've been thinking about that," she said. "If I show up at the *Times*, it will leak that I'm back and breaking a big story. If Vasquez catches wind of it, he'll do anything to silence me."

Jackson picked some grass of his own. "How long do you think it will take to write your story?"

"After a good night's sleep, a few days."

"And how long till it runs?"

She shrugged. "Depends."

"But you can get it to your editor in a few days?"

"Yeah, I think so. It's mostly in my head already."

"Good. Then it's out of your hands and you're no longer a target for Vasquez."

"What about retribution?"

"In Mexico, maybe. I doubt he'd cross into the U.S. just for revenge. To squelch the story, he'll go to the ends of the earth. But don't worry. I've got a plan."

"You always do."

Jackson nodded. "There's a boat coming."

Maggie jumped to her feet. It was just a speck, but it quickly turned into a thirty-two-foot cruiser, captained by a balding, graying man with a faded Dodgers cap sitting loosely on the back half of his head. No shirt, khaki shorts. Springsteen was thumping through a portable CD player—might have actually been a cassette player—beside him on the dash. Next to it were two empty bottles of Red Stripe. Only two was a good sign.

Larry pulled the boat up to the dock and tied her off, still humming "Hungry Heart." He acknowledged Jackson with a nod, nothing more. Jackson felt compelled to at least introduce Maggie.

"Pleasure to meet you, ma'am." He helped her onto the boat, eyed her for just a moment, then glanced at Jackson. "How long you folks been down here?"

"Too long."

Larry nodded. "Well, let's get moving. I want to be out of this toilet of a bay before dark."

For three thousand dollars, Larry provided a few services. There was cold beer in a cooler and sandwiches in the refrigerator below deck. Help yourself, he said. There was also a bed, which he offered if either of them needed it. Or both, he said, by the look of things.

Although tired, Jackson wasn't sleepy. But after several minutes of standing awkwardly beside Larry, he decided to explore the cruiser. As always, he marveled at how boat architects could cram so much into such a small space. Sleeping quarters, a bathroom with shower, a kitchen and dining room—all in a space the size of his closet. He found a coffeepot, and some coffee, and given Larry's hospitality—and the price for this rescue junket—took it upon himself to make a pot. It was hot and black, and Jackson took a cup up top, where Maggie was at the bow, watching the day fade. They had circled around the end of the bay and were cruising north of west, away from the coast. At present, they were on a course for the Aleutians, but Jackson figured Larry was just getting out into international waters.

"How you holding up?" Jackson asked Maggie.

"Okay, I guess." She glanced over her shoulder at Larry, who was nursing another Red Stripe and grooving to '80s classics. "You sure this guy knows what he's doing?"

Jackson nodded and took a drink of coffee. Add bitter to hot and black.

"You trust him?" she asked.

"Enough."

She nodded.

"But it might be best if you aren't left alone with him."

"Terrific."

Larry steered them far enough into the ocean so that no land was visible. He adjusted course slightly, veering more northward, and then called Jackson to take the helm.

"I gotta pee," he said.

Three Red Stripes down, it was no wonder.

"Just hold 'er steady. Less is more."

Jackson nodded and Larry disappeared below deck. The sun had set and the night was clear and warm, stars beginning to shine overhead. It was also a little eerie, with nothing but dark water in sight in any direction. Except straight ahead, where Maggie remained at the bow, a living figurehead, lost in thought. He watched her for a few minutes, then turned his eyes toward the dark, rolling ocean. He didn't even notice that she had come and stood beside him until she looped her arms around him and rested her chin on his shoulder.

"Hey," he said.

"We're going to make it," she said.

"I think we are."

"Something on your mind?"

He hesitated. "Can I ask you something?" he asked, turning his head.

She stood back. "Of course."

"If it's none of my business, tell me it's none of my business, but did you . . . sleep with Rafael?"

Maggie crossed her arms and leaned against the corner of the console. "Yeah."

Jackson focused his attention over the bow.

"I had to. A guy like Rafael wouldn't give me the time of day if I wasn't willing to go the distance. It was business."

"Is your story really worth that?"

"Worth what?" she asked with a shrug. "I had sex with him. It's not like I made a deal with the devil."

"Not consciously."

"What?"

"Sex changes things, Maggie. You can't take it back."

"You can't take anything back in life. And who are you to tell me about sex?"

"I'm just saying, sex isn't a casual thing."

"To you, maybe. But to me, sex isn't some great treasure to save for one special person. Sex is how you share love with somebody, and sometimes sex is just something fun. And like anything, sometimes it's a way to get what you want. Don't tell me all the saintly church ladies you know never used sex to manipulate their husbands."

"I'd really rather not know."

For a few moments, neither spoke. Then Maggie asked. "Are you jealous?"

"I don't have the right to be jealous."

"Then why does this bother you?"

"I don't know."

"You didn't think I was a virgin, did you?"

"If I say no, are you going to slap me?"

Maggie smiled. "No."

Jackson shrugged. "I didn't know. I mean, a lot of Christians think everyone else in the world is living one big orgy—which I know isn't true. And truth be told, Maggie, you don't seem like the kind of person who would hop into bed with any man that comes along."

"I'm not," she answered. "But I'm also not saving myself like you are."

"I understand that," Jackson said. "But you're not some black widow trolling for a takedown, either. I know you. This guy's a complete stranger, and this . . . You said it yourself, Maggie, this was just business. Sex isn't supposed to be a business."

"I know, and I wish it hadn't come to that. But what else could I do? This is the biggest story of my life. It's my chance, and I have to take it. And if it makes it any better, it was only a few times. Once on 'vacation' in Cabo to lure him in, and then a few times back in Acapulco to keep him hooked."

"It doesn't make it any better," he said quietly.

She shook her head. "Why does this matter to you so much? Are you marking your territory or something?"

"No."

"Then why?"

"Because I care about you, Maggie."

"Then shouldn't you want what makes me happy."

"Sex to get info makes you happy?"

She sighed.

"And no, I don't necessarily want what makes you happy? Not if it isn't good for you."

"Who are you to decide what's good for me?"

"I'm not deciding."

"I know, God is," she said. "Okay, let me ask you this?"

"Shoot."

"Have you ever kissed a girl?"

"Why do you ask?"

"Curious," she said with a shrug. "Since we're talking about relationships."

"Okay. Yes, I have."

"Have you ever been in love?"

He thought for a moment. "No."

"So you kissed a girl you weren't in love with?"

He nodded. "I guess so, yeah."

Maggie shrugged. "So how is that different than sex?"

He raised his eyebrows. "Well, anatomically speaking . . ."

"You know what I mean. You were willing to share that emotional, romantic, physical experience with someone you just said you weren't in love with. Sex is just the next rung up the ladder."

"First of all, I knew I smelled a setup. Second, it was a two-second kiss, not Hawkeye and Margaret's goodbye session, so I think your ladder is missing a few rungs. And third, sex is just different."

"Different, yeah, but the same idea."

"Plus the Bible prohibits sex outside of marriage. It doesn't say anything about kissing."

"I don't understand how you can make decisions based on a two-thousand-year-old book. Times change. The world is nothing like it was back then."

"So?"

"So, doesn't that merit a change in values?"

"Why should it?"

"Because people have changed. They've evolved."

"Don't open that can of worms now too."

"Fine, we'll table that one. But how can you live your life based on commands and principles that not only were given that long ago, but were based on life as it was that long ago? I've read the Old Testament, Jackson, and there are a lot of weird commandments in there."

"And I don't live by all of them, as you'll notice by examining the corners of my beard."

She rolled her eyes.

He shrugged.

"So you just pick and choose which archaic commands are still relevant?"

"Look, Maggie, you can pick out little pieces of the Bible and hold them up and they don't make any sense or seem archaic and crude. But the Bible isn't meant to be read as a collection of verses. It's a unified Book, one message, one theme."

"That's fair."

"And I didn't mean to condemn you."

"I know you didn't."

Larry returned with a belch, ending their discussion. He didn't make any movement to take over control of the boat. "Your business," he said, "but what brings you folks to Mexico?"

"Romantic getaway gone bad," Maggie said. "Where did you say that beer was?"

Larry nodded at the cooler, then eyeballed Maggie as she bent down to retrieve a bottle.

Jackson kept his eye out for whales.

*   *   *

9:41 p.m.

THE COFFEE kept Jackson wired long enough to give Larry a legitimate rest at the helm. He took a catnap below, telling Jackson to holler if anything went amiss. Nothing did. Maggie spent a while journaling her thoughts, now that she was no longer just writing a story but also chronicling an epic adventure, she said. Eventually, the events of the last few days overtook her, and she fell asleep on the small bench seat at the stern. (They didn't talk about sex anymore.) Two down, and Jackson was alone with his thoughts.

Was this it? A slow, simple, anticlimactic getaway, à la *The Next Three Days*? No shootout with *federales*? No father and son Vasquez swooping in on black helicopters? No border patrol seizing them at the Port of Los Angeles and "finding" kilos of coke stashed below deck? Okay, so Jackson wasn't sure they had survived that one yet. But after threats of torture, jumping from a soon-to-crash airplane, and wandering through the desert for a day, he was more than happy with anticlimactic.

Larry, now in a shirt, returned with two cups of coffee. He handed one to Jackson, letting him continue at the helm. "How long's the girl been out?"

"Hour maybe."

"Pretty."

"You should see her when she's bathed."

Larry watched her sleeping, maybe for a beat too long. "Girlfriend?"

"Not really."

"Too bad."

They caught a small crest and the boat rocked slightly.

Larry took a long drink of coffee. "You want to tell me why you folks are really here?"

"Three grand doesn't buy silence?" Jackson asked.

"Sure, if that's the way you want it." Another pull. "Just didn't peg you as the type to need this type of service. Thought you were some sort of do-gooding crime fighter or something."

Jackson nodded and tried his coffee. It was now burnt tasting too.

"If you're worried I'm going to dime you to the cops as some sort of payback, you can forget about it," Larry said.

Jackson turned to look at him.

"Back in the day, Javy and I pulled some pretty wild stuff," Larry said. "We got away with most of it, but, it's not the life I want for my kid. If I'd have known what Enrique was up to, I'd have told Landon to have nothing to do with him— Heck, I'd have kicked Enrique's tail myself." He looked up, into Jackson's eyes. "And you were just doing what you had to do. I don't hold it against you."

Jackson swallowed. "Why'd you agree to come get us if you don't want any part of that lifestyle?"

"Because I figured you weren't running drugs or nothing." Larry shrugged. "And because money talks." He waved. "But like you said, three grand buys silence. You don't want to tell me, you ain't gotta tell me."

"Not a matter of want," Jackson said. "More like can't."

"Uh-huh. Whatever." Larry took a drink.

Jackson steered a little while longer, which meant stood aimlessly at the helm a little while longer. "You read the *Times* back in L.A.?" he asked.

"Now and again."

"Make it a habit."

Larry frowned.

Jackson nodded. "Trust me. It'll all make sense one day."

"Whatever you say, *amigo*." He nodded toward the back of the boat, where Maggie was stirring. "Looks like your lady friend's awake. I'll take over."

"Watch it," Jackson said with a tongue-in-cheek wink as he relinquished the helm, "she veers a little left if you don't hold her tight."

Larry's reply was not something Maggie would be able to print in her story.

*   *   *

Tuesday, November 27
9:02 a.m.

LARRY MANNED the boat and Jackson and Maggie alternated between sleeping in the shelf-like bed below deck and drinking—him coffee, her coffee and beer. When Jackson had awakened the last time, the sun had been shining through haze, and a small island had been ahead to starboard. Catalina. They were north of the border.

A little more than an hour later, they pulled into a slip in Marina del Rey, just out of sight of Leroy's houseboat. Reggie was waiting in his Hummer H3. He helped Larry dock the boat, then handed him an envelope. A thick one.

"Second half, all cash," Reggie said.

Larry opened the envelope and thumbed through it. "Do I need to count it?"

Reggie nodded at the boat. "Do I need to sign for them or something?"

"All yours," he said, closing the envelope. "Ma'am, I don't know what you're into, but I wish you well."

"Thank you," Maggie said. "And thanks for the ride."

"Thank your friend here," Larry said. He looked to Jackson and held up the envelope. "You need my services again . . ."

Jackson nodded at Larry as he turned to leave, then he and Maggie followed Reggie to the Hummer. "You get everything?" Jackson asked as Reggie opened the back door for them.

"In the bag," Reggie said, nodding at a duffel on the seat. "You know if you use it, there's going to be consequences."

"Only for an emergency," Jackson said.

"What are you two talking about?" Maggie asked.

"Precautions."

"You mind sharing with me?"

Jackson nodded for her to get in. "On the way."

They both got into the backseat and Reggie took the wheel. "Where to?" he asked.

That had been the hundred-dollar question during their combined conscious moments the night before. Vasquez had felt a million miles away, and especially now that they were back in L.A.—back in America—continuing to hide and dodge seemed almost silly. And yet, the memories of the escape at the hacienda,

Delgado's smirk aboard his plane, and all the events of the last couple days made it almost impossible to go back to life as normal.

"McDonald's," he answered. "I need some breakfast. Then Target, a Walmart. You got a preference?" he asked Maggie "Maybe the mall."

"Whatever's close. I've been in these clothes for way too long."

"You did get the money, right?" Jackson asked, digging through the duffel bag.

"Side pocket."

Jackson unzipped it and pulled out a small envelope.

"One grand in cold, hard cash," Reggie said. "Interest free."

"As soon as I can get to a bank . . ."

"Reggie, when this is all over, I'm treating you to the biggest steak dinner on earth," Maggie said.

Jackson leaned forward. "Dude, this is the time to ask for Lakers tickets."

"Seriously, Reggie," Maggie said, "how can I thank you? Anything. Name it."

"Just make sure he pays me back," Reggie said.

They picked up some breakfast sandwiches at a McDonald's drive-thru, then hit Target, where Jackson and Maggie each bought several changes of clothes and basic personal items. They also bought some grocery staples—milk and cereal, bread and lunchmeat, fruit, various snacks. Then they were back in the Hummer, headed for the beach.

"So you want to fill me in on the details of this plan?" Maggie asked.

"There's a good chance Vasquez knows who I am now, so we can't go back to my place any more than we can yours."

"Then what, play *Three's Company* with Reggie?"

"No, we shack up at an out-of-the-way motel. You write like the dickens and I guard the door." Jackson held up Reggie's SIG Sauer P220 pistol, also from the duffel bag. "Just in case."

"Great."

"Once you have the story finished, we get it to Walter, contact the State Department or Customs or whoever, and we should be home free."

"Just like that?"

"Once you submit your story, you're out of danger because you no longer hold the cards. Walter, on the other hand, might need to watch his back. And once your story comes out, or once we put that recording in the right hands, any pressure from the Mexican authorities will die down. Compared to the last few days, it should be a piece of cake."

A few minutes later, Reggie pulled into the parking lot of a beachside motel, small and off the grid, but not too cheap and dungy. Its sign advertised vacancy, free HBO and Wi-Fi, and a price of $59.99 a night. Reggie paid for three nights in cash, and then brought them the keys. They carried their stuff inside and set up Reggie's laptop, on loan for Maggie to write her story.

"You sure about this?" Reggie asked as he logged onto the computer.

"No," Jackson said. "But I've been winging it for quite a while now."

The big man nodded. "Man, I'm going to get the full story, right?"

"In due time."

Reggie nodded again.

"You're the only one who knows we're back in L.A. Want to swing by Grandpa's place and let him know I'm all right?"

"Sure thing. You two need anything else?"

They said no and thanked him extensively. He left and Maggie exhaled. "I guess I should get to work."

Chapter Thirty-Nine

9:14 p.m.

THE DAY AND night passed uneventfully. At least for Jackson. He caught up on world events (and sports—USC had lost a heartbreaker to Notre Dame on Saturday night) and pondered Maggie's safety going forward. He was pretty sure his rationale was solid, but trusting a criminal who had orchestrated killings and kidnappings for profit to play by the rules was risky. So he also did a fair amount of praying.

Maggie typed feverishly, using Reggie's laptop and the Wi-Fi to download her evidence from the cloud. They took one break mid-afternoon to walk the beach and get some fresh air. Maggie talked about living in Mexico—the food, the culture, the pace of life. Jackson told her about working in Hollywood, having to work to convince her he wasn't pulling her leg. Rain moved in late afternoon, and they spent the night writing and watching TV muted so as not to distract her.

The events of the previous week caught up with both of them, and they were ready for bed shortly after nine. Their room had two queen beds, but being raised in a Christian home, Jackson still felt odd sharing sleeping quarters with a woman. He told himself it was in the interest of safety, and called on his self-control. Besides, it wasn't the first time.

"Can I ask you something?" he said once they were in their separate beds, lights off.

"Yeah."

"Are we back to the old Jackson and Maggie?"

"How do you mean?"

"I mean, we had our little Labor Day dispute, and we never really talked about it again. You even said our relationship had 'ended.'"

"I meant temporarily. Because I was in Mexico."

"But had you not gone to Mexico right after Labor Day . . ."

Her silence spoke volumes.

"I guess I'm asking if this issue is going to keep festering under the surface or not?"

"You mean you thinking I have a sickness because I don't believe the same thing you do?"

"I wouldn't word it quite that way," he said, "but yes."

"No," she said finally. "It just hurts, sometimes, that you think of me that way."

"I don't think less of you. Maybe my analogy whiffed. Everybody's—"

"Sick without Jesus, I get it."

"So?"

"So, it's not the most flattering description."

"I'm sorry, Maggie, but it's true. You're a realist. You know you're not perfect. You know I'm not either."

"Imperfection is a long way from sick."

"When you judge by human standards, sure. But God's standard is perfection. Not just perfection, but complete and righteous holiness, the likes of which we can't even fully understand in our sinful state. Compared to that, pretty good is downright awful."

She was quiet.

"And I don't look down on you because you don't believe. It's like somebody once said, I'm merely one beggar telling another beggar where to get bread."

"Now I'm a beggar? Maybe you should quit with the metaphors."

"Right."

"I get it, Jack, I really do. And I'm not offended, not really. But it does take some getting used to the idea."

"I get that."

"I also get your views on sex and marriage."

"Not a deal breaker?"

"No. I just have to come to grips with that being where you stand, and likely not changing, and you have to come to grips with the fact that I might not always be around."

"Meaning what?"

She shrugged. "Meaning if Mr. Right comes along and asks if I'm free, I might just say yes."

"Ouch."

"Well, you've made it pretty clear that there are certain non-negotiables for you when it comes to a serious relationship."

"Is that what you want?"

"No. But I might someday. And if that day comes, I can't guarantee I'll wait for you to change your mind."

"So where does that leave us?"

"The same place we've always been, Jack. As friends without benefits."

*   *   *

Thursday, November 29
7:27 a.m.

WEDNESDAY WAS a drag for Jackson, but Maggie made serious hay. While rain fell steadily outside, she wrote and wrote and wrote. She asked Jackson for advice a few times and ran a couple of sentences past him, but otherwise kept her story to herself. No previews, she said. By Wednesday night, she had finished her final draft, proofed it, and was ready to submit it to Walter.

Thursday dawned bright and clear. Maggie had made one final pass of her article after waking Walter with the news that she was back and had a story for him. He'd agreed to an eight o'clock meeting, so when Reggie picked them up, they headed for 25th and Santa Monica.

On the way, Reggie complained that Starbucks did not count as breakfast, which Jackson had promised when procuring a ride from him the night before. Jackson said that after the meeting, he would take Reggie wherever he wanted. How about the bank? Cute.

As they drove, Jackson and Maggie regaled Reggie with details of their adventure. Maggie gushed about Jackson's survival tactics, especially his actions aboard the plane.

"So it all comes down to turbulence," Reggie said. "If not for that . . ."

"We'd have been deep fried in Veracruz," Jackson said.

"Or you would have Jack Ryaned us out of it some other way," Maggie said.

"We've had this discussion several times," Jackson said to Reggie. "I say it's a good thing God smacked the plane with turbulence."

"And I say it wouldn't have mattered if Jack and Bill had crawled under their chairs and hid," Maggie said.

"You two trying to argue?" Reggie asked. "Man, you all've been together too long."

Walter was holding down a table at Starbucks, and jumped up with a mixture of relief and excitement when he saw Maggie. They embraced, and Jackson studied the editor. Not what he had expected. Tall, thin, at least in his fifties, with wisps of gray hair that made him look kind of like the dad on *Alf.* Without the glasses. Or penchant for cheesy lines. He wore a tan cardigan over a dress shirt, jeans, and loafers.

"Where's Bill?" Walter asked when everyone had been introduced.

"You'd better sit down," Maggie said.

For the next half hour, they talked over coffee—chai tea in Walter's case—and scones, with Maggie retelling everything, including Bill's heroic act to save her life. She said they had no idea where the plane with Bill's body had crashed, likely in the ocean southwest of San Diego. She offered to notify his sister, but Walter said he'd better take care of it, as he could better deal with any legal issues arising from an employee of the paper dying in a foreign country.

When Maggie finished her story, she provided Walter with a thumb drive (bought by Reggie, paid for by Jackson, to be reimbursed by Maggie) containing her article, and he immediately plugged it into his tablet and began skimming. A second copy was saved on Reggie's hard drive. Two more backups existed in the cloud.

While Walter read, Maggie sat back with anticipation, bright eyes smiling at Jackson. After several minutes, Walter looked up. "Maggie, this is incredible."

"Really?"

"Your best work. And talk about an exposé. This could win you a Pulitzer."

"Now you're just putting me on."

"I'm serious, Maggie," he said, dropping his eyes back to the tablet. "This is the story of the year. And your—I don't know what to call it other than a eulogy—of Bill is very good."

They talked business for several minutes, and then Walter set the tablet down. "You have copies of this, I assume?"

"Multiple."

"Good. What about Vasquez and these Mexican organizations—LOVE, GR Limited, Mexól? Are they still a threat to you?"

"We don't think so," Jackson said. "They don't want the story to come out, obviously, but now that she's passed the story to you, if anyone would be a target, it would, uh, be you."

"Assuming whoever's after her knows it's been passed," Reggie said.

"True," Walter said. "I'll put the word out that you've submitted a big story. I don't know who might possibly be after you or how they might be tapped into our circle of knowledge, but once word gets out, that should take the pressure off you."

After making a copy of Maggie's article and saving it on his own thumb drive, Walter uploaded the article remotely to the paper's servers and logged it for reference. It would need the permission of the CEO to be removed. The server would need to be hacked and Walter compromised to suppress the story, and even so, Maggie had multiple copies saved. Vasquez wasn't squelching it.

That settled, Jackson explained their plan later that day to visit the U.S. Customs and Border Protection's port of entry in Long Beach to establish their residency back in the U.S. and also provide them with Maggie's evidence, as a way of fending off any attempts at extradition by the Mexican government. Having them involved would also, Jackson hoped, give Vasquez serious pause about coming after Maggie.

"I might be able to help with that," Walter said. "My cousin works for the State Department. She's a policy advisor. I could pass the word along, grease the wheels a little."

"That would be great," Maggie said.

"Only downside is, considering all that you uncovered with the murder of several U.S. politicians and complicity by Vasquez, it might work the other way. The State Department and DOJ might begin an investigation and seek to have some members of this *Siligo* unit of Vasquez's extradited. It could end up spoiling your story, if word leaks."

"A risk we'll take," Maggie said.

"Okay. I'll give her a call."

Walter covered a few final details and agreed to be in touch. Jackson, Reggie, and Maggie lingered in the parking lot for a moment.

"You still think I need to be sequestered?" Maggie asked.

He shrugged. "I'd give it one more day. Give Walter time to get the word out, give his cousin at State time to put up a firewall. I doubt Vasquez is coming here, but better safe than sorry."

"I'm really getting sick of that motel."

"You can crash on my couch."

"I thought your place wasn't safe."

He shrugged.

"I got a better idea," Reggie said. "You can have my place. I'll crash at the restaurant for a night. Or on J's couch."

"Reggie, I couldn't."

He waved her off.

"After all you've done."

"Just add it to his tab," he said with a nod at Jackson. "Speaking of, I was promised breakfast."

"Yeah, yeah."

"I'm buying," Maggie said.

Jackson grinned. "How generous of you, seeing as how your only money is actually my money."

Reggie cleared his throat.

"Whatever. Let's eat."

*   *   *

Tuesday, January 1
10:43 a.m.

AFTER JACKSON finished his story, Detective Loyola asked him a few more questions. Why were you at the cemetery to begin with? How did the shooting go down? Details before and after the shooting were still fuzzy, and he said as much to her.

"If you do remember anything, please be in touch," she said, handing Jackson her business card.

"I will."

"Thank you for your time."

Sam had stood with arms folded, and now she slowly circled around the bed to the other side, where there was less medical equipment to get in the way. "I can't believe it," she said. "How could you not tell me all this?"

"I'm sorry, Sam."

"I'm not mad at you. I just can't believe you didn't bring it up. 'Hey, Sam, guess what happened! I went to Mexico and played the hero again.'"

"I thought it in bad taste to mention an epic adventure with one woman in front of another."

She rolled her eyes. "It's not like the two of you went on vacation together. I'm not jealous."

He nodded and decided to quit while he was ahead. He'd left out the part about Maggie kissing him multiple times on the Baja beach, her giddy and (mostly) insincere proposal, or the fact that, while Maggie wasn't his girlfriend, she was definitely more than a source.

"So you don't think there's any chance this Vasquez or one of his people shot you?" Sam asked.

"I don't think he would have failed if so. And I'm not the one who wrote the exposé."

"Maggie. You think she's in danger? I can call her."

"No, I don't think so. It's been over a month. Retribution would have come by now."

Sam sat delicately on the edge of the bed, but even so, he winced. She quickly stood.

"Are you okay?"

"I'm fine."

"Does it hurt?"

"You asking as a nurse or a friend?"

"Remember our rules?"

"I thought they only applied once we left the hospital."

"Forget I asked," she said. "I can read it in your face."

Knuckles rapped on the door, and Jackson tried to disguise the pain. But the knuckles were only Reggie's. "Hey, man, how's it going?" He held up a small duffel. "Brought you some clean clothes."

"What happened to the clothes I was wearing?"

"Well the shirt has a bullet hole in it."

"It adds character."

"And they had to cut it off you."

Jackson sighed. "Let me see," he said, and Reggie dropped the bag on his lap. Then, with one of Jackson's arms immobile, he helped him open it. Jeans, socks and drawers, and a plain button-down shirt.

"Doc come by yet?" Reggie asked.

"No, just a couple of detectives," Sam answered. "He's about having a conniption."

"Coverage starts in a little over two hours," Jackson said, "and I'm a traditionalist. I like to see the flyover and national anthem."

"Relax, man. I'm sure they'll let you out."

"I don't know," Sam said, biting her lip. "He's in quite a bit of pain."

"I never said that."

"Yeah," Reggie said, "and you look a little pale too."

"I always look pale to you."

Reggie waved. "Whatever, bro. You need anything else?"

"Just a discharge."

Reggie frowned.

"From the doctors. The other kinds have been taken care of."

Sam shook her head. "Why do guys have to talk about that kind of stuff?"

"Why do girls care?"

"I hope he lets you out soon, man. You're getting snarky."

"You try watching the Rose Bowl half-naked under paper sheets."

"You need help getting him home, change your mind, anything . . ." Reggie said to Sam.

"No, I'll manage. Thanks."

"All right. You call if you need something, J."

"Right."

"Sam."

"Bye, Reggie."

He left, passing Dr. McCarthy on his way out.

"And how are we feeling?" the doctor asked.

"Fit as a fiddle," Jackson answered.

"Um-hmm." McCarthy sat down and checked Jackson's e-chart again. Then he asked about pain, and Jackson told him it was manageable.

"What's manageable on a scale from one to ten?"

"Four," Jackson said, figuring the scale was arbitrary and therefore "four" wasn't really a lie.

McCarthy nodded, entered a few things on the keyboard, then pushed back and faced Jackson. He clapped his hands on his knees. "Well, here's how I see it. All of your vital signs are stable, and if your pain is tolerable, I think we can probably manage that pretty well going forward. But you were shot; your body experienced a major trauma. I'd really like to keep you one more night, just to make sure there aren't any complications. We're going on about ten hours since surgery. That's awfully fast."

"Please, Doc. I'll have a nurse," he said with a look at Sam. "A very good one. Very no-nonsense."

"I appreciate that, but I'm afraid I still can't advise it."

Jackson sighed. "You're saying I have no choice."

Now the doctor sighed. "We can't legally hold you against your will. You are always free to leave AMA."

"AMA?"

"Against Medical Advice. You would have to sign a waiver, indemnifying this hospital and myself personally from any liability."

"I'll do it."

"But I have to say, I strongly advise against it."

Jackson looked to Sam.

"Don't ask me to overrule a doctor," she said.

Jackson sighed again. "Can I be candid?" he asked Dr. McCarthy.

"Of course."

"Are you advising against it because you think I might die or because too many jack-wagon judges award idiot patients millions in lawsuits?"

Dr. McCarthy grimaced. "I'm advising against it because it is my professional judgment that it is not in your best medical interest to be released. I don't foresee you dying if you leave, but it wouldn't be medically prudent."

"I appreciate that, Doc." He looked to Sam again. "But I'll take my chances with Sam."

"Jackson."

"Unless you're changing your mind."

She sighed. "Will it matter? You'll just have Reggie stay with you with me on speed dial if I say no. And I already switched shifts with Tianna."

Jackson grinned and clapped his hands. "Okay, Doc, where do I sign?"

McCarthy continued the pattern of sighing. "I'll have the nurse change your bandage, we'll get you some lunch, and then I'll have the paperwork made ready for you. You'll be home in time for kickoff."

"Thank you."

"But please understand, just because you're leaving the hospital, that doesn't mean you're healed. You're going to be very sore and very tender for a while, and it is essential that you not stress your shoulder."

"Got it."

"And keep in mind, the threshold for stress is quite low. If you move it too much—even just routine, everyday movements that you'd normally think nothing of—it's going to start bleeding again."

"Understood."

"If your pain spikes, if you feel any sort of unusual sensations or are sick at all, or notice anything unusual, you call the hospital immediately."

"Check."

McCarthy nodded. "All right then. You're sure?"

"I'm sure."

"Okay." McCarthy offered a perfunctory smile at Sam and left.

She leaned in close. "How bad is the pain really?"

"You remember *The Sound of Music*?"

Sam frowned. "Yeah, why?"

"'Sixteen Going on Seventeen,'" Jackson sang. Then he grabbed her arm. "No telling. I happen to have the perfect cure at home."

"What's that?"

"A combination of the sun-splashed Rose Bowl in Pasadena, Brent Musburger, and a crockpot full of cheese-filled smokeys."

Chapter Forty

Friday, November 30
7:47 p.m.

JACKSON PAID FOR a mocha and a black coffee and began the process of finagling his way through the crowd. It was a good turnout of several hundred, which was about all that could fit on the cordoned off section of The Pier in Redondo Beach. Jackson excused himself past a group of inebriated co-eds, very much into the grunge garage band currently onstage. One of them was a blonde, at least six feet tall, with hair like Drago. She was Jackson's GPS, a signal to turn left.

Noelle was right where he'd left her, leaning against a light pole and trying not to be squished by a mob of people bigger and taller than her. She smiled when she saw Jackson, and cradled the mocha he handed her for warmth. Then she winced as the band finished their song with an aggressive barrage that sounded like a trash compactor on steroids. A third of the crowd went nuts, and the rest murmured for the next band up.

"Can't be too much longer," Jackson said, although he had no idea what time it was. They had arrived around six-thirty. Seth St. Pierre's band—Farthest First—was one of four playing that night, and had to be better than the first two. Jackson had picked Noelle up shortly before five, as a sunset was painting the sky orange. They'd grabbed a quick bite to eat and headed for The Pier. After over an hour of bad music, they were eager for a change. But apparently, there was still a little more angst-ridden grunge left to be played.

It had been nine days since *Twenty Something* had wrapped shooting in L.A.—for the time being. A slimmed-down crew had headed to Vancouver right after Thanksgiving, where they had begun shooting backstory for a new character. The rest of the crew and cast, including Noelle, was due Monday morning. There was no word on who was fetching Viggo's Canadian coffee.

It had been three days since Jackson and Maggie had returned from Mexico, a day and a half since she'd submitted her story to Walter. She had not, as of mid-afternoon when Jackson last spoke to her, been killed or kidnapped by Leonardo Vasquez as retribution. Thursday night, shortly after Noelle called to invite Jackson to the concert, Maggie had called from Reggie's to update him. Walter's cousin at the State Department had called back, announcing that both the U.S. Department of Justice and the Mexican Attorney General would be making formal announcements of an investigation as early as Monday. Jackson had been shocked at how fast the wheels of justice were turning, and somewhat relieved, for Maggie's sake. If not out of the woods yet, they were close. She'd been satisfied enough to return home Friday morning, and he'd been satisfied enough to not object.

It felt a little surreal, going out with Noelle in the wake of all that had happened, and Jackson had been hesitant to do so when she called. But he'd realized a change and a distraction would be good for him, and it would be his last chance to see her before she headed off to Vancouver. Now, as they stood on The Pier listening to below-average music and sipping warm beverages, he was glad he'd taken her up on the offer, and Mexico was the last thing on his mind.

Talking was almost impossible due to the "music" volume, so Jackson people watched. There were plenty of baby dolls, although more so from a distance than up close. It was typical in La La Land—so many of the women doctored up with excessive makeup and gaudy jewelry, wearing the trendiest of clothes. They had an appeal all right, but it was only surface-level. The overdone façades seemed to get worse the younger the girls got, and Jackson noticed more than a fair share of minors in the crowd. To be honest, there were also a few genuine knockouts dressed to the nines, which was way over the top for this little concert venue. But there were plenty with unique hairstyles and unique getups, everything from a pirate jacket to a Mardi Gras mask and beads to the supposedly stylish sweater with tights to chic tops and skinny jeans. The guys were wearing skinny jeans too, more than a few of them. Jackson saw dozens of Emo haircuts, thin lady sweaters, and at least three guys with nail polish. There was also the regular allotment of hippies and surfers and regular Joes, but on a curve, Jackson felt his masculinity rising fast.

Then there was Noelle. Beige sweater, jeans, and boots that propped her all the way up five-three or five-four. Her hair was wavy, but clipped back in a way that made her appear a little girlish, very carefree. Maybe that was just Jackson observing a lack of tension now that Rod Finley was no longer a problem. Or maybe it was an authenticity he saw in her, a down to earth mindset and natural beauty that didn't need a lot of bravado or costuming. Whatever it was, she was cute, waiting patiently and placidly, cuddling her cup for what little heat it could generate.

The grunge band finished, a few girlish squeals went up in celebration, and then there was silence. Ear-ringing, hum of conversation in the background silence, but it was something. Noelle used the opportunity to lean over, her mouth just below Jackson's ear. "Thank you for coming."

He looked at her and nodded. "Sure."

"I get sick of coming to Seth's concerts by myself."

"That happen a lot? I mean, you go to a lot of his concerts?"

"When I can. Usually they're in some undisclosed location at three in the morning."

Jackson grinned.

"Most of the people I know are either actors busy chasing glamour girls with legs as long as I am tall or crew, and there's an unwritten rule that actors don't date crew persons, and vice versa."

"I'm a crew person," Jackson said.

"You were also an actor," she answered and chanced a sip of her mocha. It was too hot, and she winced. "And this isn't a date. I mean . . ."

Jackson grinned. "I know what you mean." He nodded at the stage. "Look, they're on."

As he spoke, fire shot up from the front of the stage, the same canned little blast that had welcomed every band. It got the crowd's attention and also backed the creeps and squealers up a little. Funny, a bunch of no-name bands, and still they screamed and hollered and clamored for a touch. It spoke to the California condition.

"Oh, there he is," Noelle said when the smoke cleared. "He looks like a dork."

He kind of did, in jeans and an unbuttoned plaid shirt over a gray tee. The clothes were okay. But his hair, about the same length as Noelle's and slightly darker, was pulled back and clipped behind his head. It made room for the guitar strap. Seth St. Pierre played and sang.

Farthest First wasn't bad. They weren't Switchfoot, but they weren't bad. Seth had a sort of grainy, gravelly voice, which would have been lousy for a solo in church, but worked for rock and roll. The lyrics were about girls and having fun, freedom from responsibility, the usual. The music wasn't anything fancy, repeating a lot of the same riffs, changing a key here or there, but not varying too much. Simple, it was at least catchy. Farthest First certainly graded higher than the first two bands.

The crowd seemed to agree, clapping along, cheering, waving their cell phones like idiots during a ballad. Jackson went from watching the dervish that was the other guitarist and the stoned-looking drummer to watching Noelle. She listened to the concert as a sister, smiling most of the time, grimacing a few times when Seth's lyrics turned to screams, occasionally swaying a little with the repeating rhythms.

After four songs, they took a brief break, and Jackson nodded at Noelle's mocha. "Need a refill?"

"What? Oh . . . I completely forgot about it." She took a drink. "It's perfect."

His was long since cold.

"What do you think?" she asked.

"They're pretty good."

"They've come a long way since playing in the basement."

"That had to be fun for you."

"It was okay," she said with shrug and a grin. "They let me sing with them sometimes, and besides, I used to make Seth read scenes with me all the time."

Jackson smiled.

"What about you?" she asked, taking another sip of the mocha. "What'd you and your brother do as kids?"

"Sports, mostly. We had more of the arguing, one-upping sort of a childhood."

"But you were close?"

Jackson nodded. "You?"

"Usually," Noelle said with a grin.

The music continued, and Jackson ran his eyes over the crowd. No reason, just because they had to look somewhere. But they locked onto a shorter guy with blond hair, halfway across the pier. He was dressed in a zip-up hoodie, holding a bottle of beer. And he was staring directly at them. It was too dark to see the eyes, but Jackson knew they were green.

It was Rod Finley.

Jackson leaned down, put his arm gently around Noelle's waist, and whispered in her ear, "Don't panic, but Finley's here."

Her head snapped up, almost bumping into his. "What?"

Jackson flicked his head in Finley's direction. "Over there. Watching us."

"Is that a violation?"

"Technically, I'd say yes. I think that's less than a hundred feet."

"What do we do?"

"Right now, nothing."

"Nothing?"

"We don't want to look like we're baiting him. If he violates the order, we want it to be legit. Just enjoy the concert. I'll keep an eye out."

Noelle bit her lip, and Jackson gave her a slight squeeze before letting go. He watched the stage for a minute, and tried as casually as possible to glance over at Finley. He knew it wouldn't fool anybody, but he couldn't just turn and look.

It didn't matter. Finley was gone.

Jackson surveyed the crowd, but if somebody wanted to hide in the group, it was pretty easy to do. Farthest First exploded into their rockiest song yet, and Jackson was temporarily distracted by the noise and the activity on the stage. When he lowered his eyes, Finley was directly in front of them and coming their way. Jackson instinctively reached for Noelle, who jumped when she saw Finley.

Jackson took a step in front of her and Finley stopped less than ten feet away. "I want to talk to her!" he shouted. Jackson was still hardly able to hear him.

Jackson shook his head. "Not happening. Get out of here."

"Not until I talk to Noelle. I love her!"

Some sap beside him overheard that, and apparently thought it was romantic. She awed and they had a scene developing.

"Noelle, don't let this happen. I—"

Jackson put out his hand as Finley came closer. Several people were watching. "Stop," Jackson said firmly, but Finley pushed past his arm. Noelle shrieked, and Jackson locked his arm around Finley and jerked him backwards. He spun him around and put him to the ground, his beer bottle clanging on the wood of the pier and attracting more attention.

Jackson ignored it and flipped Finley over, pinning his arm behind his back. He put a knee in his back and Finley grunted. It came out more like a whimper.

"Hey, buddy, what are you doing?" a voice in the crowd asked.

"Get off of him," another said.

Jackson turned and addressed the first guy he saw—short black hair, not dressed like a doofus. "Get security," he said. "This guy's violating a restraining order."

"I love her."

"Shut up!" Jackson said, pushing harder.

"Hey, pal—"

"Listen, if I were the bad guy in this, would I be telling you to get security?"

The disturbance had grown, with everyone in sight watching the interaction. Including Noelle, who stood back with her hands over her mouth, eyes wide in horror and fear.

"Will somebody get security!" Jackson hollered.

Several people scurried, and a moment later, a beefy guy in black security gear arrived. "What's going on?"

That's when somebody threw a bottle.

*   *   *

9:42 p.m.

"ARE YOU sure you're all right?" Noelle asked.

They were sitting on her couch, Jackson refusing the cold compress she offered. "I'm fine, Noelle. It only grazed me."

She flopped the compress onto the coffee table and pulled her legs up onto the couch, tucking them under her and sitting sideways to face him. "I can't believe this," she said. "What was he thinking? He had to know we'd press charges."

"I don't think he cared," Jackson said. "He's 'in love.'"

"Please. He's a pervert. And I still don't get why that guy threw the bottle at you."

"Because he'd already emptied half a dozen of them." Jackson shrugged. "Get enough people together, there's always some idiot who wants to fight. He thought he had a good reason."

Noelle tilted her head. "Are you sure you're okay? Let me see that," she said, reaching for his head. She gently turned it so she could see the small bruise just above his eye.

"I'm fine. Really."

"I feel so bad about this."

"I feel bad your concert was ruined."

"It's okay," she said, leaning into the back of the couch. "They've only got four or five really good songs anyhow. I just wish you could have met Seth."

That had been the post-concert plan, but what with the mini-melee, explaining things to the security guard and then the police . . . It hadn't worked out. And seeing Jackson's head, Noelle had insisted they bypass plans for dessert. She had ice cream at her place, and she was adamant about getting an icepack on his head.

"Is he like you, a celebrity who doesn't act like the typical celebrity?" Jackson asked.

Noelle eyed him for a moment. "We're not really celebrities. And if he was, he'd act like it," she added with a smile. "But he thinks all the people I work with are like . . ."

"Shawn Thomas?"

"I didn't want to say it," she giggled. "But yeah. You're different though."

"So are you. But then again, the only other actress I really know is Jess."

"Funny you should mention her."

"Oh?"

"She's come down with diphtheria."

"Really?"

"So she claims. She also claims it was because you made us all act in the rain."

"Wasn't that like a month ago?"

"She got a cold which settled into her chest and I don't know. She's apparently seeing a specialist Monday and won't be able to get to Vancouver. Viggo's scrambling to cover for her, but from what I hear—which is ninety-nine percent gossip and rumor—it's contentious."

"I almost feel bad."

"Don't. Jess wouldn't be Jess without drama." She sat up. "If I can't get you to put ice on that, can I at least get you some ice cream?"

"Sure."

"I have chocolate or peach."

"Let's go with peach."

"It's fat free."

"It'll do."

Noelle grinned as she got up and went to the kitchen. Jackson felt the bruise on his head. It had gotten crazy for a minute, and he didn't know who had thrown the bottle. He trusted the security guard to take care of that. He had immediately jumped off Finley and stood to protect Noelle, which had been taken by several as an act of hostility, and more jostling and pushing had ensued.

Eventually things had gotten sorted out without any further injuries. But his head did kind of hurt.

"What do you think will happen to Finley?" Noelle asked from the kitchen.

"I don't know. He didn't just cross a line, he took his stalking to a new level—personal contact. And it ended in a fight." He shrugged. "I wouldn't be surprised if he gets jail time."

"I still can't believe all this has happened to me." She brought two bowls into the living room.

"Thank you."

She sat down with her bowl, at the other end of the couch but facing Jackson. "Why would he choose to stalk me? Nobody even knows me. I had one moderately successful movie and a bunch of bit parts."

"Everybody has to start somewhere."

Noelle smiled. "That's what Seth used to say. When I was depressed by just doing commercials and spot roles. He said that doing commercials was good for my career because even if I was on TV, I'd be on one of the networks and ninety percent of the world would be watching something else at the time. But commercials play across all networks all the time. He always thought it was a great way to get discovered."

"Looks like he was right."

She stirred her ice cream for a moment. "He usually is."

"My brother always thought he was right," Jackson said.

Noelle licked off her spoon. "Was? What happened?"

Jackson swallowed a spoonful of his ice cream. "He was killed in an explosion a year and a half ago. Along with my parents."

Noelle's eyes were so wide they threatened to burst. "Oh no." She let her bowl fall into her lap. "I'm so sorry."

"Yeah, me too."

"I had—We should talk about something else."

"No, it's okay," Jackson said. "My therapist says I should talk about it. About them."

Noelle took a bite of her ice cream, slowing sucking it off the spoon. "What was his name?"

"Grant."

"Did he look like you?"

Jackson grinned. "Only at birth."

Noelle spooned another bite.

"He was close-cut, clean-shaven, dressed preppy. Then there's me."

"Grayson."

He smiled. "Yeah."

"What did he do?"

"He was a police officer."

"Crime fighting runs in the family, huh?"

"Yep. And Dad worked for the Office of Naval Intelligence for almost thirteen years over two different stints."

"What about your mom?"

"She was a mom first and foremost. She was involved in church, with charities, craft fairs. She loved crafts."

"My mom likes to sew. Actually likes it. Every Christmas she'd make Dad, Seth, and me something special to wear. Shirts, hats, scarves."

"That's neat."

"Not really. She doesn't have the best fashion sense," Noelle said with another giggle.

"So what do your folks think about you and your brother's celebrity status?" he asked with a wink, expecting the look she gave him at the word celebrity.

Noelle licked off her spoon. "They've always been supportive. They encouraged us to pursue our dreams. But they were also careful to make sure we had something else to fall back on, that we knew that acting and singing weren't guarantees. They kept us balanced."

"Either of them ever come to Seth's concerts?"

"His style of music isn't really their thing. And they say concerts are too loud, but they both claim they listen to his CD."

"Claim?"

"I saw it on the shelf last time I was at Dad's house. Still shrink-wrapped."

Jackson grinned.

"What'd your parents think about you being a private eye? Were they worried?"

"They didn't know." He leaned forward to place his empty bowl on the table. "I got my license just before they died. I was going to tell them, as a surprise."

Noelle looked down at her ice cream. "I've always been lousy at knowing what to say," she said.

"You're doing just fine."

She looked up. Then at his bowl. "You want some more?"

"No, thanks. I should probably get going, actually."

"You don't have to," she said, and promptly yawned. It scrunched her nose, very adorable, and caused Jackson to grin. "I mean it," she said. "It's nice to have a real conversation with somebody, something that isn't about contracts and plastic surgeries and who's sleeping with whom."

Jackson shrugged. "Okay."

Noelle grinned and settled sideways into the couch again.

They talked more about their childhoods and siblings, Noelle's parents' divorce, career aspirations, and skirted around the edge of a discussion about marriage and a future family. Before Jackson knew it, it was midnight, and Noelle's cute yawns were more frequent. He again said he should be going, and this time stood.

Noelle walked him to the door, and seemed to bounce on the balls of her feet as they said goodbye. "Thanks for tonight," she said. "I mean, for stopping him. I'm really sorry about your head."

"It's all part of the job," Jackson said.

"That's just it. It wasn't a job. It was a favor. And I insist you tell me how I can pay you back. That was the original deal, remember?"

"Let's try for dessert again sometime," Jackson said. "If I can avoid a head injury."

She laughed.

"Not that I didn't enjoy the ice cream," he added.

"It's a deal. And seriously, thank you for everything."

"You're welcome."

"Um . . ." She leaned on her other foot. "Don't take this the wrong way, okay?"

"Okay," he said hesitantly.

Noelle stood on her toes to reach up and give him a quick nip on the cheek. She smiled as she stepped back. "Good night."

"Good night."

The midnight air was cool and crisp, and Jackson hesitated on the stoop of the apartment building. Funny, he thought, how a kiss on the cheek could take away the pain in his forehead.

Chapter Forty-One

Sunday, December 9
1:44 p.m.

PHILADELPHIA HAD JUST nipped Washington in an overtime thriller, and, after going to the bathroom and refilling his drink, Jackson had settled back onto the couch for a Chargers-Raiders tilt when the doorbell rang. He watched the rest of the play on his way to the door, expecting Connie. She needed help with her Christmas tree, a twelve-foot-high monster that she could never get out of storage or erected in the living room without help. She'd been hinting at it for weeks, and he knew that sooner or later she would call in another favor.

Instead it was Maggie. She wore jeans and an orange Henley under a leather jacket. In one hand, she held a six-pack of Coors. In the other, a rolled up newspaper.

"What's up?" Jackson asked.

"Brought you a paper," she said.

He took the paper from her, that day's *Los Angeles Times*. Inch-high black letters across the top proclaimed MEXICAN OIL CONSPIRACY LINKED TO POLITICAL MURDERS. Jackson looked up. "So, uh, what, did you pick up a route for some extra cash?"

"Ha-ha. Invite me in."

"Say, Maggie, would you like to come in?"

He followed her into the house and they sat on the couch. He muted the TV and Maggie waited silently while he read.

> *In 2008, North Dakota Senator Ted Simpson was pulling a wagon of hay across his ranch outside Minot, North Dakota, when he lost consciousness and drove his tractor into a muddy ditch. His son found him unresponsive and called 9-1-1, only to realize his father was already dead. Senator Simpson's cause of death was determined to be a massive heart attack, even though he was only 57 and in peak physical condition.*

In 2010, Mississippi Congresswoman-Elect Dominique Jolie was driving her newly leased Honda Accord along a desolate stretch of The Natchez Trace Parkway northeast of Jackson, Mississippi, when she lost control, drove off an embankment, and plunged into the Ross R Barnett Reservoir, dying almost instantly. The coroner found nearly twice the legal limit of alcohol in her system and pronounced her death a casualty of drunk driving. But Congresswoman-Elect Jolie was not a drinker.

Earlier this year, Texas Congressman Booker Dade was flying his single-engine Cessna 152 aircraft from Houston to the capitol in Austin when he crashed in a field just north of La Grange, Texas. Dade was killed on impact, and the NTSB ruled (due to perfect weather conditions and no discernable mechanical failures) that pilot error was to blame. But Dade was an accomplished pilot with over 2,000 hours of stick time.

Three U.S. politicians. Three seemingly accidental deaths. Three families who don't buy it.

And they aren't the only ones.

He looked up. "Killer opening."

Maggie raised her eyebrows in response.

Mexican politicians have also recently fallen prey to an unusually high mortality rate, even for their country. Three more deaths, two kidnappings where the victim was never seen again, and more bribes than, well, is typical for the Mexican government. Who is behind these seemingly random deaths, and why? And what's the connection to Senator Simpson, Congresswoman-Elect Jolie, and Congressman Dade?

The answer goes back six and a half years, to the discovery of a potentially enormous oil reserve beneath a four-hundred-foot-deep cenote* *in the Mexican province of Veracruz. What follows is an epic tale of collusion, corruption, and carnage by various Mexican corporations and private individuals, all in the name of profit. Sadly, it is not fiction.*

Jackson looked up again. "You have a very foreboding style."

"I tease."

"I hadn't noticed."

"You want a drink before they get warm?" she asked.

"I'm all for congratulating you, Mags, but I still don't imbibe."

She spun the six-pack around, revealing a trio of cream soda bottles. Jackson grinned and reached for one. "Now you're talking."

316

Maggie removed a Coors and carried the remaining four bottles to the kitchen. "You didn't have plans today, did you?"

"Um, I do sort of later. A double date."

Maggie raised an eyebrow.

"Remember Brady Kane?"

"The guy whose wife you rescued?" She returned to the living room as the refrigerator door closed behind her.

He nodded. "I've been monitoring his rehab for a few months, and tonight he gets to see his wife for the first time, with me as chaperone."

"He ready?"

"We'll see. I think so, but you never know. Anyhow, that's not until later."

"Good. We had a little party down at the office, but I feel like celebrating some more."

"What'd you have in mind?"

"First I want your review."

Jackson took a swig of soda and returned to the article. Maggie gave a little more setup, just enough to entice the reader, before recounting her journey to Mexico back in September. Part one of her story spanned her initial investigation to the point of being hired by Mexól VP Rafael Vasquez. (It did not stipulate how she acquired the job.) In typical Maggie style, she ended with something of a cliffhanger, leaving the reader wanting more. He or she would have to wait another week until the second half of her story released.

Jackson folded the paper and reached for his bottle. Maggie faced him on the couch, beer in hand. "What'd you think?"

"Walter's right . . . Pulitzer stuff."

"Do you even know what they give a Pulitzer for?"

"Apparently almost anything."

She backhanded him.

He tossed the paper on the couch "So how do we celebrate?"

"I thought I'd take you out for dinner," she said, "but if you have plans, that can wait for another time."

"Take *me* out for dinner? Isn't it supposed to be the other way around?"

"Yeah, well, I still figure I owe you."

"Forget it, Maggie."

"Besides, that's not what I meant. You risked your life, Jack."

"There've been larger wagers made."

Maggie's eyes bored into him. "You're not still beating yourself up over what happened back in September, are you?"

"That, and it's almost Christmas. Holidays get me down lately."

Maggie answered by taking a swig of beer.

"How have you been?"

She sighed. "The funeral was hard. I was okay until . . . until I saw Bill's sister. I couldn't help feeling it was my fault she had to go through that."

"It's not."

"I know, but still. I talked to her for a while, at the dinner. I felt I owed her an explanation. She was so gracious, so understanding, and yet . . . I could see it almost destroyed her not knowing what had happened to him, where his body was. The loose strings."

"Tell me about it."

Maggie put her hand on his arm. "I'm sorry, Jack. I didn't—"

"Forget it. And enough sadness. This is the day of your life, so let's celebrate."

She nodded her assent.

"What do you want to do?"

"It's a nice day." She shrugged. "The beach, the pier, maybe get on my bike and blast through the desert."

He nodded at her as she tipped up her bottle of Coors again. "How many of those have you had?"

"First one."

"And how many Bloody Marys at the little luau with the folks from the *Times*?"

"Bloody Marys? Really?"

"How many?"

"I had a little champagne."

"I'll pass on the bike ride, thanks."

"So you can drive then."

"Never driven a motorcycle."

"Then we'll take your car. I don't care. I just want to do something."

He cast one more glance at the TV, then nodded. "Okay. Let's go."

*   *   *

7:27 p.m.

JOHNNY ROCKETS was not some sophisticated, upscale, Santa Monica original, but their burgers were good. Jackson picked up Brady, and they met up with Sam and Stephanie out front. After not seeing his wife for almost four and a half months, the first thing Brady did was take her hand and drop to his knees in front of her. Jackson assumed Brady was apologizing, and kneeling also put him on the same level as his unborn child. Stephanie was showing enough to be obvious, and they spent a few moments hugging and crying. It was all a good start, but nothing more.

It had been 135 days since Jackson had delivered his ultimatum to Brady: get help or never see your wife and baby again. Brady had spent the subsequent four months working on dealing with a violent temper, and, according to Jackson and the counselors with whom he routinely checked in, had made substantial progress. Still, Jackson had trepidation about allowing him unrestricted access to Stephanie. His plan was to supervise a few more meetings before allowing her to move back into their apartment sometime before Christmas. Then, it would be all on Brady.

The four ate dinner, the conversation at times stilted, at times awkward. But as the meal wore on, it became obvious that Brady wasn't hiding anything because of shame. He owned up to his mistakes and took full responsibility in front of everyone. He claimed he hated the old Brady, and would do anything to make sure he never resurfaced.

After eating, they took a walk along the Third Street Promenade. Two weeks before Christmas, the promenade was festive and lively, with lights on the trees and the old-fashioned lampposts creating a cozy, Hallmark-movie sort of feel. Jackson and Sam lingered a little ways behind, giving Brady and Stephanie some privacy.

As they walked, Jackson's mind played over the last few weeks, which had seen something of a return to normalcy. No acting. No trip to Mexico to rescue journalists. No hiding away in off-the-grid motels. While Maggie had remained safe over the last two weeks, as of that afternoon she'd heard nothing more on the joint Department of Justice-Mexican AG investigation into Vasquez, Mexól, or the rest of that rat's nest.

Along with the relaxed pace of life, boredom had crept in, and with it, memories and images from Nevada. Jackson had made progress in three months, but what he had done still haunted him. So did the loss of his family, an excruciating reality driven home each holiday. He'd made progress healing there too, but was starting to wonder if he was destined to be consumed by an aching pain the rest of his life.

The night was cool and crisp, and as they trudged slowly along, Sam wrapped her arm around Jackson's. "In case you were wondering, this is the real Jackson," she said.

He looked down at her vivid blue eyes. "How's that?"

"All that happened in Nevada, all that you did . . . That's not you. It's what you did—what you had to do. But this . . . this is you. What you did for them."

He narrowed his eyes, wondering if she had read his mind. They took a few steps.

"I beat up a guy, threatened him, and then checked in with his counselor twice a month," Jackson said. "You're the one who took her in for four months."

"Downplay it if you want," she said. "But I know the truth about you." She hugged his shoulder as they slowed their pace slightly. "And deep inside, I think you know it too."

Deep inside. Where he was hurting. Where he was still raw.

He didn't bother to correct her.

Deep inside was where it was worst of all.

*　　　　　*　　　　　*

Sunday, December 16
7:01 p.m.

SNOW WAS falling in New England. Hard. Hard enough that the Sunday night game between the Patriots and the Jets had disintegrated into a backyard free-for-all. Artistically awkward, it was still entertaining, and the football-minded patrons at the bar at Finn McCool's Irish Pub on Main Street were hollering like they had a legitimate rooting interest. Nobody in California cared about the Jets, but a lot of people everywhere hated the Patriots. Hence the hollering.

It had not been snowing in Santa Monica or along the Malibu Coast. The day had been brilliantly sunny and unseasonably warm, and Jackson and Maggie had celebrated the release of the conclusion of her article by enjoying a drive along the base of the Santa Monica Mountains and watching a crisp sunset from a scenic overlook off the famed Mulholland Drive. Then they'd headed to Finn's, where Maggie had treated Jackson to all of the potato skins he could eat—along with a delicious steak sandwich. They had kept an eye on the game and an ear on the Irish brogues of the staff and many of the patrons, as well as live music from a local Irish folk band.

The Jets scored on a fourth-and-one touchdown run by Tim Tebow. At the bar, half of the patrons cheered, half cursed, all drank. In their booth off toward the corner, Jackson and Maggie had long since finished dinner. She had paid the bill and drained her last drop of Draught Guinness. It was her third, and while Jackson didn't think she was drunk, she certainly was a little looser than normal.

"You ready to go?" he asked.

"Sure."

They headed outside and halfway down the block, to where Jackson had parked in front of the Omelette Parlor. The night was still balmy, and they took their time. Maggie's face displayed the same, subconscious smile it had all day, an afterglow born of success and accomplishment. When they reached the Granada, she stopped and leaned against the passenger door. "Where to now?"

"I thought I'd take you home," he said.

"My home or your home?"

"Yours," he said.

"What about my bike? It's still at your place."

"I don't know, you think you can balance right now?"

Maggie eyed him. "You wanna try me."

"I don't hit drunk girls," he said, walking around the car.

Maggie turned. "I am not drunk."

"Spell Ecclesiastes."

"You first."

"I wasn't the one throwing back pints like Samwise Gamgee."

"I've got a better idea," she said across the roof of the car. "Dessert."

"You got a place in mind?"

L.A. had tons of unique, *Food Network*-praised eateries that boasted vast and inventive dessert options. But they settled for a Baker's Square on the way back to Maggie's apartment. After ordering slices of pie, Jackson asked what was next for her, the rising star.

"Well," she said, folding her hands, "Walter has hinted several times at my very own column."

"A column. On what?"

"Whatever," she said. "I won't be tied down by having to report. I can opine on the news, current events, politics."

"That's great, Maggie."

"And I didn't even tell you yet, but I got a call from CNN. They want an exclusive interview."

"You're serious?"

She nodded and grinned as a waitress brought them pie.

"What about you?" she asked. "What's next in your life?"

"That is the question," he answered cutting into a wedge of cherry pie. "I'm certainly not getting a reprisal on *Twenty Something.*"

"I watched it this week," she said.

"You didn't."

"It's pretty awful."

"I know."

"Which one's your girlfriend?"

"That's cute, a put-down to disguise your jealousy."

Maggie deposited a decadent bite of chocolate cream pie into her mouth.

"She's the incredibly cute blonde," Jackson said.

"The angry one who likes leather?"

"Yep."

"She is cute."

"Even more so when she's not playing Roxie."

"Crushing on an actress. You're such a cliché."

"Hmm, and here I thought it was the light making your eyes green."

They finished the pie and returned to the car. As they were buckling in, Maggie's phone dinged. She looked down at it as her other hand absentmindedly inserted the seatbelt into the buckle. "Hmm."

"What's 'hmm'?"

She turned the phone so he could see the text on the screen.

They are coming.

"They," Jackson said. "They who?"

"I don't know. Third one this week. Same number. First one just said 'They know.' Second one, 'Your in danger.' Your, not you're."

"Same number for all three?"

Maggie nodded.

"They being Vasquez?"

"Maybe. But why would he be coming now? And who would be warning me? My only source in Vasquez's circle was Rodrigo, and he's been compromised."

"When did the first one come?"

"Last Sunday, late. Eleven, eleven-thirty."

"And the second?"

"Thurs—Wednesday. Same time. I saw it the next morning."

"'They know,' 'Your in danger,' and 'They are coming'?"

"Yeah."

"Have you called the cops?"

"They're just texts, Jack."

"That could be seen as death threats. Given what you've been through . . . At least let me have Mouse track them down, see where they came from. We're getting good at that sort of thing."

"We'll see."

Jackson drove back to Maggie's apartment complex, feeling suddenly tense. And upset that his lovely afternoon and evening had been ruined by this anxiety.

As always, Jackson walked her up to her apartment on the third floor. As almost always, she lingered by it. "Want to come in for a little while? No tricks."

"Sure."

She punched in the code and opened the door. Entering the apartment first, she flipped on the lights and immediately screamed.

Chapter Forty-Two

8:49 p.m.

IT WASN'T A terribly girlish scream—more an exclamatory shout of surprise. As a result, Jackson wasn't quite as on edge as he should have been.

"What is it?" he asked, pushing through the door. He stopped in his tracks when he saw two men snooping through Maggie's stuff. One was in the darkened bedroom, going through her bureau drawers with a flashlight. The other was in the living room, sorting through mail, magazines, and books.

Or rather, that was conceivably what they had been doing. Both now looked at Jackson and Maggie, and for a few seconds, the foursome stared at each other, frozen, wondering what to do and what the others would do. Jackson reacted first.

Elbowing Maggie to the moderate safety of the galley kitchen, he charged the guy in the living room. Neither of the men had weapons that he could see, and while this guy wasn't small, he didn't look like a heavyweight either. Jackson leapt through the air, over Maggie's coffee table, and crashed into the guy as he stood to fight. They fell to the ground, grazing the edge of her entertainment console with a crack and rolling hard into the wall.

The guy smelled funny, like fish and either cheap cologne or cheap booze. As they grappled to gain control, Jackson quickly determined the guy wasn't a skilled fighter, but he had a brute strength that was slowly gaining the upper hand. He reached for Jackson's neck, which provided an opening for Jackson to swing his left arm. It missed its intended target, the man's jaw, but draped over his arms and pulled them down. The guy lost his balance and his control, and Jackson rolled until his right shoulder was off the floor. Then he threw a hook that landed flush on the cheek.

The man rolled over, dazed at the least, and Jackson stood to pounce. Before he got the chance, a mass collided into him from the side, knocking him against the wall. He hit his head, not hard enough to stun him, but hard enough to hurt and to fuel his rage.

Ignoring any tactical fighting points he had learned, Jackson brawled like a caged animal, punching, kicking, and sending his hardest body parts in the general direction of their softest. And he was holding his own, too, until the threesome lost their balance and tumbled over.

Tasting blood in the corner of his mouth, Jackson threw an elbow at the nearest thing to him and pushed to his feet. He never made it.

Out of nowhere, something cracked against the side of his head. His last thought as he pitched backwards was to hope that Maggie had taken the opportunity to make an escape, because there was nothing more he could do to protect her.

*   *   *

9:36 p.m.

"YOU SURE you don't want us to call an ambulance?"

Jackson looked at the trio of police officers, then blinked his right eye to make the two flanking officers disappear. "Yeah, I'm fine."

The officer nodded without conviction and made eye contact with his partner—a real one, not a blurred copy. The two of them headed for the door. A guy in a navy jacket was dusting for prints in Maggie's bedroom, while a guy in a polo shirt that matched the jacket was taking pictures in the living room. A detective with a loosened tie, no jacket, was reviewing his notes on his tablet, while his lady partner was in parts unknown. Jackson leaned against the wall and tried to keep the room from spinning.

The last hour was a blur. He remembered Finn-Skins, Tim Tebow in the snow, pie, and returning to Maggie's apartment all with relative clarity. And he remembered blow-for-blow the fight with the two intruders. And then something had cracked against his skull, and from that point on, it was only fragments: Waking up and feeling like a freight train was chugging through his head trying to get out. Police sirens that made the pain in his head worse. Introductions. Questions. He may or may not have asked the female detective for a refill of coffee. The only constant was dizziness—he was dizzy now and pictured all of those fragments taking place in a Tilt-A-Whirl.

The male detective chatted with the photographer for a moment, and that seemed to signal the departure of the crime scene guys. They brushed past Jackson with a nod, and then the detective sauntered over. "Anything else you can remember, Mr. Douglas?"

Jackson frowned. He couldn't remember how much he'd even told him. So he shook his head—big mistake—no. The detective handed him a card. "Call me if that changes."

Jackson refrained from nodding and pocketed the card. The detective hollered for his partner—some complex name that sounded like Jasmolina—and she appeared through the kitchen. They gave Jackson the cop nod and left. He had the vague sense to lock the door behind them. Then he leaned back against the door, closed his eyes, and willed himself to remember more since the fight.

He knew he had blacked out for quite a while, because the cops had already been on their way in when he woke up. And Maggie—she had been there. She had been crouched over him when he woke. So where was she now? When had she gotten lost in the shuffle?

Jackson pushed away from the door. "Maggie?"

Nothing.

He checked in the bathroom and bedroom, both empty, lights way too bright. He pushed through the living room and into Maggie's small dining room. The windows were black, reflecting everything inside, and he didn't spot her until he pulled open the sliding glass door.

She stood on her small balcony, staring blankly out at the city below. The breeze ruffled her hair and helped revive Jackson's groggy brain. He stepped beside her. "You okay?"

"He came for me," she said without turning.

"Who?"

"Vasquez."

"You recognized those guys?"

"No."

Jackson looked down over the railing and wanted to puke. He lifted his head and stared out at the distant mountains, a black form separating the million lights of the city from the glow of the San Fernando Valley beyond them.

"Then how . . ."

"Who else would it be?" She shook her head. "I need to disappear."

"Disappear?" Jackson knew his mind was functioning a little slowly.

326

Maggie finally turned to face him. "They obviously found me. And we were wrong—they didn't just want to suppress my story. I don't know why they waited, but—I have to vanish until . . ." She threw out her arms and dropped her shoulders, then turned and went inside.

Frowning, Jackson followed. Maggie stopped in the living room, looking around in disbelief for a few moments. Then she headed for the bedroom. Jackson followed again.

"What are you doing?" he asked.

"Packing. I've got a short window now. They'll lay low since the cops were here, but by daybreak, I've got to be in the wind."

He sat on her bed, trying to hold his head together and trying to make sense of Maggie's fears and the nagging in his brain.

"Where can I go?" she asked. "I have nobody to turn to." She turned around. "And don't take that the wrong way, but you're as hot as I am."

Jackson ran his fingers through his hair.

"What, no smart-aleck reply?"

He raised his eyes.

"Jack, are you okay?"

"I've been better."

She dropped her clothes back in her drawer and knelt in front of him. "I thought—I'm sorry. You told everybody you were fine, so I didn't think anything was wrong. I completely forgot."

"I'm having a little trouble remembering myself."

Maggie looked at him for a moment. "We should get you to a doctor."

"I'll be okay, Maggie."

"You look hungover."

"I wouldn't know." He pushed himself up. "I'm fine. Just a little dazed."

She nodded and resumed ransacking her drawers.

"Possibly concussed. Any idea what they were looking for?"

She shook her head. "Not a clue."

"Doesn't that strike you as odd?"

She shrugged. "Where would you go?"

"Huh?"

"If you had to disappear. Which might not be a bad idea, you know?"

"Hawaii."

"Hawaii?"

He shrugged. It didn't hurt too bad. "I was born there. I'd get a shack by the beach and buy a few Kamekona types to keep an eye on any muscle coming in from the mainland."

"Not bad. But I'm thinking somewhere a little less American."

"So what, you're just going to go all 'Holiday in Cambodia' for the rest of your life?"

"I don't know," she said, dropping a pile of clothes on her bed and moving to the closet. "You'll forgive me if I'm panicking a little bit."

"I don't know. Something doesn't wash here, Maggie."

She didn't turn from her closet. "How do you mean?"

"I mean, these guys weren't lying in wait to kill you. They were searching for something. And after they clobbered me, they didn't whack you. They ran."

She turned and leaned against the wall. "Meaning?"

"Meaning, if this was a hit, you'd be dead."

"Maybe they were afraid of witnesses showing up. You were fighting with them for a while."

"Okay, but if this was Vasquez, like you said, why'd he wait so long to come after you?"

"I don't know. Letting the heat die down."

"And those guys—they weren't Hispanic. I didn't hear what he said, but the one guy sounded Baltic. Maybe Russian."

A shadow passed over Maggie's face, but she said nothing. Instead she crossed her arms and leaned a little harder into the wall.

"And Vasquez wouldn't be looking for anything. The story's out— everything you have is in last week's and today's paper, and they were more than incriminating enough. What could you have that they would want?"

She shrugged.

"I don't know, Maggie—My thoughts are kind of like Samson's foxes right now, but . . . this doesn't add up."

"So what, you think it was just a random break-in and robbery? My apartment?"

"I don't know."

"Common refrain."

"I know. I just think—Before you do something rash like running off to Goa, you should take a few minutes to think about it. Sleep on it, maybe. See what the cops turn up tomorrow. They run the prints, and maybe it's local thugs after all. Misguided Russian terrorists or something."

Maggie's eyes narrowed. "By morning, my best chance to get away unseen is gone. I'm nervous every minute that goes by."

"I'll stay," he said.

"What?"

"I'll stay and make sure you're safe tonight. Tomorrow we'll check in with the cops and see what they've found. And then, if you still want to go all Richard Kimball, you can do it with a little planning and backstopping."

Maggie chewed her lip for a moment, thinking. "Okay. But if I end up dead, my blood's on your hands."

"It'll have to take a number."

Chapter Forty-Three

Monday, December 17
1:48 a.m.

JACKSON COULDN'T IDENTIFY the exact moment, but the ringing in his head silenced. And his constant pacing and thinking—and maybe the three cups of coffee—had alleviated the dazed and dizzy feeling. However, all his thinking had muddled his brain. If Vasquez and his cronies had been behind the break-in, there were too many unanswered questions. Why hadn't they killed Maggie if revenge was their motive? Why had they waited to come until now? What had the duo been looking for? As much as he hated coincidences, Jackson couldn't help thinking the break-in was related to something else.

But what?

A random robbery, while plausible, didn't seem likely. Not at nine o'clock on a Sunday night. And not when the intruders had been found going through Maggie's documents and clothes drawer. On top of which, Maggie had confirmed nothing was missing.

That left Maggie's past. Jackson knew little, other than that she had grown up in New York State and had left home under less than ideal circumstances. She hadn't revealed anything else. And frankly, teenagers come of age left home under less than ideal circumstances all the time. It didn't mean anything sinister was going on.

The fourth cup of coffee didn't help much. It did manage to keep Jackson awake, as did the muted TV and his continuous pacing and mulling. Aside from the presence of a Korean family, he felt like Hawkeye in the self-named episode of *M*A*S*H*.

Maggie's door opened and she stepped out, wearing boxer shorts and a tank top. She ran a hand through slightly mussed hair and spotted Jackson, currently in the living room. "You're still up," she said.

He turned from the window. "I think there's some Chinese proverb about sleeping guards. What about you?"

"Can't sleep." She looked at his coffee cup. "There more?"

"I made a full pot."

Maggie poured herself a cup and sat on the arm of a living room chair. She took a long, slow drink of coffee. "How's your head?"

"Still attached."

She nodded, took another drink. "What are you thinking?"

"I still don't think this is Vasquez."

"Then who?"

"I don't know," Jackson said. He waited for her eyes to cut to him before asking, "Who else could it be?"

"You're asking me?"

Jackson nodded.

"How would I know?" Maggie asked.

He shrugged. "You're twenty-eight. I've known you less than two years."

Maggie stared into her coffee mug.

"Is there something I should know?" he asked quietly.

"It's ancient history," she said. "At least, I thought it was, until you said the guy had a Russian accent."

Jackson leaned back on the arm of the other chair and waited. Maggie took another drink of coffee, then stood up. "I'm going to need something stronger."

She dumped the coffee and grabbed a bottle of Coors from the refrigerator. Jackson said nothing while she popped the cap and took a long swig. Then she dropped into the far chair. Jackson took the near one and waited for her.

"My family runs a restaurant outside of Kingston," she said.

"Jamaica?"

"New York. Upstate. It's named Troika, which is Russian for three or a triumvirate. It's been in the family for years. Like everybody, I worked there part-time while I was in high school, waiting tables, bussing, in the kitchen. On school nights, I'd bring my homework along and do it in the back or at a table before or after my shift. Sometimes I even just hung out and studied there on free nights."

Jackson nodded along. Maggie continued. "My uncle Konnie—"

"Uncle Konnie?"

"Short for Konrad. He let me use his office, attached to which was a small, private room."

"What kind of private room?"

She shrugged. "A hovel really. Pull-out sofa, juice can of a bathroom." She shrugged again. "Anyhow, finals week my junior year I was dead. Stressing over tests, working tons of hours. I was trying to study one Sunday night, but I just couldn't. So I thought I'd take a catnap on the sofa in the back." She took another pull on the Coors. "It turned into more than a catnap. When I woke up, the place was completely dark. They must have forgotten I was there and missed me when they were locking up, never thinking that there would be anyone on the sofa in Konnie's room."

Jackson exhaled. He'd had this nagging feeling—for more than just the last few minutes—that Maggie's past had a secret, and one that was kind of dark. Hearing about an uncle's private sleeping quarters gave him chills, but it didn't sound like the story was going that way.

"Then I heard something. I was not a jumpy teenager," she said, making eye contact with Jackson for the first time. "And this wasn't a bump in the night. I froze, and that's when I saw a guy dressed in black entering Uncle Konnie's office."

"Burglar?"

Maggie nodded. "He was there for like three minutes, and I didn't dare breathe."

"He didn't see you?"

"It was completely black except for his flashlight, and I was in the back corner of the room. I couldn't see much of what he was doing without moving, but I suspected he was opening the safe. And when he left, there was a knapsack or a backpack over his shoulder."

"They keep a lot of cash in the restaurant?"

"Not usually. But Sunday would be the night to hit it, because they take everything to the bank in the morning for the previous night. On Sundays—"

"Everything since Friday would be in there."

Maggie nodded. "Well, I figured if somebody was robbing Uncle Konnie, I should see if I could ID the guy, be the hero. I snuck out of the back room after him and crept over to the front window. I saw the guy getting into the passenger seat of a car. Real idiots, they'd parked under a streetlight, and I could see his face." Maggie looked up. "It was my cousin Brendan. Konnie's son."

"Whoa."

"Yeah, whoa."

"What'd you do?"

"I told my dad. He said he'd take care of it, but nothing happened. I asked him about it later, and he said not to worry about it. Again nothing happened."

Jackson nodded. Maggie took a drink. "So I went to the police. I know it's the lousiest of the lousy who squeal on family, but he was stealing from Uncle Konnie."

"You know he was stealing?"

"Yeah. I heard people talking, coworkers. Word was out, Troika had been robbed."

Jackson nodded again.

"The police said they would look into it, but—"

"Nothing happened."

"You got it."

"Why?"

"Because my family is big in those parts, Jackson. The cops ask for permission before investigating."

"I see."

"It's a mess. But impetuous little Miss Journalist-to-be wasn't about to be outdone by local politics and cover-ups. I wrote about it all in the school paper. To this day I'm not sure how somebody didn't keep it from going to print, but it was my first exposé."

"How'd that go?"

"Not great. I outed my cousin for robbery, my family for covering it up, and the local cops for bowing to the family. And my story was explicit. I gave details. I've never seen my dad so mad. I thought he was going to crack my skull."

Jackson felt compelled to ask. "Did he . . . hit you?"

"No, he never did. I was lucky that way. I think hitting is pretty common among my relations. But Dad didn't need to. He could hurt with his words and his eyes. I got reamed for half an hour and then grounded until about a week from tomorrow."

"Is that why you left?" Jackson asked.

Maggie looked up. "No." Her eyes went down to her bottle, and she picked at nothing on the label for a while. "The school paper came out on Wednesday. Took till Thursday before the stupid thing made the rounds and everybody saw it. Dad read me the riot act Thursday night, I cried myself to sleep, and got up Friday ready to have the local paper print a retraction. Never got the chance."

On the muted TV, Mary Tyler Moore was chucking her hat into the air—the start of another episode. The TV provided the only light in the room, and wasn't sufficient for Jackson to make out the complexities of the expression on Maggie's face.

333

"Mom and Nicky were sitting at the table crying when I came down for breakfast. Dad was on the phone. Brendan was in the hospital. Somebody had beaten him almost to death the night before."

Jackson felt sick to his stomach.

"A cop on patrol saw a couple of guys pounding him in an alley and chased them away before they could kill him. It didn't matter. Brendan . . ." She sighed, then scratched her temple with the top of the bottle. "Brendan had Type 3 Von Willebrand disease." She looked up. "It caused him to bleed excessively. He had to go to the emergency room for nosebleeds. Once he lost a tooth and it bled for four hours. A normal person probably survives the beating with some bruises and breaks. He bled internally and . . . there was nothing they could do to stop it."

"I'm sorry."

Maggie sighed again. "Dad came back from the hospital and that's when I really thought he was going to kill me. Instead, he just got real close in my face and said he hoped I was happy. At the funeral, nobody would even talk to me."

"They blamed you for his death?" Jackson asked, incredulous.

"Yeah. Uncle Konnie even came over one night. I was in my bedroom doing homework, but it sounded like he and Dad were going to come to blows. He ended up leaving and I never saw him again."

Jackson tread hesitantly. "What happened?"

"I left. Sort of ran away. I stayed with my grandma—on Mom's side—in Syracuse for a while, then some friends in Albany, finally a cousin—again on Mom's side—in New York City before back to Grandma again. The day I turned eighteen, I split. Haven't been back since," she added, looking at Jackson. She tipped her bottle and drained it.

"Wow."

"That's one word for it."

Jackson exhaled slowly as Maggie got up to get another beer. He thought of advising against it, but knew he'd lose the argument. So he waited for her to return. "Is it possible someone in your family would come after you?"

Maggie shrugged before she took a drink. "I doubt it. Maybe right away, but why a decade later?"

"How much contact have you had with your family?"

"None."

"None?"

"Mom and I talked once or twice, but when she married into the family, she became part of it. I think she blames me too. I've sort of kept up—I know everybody's still alive, know they're still in the Kingston area, but that's about it."

Jackson nodded.

"Besides," she said, "if they were responsible, why would they be tossing my place? If they wanted revenge, they would have come for revenge."

Jackson stood and paced for a few minutes, trying to put the pieces together. They didn't fit.

He turned back to Maggie. "What's your gut say?"

"My gut's as confused as my head. The only thing working right now is my amygdala."

"These texts you got, can I see them?"

Maggie shrugged and got out of the chair. She headed for the bedroom and returned a moment later with her phone. "I saved them all," she said, scrolling on the screen. She passed it to Jackson.

He scanned the texts Maggie had quoted to him earlier.

They know. Sent December 9 at 11:28 p.m.

Your in danger. Sent December 12 at 11:21 p.m.

They are coming. Sent December 16 at 8:27 p.m.

All were from the same number, an unfamiliar string of digits with no area code Jackson knew offhand.

"'They know,' 'Your in danger,' and 'They are coming'?" he read. "Is this a New York area code?"

"No. I did a Google search Thursday night. It's not from anywhere. A burn phone or routed through a server in Morocco or something."

He sighed. "It's funny, they sound like warnings."

"Sent by whom?"

"Someone sympathetic to you?"

"Not sure there is anyone like that. And warning me of what, that a couple of fishermen were going to come conduct a panty raid?" Maggie sighed. "I thought moving to L.A. would be far enough to get away from that bunch, but I guess not."

Before Jackson could answer, the phone in his hand began to vibrate. "For you," he said, handing it to Maggie.

"Not a call. It's my text alert."

"A text?"

The light was still dim, coming only from the TV and the bedroom behind Maggie. But Jackson could still see her face blanch.

"I don't believe it," she said. "It's him again."

335

Chapter Forty-Four

6:47 a.m.

A NOISE CAUSED Jackson to startle, which made him realize for the first time he had fallen asleep. He'd known he was close, drifting along the border between consciousness and unconsciousness, but thought he'd kept from crossing it. Apparently not.

He took a moment to identify what was on TV—a rerun of *Mad About You*—and then turned to see what had caused the noise.

Maggie stood in the kitchen, leaning on the counter with one hand, fiddling with the coffeepot with the other. Yawning, Jackson pushed himself out of the chair and joined her. "Morning."

"Ugh," she said, displaying red eyes.

"Sleep at all?"

"A little."

"Still feel like running away?"

Maggie sighed. "I don't know. What do you think?"

"I think we should see what the cops turn up."

"And in the meantime?"

"In the meantime, you should probably hang out elsewhere."

"Great. Where? And don't say your place."

"What, now you're the prude?"

"Funny," she said, forcing a smile. "Would you do this? I can't see straight."

Jackson picked up the canister. "You want it strong?"

"Very."

He dug for a filter, then spooned out the coffee grounds. "Why not my place?"

"Because they'll find me there, whoever they are. I need to be off the grid."

"There's always another fleabag motel."

"I was thinking more like Seattle."

"Isn't that a bit drastic?"

"You start getting death threats, you tell me."

It hadn't exactly been a death threat, but Jackson decided not to quibble with Maggie's early-morning disposition. Instead, he invited her to have a seat while he made breakfast. She opted for a shower instead, and Jackson groggily set about making eggs and toast.

The text the night before had been succinct. *On there way. Run.* "There" had been spelled incorrectly, which didn't do much in the way of indicating who the sender was. It had come in the middle of the night, L.A. time. Which would be early morning on the east coast, if indeed that's where the warnings had originated.

Jackson replayed Maggie's story from the night before. A young girl tried to do the right thing, exposed a cover-up, and was blamed for a tragedy. He could understand why she'd never told him. Maybe there was something worse than losing your family to death—losing them in life.

Showered and dressed, Maggie filled a mug with coffee and sat down at the table just as Jackson placed a plate of scrambled eggs and a couple slices of toast in front of her.

"Thanks."

"Um-hmm." He grabbed his own plate. "Not to open old wounds, but did they ever figure out who killed Brendan?"

Maggie swallowed a bite of toast. "No. But the general consensus was that the family did it."

"The family. Your family?"

She nodded.

"Why? I thought they were protecting him."

She shrugged and took another bite of toast.

"Maggie, when you say 'the family' . . ."

"Yeah, pretty much."

Jackson sat back, digesting. "So they punish their own, that sort of a thing?"

"Yeah. Which is why Dad didn't fight me running away. He didn't want Kasper to decide I deserved the family treatment too."

"Who's Kasper?"

"The patriarch. He's the oldest. The 'don.' Then Konnie. Dad's the baby."

"Would Kasper do this?"

"Like I said, maybe a decade ago. Not now."

"So what does Kasper do?"

"Takes a cut off the top. The family has a number of businesses. Konnie ran the restaurant—among other things—and Dad managed a series of small to midsized grocery stores, hardware stores, Ma & Pa bakeries. Kasper had his fingers in it all."

"And paid off the local cops?"

"Bingo."

Jackson finally cut into his eggs. "So who would be sympathetic to you? Assuming the family is after you, who would warn you?"

"Like I told you last night, I'm not sure anyone would."

"Assume somebody did."

Maggie shrugged. "Maybe Mom, Nicky."

"Your sister?"

"Younger brother. Nikolas. But why would they hide behind a phony number and vague messages?"

"Because they didn't want to get busted by the family."

"If they thought they would, they wouldn't warn me. You don't get it, Jack. They're in. I'm dead to them."

"We'll figure it out," he said. "I'll send the text number to Mouse. If anybody can track them down, he can. And we should probably give them to the cops too."

"Already did. When you were dazed last night."

He nodded and they ate for a few minutes.

"What if you stayed here?" Maggie asked.

"Huh?"

"Until things get sorted out. Kind of as my bodyguard."

"I think you'd be safer somewhere else."

"Like where?"

"My place. A hotel."

"I'm sick of living in other people's houses."

"I thought you were planning on going to Seattle."

"I don't know what to do, Jack." She pushed in her plate. "I just want this to be over."

"I know."

She sighed. "I've got a nine a.m. meeting with Walter, my performance review."

"Today?"

Maggie nodded. "I'll call you this afternoon, see where things are?"

"Okay."

"Besides, I'll need to get my bike."

After a quick clean-up of dishes, he drove Maggie to work before returning home. He was promptly assailed by Connie, who had plenty of questions about where he'd been and why there was a motorcycle in front of his house. He dodged them for a few hours while helping her with her Christmas tree. Then she made him lunch. He finally made it back to his house and was about to hop in the shower when Maggie called.

"I'm working a full day, so pick me up around five?"

"Okay."

"I've thought about it, and if the offer's still good, I'll crash at your place, at least for tonight."

"It's still good."

"You're a prince, Jack."

Since he had the afternoon, he decided to bum over to Mouse's house. But his pal had to work, so he gave him the number of Maggie's texter over the phone and asked him to look into it, when he had time. Then he called Ashley. He had to leave a voicemail, but she called back almost immediately.

"Hey, Ash, I've got a favor."

"Good, because I have nothing to do," she said flippantly.

"You hear about the break-in at Maggie's last night?"

"Do you even understand the concept of divisions within a police department?"

"I thought maybe because of who it was—"

"I don't get notified of every report involving one of your girlfriends, Jackson."

"Me-ow. Everything all right?"

Ashley exhaled. "Sorry, one of those days. We just busted a nineteen-year-old mother of three for possession with intent to sell."

"The hippy lettuce?"

"Half a kilo of cocaine. Laced with PCP."

"Nice."

"Yeah. But that's no excuse. What happened at Maggie's?"

He gave her the rundown.

"Is she okay?"

"Physically, just fine."

Silence.

"Ashley?"

"No, sorry, just waiting for you to follow that up with some crack about how she's not just fine but 'smoking' or something."

"You pigeonhole me so."

"Let me guess, you want me to see if we've made any progress in our investigation?"

"Could you please?"

Her sigh thundered through his ears. "I'll call you back."

"Thank you."

With nothing better to do, Jackson fired up his Xbox for a crucial Rams-49ers game. Jim Everett was defying Father Time in an effort to lead virtual Los Angeles to a fifth straight Super Bowl. It was amazing, Jackson marveled as he took a halftime bathroom break, how a thirty-year-old man could become so engrossed in a video game so as to forget all the problems of life around him.

Ashley called back in the third quarter, much friendlier and less snarky. Unfortunately, she didn't have good news. As of yet, the cops had no leads. Frankly, with all the crime going on in Los Angeles on a given night, he wondered how high a smash-and-grab where nothing was missing would rank on their scale.

He picked up Maggie at five. They grabbed a take-and-bake pizza for supper, and ate at his table as a rainstorm moved in off the Pacific.

"You gonna decorate for Christmas?" Maggie asked, reaching for another slice of pepperoni and black olive.

"No. Christmas decorations always remind me of Mom."

"Not in a good way?"

"There isn't a good way," he said before stuffing his mouth. He chewed a few times and gulped the piece down. "Still too much pain that comes with any memory. The bitter drowns out the sweet."

"Most of my memories got tarnished," Maggie said. "Not that they were all that spectacular to begin with."

He looked at her. Maggie was the antithesis of touchy-feely, and had never opened up about her family. He said nothing, letting her decide how far to go.

"It wasn't bad," she said after swallowing, "but we never had that wonderful, tight-knit quality. We loved each other, sure, but nobody completed anybody's world. We were more functional than anything."

Jackson said nothing.

"What?" she asked.

"What do you mean 'what'?"

"I saw that little tug at the corner of your mouth. You've got something to say."

"And chose not to. Discretion and valor and all that."

"Out with it."

He shrugged. "I was just going to say, you are Russian."

"No. My grandparents and great grandparents were Russian. I'm as American as Abe Lincoln and John Wayne and Mike Eruzione."

"That's my girl."

They finished eating, put feelings aside, and sat side-by-side on his couch watching Monday Night Football.

"You know something, Jack?" Maggie said during a commercial break. She hugged her knees to her chest, dangling the remains of a bottle of Coors with one hand.

"Hmm, what's that?"

"You remember what I said that night in the hotel, about being friends without benefits?"

"Yeah?"

"I've been thinking about that the last few weeks."

"Have you?"

"Yeah. And I think for the time being, I'm comfortable with it."

He turned his attention fully toward her. "Yeah?"

"Yeah. The fact is, if I talked you into something I know you didn't believe in, I'd lose respect for you and for me. So, I'm glad you haven't caved."

He nodded. "So just to be clear, after repeatedly giving me a hard time and practically breaking up with me because I wouldn't sleep with you, you're now praising me for not sleeping with you?"

She offered a sly grin. "Yeah."

"Maggie, you are what Churchill would call a riddle inside a mystery inside an enigma."

*   *   *

Tuesday, December 18
12:23 p.m.

JACKSON'S ENTIRE body ached. Except for his eyes. They were in ecstasy.

In every direction, there was nothing but desert. Barren, blistering, beautiful desert. Distant purple mountains were partially obscured by haze, and none of the namesake Joshua trees were visible at present. It was still beautiful.

Maggie popped off her helmet and stuck it over the handlebars of her Yamaha FJR1300. She shook out her hair and grinned, then peeled off her leather jacket. The December sun wasn't at full power, and Jackson guessed the temps were only in the eighties in the desert. But with no shade, and he in long sleeves to protect against windburn, they felt much higher. The jacket couldn't have been comfortable.

"Nice hair," she said.

Jackson tousled his windblown mane. "Yeah, well, somebody took the only helmet."

"I offered to stop and get you one."

"The word 'get' usually implies payment."

"You're the one with forty grand in poker winnings under your pillow."

"I only cleared sixteen plus, and you may remember I spent a few stacks of that already."

"Yes, I remember."

"Besides, if we crash at seventy miles per, the only thing a helmet's going to do is keep my scrambled brain all in one place." He stretched and winced. "These things definitely weren't built for two."

"You didn't seem to mind earlier, judging by how tight you were squeezing."

"I didn't want to fall off, what without a helmet."

"Uh-huh," she said with a grin.

After an uneventful (on all fronts) night, and after inquiries with Mouse (who wasn't happy to be awakened so early) and Ashley turned up nothing, Maggie's cabin fever had reached critical mass. She'd been scheduled to work "from home" anyhow, and was still in a lull after returning from Mexico and completing her masterpiece exposé. So Jackson had actually suggested they go for a ride, get away from it all. She'd been easy to convince, and they'd set out without a destination. Three and a half hours later, they were in the midst of Joshua Tree National Park on the edge of the Mojave Desert.

Jackson grabbed a bottle of water from a holder on the bike and took a swig. He tossed it to Maggie. "Now where?" he asked.

"Vegas?"

"Sure, that'll keep a low profile."

"I gotta work—"

Her phone interrupted her.

"You get service out here?" Jackson said.

"Apparently," she said, flipping the bottle back to him. She pulled the phone from her pocket. "Hello? . . . Yeah."

Maggie's face drained of color, and Jackson thought for a moment she was going to collapse. He stepped beside her in case, but she kept her composure and continued the conversation. "Thank you. We will," she said, then lowered the phone.

"Who was it? Another warning?"

"No. Detective Nichols."

"Who?"

"From last night."

"Right. Of course. They catch the guy?"

"No. IDed him from a partial facial image on apartment security."

"Took their time, but good. Who is it?"

"Alex B. A small-time hood from out east. I don't remember the charges and they don't matter."

"Who's Alex B?" Jackson asked.

"Full name is Alexander Bocharov," Maggie answered. "He's—or at least he was—an underling for the Baby Crime Family."

"Baby Crime Family? Is that like Baby Face?"

"No, Baby's their last name. It's Russian. Or Ukrainian, actually, I think."

Jackson nodded. "Do I want to know how you know them?"

"They were rivals of my family. Still are for all I know."

"And Bocharov worked for them?"

"Yeah." She shrugged. "I heard things when Dad was on the phone, or when Uncle Kasper and Konnie came over. Names, titles. I used to spy on them as a little kid, until they caught me. Anyhow, Bocharov was one of the names that stuck with me."

"Well, good news and bad news," Jackson said.

"Yeah, how's that?"

"It's not Vasquez."

"No, I'm just involved in an East Coast crime war."

Jackson kicked at a rock. "What else did Nichols say?"

"They've got a warrant out for Bocharov. And he wanted us to swing by and ID him, just to verify it's one of the guys."

"I guess the joy riding's over," Jackson said. "Mount up."

*   *   *

2:10 p.m.

CHRISTMAS MUSIC seemed out of place at a Taco Bell on the outskirts of San Bernardino, especially after spending hours driving through the desert. But in the middle of the afternoon, it fought off silence as Jackson and Maggie refueled.

"Tell me what you know about the Baby family," Jackson said.

"After ten years, not a lot."

"Tell me what you knew then."

"Not a lot either," she said, taking a sip of soda. "I knew they were in the same lines of business as my family, they weren't friendlies, and I caught some names now and then. No specifics."

"Did you have any dealings with them?"

"Dealings?"

He shrugged. "I'm fishing, Maggie. Maybe you and Bobby Baby kissed behind the gym when you were twelve, or you and Susie Baby used to play Barbies before you realized your families were at war, anything."

"I knew a few Babys at school, but I don't know how they were related to the Baby Crime Family. Maybe they weren't. And that's it. If I rack my brain I could come up with five to ten names of family members. There's nothing more."

Jackson bit into his chalupa. It didn't add up. Could there be two Alexander Bocharovs? Sure, but what were the odds?

Jackson's phone interrupted him, playing the James Bond theme. Jackson fished it from his pocket. "Yeah, Mouse."

"Where have you been, dude? I've been trying to reach you for like two hours."

"On the road, sorry."

"Yeah, well, I couldn't trace the phone number you sent. Probably a TracFone or something."

"We figured it was a burner."

"But get this, whoever bought it, paid with a credit card. Well, debit card, actually."

"And you determined this how?"

"You really want to know?"

"Actually, nope. What's the name?"

"Sasha Baby."

Chapter Forty-Five

Tuesday, January 1
12:31 p.m.

CHANGING FROM HIS hospital gown to the jeans Reggie had brought nearly killed Jackson. Sliding into the shirt wasn't much easier, but he kept his left arm limp at his side and buttoned the shirt over it. With one hand available, that took some doing. By the time he was dressed, he felt worse than he had all night.

He emerged from the bathroom to find Sam standing behind a wheelchair. She was smiling, but when she saw him, she frowned. "Your buttons are crooked."

"It's closed. What's that for?"

"Getting you to the car."

"Sam, I can walk."

"Twelve hours ago you were shot, Jackson. You don't need any additional stress."

"Then I should have had Wardrobe help me in there. And more like fifteen."

The frown intensified. "Are you hurt?"

"I'm fine, Sam."

"Jackson."

"Yes, it hurts. But it's going to hurt; I was shot. I'm fine."

She set her mouth and stared at him for a moment. But she didn't push the issue.

"Now, you want to find some frail old lady that needs this thing," Jackson said, nodding at the wheelchair as he scanned the room for anything left behind. He hadn't come with anything, so he didn't know how it could be left behind. Except a half roll of Rolos.

"Quit being macho, Jackson."

"I'm not. I just don't need a wheelchair."

"Sit."

"Sam."

Her eyes bored into him, her wrists on her hips. "Do you remember our rules? Sit."

He pouted internally for a moment, then remembered the Rose Bowl and chalked it up for the greater good. With a sigh, he sat down, and munched on candy as Sam wheeled him out of the room.

"I really do appreciate this, Sam," Jackson said as they entered the elevator.

"I know. You're welcome."

"You're welcome to share my smokeys."

"That's very magnanimous."

The elevator dinged at the ground floor. "What time's kickoff?" she asked.

"Two."

"Good. Then we'll have time to stop at the pharmacy."

"I don't want to miss the flyover."

The checkout procedure was fairly hassle-free until Sam insisted Jackson take the wheelchair out to the car. He didn't fight, only because that would take more time. A pretty redheaded nursed accompanied them, and Jackson smiled as he passed through the automatic doors and out into bright, warm sunlight. The year before, it had rained during the Rose Bowl. Sacrilege.

The nurse helped Jackson into the passenger seat of Sam's Ford Fusion, smiled, and took the wheelchair back inside. Sam buckled him in and made sure the seatbelt wasn't coming anywhere near his wound. When he assured her he was fine, she finally started the car.

Jackson's prescriptions had been called in to a Walgreens a few blocks east. The drive took five minutes, and Jackson unbuckled his seatbelt as they pulled into the lot.

"Jackson!"

"What?"

"Wait until we're stopped."

"We're kind of up against the clock, Sam, and you know how pharmacies are."

She parked and he started to get out. She hollered again.

"Come on, Sam. I can do this."

She grabbed his knee. "Jackson, you were shot."

"I know."

"Do you? Because you seem more concerned with your smokeys than with the fact that someone tried to kill you last night."

"I don't know that—"

346

"You may not be taking this seriously, but I am. And I know you think I'm babying you, but you need to be babied right now. So relax, let me help you, and we'll make it in time for the flyover."

"Let's hope so."

She patted his knee. "Wait. I'll help you out."

He sighed as her door closed behind her. She was right. He had almost died last night. Almost being a relative term, but in his life, taking a bullet in the shoulder counted as almost dying. And he was making light of it, but maybe that was because he was stymied as to who had pulled the trigger. Or because he was still sort of in shock. Or maybe because, despite the fact that he was ready in several ways to die, he was still scared of it.

As Sam fully opened his door, he resolved to have this out. Sort his feelings, respond properly emotionally. It would be therapeutic.

But not until after the Rose Bowl.

*   *   *

Wednesday, December 19
7:23 a.m.

JACKSON SAT in the LAX terminal, thinking over the events of the last few weeks—since Thanksgiving: Bill's phone call, their trip to Mexico, their escape, Bill's death, Maggie's story, the texts, the break-in, and her family history. If he wasn't prepared to board a flight to New York, it would be hard to believe it all.

He had talked Maggie into staying at his house and using his car while he was gone. No, it wasn't exactly a CIA safe house, but then again, on TV and in the movies they were never safe anyhow. He had also asked Connie to keep an eye on things, you know, in case guys in a van show up to kidnap her while you sip daiquiris on the deck?

He'd briefed Reggie as well, who had commented that Jackson's life was unfolding like a soap opera of late. Speaking of, he had met with Dr. Zachary the day before. Jackson hadn't felt like squeezing in a psychiatric appointment before heading east, but had gone nonetheless. They had discussed repercussions of the events in Nevada, acting, Mexican exfiltrations, and stalkers. The net result had been a distraction (in session and in real life) from the reason Jackson had first started seeing Zachary in the first place, the death of his family.

They called his row, so Jackson pushed himself out of the chair and filed onto the plane. His was a window seat next to a guy in a suit who was engrossed in his tablet, and Jackson settled in and tried to sleep. He was almost there when the plane shook and began backing up from the gate. And from that point on, Jackson was wide awake.

He sighed, thinking of how much Maggie owed him for making him fly again. He didn't have a phobia, really. He just didn't like flying. Sure the bird's-eye perspective was neat, but he wasn't comfortable enough with the science of flight to totally relax. And he always seemed to catch a touch of airsickness and disorientation. To combat that touch, he ran through all the facts again.

Mouse's revelation that Sasha Baby, presumably of the Baby Crime Family, had been the one to send Maggie a total of four warning texts was the final clue that Leonardo Vasquez was not behind the break-in at her place. But it also brought the mob and Maggie's past into play, and asked more questions than it answered.

Alexander Bocharov and his partner had yet to be apprehended by the police, but they hadn't showed up again either. Maggie had thought long and hard and couldn't figure out a motive for anyone to come across the country to search her apartment or do her harm. She had told Jackson everything she knew, and while the events of a decade ago had destroyed her family, they didn't seem to be motivation for any malevolence now.

So Jackson was off to New York to investigate. Maggie wasn't wild about him stirring things up with her family, but he promised to be careful. If she wasn't going to enter her apartment with trepidation for the rest of her life, it was necessary, he argued. Besides, it didn't appear that her family was behind the break-in, but rather her family's rival family. It was positively Shakespearean.

After they crossed the Desert Southwest and the southern tip of the Rockies, the landscape got boring and flat. Jackson really pitied Midwesterners. Somewhere east of the Mississippi, cloud cover obscured any vision of the ground until the jet's engines had throttled back and they were descending into La Guardia International. Jackson was on the wrong side of the plane to see any landmarks, instead having a view of a gray and choppy Atlantic, then the expanse of Long Island.

Wheels touched down, but it was another half hour before Jackson was off the plane. He found a McDonald's and bought lunch. Or maybe dinner. The clock in the concourse read 3:28. What a way to spend a day.

His only bag was a carry-on duffel, so with his Quarter Pounder in tow, Jackson stopped to buy a New York City map, then headed for the car-rental counter. Forty minutes later, he was in New Jersey—via Manhattan and the George Washington Bridge—and heading north toward Kingston. Flurries had been spitting in Manhattan, and continued as he drove through familiarly named towns like Hackensack and Paramus. By the time he finally left the sprawl, darkness had fallen and he was back in New York State.

The flurries relented, and he phoned Maggie.

"Hey," she answered.

"Hey. I'm here."

"Kingston?"

"New York. Weird place."

"How's the weather?"

"Snowing."

"Sixty-four and sunny."

"Nice talking with you."

"Thanks for doing this, Jack."

"Thank me if I have success."

"I'm thanking you for the effort."

"In that case you're welcome."

"What's your plan?"

Jackson checked his blind spot before passing a semi. "I'll look up Sasha first. Maybe she can explain everything for me. If not, I'll play it by my gut."

"Be careful."

"You too."

"You'll call me when you know something?"

"I will."

They said goodbye, and Jackson settled in for another hour on . . . He'd lost track of the freeways by now. Or rather, tollway as was soon to be the case. Stupid New York.

At quarter after six, Jackson finally reached the outskirts of Kingston. His research indicated that Sasha Baby lived in an apartment a few blocks from the river. He identified it, made a lap around the block, and parked a few houses down. There was nothing to indicate Sasha was married, but that wasn't to say a boyfriend in an unbuttoned flannel shirt wouldn't open the door and greet him with a shotgun. He thought of Maggie, said a prayer, and willed himself up the front walk. He noticed for the first time patches of snow here and there, and nearly slipped on a low point in the sidewalk where ice had formed. Stupid New York.

Sasha's apartment was an upper in an old Victorian house that been split into four apartments. He rang the doorbell and waited, regretting his decision to listen to Christmas music on the drive up. He'd heard a Britney Spears cover of "Santa Baby" that now played through his head every time he thought of Sasha Baby. And he had plenty of time for it to run as nobody came to the door. Determined to be persistent, Jackson rang the bell again, then pounded on the wooden door with his fist. A moment later, he heard a series of thumps behind the door. The latch turned, and the door opened a crack.

Backlit by a yellow lamp was a skinny woman who didn't look a day over twenty-five. Her dirty blond hair had strands flowing everywhere, including over a flannel shirt, sleeves rolled up, accompanied by black sweatpants. (At least he'd been right about the flannel.) Her eyes were blue, wide, with shadows beneath them. A slightly upturned nose was red, and Jackson wasn't sure if she was sick, had been crying, or was just succumbing to the smell wafting down the stairs. Day-old borscht?

Jackson cleared his throat. "Are you Sasha?"

The girl swallowed. "Y-yeah."

"My name's Jackson Douglas," he said, having decided earlier to use his real name and avoid a cover story. If the Babys wanted to come after him, fine. Better him than Maggie. "I'm a private investigator from Los Angeles," he continued as Sasha just stared at him. "I'm here on behalf of a friend. I think you might know who it is."

Her eyes answered for her mouth.

"Could I come in for just a minute?" Jackson asked.

Sasha hesitated a moment before nodding and opening the door wider. He followed her up creaking, steep steps, and resolved to make the interview quick as the smell intensified.

The apartment was threadbare. A living room and kitchenette flowed as one to his right, a bathroom was straight ahead, and presumably two bedroom doors were to his left. Six, seven hundred square feet max. Sasha offered him a seat in an end chair that didn't match the old, plaid couch. The room was devoid of any decoration, save for a cheap oil painting above the couch and a small five-by-seven photo on the end table. It showed a smiling, gushing Sasha with her arms around a nine- or ten-year-old. Hair unkempt, eyes also wide and blue, a toothy smile on his face. He looked like a model in a toothpaste ad. Or the *Mad* cover boy.

"Your son?" Jackson asked.

"Ruslan."

"How old is he?"

"Eleven just last week. Can I offer you something to drink? Coffee or tea?" She had an accent, Russian, it stood to reason, but it wasn't thick like the Russian girls in the movies. She also wasn't smoking hot, which was another female Russian myth Jackson had long ago debunked.

"No thanks," Jackson said, realizing he still hadn't answered. "I won't take up much of your time."

"You want to know about the text messages I sent?"

"I do."

Sasha looked down. "How much do you know?"

"I'm afraid not too much. It might be better if you just told me things from your perspective."

Sasha nodded and receded a little farther into the couch. "Do you know about Brendan?"

"I know he was caught stealing from Troika, that somebody beat him up and that he died from Von Willebrand disease."

"Brendan and I were dating," Sasha said "I was with him the night he robbed the restaurant, but I had no idea what he was going to do. I . . . I tried to make him stop, to put the money back, but he insisted I drive. I . . ."

"It's okay, Sasha." He sat back and did the math. "Is Brendan Ruslan's father?"

She nodded.

"I'm sorry."

"We knew if our families found out they would not stand for it, but we were young and in love. I did not know I was pregnant until after Brendan died. I did not tell anyone that he was the father. I . . . I said I did not know who the father was. An illegitimate child was better than an illegitimate child of an enemy."

Sasha took a deep breath. "A few months ago, Ruslan was tripped during a soccer match. He cut his chin, and it kept bleeding He has had nosebleeds before, and the doctors wanted to run some tests. They diagnosed him with Von Willebrand Disease. They said it was . . . her . . ."

"Hereditary?"

Sasha nodded and looked up. "Then my family knew the truth."

The pieces were starting to click, but it still didn't lead to anyone coming after Maggie. So Jackson let Sasha keep talking.

"A decade ago, our families were bitter rivals. Now my family works for Brendan's family."

"Works for them?"

"Yes. They have 'let bygones be bygones.' All in the name of profit."

"Blood enemies are blood enemies, but money's money," Jackson said.

"Something like that. My Uncle Maxim was very angry when he learned the truth about Ruslan. I did not know why, if our families are now working together. But he kept speaking of your friend and her article. He said the truth would be disastrous. I do not know why, but as I overheard things, I began to fear she was in danger. I sent the messages to warn her."

"Why were you so secretive?" Jackson asked. "Why didn't you tell her what you told me?"

"Uncle Maxim is not a kind man, and he has a temper. I was afraid if he thought I was interfering—I was afraid of what he might do."

Jackson couldn't hold it against her. The fear was played out all over her face.

"Sunday night, I found out he had finally sent Alex and Dmitri to Los Angeles. I work most nights at the soap factory, and as soon as my shift ended, I sent the final text. I did not know why else they would be sent, but to cause her harm."

"Alexander Bocharov?"

Sasha nodded.

"Who's Dmitri?"

She bit her lip.

"No one will ever know I talked to you," Jackson said.

"Dmitri Fischer. He is one of Uncle Maxim's henchmen."

Jackson nodded.

"Where can I find Uncle Maxim?"

Sasha's chin trembled. "Please do not."

"I won't tell him how I found him."

"That will not matter. If you bring a fight to him, he will finish it. It is best to run away."

"The problem with running is you can't stop."

Sasha looked down, and Jackson stood to leave. "I won't trouble you anymore." He pulled out a business card with just his name and cell number on it. "If you think of anything else . . ."

Sasha took the card, blinking back tears. "I'm sorry."

Jackson shook his head. "You've got nothing to be sorry for. Thank you for your help."

She forced a thin smile as she nodded.

"I'll see myself out," Jackson said.

At the door, he braced himself for the cold, still wearing the long-sleeved tee and jeans—no coat, gloves, or hat—that he had donned that morning in L.A. He also braced himself, half expecting Uncle Maxim's thugs to swing a tire iron at his knees as he walked to the car. It didn't happen.

It took Jackson ten minutes to find a cheap motel, the Bonne Belle, off one of the turnpikes. Rooms were $49 per night, and Jackson paid for two nights. It was just after seven-thirty, which meant four-thirty Pacific Time. Even considering he had been up early to be at the airport in time for his flight, Jackson was far from ready for bed. But Sasha hadn't been the piece that caused all the others to click into place, and he was left with more questions—questions that would have to wait until tomorrow.

Having lost Detective Nichols' business card, he called Ashley and told her to add the name Dmitri Fischer to the APB Nichols had put out. He thought about calling Maggie again, but decided against it. He walked down to a nearby hole-in-the-wall restaurant, ordered a burger and fries to go, and took them back to his room. ESPN had a bowl game on, a typical pre-Christmas contest pitting two no-name teams with mediocre records against each other. Jackson watched until the start of the fourth quarter, when his faint interest dissipated and he fell asleep.

Chapter Forty-Six

Thursday, December 20
8:12 a.m. (EST)

JACKSON WAS HAPPY to find that Troika served pretty standard breakfast fare. He ordered a ham and cheese omelet and white toast with plenty of coffee. The pot in his room didn't work, and with the skies overcast and the air cool, he wanted coffee. And sunshine. And pretty California girls.

He settled for the waitress. Her name was Carli, and she was cute, energetic, and flirtatious. She was also good. She topped off his coffee twice before bringing his plate. Then she set down a bottle of orange-red sauce.

"What's that?" Jackson asked.

"Our special sauce."

"What's in your special sauce?"

"Can't tell you. It's a secret recipe. Been in the family for years. They won't even tell me what's in it."

"But it's good?"

"You tell me."

He nodded. "Thanks. I'll give it a try."

Carli winked as she left, and Jackson tried the sauce. It wasn't bad, but it also didn't suit his breakfast palette.

He'd asked for a corner table, and as he ate, he kept an eye on the restaurant and its patrons. Aside from the name over the entrance and a few decorations here and there, it looked like any other family-owned restaurant across America. No Soviet flags or photos of the Kremlin, no Russian folk music playing in the background, no Communist propaganda on the walls. And most importantly, no smells like in Sasha's apartment. To be fair, Jackson had lived in apartments before. The smells couldn't always be traced to a particular tenant.

Jackson did not see Kasper, Konrad, or Kurt, the famed *troika* of Maggie's family. Then again, Maggie had given him descriptions, not photos, so he

354

couldn't be sure. For all he and Maggie knew, Konrad didn't even run the place anymore.

"How's the omelet?" Carli asked.

"Good."

"You try the sauce?"

"I did."

"And?"

"Maybe on a burger."

"So come back for a burger."

"I just might."

Carli smiled. "Can I get you anything else?"

"Actually, yeah. Does Konrad still run this place?"

"He owns it," she said. "But the day-to-day stuff he delegates. Why?" she asked, forming a pouty smile. "Did you not like the service?"

"Quite the opposite. He's an old friend of a friend. I was hoping to catch up with him."

"From what I hear, he spends most of his time at home these days."

"Where's home?"

"He's got a place out on Highway 37, overlooking the river. Pretty nice, I hear."

"You hear quite a bit."

"Just gotta know how to listen," she said with a sly grin.

"I'll remember that."

"I'll be back with your check and top off your coffee," she said.

Jackson took a few minutes to savor his coffee, left Carli a ten-dollar tip, and stopped in the entry to check for Konrad's address in the phonebook. Surprisingly, it was there. Fifteen minutes later, he was at the end of a winding asphalt driveway that led through the barren trees to a small mansion on the banks of the Hudson River.

He rang the bell and, as he had on the drive over, tried to figure out what to say. Hi, Konrad, do you still hold a grudge against Maggie, and have you by any chance teamed up with your old enemy-turned-friend Maxim to kill her? Or maybe something a little more delicate.

A young woman opened the door. Long, straight brown hair, matching eyes, soft features that did not look Russian. Then again, neither did Maggie. She wore jeans and a loose sweater and carried a small cup of yogurt. "Can I help you?" she asked, spooning a bite to her mouth.

"Is Konrad home?"

The woman shook her head. "Who's asking?"

As tactfully and as simply as possible, Jackson explained who he was. The woman's eyes flickered, but her face remained stoic at the mention of Maggie's name. Same when he expressed his sympathy for Brendan's death.

"It was a long time ago," she said. "What do you want?"

"Do you mind if I come in? It's a bit cold out here."

"Cold isn't for another month," she said, but stepped back. The house was open, with stairs to the right and a living room with crackling fireplace to the left. The living room flowed into a dining room and kitchen, both backed by spacious windows looking out on a deck and a gentle incline down to the river. Forlorn and gray, a few ripples were highlighted by rays of sun that peaked through the cloud cover. The orange-yellow gaps in the clouds were teasers—the skies showed no signs of clearing.

The woman nodded at padded stools on one side of the kitchen counter, beyond which sat a St. Bernard that slowly lifted its head to look at Jackson. He didn't bark or growl, but the warning was conveyed simply enough.

Jackson sat down while the woman strolled around the counter, placing her empty yogurt container and spoon in the sink. She stood opposite Jackson and introduced herself as Patricia, Konrad's daughter. "What did you want to talk to my father about?" she asked.

"Sunday night, two men broke into Maggie's apartment. Police were able to identify one of them as Alexander Bocharov, who I understand is a henchman for Maxim Baby."

Patricia's body bristled, but her face was still void of expression. Cold as the Hudson behind her. "I'm still not hearing a question."

"I understand things were tense after your brother died. But Maggie herself said she didn't think her own family would come after her."

"So why are you here?"

"Because your family and the Baby family now work together. And I'm trying to put the pieces together."

"You think my father sent this Bocharov character after her?"

Jackson made a mental note that she didn't even use Maggie's name—her own cousin—and filed it away.

"I'm trying to rule out that possibility," he said.

Patricia shook her head, for the first time showing emotion. "Look, I don't know where you got your information, but our families don't 'work together.'

356

And if my father wanted to do her harm, he wouldn't send Maxim Baby's goons to do it."

Was she implying that Konrad had his own goons?

"What about Kasper?"

"What about him?"

"I understand he's the head of the family."

"He's the oldest, yeah."

Jackson looked out at the river, then back. "I didn't just mean the oldest."

Patricia nodded. "I think maybe it's time you leave. I don't like your implications."

"Fair enough. I didn't mean to insinuate anything."

"Yeah, I think you did."

Jackson was already on his way to the door. "I apologize for upsetting you."

"When you see her, tell her we had nothing to do with it."

"I will," Jackson said, noting again that Patricia couldn't bring herself to use Maggie's name. "Thanks for your time."

The door practically closed on his heels, and Jackson returned to his car wondering who to believe—Sasha Baby, who said her family was working for Maggie's, or Patricia, who denied it. Then again, Patricia hadn't really denied it. She had just said the families weren't working together, not that the Babys weren't working for her family. Semantics? Maybe.

His cell rang as he turned back onto the highway. "Hello?"

"Mr. Douglas?" He didn't need to hear, "It's Sasha Baby," to know who it was. Nor did he need the Britney Spears that began playing in his head again.

"Sasha. What can I do for you?"

"I thought of something else you might want to know. But you have to promise me you will not tell where you heard it?"

"You have my word."

Sasha hesitated, long enough that Jackson was about to ask if she was still there. Then she said, "About two months ago, a man came to me. Several times. Asking me all sorts of questions about my family, about Brendan and his family and the robbery. He said he worked for the FBI and was trying to bring down the Baby Crime Family. I was scared. Uncle Maxim . . ."

There was another long pause.

"I told him all I knew, and he promised he would protect me. I have not heard from him since."

"Do you know his name?"

"Agent Joseph."

"Thank you, Sasha."

"You are welcome."

"As far as I'm concerned, we never spoke."

"Thank you."

He closed the phone and pulled off to the side of the road. Two phone calls confirmed his hunch, and he made a U-turn and headed north to Albany. A third call put him in touch with FBI Special Agent Jamie Joseph, who agreed to meet him for an early lunch. He gave Jackson directions to a local diner. An hour later, Jackson was sitting across the table from a clean-cut, close-shaved man in his thirties. He wore a suit and tie—light blue and dark blue stripes—under a long, dark coat. All that was missing were the traditional Fibbie shades, but it was cloudy.

They both ordered coffee and sandwiches—Joseph first, and Jackson when he saw how tasty Joseph's looked. Then they got down to business.

"You said you had information on the Baby Crime Family," Joseph said.

Jackson explained again, telling everything he knew, leaving out Sasha's name. It didn't fool Joseph. "You've talked to Sasha?"

"On the record, no I have not," Jackson said, making eye contact with Joseph.

"I hear you," the agent replied. He took a bite of a Reuben sandwich and savored it, working on government time and all. "Here's the deal," he said, pausing to take a drink of coffee. Jackson took one too and found it was almost gone. Where was Carli when he needed her?

"This all hinges on the robbery at Troika a decade ago," Joseph said. "And I didn't hear an admission in so many words, but I'm confident enough in my intel to say that Brendan was working for the Babys when he robbed the restaurant."

"He was working for the Babys?"

Joseph nodded. "His brother, Konrad Jr., was set to follow in his father's footsteps, take over the restaurant, run the family business. Brendan resented it, fell in love with the wrong girl, and met her uncle."

"Maxim?"

Joseph nodded.

"So Maxim knew who Sasha was dating?"

"He knew. And he saw Brendan's mindset and decided to use him."

"So Brendan knew he was working for the Babys? This wasn't a guy getting instructions by phone or by some envelope taped under a bench?"

"No, he knew," Joseph said. He scanned the room, looking for eavesdroppers or else a coffee refill. He gave up and leaned forward. "When your friend wrote her little exposé, it opened Pandora's box. If the KKK—and it's politically incorrect, but forgive me, it's what I call them—found out that Brendan was working for the Babys, it would have been war. So the Babys made sure he was never traced back to them."

"You're saying the Babys killed him?"

Joseph nodded. "Tried to, were stopped by an inconvenient cop on patrol, but then he died in the hospital anyhow from VWD. They wanted it to look like members of his own family had caught him and punished him for robbing from them. But it was the Babys."

Jackson sat back. That should be a relief to Maggie at least, knowing her family hadn't killed her cousin.

"So is Sasha or Patricia right?" he asked. "Are the Babys working for the KKK?"

"Yes. And that's the kicker now. If anyone ever uncovered the truth—that Brendan was working for the Babys—it would blow the entire deal. There'd be war again. The Babys would be hosed and the KKK would take a hit but keep on ticking."

"So how does that tie to Maggie?"

"Have you read the article she wrote back then?"

"No. She summed it up for me."

"Read it," Joseph said. "She's got a style that's . . . inflammatory."

"Personality too."

Joseph grinned. Maybe he wasn't a real Fibbie after all. "You read between the lines, you get the impression she might have known more than she penned. Like the identity of the girl driving Brendan's getaway car."

"Sasha."

Joseph nodded. "From talking to her, I don't think she knew what he was planning until he came out of the restaurant with the cash."

"That's what I gathered too."

"But if your friend could tie Brendan to the Babys—even just that he was dating one of them—when he robbed Troika, it could be enough to dissolve a fragile partnership." He finished off his sandwich and pushed his plate to the side. He leaned on the table. "And let me tell you, the Babys are making a pretty good go of it right now."

"What kind of go?"

"A little of everything. They make the big money through extortion and trafficking."

"Trafficking what?"

"Humans, mostly. Little Russian girls."

"They should be shot in the neck."

"Find me a lenient judge and I'll pull the trigger."

Jackson sighed. "That's what they were looking for."

"How's that?"

"Maxim's thugs. They were searching her apartment for information she had on the robbery, Brendan, the Baby connection."

"Makes sense," Joseph said. "Only why now? It's been a decade."

"Ruslan Baby."

"Sasha's boy?"

"Recently diagnosed with Von Willebrand Disease. It's hereditary."

Joseph leaned back. "Naturally, it would lead to suspicions—"

"The Babys feared Maggie could confirm," Jackson finished.

Joseph took a long draw on his coffee. "You said you IDed one of them as Alexander Bocharov?"

"Footage on an apartment security cam," Jackson said. "LAPD put out a warrant for his arrest, but he hasn't turned up."

"Not a surprise."

"Pretty sure the other is Dmitri Fischer. My unnamed source."

"Sasha," Joseph said. "It would track."

"So where does that leave us?"

"Unfortunately, with not enough to act on. I learned a lot undercover, but I didn't gather a lot of evidence. These guys are good at what they do, Mr. Douglas."

Jackson nodded. "Well, thanks for your time, Agent Joseph."

Joseph nodded in return. "You've got my number," he said. "If anything turns up, please let me know."

"I will."

"But be careful. People like this don't take prisoners."

"Neither do I, Agent Joseph. Not when I'm playing for a friend."

They shook hands and Jackson headed back out into the cold. And now, delightfully, snow.

*   *   *

360

11:41 a.m.

THE SNOW lessened as he drove south, but the flurries continued all the way to Kingston. Jackson made two calls on the hour drive along the New York State Thruway. The first was to Maggie. He briefed her on what he'd learned thus far, and double-checked to make sure there wasn't anything she knew and had been sitting on for a decade. She assured him there wasn't.

"Where can I get a copy of that article?" he asked.

"Probably a birdcage somewhere."

Jackson stuck his tongue in his cheek and waited for her to continue.

"I can dig up a copy. How should I get it to you and your outdated phone?"

"Just e-mail it. I'll find internet access somewhere."

"Okay. What are you going to do next?"

"Call Reggie. See if he can keep an eye on you."

"I don't need a babysitter, Jackson," she said in a hushed but forceful tone.

"These guys play hardball, Maggie. I don't want to take any chances."

"I'll check into a hotel."

"Hotels have security cameras and bribable desk clerks."

"Then I'll go camp out in the desert."

"He'll sleep on the couch, Maggie, play the guard dog."

"He has a life to live. I'll be fine. You send him over, I'll make him go home."

Jackson sighed. She would, too. "Be careful," he said.

"I will. You too."

"Yeah. I'll call you when I know more."

He closed the phone, waited five minutes, and then called Reggie anyhow. He gave a brief explanation and asked him to just pop in after work. If nothing else, he would show a little muscle in case the place was being staked out. It wasn't much, but from across a continent, it felt like something. Reggie, as always, agreed.

Jackson found a strip mall café with free Wi-Fi. Maggie had sent a copy of the article, and looking over his shoulder a few times, Jackson read it twice. Agent Joseph was right—Maggie's writing was inflammatory.

> *He ran to the getaway car, driven by a light-haired woman. His partner? His lover? Or both?*

Family members do nothing. Local police officers do nothing. You'd almost think we were back in Mother Russia, not in the constitutionally-governed United States of America.

People don't cover up crimes for no reason. They either gain from the cover-up or avoid losing because of the cover-up. I wonder which it could be in this case?

Technically, it wasn't the best writing ever. Not nearly as good as her stuff now. But for a small town school newspaper, it was a page-turner. And throughout, it implied that Maggie knew more than she was telling. Then again, it was just an implication, and reading between the lines with a different bias would suggest that an angry, aspiring Maggie was just trying to draw in readers. Either way, he could understand why her family had been upset. She hadn't pulled any punches. He was actually surprised a school newspaper had printed it, but what did he know about high school journalism?

Jackson left the café and went to get a second lunch, the small sandwich he'd eaten with Agent Joseph not cutting it. He didn't go back to Troika because he didn't need the distraction of Carli, her smile, or her secret sauce. He found another local diner and sat at the bar hoping to pick up some gossip. Not surprisingly, no one blabbed the answer to his problem.

He reviewed the facts. Maggie's cousin Brendan stole from the family while, unbeknownst to them, working for their rivals and dating one of them. Maggie exposed the lack of action on the part of her family, and did so in a way that implied she knew more than she did, like perhaps the identity of the getaway driver and the connection between Brendan and the Baby family. The Babys silenced Brendan, and once they formed a lucrative partnership with Maggie's family, remembered her story and decided to make sure she didn't reveal the damning facts she didn't actually have. Jackson wasn't sure it was a perfectly accurate picture of what had happened, but all the pieces at least fit together.

So now what?

He left the diner and called Maggie again. He went over specific excerpts from the article, hoping to jog her memory or her subconscious. But she was adamant that she didn't know any more than she had told him or than she had put in the article. He believed her, he said. The trouble was getting Maxim Baby to believe that.

Jackson stuffed his phone back in his pocket and started walking. The flurries came and went, but it wasn't bitterly cold, the wind wasn't blowing, and Jackson figured a little chill in the air might clear his mind.

As he strolled through downtown, he asked himself, how do you convince somebody that a person isn't keeping a secret? The old maxim (pun intended by his cold-riddled mind) said you couldn't prove a negative. Maggie didn't know anything, but that was just her word, and she had every motive to lie.

A jogger and his tiny little dog approached, and the dog began yapping at Jackson, nipping at his shoes and pant legs. Its bark was shrill, piercing, and almost as annoying as the stupid jogger who, instead of pulling his mutt away, stopped to let him yap and attack Jackson's ankles. So Jackson turned around and gave the heartiest snarl and growl he could. The dog whimpered once and then darted off in the other direction.

With a smile befitting Scrooge, Jackson resumed walking. But only for a few paces before he stopped in his tracks.

Maybe . . . Just maybe.

Slowly, he started walking again, the wheels turning.

The problem was that Maxim Baby suspected Maggie had knowledge that could ruin his illicit business, and the logical solution was to prove to him somehow that she didn't. But Jackson had been looking at it wrong. His only concern was to get Maggie off the hook, to rig things so that Maxim had no reason to go after her. Convincing him she didn't know anything was one way to do it. But so was exposing whatever knowledge Maxim feared she had. Once the cat was out of the bag, the bag was suddenly irrelevant If Maggie would forgive him for calling her a bag.

Jackson hurried back to his car, turned on the heat, and locked the doors. Then he called Agent Joseph.

"Mr. Douglas. What can I do for you?"

"How's your social calendar for tonight?"

"Excuse me?"

"I think I might have an idea how you can finally collar the Babys."

Chapter Forty-Seven

2:40 p.m.

JACKSON AND SPECIAL Agent Joseph shared an isolated table at a McDonald's off Route 212, a dozen miles north of Kingston. They drank coffee again, and Jackson knew sooner or later all this coffee would catch up with him and he'd have to pee every fifteen minutes. For the moment, he had bigger things on his mind.

"You realize what you're proposing?" Joseph asked.

"I do."

"There's no guarantee this works." He shook his head. "This could blow up too."

"Blow up how?"

"A war between two crime families."

Jackson shrugged. "I don't much care. My only goal is to insulate Maggie."

"And you think this will do it?"

"You want to protect a secret," Jackson said, "you have to protect the secret keeper. They get caught, they might blab, might squeal if they're tortured, might accidentally reveal something without meaning to. But I don't care about the secret. I want to protect the secret keeper. Best way to do that, destroy the secret. If I have to, I'll take out a full-page ad in *USA Today*."

"What about the innocent victims?"

"Which innocent victims? The ones selling Russian girls into the sex trade or the ones extorting their neighbors? Or do you mean Maggie's family, the good old bunch that sold her down the river because she had the gall to out a guy for robbery?"

"I mean everybody else. These families are huge. Uncles, aunts, cousins— and they're not all criminals. Most of them probably don't even know what's going on."

Jackson shrugged. "Then why are they targets?"

"Because innocent bystanders get killed, Douglas. All the time."

"That's not on my head. I can't live my life worrying about how the mafia will react to the choices I make in the best interest of me and my friends."

"Unfortunately, that's exactly how I live my life," Joseph said.

Jackson sat back. Joseph took a drink of coffee, never breaking eye contact with Jackson.

"So does that mean I walk alone?" Jackson asked.

"Not necessarily. But this has to be done right."

"What does that mean?"

"We need to think it through. Maybe lay some feelers. This can't be a rush job."

"Yeah, well, every minute that goes by, Bocharov and Fischer run around loose and Maggie's life is in danger. I don't have that kind of time."

"Can you give me twenty-four hours?" Joseph asked.

"I was thinking more like sundown."

"That's two hours."

"Less. It's overcast."

Joseph sighed. He slouched, for the first time. "I can't decide if I really like you or really dislike you."

"I don't mean to be a jerk," Jackson said, "but every decision I make, I'm making with Maggie in my head."

"You really care for this girl, huh?"

"She's a good friend."

Joseph's eyes pried for a moment, then he let them fall. "Okay, let me make a call. Buy me another."

Joseph stood and headed for someplace private to make his call. Jackson bought two more coffees and returned to the table. Joseph was nowhere to be seen, so Jackson stared at the snow falling outside. It was snow now, not just flurries, starting to accumulate on the grass, bushes, and dirt. The streets would be next. Jackson really missed L.A., even if it had been a sort of drizzly autumn.

Ten minutes passed before Joseph slid back into his booth. "Agents Weatherford and Murphy are on their way down from Albany," he said. "When they get here, we'll move."

"So is this the part where you tell me to go stay out of the way?" Jackson asked.

"Ideally, yes. But I'm afraid if we're going to sell this, you're going to have to play a role. So let's talk strategy."

*   *   *

7:43 p.m.

TWO INCHES of snow blanketed Kingston. It had fallen all afternoon and evening, slow and steady, eventually accumulating. It would make a nice contrast to the blood, Special Agent Weatherford said. He was tall and cocky and chomped gum all the time. Special Agent Murphy was short, a little stocky, with a voice like a white Dave Stewart. Both of them regarded Jackson as a pimple on prom night.

But Jackson had to give the FBI credit. In the three and a half hours since Weatherford and Murphy had joined Joseph, they had put together a comprehensive plan. Research, scouting, failsafe upon failsafe. Had it not been for his singular purpose of protecting Maggie, Jackson would have been overwhelmed with what lay ahead.

The first element of the devised plan commenced at quarter to eight when Jackson called Kasper's cell phone, a number supplied by FBI research. He told him he had vital information about Maxim Baby, the Baby Crime Family, and several members of his own family. Threateningly, he said it was in Kasper's best interest to meet with him as soon as possible.

"I'm afraid I don't respond well to threats," Kasper said. His voice was thick and slow, and Jackson pictured a hulking body and lots of scraggly facial hair.

"Okay, well then if you'll excuse me, I have to go make this same deal to Maxim. You have a nice evening. Don't strain yourself shovel—"

"Can the act. What do you want?"

"Meet me and my friend, and we'll explain it all. Your place?"

"How do you know where I live?"

"I'm connected," Jackson said.

"Where are you now?"

"In my car. Do we have a deal?"

"Eight-thirty."

"We'll be there."

Jackson closed the phone and smiled. Agent Weatherford wiped the smile away. "You realize you're going to be walking into the teeth of the Russian mob, right?"

"Yes, but I have leverage. I hate the Babys almost as much as they do."

366

"We should get moving," Murphy squawked, tapping Weatherford's shoulder. "Be careful," he said, looking at Joseph and very much not at Jackson.

"We will," Joseph said. He sipped more coffee—a bladder like a sponge. "You sure you're ready for this, Douglas?" he asked when his partners were gone.

"Ready as I ever will be."

"That's not exactly a rousing yes."

Jackson shrugged.

"Okay," Joseph said. "Run the script one more time."

They ran it twice, then headed out into the Catskills. Kasper and his wife, Tamara, lived in a luxurious cabin on the side of a mountain. His son, Kasper V, and daughter, Valerie, both lived in the area, and were known to frequent the house. Amazing, the depth of FBI research. There were also servants and henchmen and any number of family members who may or may not be present, ready to bury Jackson.

Snow was still falling, and the mountain roads were a little slippery, so they were already late when Joseph turned into a narrow driveway and stopped at a gate. He rolled down his window and leaned toward an intercom built into the stone surface. "Douglas, party of two."

No response came from the intercom, but the gate slowly opened. Joseph drove forward, up the side of a hill, then back around in front of a house that made Konrad's look like a Mongolian yurt. The massive front was lined with a stone façade, creating the appearance that the house was part of the side of the mountain. Giant pines towered over the structure on either side. Behind the house, the terrain was bare, allowing a view up the hill. With the falling snow, it looked just like an Austrian ski chalet.

"You've got this, Douglas. Just like we practiced."

He nodded. "Let's roll." He wasn't sure, but he thought he heard a sigh in his comm. Weatherford.

Jackson and Joseph got out and headed up the front steps of the house, Jackson leading. The front porch was protected from the snow, but several inches had accumulated on the waist-high stone wall around the perimeter.

"Heat signatures show six to eight people inside the house," Murphy reported quietly as Jackson pressed the doorbell. He was in awe of the FBI's technology, and also a little skeptical. Six to eight? Were there a couple of Great Danes walking around the house on their hind legs? Had they mistaken a fireplace for a heavyset aunt?

Kasper himself opened the door. His eyes were dark and menacing, but he forced a smile to his face. An alligator circling a canary. He wore a thick tan sweater, like an Alaskan ice fisherman might wear, and corduroys. Loafers. The casual mafia look.

Kasper stepped back and allowed Jackson and Joseph to enter. Immediately, a man in a suit stepped forward and patted them down. He didn't find any weapons, because there weren't any to be found. Satisfied, Kasper turned and motioned for them to follow. Without introductions, he led them through a massive great room, down a hallway past the kitchen, and into a study. Rich red carpet offset the dark wood of the bookcases (albeit filled with far more than books) that lined three walls. The other was a massive bay window looking out at a snow-capped forest of pines.

"Have a seat," Kasper said, motioning at several couches in the middle of the room. Jackson and Joseph sat side by side. Kasper sat adjacent to them. His friend in the suit stood by the door.

"I typically offer my guests cigars or vodka, but given the nature of your visit, you'll excuse me if I smoke alone," he said, deliberately lifting a cigar from a humidor on the bureau behind the couch. He clipped it, then pulled a lighter from his pocket and puffed a few times until the cigar lit. He inhaled twice, then returned the lighter to his pocket and sat back. His eyes, if possible, narrowed farther. "What do you want?"

"I have a deal for you," Jackson said.

"A deal?"

"That's right."

Kasper puffed on the cigar. "Please, go ahead. Share with me your deal."

"I should preface it by telling you I know everything. I'm a close friend of your niece—the one your family exiled because she had the nerve to report the truth. I know about the robbery at Troika, Brendan's death, and your current—ahem—partnership with the Baby family."

The eyes narrowed some more. Slits just wide enough to let out black hatred.

"But I'm not breaking any news," Jackson said. "So try this: I also know that Brendan wasn't working on his own when he broke into Troika. He was working for Maxim Baby."

Finally, a crack in the dam. Kasper licked his lips. Then he slowly brought the cigar to his mouth and took a long drag.

"The Babys killed Brendan before he could talk and reveal he was working for them. They knew if it came out, your family would destroy them."

Kasper glanced at his watch. Jackson paid no attention to the gimmick. He knew he had the big man, and continued, explaining that Bocharov and Fischer had broken into Maggie's apartment, presumably on Maxim Baby's orders. "You see, Maxim thinks Maggie knows more about what happened than was in her article. He thinks she knows that Brendan was working for him. And if she were to ever reveal that to you, well, that would really put the kibosh on your profitable little partnership, wouldn't it?"

Kasper had taken another drag on the cigar, and he slowly removed it from his mouth.

"And I'll be honest," Jackson continued, "I don't give a crap about you and your enterprises or Maxim Baby and his crimes. I'm just here to protect Maggie. And I figure if her secret is out—or rather, the secret people thinks she has, which she really doesn't—then nobody has any reason to come after her."

Kasper finally spoke. "I am not the one who sent Mr. Bocharov and Mr. Fischer to her apartment. Why are you talking to me?"

"I have a deal, remember? The Babys work for you. You have to have something on them, something you're holding for a special occasion. Well, this is it. You turn them in, and not only is Maggie safe from them, but so are the little girls they've been abusing with their sex trade."

"I must admit, sir," Kasper said after a moment's pause, "that you are well-informed."

"Didn't I tell you?"

"But there's a flaw in your deal."

"Oh, what's that?"

"You yourself said it, we have a lucrative partnership. Why would I jeopardize that to help you?"

"Because you were making it hand over fist before the Babys came into the picture," Jackson said, relying on what Joseph, Weatherford, and Murphy had dug up. "And because if you don't go to the feds and turn in the Babys, then you'll seek retribution some other way for what they did to Brendan. A guy like you doesn't take betrayal and murder lying down. So you can either do it your way, and then go to prison for the rest of your life, or you can do it my way and send Maxim Baby and his goons to prison for the rest of their lives."

Kasper exhaled a thick tuft of smoke.

"And you should know," Jackson said, "that I've already contacted the FBI. They know everything I know, so they'll be all over you. You smoke Maxim, they'll have you in cuffs before the echo of the gunshot."

"Your deal seems more like a threat," Kasper said.

"Semantics. And frankly, if you roll on Baby or bury him under the Meadowlands, it's all the same to me. I just thought staying out of prison might appeal to you."

Kasper leaned forward. "I don't like being handled," he said.

"Life's full of things we don't like, isn't it?"

"You're awful smug."

"Never said I was perfect, just well-connected."

Kasper thought for a few minutes. "You have proof of all this?"

Jackson nodded at Joseph. "That's where my friend comes in. Meet FBI Special Agent Jamie Joseph. He's got more dirt on Maxim Baby than anybody, except maybe you. Your combined testimony should nail him to the wall."

"You lied to me," Kasper said.

"I did no such thing. You were the one who never asked for introductions."

Joseph edged forward. "I spent three months undercover with the Babys," he said. "I know what they're doing, but I don't have the proof. With your cooperation, we can, as Mr. Douglas said, nail Maxim Baby and his organization to the wall." He sat a little farther forward. "That may seem bad for business for you, at first. But not nearly as bad as being tied to Baby when we finally bring him down. And I assure you, that day is coming."

"You have identification?" Kasper asked.

Joseph reached for his wallet and showed Kasper his badge and ID. Kasper studied it, then stood and paced for almost five minutes, puffing on his cigar all the while. Jackson and Joseph exchanged a few nervous glances and watched the snow fall outside.

Kasper returned and sat down. "What do you need from me specifically?"

Joseph spent half an hour laying out the details of the case against the Babys, what they needed from Kasper, what protections they could offer, etcetera. A little before nine-thirty, he and Jackson walked out of the house into hangover flurries floating erratically toward the ground. They didn't speak until they were in the car and out of the driveway.

"Well, that went well," Jackson said.

"He seemed to buy it," Joseph said. "Looks like he'll cooperate. Guys, you get all that?"

"We got it," Weatherford said. "We'll keep eyes on the house."

"You get the wiretap warrant?"

Murphy replied. "Yeah. In place. If he makes a call, we'll know about it."

"Good. We'll be in touch."

"Enjoy your warm beds," Weatherford mumbled.

Jackson couldn't resist. "Enjoy sleeping in your car." He pulled out the comm before Weatherford finished cursing in reply.

"I've made up my mind, Douglas," Joseph said with a quick grin. "I like you."

"That puts you in a select group, Agent Joseph."

They returned to town and Joseph dropped Jackson at the Bonne Belle. "Seven o'clock tomorrow?"

"I'll be ready," Jackson said.

Joseph nodded. "Good work tonight."

"Thanks." Jackson closed the door and trudged to his room. The snow was still falling in the valley, and he stopped a moment outside his door to admire the view. Then he reached for his key. Good work, yeah. But the real test would come in the morning. That's when the train was in danger of coming off the tracks.

Chapter Forty-Eight

Friday, December 21
7:16 a.m.

MAXIM BABY HAD breakfast, consisting of a cup of coffee—cream, two sugars—and white toast with butter, every morning at a small diner by the river. He had a back table, all by himself, where he read the newspaper, made calls, or just ate in silence. But he was not alone. Two of his thugs staked out an adjoining table, making sure Maxim was not interrupted unless he chose to be. Which made Jackson's task a little more challenging.

So too did the fact that he would be going alone. Joseph could supply information, but couldn't risk showing his face to Maxim Baby, not right away. He and Murphy would be stationed nearby. Weatherford would be in the diner, but not with Jackson.

The other problem was that Brendan had been working for Maxim, which gave Kasper motive to turn on his partner. There was no such motive the other way around. Joseph, from his time undercover, knew some of the skeletons in Kasper's closet, and was sure that Maxim knew even more. But how dark those skeletons were was something of a mystery—a mystery on which Jackson's plan hinged.

He'd been debating his exact strategy all morning, and had talked over several possibilities with Joseph on the drive over. As he entered the diner, however, and spotted Maxim in the back corner with his coffee and toast, a new plan came to mind. One he embraced.

Maxim didn't look like a mafia don or mob boss. He was thin, mostly bald, with a rim of hair around the top of his head and in back. He wore a suit coat over a sweater vest and slacks. And boots, to combat the snow. Quite a fashion statement. Jackson would have guessed him in his upper fifties. Joseph said he was sixty-nine. Too bad—his life without parole sentence wouldn't be nearly long enough.

Jackson ordered a cup of coffee, black, and took the lid off under the pretense of blowing on it. He walked toward Maxim, cutting his eyes to the restroom hallway to the right. At the last second, he veered left. A guy in a black trench coat popped out of his chair. Jackson stopped and, before the thug could reach him, flung his coffee toward Maxim. It hit his paper, drenched his toast, and caught him on the chin and neck.

The old man howled with pain as the burning coffee soaked his flesh. Jackson didn't even see it all, because the guy in the trench coat put him on his back, nearly knocking the wind out of him. "Kasper," was all Jackson could get out before the guy grabbed him by the neck and picked him up, pinning him against the wall. Jackson's eyes observed the majority of patrons looking his way, including Weatherford. With his eyes he tried to send the agent a message that he had things under control.

"What did you say?" the thug asked. His pal was tending to Maxim, who was cursing under his breath as he tried to blot the coffee off his skin and clothes.

"I have a message from Kasper," Jackson wheezed.

"You're a dead man," Maxim mumbled, stepping away from his table. "Take him into the back room."

Jackson was ushered through a doorway he hadn't even seen before and thrown to the floor. He started to get up, but before he had the chance, Maxim stood over him. He looked like an angry hawk, sharp eyes peering down at him. While not physically imposing, his external "muscles" were.

"What about Kasper?" he asked.

"He's going to kill you."

Maxim swore, implying he didn't believe Jackson.

"Cat's out of the bag, Maxim. He knows that Brendan was working for you when he robbed Troika eleven and a half years ago. He knows he was dating Sasha, that their son is as much his as yours. He isn't happy."

"And I suppose you're the pigeon that squealed to him?"

"Me and an old friend of yours. Special Agent Jamie Joseph?"

Maxim nodded over his shoulder. "Mikhail, sweep the perimeter."

Jackson looked up at Thug Number One. Plenty of muscles left. Maxim nodded at him, and he frisked Jackson, thoroughly and roughly. "He's clean."

"I'm not an idiot," Jackson said. "I came here to make you a deal."

"I don't make deals with peons like you."

"Suit yourself. I'll see myself out. I assume you have to book out of here so you can go pack up your existence and head back to Moscow before Kasper sends you and your pals here swimming with some cinderblocks."

"You talk big."

"Yeah, I act big too. And twenty people, including a federal agent, saw you and your goons bring me in here. If I don't come out in similar condition, you'll at least spend the night in the local lockup. Which should be plenty of time for Kasper to formulate an extinction plan and mobilize it."

"You want me to ice him?" Thug Number One asked.

"Ice? Really? How original," Jackson said.

He was rewarded with a kick in his side that had to have hit an organ. Jackson rolled over, holding his ribs. He looked up at a crouching Maxim.

"Yuri here is capable of inflicting great pain—pain that leaves no external marks."

"Sure, but tell him to hurry, will you. I get queasy around blood, and I hate to have to watch Kasper slit your throat."

"He will not slit my throat. Our business—"

"Your business means nothing to him, old man. He was doing fine long before you ever came along and will be doing fine long after you're gone. At least, that's what he told me."

Maxim's coal-like eyes searched Jackson. "You're lying."

"Right. I got up this morning and said, 'Hmm, what can I do to get a beating? Oh yeah, I'll go mess with Maxim Baby.'" He shook his head. "You really dumb enough to think I'm that dumb?"

Maxim stood slowly. He was caving.

"Why?" he asked.

"Because you sent your goons to my friend's place out in L.A. See, the way I figure it, you think Maggie has the goods that can ruin your relationship with Kasper. But I've already ruined it. And either one of two things happens: Kasper kills you, which, considering you're about the lowest slime on the earth, works for me. Or else you go to the feds, tell them everything you know about Kasper and the extended family that disowned Maggie. You cut a deal, and they all go away. That works for me pretty good too. The ball's in your court, Max."

The eyes actually started to smolder. "Who are you?" Maxim asked.

"Consider me a broker. I put deals together. Now, if you choose option B and decide to dime Kasper—and that's my bet, because if you're like me, your self-preservation instinct has probably kicked in by now—I can get in touch with

Agent Joseph. You can call him a few dirty words and then get down to business. Else, it's been real."

Maxim turned away. Yuri looked like he wanted to beat Jackson to death—and probably could. Jackson hoped his pounding heart wasn't showing through his shirt. His bluff was about to work, so he kept up the cocky sneer. "Poop or get off the pot, Max. Kasper's been sitting on this for twelve hours. If I'm his crony, carrying a gun instead of coffee, you're toast."

Maxim cursed as he turned back. "Call Agent Joseph."

"Your hound here isn't going to cap me when I reach for the phone, is he?"

Maxim took a step forward. "But if you are being dishonest, if you are cooking something here, you will suffer unimaginable pain."

Jackson stared stone-faced at Maxim as he reached for his phone. Joseph was on speed dial, and answered right away. "Douglas?"

"We're a go. I'll set up the meet."

"All right. Good work."

Jackson closed the phone. He looked at Maxim. "How soon can you be in Albany?"

*   *   *

10:13 a.m.

INTERROGATION ROOM #2 at the FBI Field Office in Albany had two doors, one on either end of the plain gray room. Jackson stood with Special Agent Jenna Hastings on the other side of a two-way mirror, both drinking coffee. Hastings was pretty and kind, a refreshing change from Weatherford, who'd given Jackson guff all morning. Sure, the coffee stunt with Maxim Baby had been a little dicey, but it had worked, hadn't it?

Fortunately, Weatherford had been occupied for the last forty-five minutes, debriefing Maxim Baby. Joseph had spent the time with Kasper and Konrad, who were both testifying against Maxim. As of yet, neither party knew the other was in Albany. Maxim had been ushered in through a rear door from a side street parking lot. Kasper and Konrad had waltzed in the front door. All three had waived the right to have an attorney present, likely because they knew lawyers wouldn't let them say most of what they had to say to indict the other party.

The right door opened first, and Kasper and Konrad walked in. They were offered seats on Jackson's right, at a table that had been turned sideways.

375

Normally it was placed so that anyone watching from behind the glass would get a look at the suspect being interrogated. This was different.

Joseph stood at the far end of the table, looking at Jackson and Hastings, even though he couldn't see them. Jackson sipped his coffee, trying to force the nerves out of his body. They should have been gone—he'd done it. Kasper and Konrad had rolled on Maxim, and he on them. But Jackson's concern wasn't an indictment and making it stick and cleaning up corruption and all that. That would be nice. His real concern was Maggie's safety.

The left door opened and a downtrodden Maxim shuffled in, ushered by Weatherford. He stopped suddenly when he saw Kasper and Konrad at the table. They both rose.

"What's going on here?" Maxim asked, his voice muffled somewhat by the old speaker system carrying it to Jackson and Hastings.

"What is he doing here?" Kasper asked.

"Did we forget to tell you?" Joseph asked innocently. "We thought we'd bring everyone together, to really get at the truth."

"I told you the truth," Kasper replied.

"As did I," Maxim shouted.

That led to more shouting, protests of innocence, accusations of lying, louder shouting, finger pointing, and plenty of swearing.

"You ever seen *Enemy of the State*?" Jackson asked.

"With Gene Hackman?" Hastings said.

"I was thinking Will Smith, but yeah. In the kitchen of the little Italian restaurant, right before everyone got shot . . ."

"We have all the guns," Hastings said.

"Yeah," Jackson said, tipping his cup up. His third of the day—not counting the one he had spilled on Maxim—and he was at least a little wired. The exact opposite of what he needed. Should have just asked for warm milk.

Joseph finally got everyone to be quiet. "Sit down," he said.

"I will not be part of this," Maxim said.

"Fine," Weatherford said from behind him. "Let them tell the whole story."

Maxim spat another curse and reluctantly took his chair.

"Here's the deal," Joseph said. "You're all going to jail. It's up to you to determine for how long."

"This is entrapment," Maxim said.

"You had a choice to bring a lawyer."

"I wasn't aware they would be here," he said, nodding across the table.

"So you're poorly informed," Joseph said with a shrug. "Not my problem."

"I want my lawyer. Now."

Joseph nodded at Weatherford. "Will you get his lawyer on the phone? And take him out of here. We'll question these two while he waits. We should have enough before Mr. Baby's lawyer arrives."

"Wait," Maxim said.

"Change of heart? You want to stay?"

"This is entrapment."

"It's nothing of the sort, Mr. Baby. You are free to stay, or free to wait to be questioned until your attorney is present. Your choice."

Maxim swore again, then sat.

"Here's how it's going to work," Joseph said. "You're both going to jail, like I said. You've each testified against each other, enough to corroborate other evidence that's been gathered over the years. I may have a baby face, but I've been doing this a while. We have enough to get indictments. I've also been around long enough to know that if you disappear, your . . . 'businesses' will be run by somebody else. So here's your chance. I think you've been holding out on me. You come clean, put everything on the table against the other guy, I see what I can do about a plea deal."

Three sets of glaring eyes bored a hole in Joseph.

"Only one deal out there," he said. "Whoever gives me the scoop first wins."

Maxim cursed. "This is outrageous. I ref—"

"Baby has a safe house outside Marlboro, overlooking the river," Kasper said. "You're looking for Bocharov. He might be there."

Maxim popped out of his chair, calling Kasper every name in the book. He looked as if he might crawl across the table and attack the big man, but Kasper rose from his chair, to full stature. Maxim just swore some more.

"Sit down, both of you," Joseph said.

They did.

"The *Chatsha*," Kasper said. "A Russian freighter. It is how he smuggles girls to this country."

"You—" Maxim's face boiled.

"He brings them to Port New—"

"He only knows this because he has taken over twenty-five percent of human trafficking operations," Maxim nearly shouted. 'Or should I say, twenty-five percent of the profits."

"Port Newark-Elizabeth Marine Terminal," Kasper continued. "From there he transports them via railroad to—"

"Kasper has brought in Ukrainian mercenaries to run several of his shipping corpor—"

"You want a man named Malinov," Kasper said. "He directs the shipments after they leave Port Newark."

And so it went for the next twenty minutes, with Kasper and occasionally Konrad telling all of Maxim's dirty secrets, and he telling all of theirs. Neither was smart enough to suggest they both shut up and wait for attorneys. Instead, they tried to reveal enough to satisfy Joseph, not realizing the dirt they were using to bury the other guy was coming from the hole they were digging for themselves.

Finally, at quarter to eleven, Joseph stepped forward and stopped the onslaught. Jackson had heard more curse words in the last half hour than in his cumulative life. Maxim was shiny with sweat, his face red, his language having grown fouler and louder until he was almost reduced to tears. Joseph had Weatherford escort him out, then left following Kasper and Konrad. A minute later, a door behind Jackson and Hastings opened and Joseph entered their half of the room. He had removed his suit jacket, and stuffed his hands into his pockets. "We got 'em," he said.

"How well?" Jackson asked.

Joseph shrugged. "Hard to say. Depends on the judge, the jury, deals. But I doubt Maxim Baby will ever see the light of day again."

"Bail?"

"No. Not likely."

"What about his organization?"

"We'll go after them next. That will be part of the deals I mentioned. He might rat them out. Or they might rat each other out. The KKK knows more yet, and might give us details to lessen their sentences. But they're all going away, and the human trafficking charges will make for very sympathetic judges and juries. They will get hit hard."

"Good." Jackson exhaled. "You need anything else from me?"

"You gave Agent Hastings your full statement?"

"Every word."

"Then for now, I think we're good. Depending on how things play out, you may be a key witness at trial."

"You've got my number."

"I do," Joseph said. He stuck out his hand. "I still don't get how you got in the middle of all this, but I'm glad you did."

Jackson shook his hand. "I appreciate all your help. Sorry I caused you guys some headaches."

"Worth it in the end."

"You'll give Agent Weatherford my best?" Jackson said.

"Might as well, since you haven't."

They both grinned.

Special Agent Hastings walked Jackson out of the building. The sun was shining and the snow cover was blinding, but perhaps starting to melt. At least the foreboding gray skies were gone.

Jackson took a few deep breaths and headed for his rental car. It was time to get out of New York. The sun out west was surely warmer.

Chapter Forty-Nine

Tuesday, January 1
1:14 p.m.

SAM DROVE PAINSTAKINGLY, slowly and carefully, but they turned into Jackson's driveway at quarter after one—fifteen minutes before the Rose Bowl coverage began on ESPN, and three-quarters of an hour before kickoff. Sam hurried around to open Jackson's door and gingerly helped him out of the car.

"Keys?" she asked as he leaned on the open door.

He dug them out of his pocket and handed them to her.

"Are you okay to walk?" she asked.

"Just point me to the TV."

"Here," Sam said, sliding under his right arm and looping her left around his waist.

"I can make it, Sam, really."

"Quit pretending you don't like it."

"Liking and needing are two very different things."

They trudged toward the door, making it only a few steps before something akin to a shriek sounded from next door and Connie came bustling across the lawn. "Jackson, what happened?"

He stopped. "Do I look that bad?"

"You didn't come home last night, and then that football player friend of yours came by, and now . . ." She saw the bandage under his shirt. "Oh my goodness, are you all right?"

"You keep tabs on when I come home?"

"You're a private investigator. You have a dangerous job and I'm a concerned citizen."

"And I'm fine, Connie."

"Jackson Douglas, you are not fine." She looked to Sam. "What happened?"

"He was shot."

Connie gasped with the intake of a jet engine. Then she mumbled the name of some Italian saint. "Are you—Is he—My goodness!"

"He's okay," Sam said.

"You should be at the hospital."

"I was. Sam's a nurse. And shouldn't there be some confidentiality or something?"

"What happened, Jackson? Who shot you? Where?"

"I don't know, Connie."

"You don't know! How can you not know? Was it a robbery? A gang?"

Jackson turned to Sam. "How does one faint?"

"I really need to get him inside," Sam said.

"Of course, of course. You take good care of him. If you need anything, Jackson, anything, you just let me know."

"I'll call, Connie. Thanks."

She stood in the lawn and fussed while Sam helped Jackson inside. He sat down on the couch and immediately reached for the remote.

"Hold on," Sam said.

"To what?"

"You're not just sitting there and watching TV."

"I thought we had a deal."

"And the deal is, I'm in charge, remember."

"Contrary to popular belief, bossy girls are not hot."

Sam's hands went to her hips. She sighed. It was for show, and Jackson stifled a grin.

"You should probably lie down, or at least recline in some way." She looked around. "No pillows?"

"Dudes don't have pillows on their couch."

"Of course, I forgot about the almighty Dude Code. Well, do dudes keep pillows anywhere in their home?"

"Some use them in bed."

Sam sighed. "I'll be right back."

Jackson waited until she was up the stairs and then flipped on the TV. Georgia was playing Michigan, and he sat back to enjoy the final few minutes of a shootout. The sitting back hurt, and he considered that maybe Sam was right.

Michigan called timeout before a fourth down, and Jackson tried to push himself off the couch. The smokeys weren't going to slow-cook themselves.

"What are you doing?" Sam asked, bounding down the final few steps. She took the pillow from under her arm and tossed it in the chair.

"Going to the kitchen, Sam."

"No. You sit down," she said, and quickly grabbed the pillow to prop behind his back. "Here's the remote. Watch your game and your flyover and your national anthem. I will make your smokeys, get your drink, whatever you need. Okay?"

He paused for just a moment, as if he still wanted to resist such an offer. Then he settled back. "They're on the second shelf. Barbecue sauce should be in the door. The Crock—"

"I'll find everything, okay?"

"Okay."

She stood there for a moment, then bent down beside the couch. She cupped Jackson's head in her hands. "I'm so glad you're okay," she said, kissing his forehead.

"Me too."

She smiled.

"But you're blocking a critical fourth down."

Sam shook her head. "You are impossible."

*   *   *

Friday, December 21
3:20 p.m.

IT WAS only mid-afternoon, but already the sun was sinking in the southwestern sky, creating long shadows across Manhattan. Jackson's flight left a little after five, and he had decided to take the time to actually see a few sights. He'd followed the same path into the city, crossing the Hudson via the George Washington Bridge, before veering off onto the Henry Hudson Parkway. He'd followed that all the way to Battery Park at the southern tip of Manhattan Island, then jogged over to the FDR which had taken him back north. Past the Brooklyn, Manhattan, and Williamsburg Bridges, and past dozens of landmarks Jackson knew but couldn't identify. What stuck with him most was the contrast between bright sunlight and city shadows. That and the way the setting sun turned the old brownstones a fiery orange.

His marveling at the architecture had been interspersed with thoughts about Maggie. He'd called her to tell her he was coming home. Everything was fine, but he'd give her the details in person.

Truth was, he didn't know if everything was fine. What if Maxim Baby had a Johnny Cochrane up his sleeve, or was one of those mob bosses who still called out hits from behind bars—hits on the people responsible for him ending up in the slammer? Or what about old Uncle Kasper and Uncle Konrad? They had been indicted, admittedly on lesser charges than Maxim, but they would still do hard time. So might Maggie's father, for that matter. Would she care? And how did he tell her either way?

Jackson had a five-hour flight chasing the sun back to L.A. to think about what to tell Maggie. In the meantime, he concentrated on navigating New York traffic through Queens and on to La Guardia. There he agonized through the slow security lines, then waited in a cramped terminal before boarding his plane and sitting on the runway for forty-five minutes. He overheard another passenger saying that was typical and was actually factored into departure times at La Guardia. Stupid New York.

When the plane finally took off, Jackson was afforded a brilliant dusk view of the Manhattan skyline. He continued to stare out his window as they climbed several miles into the sky, which was still lit in the west. Slowly, the blue faded to black, and when the entire sky was dark, Jackson drained his cranberry juice and succumbed to sleep.

*   *   *

7:38 p.m. (PST)

LIKE EVERYONE else, Jackson filed off the plane in L.A., feeling dead. Clocks told him it was just after seven-thirty. His brain told him it was midnight. Well, at least a little after ten-thirty. An early wakeup call and twenty-four strenuous hours of fighting organized crime had taken their toll. He wanted nothing more than to go home, fall into bed, and wake up on New Year's Day for the bowl games.

Instead, he bumped into a guy in a suit who had hassled the flight attendant all across the Heartland. Jackson apologized once, and would have a second time, but he determined the guy was being a jerk, and turned the other way. He almost ran into Noelle.

"Jackson. Hi!"

"Noelle. What are you doing here?"

"Just got in from Vancouver," she said, shrugging a heavy-looking bag off her shoulder. It fell beside a behemoth rolling suitcase that was almost as tall as her.

"Shooting finished?" Jackson asked.

"We just wrapped episode one-eleven. Now we're off until the new year. What about you?" she asked. "Coming or going?"

"Coming. New York."

"New York? Business or pleasure?"

"Neither. More of a favor for a friend. A long story."

"You at least get a pretzel out of it?"

He laughed quietly.

"You look exhausted," she said.

"You look great."

Noelle smiled. "Thanks."

She did too, wearing a reddish sweater, black pants, a long black coat, and a white scarf. Her hair was crinkly, a little longer than before, still short of her shoulders. They were high, her eyes bright, her smile unwavering. Cute as the proverbial button.

"You have a ride home?" Jackson asked.

"My neighbor's going to pick me up," Noelle answered.

"Then can I help you with your bags?"

She grinned. "That would be great."

He took the handle of the rolling suitcase, then hung her other bag over his shoulder. They started walking. "Do you have Christmas plans?" Noelle asked.

"Not really," Jackson answered. "Grandpa's headed to Houston to see my uncle, and he's the only family I have in the area." He shrugged at Noelle's downturned face. "Reggie—the guy with the restaurant—he's having some get-together, I think. Most of my friends have nowhere to go."

They boarded an escalator. "How about you?" he asked.

"Seth and I are visiting Mom this weekend, then going to San Diego to Dad's for Christmas. He has a big family, so I'll just find a corner and hide for a few hours."

"Sounds great."

"It's not bad." They stepped off the elevator. "We should get together. Grab a drink or something. You can fill me in on life after *Twenty Something*—let me know what I have to look forward to."

"My schedule's wide open," Jackson said. "Just name the time and place."

"Okay." Noelle cast her eyes about. "There's Kendra."

Jackson followed her, was introduced to a short, middle-aged woman with a motherly disposition, and helped load Noelle's luggage into the back of Kendra's hybrid. "Thanks," Noelle said.

"Not a problem."

"I'll call you?"

"Sounds good."

She gave him a quick hug, and he watched her into the car. Then he headed for the extended stay lot where he'd parked his Granada. Maggie was waiting.

*   *   *

9:14 p.m.

MAGGIE TOOK the news stoically.

Maxim Baby was going to jail. Alexander Bocharov and Dmitri Fischer couldn't be far behind. The secret Maxim thought she held had been exposed, giving him no motive to come after her. If he wanted revenge, he would come after Jackson. Or rather, dispatch goons from prison to come after Jackson. Or so Jackson hoped.

Maggie's two uncles, and possibly her father, would also be going to prison. Of all the members of the "KKK," Maggie's father seemed to have the least liability. But it wasn't beyond the realm of possibility that he could go to prison. And Jackson said as much, with an apology.

"Let him," Maggie said. She'd sat at his kitchen table, drinking from a bottle of Coors the entire time. She tipped it up again. "If he's involved in what you say he is, let him go to prison." She shook her head. "I don't blame you."

"Still, I'm sorry."

"I'm just glad this is over," she said. "My family has been an absentee family forever. What difference does it make if a few of them have a new address?"

Jackson sighed as she stood and took her empty bottle to the trash. She came back and dug her hands into his shoulders.

"How'd you know?" he asked.

"I've flown across the country before."

He nodded and tried to relax tense muscles.

"I'm going to Las Vegas for Christmas," she said.

"That should be nice and quiet."

She lightly bapped him on the head, then continued the massage. "I just need to get away. I can ride my bike there, relax, maybe flirt with a few guys."

"Go ahead. I winked at the stewardess over Utah."

"I'm staying at the Mirage, in case you need to get a hold of me for some reason. If they need my testimony to pin somebody to the wall or something."

"Noted."

She stopped. "Thank you, Jack. I'm going to pay you back."

"Just don't do something stupid in Las Vegas."

"Like hook up with a bartender or something?"

"I'm not telling you what to do, Maggie. I'm just saying, you've had quite a couple of months. I'd hate to get a wedding notice in the mail Wednesday morning."

"I won't do anything stupid."

He sighed. "Ready to go home?"

"Yeah."

She was all packed, and in five minutes they were on the road.

"What about Sasha?" Maggie asked. "What's going to happen to her?"

Jackson shrugged. "She was an unwilling accomplice, so we kept her name out of things. I'm guessing she'll continue on with her rather miserable life."

"You think she's safe?"

"As far as Maxim knows, she had nothing to do with his getting busted."

"But she was part of the relationship with Brendan that started it all."

"I doubt that's even on Maxim's radar right now. She's as safe as she can be in that family."

Maggie sighed. "Sometimes life is a real bummer, you know that?"

He looked at her. "I do."

Chapter Fifty

Monday, December 24
7:44 p.m.

A LIGHT DRIZZLE had been falling all day, but had relented by the time Jackson pulled his Granada into the parking lot at Cameron's. The rain had been replaced by a low layer of fog that had moved in off the Pacific, giving the Santa Monica Beach a film noir ambiance.

"This is depressing Christmas weather," Sam declared from the passenger seat.

"It sure is, sweetheart."

She turned his way. "And that's a pretty lousy Sam Spade."

"Phillip Marlowe, but what's it matter?" Jackson opened his door and got out. A hundred yards of sand away, thin white lines separated one dark wave from the next. They rolled ashore in perfect perpetuity, an endless supply of incoming water, a constant in a world of change. Maybe that's why people found them so soothing.

Sam appeared beside him. "You ready?"

"Yeah." He didn't move.

"What?" she asked.

"I was just thinking."

Sam relaxed her posture. "About what?"

Jackson made one of his George Clooney faces—a slight raise of his cheek and a tiny furrow of the chin and brow, creating a smile so small that it couldn't really be called a smile. "You."

She relaxed a little more. "What about me?"

Jackson turned his eyes toward hers. "How adorable you look tonight."

And she did. Sam's long, blond hair had been cut several inches to just beneath her shoulders. Tonight it was straight, flared at the bottom. Her eyes were a blue the sky hadn't been, and her smile caused her entire face to glow. The cowl neck on her burgundy sweater seemed to swaddle her neck, and provided the perfect frame for the mental snapshot Jackson took of her face.

Sam's smile faded slowly. "You don't look so bad yourself," she said, reaching out a hand to smooth the collar of his white dress shirt. Worn under a Dodger-blue sweater, it was about as dressy as Jackson got.

Sam let her hand linger a second longer than necessary, then turned toward the restaurant. "Shall we?"

Reggie had reserved the Cameron's banquet room for a private celebration for friends who, like him, had nowhere else to go on Christmas. With Leroy in Houston until Monday, Jackson fit into that group. Sam had family in San Francisco, and was flying up to see them on Wednesday. But first she had to work a twelve-hour Christmas shift. Stephanie, her houseguest for the last four and a half months, had just moved back in with Brady, and thus was off the list. Knowing Reggie's generosity, he would have made room for her had it been necessary.

Wearing a bright red polo shirt, Reggie was the first to greet them when they reached the upstairs banquet room. "Hey, merry Christmas, J," Reggie said, extending a fist toward Jackson.

"Merry Christmas, Hoss," Jackson replied, bumping Reggie's knuckles with his own.

"Hoss?" Sam asked.

Jackson shrugged. A former All-Conference defensive end at Nebraska, Reggie still looked ready to take down opposing quarterbacks, and fit the description well.

"Thank you for the invitation," Sam said.

Reggie nodded. "My pleasure. Drinks are on the table in the corner, hors d'oeuvres too. Help yourselves. Dinner should be out in ten." He extended a bear-like hand in Sam's direction. "Sam, I'm glad you could make it. And you," he said, punching Jackson in the shoulder, "and I will catch up later."

Jackson nodded as Reggie headed off to greet another newcomer. So far, there were maybe a dozen people in the room. The only one Jackson recognized was Pam, Mouse's overweight, under-medicated sister.

"You want something to drink?" Jackson asked.

"Um, I'm actually going to freshen up," Sam said.

She slipped out of the room and Jackson found his way to the punch. He filled a cup and drank it while staring at the fireplace in the corner. It was trimmed with garland and holly. A professionally decorated tree stood in the corner to the left. Thanks to the cool weather, most of the guests were in sweaters and long sleeves. Jackson almost forgot he was in L.A.

"Hey, dude."

Jackson turned to see Mouse, also holding a cup of punch. He and Reggie were little more than acquaintances. But Mouse and Pam had no family to speak of, and Reggie's heart was as big as he was.

Jackson nodded at his pal. "Who's the guy with Pam?"

"Clark."

"I thought they split again. For good."

"They did. That was last month."

Jackson sipped his punch.

"How you been?"

"Busy. I bought myself the new *Call of Duty* for an early Christmas present. You ever feel like getting back at it, it's killer."

Pam materialized in front of them, hips everywhere. "Jackson."

"Merry Christmas, Pam."

"Have you met Clark?" she asked, looking over her shoulder, sounding bored. In true lackey fashion, Clark trailed a pace behind.

"No, but Mouse has told me a lot about you," Jackson said, offering his hand.

Clark cleared his throat and shook Jackson's hand. He frowned. "Mouse?"

Pam rolled her eyes. "It's some dorky nickname they use."

"I see."

Jackson turned over his shoulder as Sam returned.

"Your girlfriend?" Pam asked.

"This is Sam," he said. "Sam you know Mouse. This is his sister Pam and her boyfriend Clark."

"For the moment," Mouse muttered as Sam shook hands with Pam and Clark.

Reggie called for everyone's attention and announced that dinner was on its way up. The group filtered to a pair of tables, and Jackson found himself between Sam and a girl he was pretty sure was a new waitress at Cameron's.

"Girlfriend?" Sam asked.

Jackson made another George Clooney face, this one a little more pronounced, as Reggie clanked a fork on a glass. Behind him, several servers had appeared with rolling carts of food. He stood. "I want to thank you all for coming. Eat and drink as much as you like. I assure you we ain't running out." The big man smiled, holding up a glass of water. "A toast . . ."

Jackson reached for his plastic cup of punch.

"To celebrating with family and friends," Reggie said, "and to family and friends that, for whatever reason, cannot celebrate with us."

Jackson looked down, unable to fight back the memories of Christmases with his family.

"And to the Baby in the manger," Reggie continued, "in whose Name we gather tonight." He lifted his glass, as did the majority of the group. Jackson drained the rest of his punch and set his cup down.

"I've never toasted Jesus before," Sam said.

"It's fine as long as you don't use hard liquor," Jackson replied.

From then on, Cameron's beef tenderloin stole the show. Perfectly seasoned, grilled to a crisp on the outside, red and tender inside. Jackson ate until his stomach was about to burst. Dinner was followed by a round of tasty desserts, and he topped off the tenderloin with several slices of cake and pie as the evening progressed. Sam struck up a conversation with some woman Jackson had never met, and Jackson got up to intercept Mouse as he trailed behind Clark and Pam to the exit.

"You leaving already?"

"When you bum a ride with somebody . . ."

"I can run you home."

"You've already got a passenger, dude," he said with a nod at Sam. "Forget it."

"Kyle, come on," Pam said.

"You have a good Christmas, Mouse."

"Yeah, all mirth and merriment."

Jackson refilled his punch, snagged a couple slices of cold tenderloin, and returned to his seat. Reggie, having made his rounds, pulled out an empty chair.

"Nice toast," Jackson jibed. "Who knew you had a touch of the poet in you?"

"Practiced all afternoon," Reggie answered as he straddled the chair, backwards, as if it was still 1994. "So catch me up, man."

Jackson did. It had been a busy few weeks for Reggie, what with Christmas scheduling and preparations to get work done ahead of several holidays. Aside from a quick call to confirm the party time, they hadn't talked much of late. Jackson briefed him on Brady's assumed reformation, the break-in at Maggie's, and his trip to New York. Reggie listened quietly, just shaking his head. When Jackson was finished, he rubbed his hand over his head. "Man, the things you don't get into."

Jackson shrugged.

"How was church today?"

"Well, it depends. If you're a real stickler, it was biblically inaccurate."

"How so?"

"Wise men came to the manger."

"Ah."

"Sam fussed the whole way here. And Baby Jesus spit up halfway through Mary's solo, but that's probably not inaccurate. A sinless nature doesn't preclude spitting up."

"So how is Sam? I haven't seen her in a while." His eyes drifted across the room to her.

Jackson shrugged. "Same as always."

"She looks good."

Jackson turned his head. "Yes she does."

"The two of you have Christmas plans?" Reggie asked with a hint of suggestion.

"Yeah. Unfortunately not together. What about you?"

Reggie sighed. "Working, man."

"Bummer."

He shrugged. "Else I gotta pay double-time to somebody else. What about you, J? You got any work lined up?"

"Not really. You mind if I line my pockets when I leave?"

"Please do. Seriously, tell Sam if she needs a Christmas dinner, Ameer can whip up a little something for her."

"Sounds delightful."

Reggie took a deep breath. "And I can always make room for you. Something semi-permanent."

"No offense, but I'm hoping for more than busboy."

"Shoot, I wasn't even going to start you at busboy."

Jackson looked out the window. "They never really told me how long my license would be suspended . . ."

"You heard anything?"

He shook his head.

"Hang in there, J. Things will turn."

"My experience is they keep turning south."

Reggie placed a hand on Jackson's shoulder. "I used to think that too."

"Am I interrupting?"

They both looked up at Sam. Reggie lowered his arm. "Not at all," he said, pulling out a chair for her.

She gracefully dropped into it. "Reggie, thank you so much for dinner. It was fabulous."

"I'll tell the chef."

"Rumor has it you were the chef."

"More like executive producer."

"Well it was wonderful," Sam said.

Another guest stopped to thank Reggie on his way out, and the two of them slapped hands. Sam sipped her punch, eyeing Jackson over her cup.

"So J tells me you're headed to Frisco for the week," Reggie said when the guest was gone.

Sam nodded and broke her eyes away from Jackson. "I leave bright and early Wednesday. And I can't wait. I haven't seen my family since late summer."

"I thought about going home," Reggie said. "But with the restaurant, and . . . it's complicated."

"Yeah, well, at least you have the option," Jackson mumbled.

Reggie backhanded Jackson in the knee. "Hey, you guys going to stay a while? I should see a few more people, but if you're up to it, you're both invited to the after party."

"The after party?" Sam asked.

"Yeah, very exclusive, by invite only. You'll recognize it by the dessert tray getting passed again."

Jackson looked to Sam, who gave a slight nod. "Yeah, man, we'll be here."

"Great." Reggie stood. "Then I'll catch you later. Sam, I like your hair."

"Thank you," she said over her shoulder. She flicked it out of her face as she turned back to Jackson. "You all right? You've been contemplative all day."

He looked at his hands. "Holidays are hard."

Sam nodded, reaching her hand for Jackson's. "I know." She squeezed. He squeezed back. "You want to take a walk?" she asked. "Before the 'after party'?"

"A walk?"

She shrugged, eyes a touch beguiling. "I thought a stroll on the beach might be the perfect ending to a very good day."

"Except that the after party is actually the ending."

"Except for that," she said, her eyes now a friendly glare.

Jackson smiled and reached for her hand. "Sure."

They exited unnoticed and wandered south from Cameron's, toward the famed Santa Monica Pier. They had the beach mostly to themselves, and for several minutes, neither of them spoke. Jackson kept his hands in his pockets, his eyes out at the ocean. Movement caught his eye, and he turned to Sam. Even in a thick sweater, she was shivering. And with good reason. It had started to spit again, a drizzle so faint it was more like a thick, invisible cloud. Maybe it was just the fog, but whatever it was, it was damp and cold.

Jackson nodded up the beach at a small gazebo nestled among dormant flowerbeds and shrubs, with giant California fan palms towering overhead. They quickened their pace and reached it as the drizzle materialized. It was heavy enough to create a soft hiss as it pattered on the palm fronds, surrounding bushes, and the shingles of the gazebo. Sam shivered again, and Jackson instinctively put his arms around her.

Instead of squeezing his arms or giving them a pat, Sam sighed and settled back into his arms. For another few minutes, they stood there, listening to the rain, sheltered from the world around them. Then Sam leaned her head against Jackson's arm. "I wish I knew what to do to make things better."

"Well, you're doing a pretty good job right now," Jackson replied.

She turned around, and Jackson locked his fingers behind her back. For several moments, her big blue eyes studied him. Then she returned her head to his shoulder.

The drizzle turned to outright rain. "I think we might be stuck here a while," Jackson said quietly.

"I don't mind."

They stood and listened to the rain, in unusual territory physically. Their relationship had always been tinged with romance, but it had never developed into excessive hand holding or cuddling on the couch or long hugs in the rain. And yet, this felt perfectly natural.

"Jackson?"

"Mmm?"

"The rain's stopped."

"So it has. I suppose we should head back."

"I suppose we should," she answered.

Jackson stared into her eyes. Even in the darkness, they were pools of azure, and he felt like going for a swim. He reached his hand up and swept a strand of hair off her cheek, tracing it with the back of his hand in the process. He made the first move, lowering his head slightly. She raised hers in response. Their lips brushed, and then they kissed.

They separated after several seconds, again locking eyes. Jackson was aware of the mist around them, of the distant lapping of waves against the shoreline behind him, of cars passing on the rain-slicked Pacific Coast Highway. But it was as if it was all a giant fresco surrounding the gazebo. None of it seemed to penetrate.

He studied Sam's face, not smiling but still aglow.

"Sam . . ."

"Shh," she said softly, placing the tip of her index finger over his lips. "Don't say anything," she breathed.

This time she made the first move, reaching up to embrace him. She wrapped her arms loosely behind his neck and they kissed a second time. Longer, slower, three or four kisses combined into one. Jackson pulled her close, and Sam raised herself onto her toes, her hand clasping the back of Jackson's head. The fresco faded away, and the only thing in Jackson's world was Sam.

She withdrew and settled in against him with a soft sigh. Jackson held her, stroking the back of her head for several minutes that could have been hours. Finally, with another sigh, she stepped away. Without a word, she took Jackson's hand and led him out of the gazebo and back toward the restaurant.

He allowed himself to be led along, doubting there was any way Reggie's after party could compete with the one he and Sam had just celebrated.

Chapter Fifty-One

Tuesday, January 1
1:51 p.m.

THE ROSE BOWL in Pasadena was awash in brilliant sunlight. The sky was pure blue and the air crystal clear, adding distinction to the San Gabriel Mountains in the distance. Down on the field—a grass surface that resembled a fairway with a giant rose painted in the middle—the cardinal and gold jerseys and pants worn by the Trojan players caught every ray of sunshine, and contrasted perfectly with Iowa's black and yellow. USC's marching band played the national anthem, and as the final notes echoed around the old stadium, a B-2 Stealth Bomber buzzed overhead. The crowd erupted in patriotic fervor.

"Happy?" Sam asked. She stood at the foot of the couch, in between tending to the smokeys and monitoring Jackson's pain. She was also whipping up some other snacks, because miniature hot dogs were not a suitable dinner for a man recovering from a gunshot wound. Jackson had concurred, and said he thought there were pizza rolls somewhere in the freezer.

"Yes, I am," he answered.

Happy didn't begin to describe it. He had watched a thrilling finish between Michigan and Georgia—touchdown, touchdown, field goal in the final three minutes—and then caught a defensive stand by Texas A&M to seal the Gator Bowl. And that was just the undercard.

"Well, the smokeys are warm, the pizza rolls are in the oven, and you didn't have much else on hand, but I'm putting together a tray of cheese and crackers. Don't you have any veggies in the house?"

"Check the crisper."

"I did."

He shrugged, which hurt. She shook her head and returned to the kitchen. Jackson watched the coin toss, presided over by Michael Phelps, the Tournament of Roses Grand Marshal. As the players took the field for the opening kickoff,

Jackson's cell began playing CCR. Maggie. Calling now? He wasn't about to answer it, especially with Sam in the next room.

"Is that your phone?"

"Yes."

"Aren't you going to answer it?"

"Ball's in the air," Jackson said as the Trojan kicker booted the opening kickoff to the goal line. Iowa's return man only managed the eighteen yard line. Jackson sat up a little straighter as the USC defense took the field.

Sam appeared in the doorway. "'Bad Moon Rising'?" she asked. "Whose ringtone is that?"

"A friend."

"And you're not answering a call from a friend?"

Iowa ran a play-action pass, and under duress, the quarterback threw the ball away.

"Bad timing," he said, looking quickly to her.

Sam's hands went to her hips. Iowa ran a delay into the line for a yard. Third and nine, and the Trojan defenders were already woofing.

"What's my ringtone?" Sam asked.

"Seriously, Sam, can this stimulating conversation wait?"

She made a face as she returned to the kitchen. Iowa ran a rollout, and the quarterback had to throw the ball away again. Jackson pumped his fist, then thought better of any physical displays of emotion. Fist pumps led to hands raised which led to jumps off the couch which led back to the hospital.

Iowa punted, and as the ball sailed out of bounds around midfield, Jackson's phone started again. This time it was Point of Grace, singing the chorus of "By Heart." He swiped it off the table as Sam peeked around the corner. "That's my ringtone?"

"Really?"

She grinned. "That's very sweet, if not perhaps sacrilegious."

Jackson shook his head. "How are those smokeys coming?"

"Almost ready."

She returned to the kitchen and Jackson continued shaking his head. "I think the hospital would have had less interruptions."

"I heard that."

*   *   *

Tuesday, December 25
11:55 a.m.

JACKSON SLEPT till noon. Consciousness slowly washed away the sleep, in the process reminding him that he was alone. No wife lying beside him with a thin, contented smile. No kids kicking at the door, anxious to open presents. No brother, sister-in-law, and nephews and nieces loaded into a minivan to come over, or filling a house with laughter and cheer for him to visit. Most painfully of all, no parents.

No Mom cooking a turkey dinner and saturating the house with its aroma, ornamenting the walls with all manner of festive decorations, or pushing cookies and candy like a used car salesman behind on commission. No Dad brewing an early pot of coffee, wearing old sweaters, guiding the family to the biblical meaning of Christmas, or with whom to have a casual chat that turned into serious, cherished conversation.

Leroy was in Houston through the end of the week, Reggie was working, Mouse was "stuck" with Pam, Sam was working then headed to San Francisco to be with her family, and Maggie was in Las Vegas.

For a few moments as Jackson staggered out of bed and into the bathroom, he contemplated what life might be like had he taken a different path. He would be with Maggie in Vegas, enjoying all the pleasures that it—and she—had to offer. Forget the sensual, just kicking it with her for a few days in America's Playground would be a blast. Pulling all-nighters on the Strip at various casinos, clubs, burger joints; bumming through the desert on her bike; lounging in the shade of poolside palms, cold drinks in hand; sharing the atmosphere of Vegas with a fun and feisty woman.

Nope. He was too virtuous for that. No sex till marriage. No shacking up with a spunky brunette. No weekend getaways to Sin City. He didn't regret his standards or the conviction—wavering as it was at times—to adhere to them. But he also couldn't deny that there were times he missed that which biblical living denied.

Then again, Vegas was tainted after what had happened back in September. In fact, he was something of a persona non grata with the local authorities, so it was best he stayed away.

As he showered, his thoughts turned to Sam, to their kiss the night before. Kisses, technically. It had been so unexpected, so out of the blue. And yet, it had felt so right. He contemplated what life might be like if he and Sam were more than friends. He would be driving up with her to San Francisco to meet the family, her adorably cute in a seasonal sweater. He pictured a warm house with a soft glow emanating from the tree and a fire in the hearth, classic Christmas music in the background, delicious food and laughter at the table, exchanged looks of love and happiness across the living room. Afterwards, he and Sam would take a walk outside. She'd shiver in the cold. He'd hold her. They'd do some more kissing.

Nope. Theirs was just a casual relationship. Sometimes he didn't know why. Did he possess that stereotypical male fear of commitment that subconsciously kept him from making their relationship official? Was it because of Maggie—was he not ready to be a "one-woman man"? Was it something on Sam's end? She'd never really pursued anything more serious or committed either. Unless you counted practically making out in a gazebo in the rain the night before.

Jackson shut off the water. He didn't really like analyzing his relationships. That was Dr. Zachary's domain. Besides, it was depressing today. Whatever the reasons, he was alone.

He dressed and headed downstairs to the cold, undecorated living room and into the kitchen, where he found the tinfoil "duck" of tenderloin and sides Reggie had sent home—but certainly not wrapped himself—the night before.

Merry Christmas.

*   *   *

Wednesday, December 26
10:07 a.m.

JACKSON ONLY slept till ten the following morning. Then, for a reason he couldn't really explain, he got up and went for a long run. It was something he did every once in a while, usually when he had a lot on his mind. In this case, he figured it had something to do with knowing that if he just sat around all day— with prospects for little else the rest of the week—he'd slip into another quagmire of depression. He was getting better at handling said quagmires, but he also knew there was a chance that one day he'd fall into one and never climb out.

Connie had come to the rescue the night before, inviting him over for a delicious dinner. Unbeknownst to Jackson, her niece Gina was visiting, and the three of them had stayed up into the morning hours catching up, talking about nothing, and filling the void in Jackson's heart reasonably well. It had beaten sitting home by himself all day and all night.

The air was cool, the sky marred by a marine layer that didn't dissipate throughout his run. He covered a few miles, thinking a little bit more about Maggie, Sam, love, sex, and his future. His thinking didn't accomplish much.

After returning home, he showered, made himself breakfast, and then sat down with his case files. He hated taking notes, and with his memory and easygoing nature, didn't really see the point in all the paperwork that went with being a P.I. But he knew it was good practice, especially if the State of California ever inquired, so he spent the afternoon coalescing his assortment of notes, thoughts, receipts, and the like and entering them into a somewhat organized format on his computer. In the background, several low-level, largely irrelevant bowl games played on the TV, occasionally distracting him. Once again, it beat just sitting around all day.

"Bad Moon Rising" began playing from the coffee table. Jackson had finished up on the computer and turned all his attention to a shootout between two mediocre teams—hey, it was football—and hadn't noticed that it had gotten dark outside, the only light coming from the TV and the glow of his laptop screen.

He muted the TV and scooped his phone off the couch beside him. "Hey, Mags, how was Veg—"

"Jack!"

He sat up. "Maggie, what's up?"

"You need to get over here right away."

"What happened?"

"I just found a horse's head in my bed."

Chapter Fifty-Two

6:13 p.m.

"WHAT?" JACKSON ASKED. "What do you mean by a horse's head? Are you okay?"

"I'll show you. Can you come over?"

"I'll be there as soon as I can. Are you safe?"

"The cops are on their way."

"I'm heading out the door."

Technically, he was headed upstairs to his room, where he grabbed his Glock, making sure it was loaded and the safety was engaged. He stuck it in his pants. Just in case. Then he headed out the door.

It was a twenty-five minute drive to Maggie's apartment, on a good day. Jackson made it in twenty. A uniformed officer stopped him at Maggie's apartment door, and appeared ready to clobber him with his nightstick. But Maggie intervened and the officer grudgingly stepped aside to allow Jackson into the apartment.

"Thanks for coming, Jack," Maggie said. She wore jeans and a Yankees T-shirt. Her hair was creased, as if it had been in a ponytail all day, and her skin was a shade paler than normal. A suitcase sat by the bedroom door, a reminder that she had just returned from Las Vegas.

"Yeah," Jackson answered. "What's going on?" He looked around the apartment. Detective Nichols and a man with a camera stood around the table in the dining room. Nichols, tonight with a jacket but no tie, was focused on his tablet screen. The guy with the camera was just standing there, staring at nothing. It was eerily similar to a week and a half ago.

"Come and see," Maggie said. She led him to the dining room and quickly reintroduced him to Detective Nichols. He eyed Jackson with cold detachment, then stepped aside.

"She made us wait," Nichols droned. "Said you'd want to see this."

The cameraman also took a few steps back from the table and Jackson eyed a square brown box, eight or nine inches in length, width, and height. It had been opened down the middle, the flaps sticking out to the side. Jackson took another step and peered inside. And did a double take.

Nestled in shredded newspaper was a rat. Dead, covered in blood, likely its own because it appeared to have flowed from the slice across the neck.

Jackson looked up at Maggie. "Who sent this?"

"I don't know. No address."

Jackson turned to Nichols. "What else do you know?"

"Nothing yet." He looked at Maggie. "May we?"

"Yeah," she said, and pulled Jackson into the living room.

"Are you okay?" he asked.

Maggie nodded. "I'm okay. I just thought this was over."

"What happened?"

She shrugged. "I came home from Vegas and this was in my box. I didn't think much of it, just brought it in and set it on the counter. I was kind of tired and jetlagged, but curious too. So I sliced it open."

"No note or anything with it?"

She shook her head. "I saw it and called the cops right away. You next. I hope you weren't busy."

"No. You look a little pale. You need something to drink?"

"I'm okay," she said again. "Just a little surprised." She leaned against the back of the chair.

"Looks like we ruffled some feathers."

Her eyes met his. "You can say that again."

"Ma'am?"

Jackson turned and stepped aside so Nichols could address Maggie. "We're going to take everything into the lab, examine it there."

"Okay. Do you need anything else?"

"Not at the moment. Unless there's anything else you can tell us."

He said it as if there should be, but Maggie just shook her head.

Nichols nodded. "We'll be in touch if we find anything."

"Thank you."

He nodded again, then left, taking the cameraman and the officer by the door—and the rat—with him. Maggie closed and locked the door behind him.

"What all did you tell them?" Jackson asked

"All we know," she said. "Which isn't much as far as why there was a dead rat sent to me."

"It was addressed to you?"

Maggie nodded.

"Address and everything?"

She nodded.

"So it was mailed."

"Overnighted. With New York City postmark," she added before he could ask.

Jackson sighed.

Maggie reached into a drawer and pulled out a spray bottle and some paper towels. She proceeded to wipe down the dining room table.

"Is there anything I can do?" Jackson asked.

She looked up. "Can you stay tonight? I feel like a wimp asking, but . . . this has me scared."

Jackson nodded. "Of course."

Neither of them had eaten, so they ordered Chinese takeout. Technically delivery, which was slow in coming. When it finally arrived, they sat down at Maggie's well-cleaned table and enjoyed mounds of Kung Pao chicken and steamed rice.

"Now I know how you must feel all the time," Maggie said when they had finished.

"How's that?"

"Owing me."

Jackson grinned and sat down on her new loveseat. "Friends don't owe friends, Maggie. It comes with the territory."

She pitched her container in the garbage and joined him. "You mean that, or are you just laying the groundwork for the next time you need a favor?"

"Both."

Maggie sighed. "What did I do to bring all this on me?" she asked, slouching and dropping her head onto Jackson's shoulder.

"You write feisty exposés," he said. "You should write nice little pieces on old grandmothers and their charities or the Girl Scouts or something."

"Else not be born into the mob."

"Well, there's that."

Jackson ran the last few weeks through his mind. The bloody rat fit, and yet it didn't. The why wasn't making sense. Nor the who. He turned to ask Maggie a question, but saw her eyes closed. Her breathing was rhythmic and shallow, and he concurred that tiredness had won out over curiosity.

*   *   *

9:20 p.m.

MAGGIE WOKE up after about an hour, apologized, and then tried to get Jackson to sleep in her room while she took the loveseat. He declined, instead asking if the TV would keep her up.

"You're not going to sleep?" she asked.

"It's kind of early."

She glanced at the clock. "So it is. I'm beat though."

"That's fine, you can sleep. I'm too wired right now."

She had stood, but now dropped back down beside him, turning sideways to face him. "How was your Christmas?"

"Thrilling. I caught up on *Twenty Something.*"

"You hadn't been watching?"

"It's really not that good. And I was terrible."

"You hang out with Reggie at all?"

"He worked all day, but he had some people over for dinner Christmas Eve."

"That sounds nice."

"Yeah," Jackson said, still thinking about his kiss with Sam. He tried not to linger. "You?"

"It was eighty-four in Vegas, so I hung out by the pool, ate at BLT Burger and Landry's, saw Penn and Teller."

"It's not very Bing Crosby, but sounds fun."

"It was, and yet . . ." She ran a hand through her hair. "It was kind of empty."

He looked, waiting for her to continue.

"All this deal with my family has got me thinking lately, especially on the four-hour ride to and from Vegas. I'm spending a lot of holidays alone."

"Have you ever thought about trying to get in touch with them again? Maybe time has healed old wounds."

"You were just there. Did it seem like a lot of healing had taken place?"

"No, the wounds seemed rather fresh."

403

"I've accepted my family isn't my family anymore, isn't part of my life. I'm just . . ." She took a deep breath. "Sorry, I'm just thinking out loud. Death threats tend to make a person contemplative."

"It wasn't a death threat."

"No? How would you take a decapitated rat in the mail?"

"Hmm. Fair point."

"Anyhow, nothing can make you feel alone quite like a huge crowd of people. Couples, families, even frat boys on the prowl."

"You're preaching to the choir, Maggie. Why do you think I spent my Christmas watching four episodes of a mundane serial drama?"

"Next Christmas," she said, patting his knee. "You and I will celebrate together."

"Point of order, but do you actually celebrate Christmas?"

She shook her head. "Or maybe I'll call up Jake."

"Wh-who's Jake?"

Maggie winked. Then yawned. "I'm going to bed. Sure you don't want my room?"

"I'm sure. The guard should be by the perimeter anyhow."

She smiled and leaned over, quickly pecking his cheek. She withdrew her head a few inches. "Merry Christmas, Jack."

"'And to all a good night.'"

"You're such a dork," she said as she retreated toward her bedroom.

Jackson sat in place for several minutes, thinking about her. He loved Maggie's lively, aggressive, flirty side, but this new vulnerable, little-girl-asking-for-help side was kind of appealing too. It certainly stroked his male ego.

Having slept in the last two mornings, he wasn't at all tired. And Maggie's loveseat wasn't exactly a Tempur-Pedic. He channel surfed through several so-so options, then stumbled upon *Rio Bravo* just starting. Positioning a throw pillow against the armrest and extending his legs over the far arm of the loveseat, he settled back for a couple hours of action.

As always in Westerns, the good guys prevailed. While the credits rolled, Jackson stood, stretched, and walked over to the dining room and out onto the balcony. A siren sounded in the distance. Mechanical units on the apartment hummed. Cars started and stopped, and somewhere a horn honked. Jackson let the noise become static in the background, and spent a few minutes pondering Maggie's situation.

He'd feared some sort of retribution from her family or the Babys, but there was no provable link this was that. Nor was the meaning obvious. Was it a death threat? Was it just to scare her? Was the rat retribution or did it signal its coming? That was the real question. He sighed, realizing he had no clue.

Beginning to feel tired, he went back inside and carried the TV. He stepped out of his shoes and stretched out on the loveseat, his head and back flat, his legs bent over the arm.

Sleep didn't come right away. Instead he found himself thinking about Maggie some more, wondering if her feeling of loneliness wasn't so much because of her family as due to a spiritual awakening, a sense of a "God-shaped hole." If so, what could he do to help her awaken further? Sleep finally interrupted his musing, and he dreamt he was John Wayne, on an adventure with Indiana Jones and Dr. Elsa Schneider, fighting bloody rats and Turkish guys with fezes in the sewer beneath Venice, all the while trying to save Maggie's life.

*   *   *

Thursday, December 27
8:41 a.m.

MAGGIE WENT into work Thursday to do some year-end tidying up, as if nothing had happened the previous night. Jackson had tried to talk her out of it, saying they could hang. She said she really did have a few things to take care of post-vacation, and she could use the distraction.

So he headed for home, a shower, and a change of clothes. On the way, he gave Ashley a buzz.

"Detective Larson," she answered chipperly.

"Merry Christmas, Detective."

"Jackson?"

"Guilty as charged."

Her tone dropped. "What do you want?"

"Are my seasons' greetings insincere?"

"No, just your motives."

"That hurts."

"I know you, Jackson."

"Fair enough," he said, then launched into a brief explanation about the rat. He left out the details about his mob takedown in New York.

"And you're checking in on our progress, right?" Ashley asked.

"I am transparent."

"Very. I'm sorry, Jackson. I happened to talk to Detective Nichols this morning. He mentioned something about a suspicious package case. They passed it on to the feds."

"The feds?"

"Sending dead rats through the mail is serious business."

"I guess so. Any chance you can see what they've turned up?"

"Jackson."

"I'm not asking for me, Ash. For Maggie."

"Does asking one girl to do you a favor for another girl often work?"

"When it's a professional favor, yeah."

Ashley sighed.

"Come on, Ash. Without Maggie's help, I might never have found you and Dylan in time."

She sighed again. "I'll see what I can find out."

"Thanks."

"No promises. The feds don't like reading in local cops on their progress."

"Try my methods."

"Yeah, well, I don't have any favors to cash in over at the FBI, so I'll see if there's anyone I can sweet talk. I'll call you."

"Thanks, Ash. And I did mean it. Merry Christmas."

"Yeah, yeah. Same to you."

Jackson closed his phone with a grin. He still had it.

Chapter Fifty-Three

Tuesday, January 1
3:48 p.m.

ASIDE FROM THE bullet hole just above his scapula, Jackson's afternoon could not have been more perfect. The smokeys, pizza rolls, and cheese and crackers hit the spot after hospital food. His women stopped calling him. And under perfect, storybook conditions, USC was mauling Iowa. They had scored on five of six possessions, turned the Hawkeyes over twice, and blocked a punt. They led 27-7.

Sam stood and cleared their plates, stacking them in the kitchen and promising to do the dishes later—during the fourth quarter, when the game was for all intents and purposes over and Jackson was still watching because he was obsessed. She returned, biting her lip, standing between the dining room and the living room, backlit by the late afternoon sun. She was almost as pretty as the Rose Bowl.

"Is there some pageantry you need to watch at halftime?" she asked.

"Can't say as there is," Jackson replied. "Why, is it bandage changing time?"

"That can wait till before bed," she replied. She sat down on the coffee table. "But, there is actually something I wanted to talk about."

Jackson muted the TV and sat up a little straighter. "Sure. What's on your mind?"

"I know this probably isn't the ideal time, and I meant to talk about it last night, but, what with you getting shot . . ."

"It's a terrible inconvenience, isn't it?"

Sam smiled. "Can you not be a smart aleck for like two minutes?"

"I can try."

She gave him the look.

"Sorry. What's up?"

She took a deep breath. "I think we should talk—"

407

The doorbell interrupted her.

Sam quickly stood.

Jackson winced. Please don't let it be Maggie. He really should have answered her call.

"Oh, hi," said a somewhat high-pitched female voice when Sam opened the door. She was blocking Jackson's view of the visitor's small frame, but he knew her by the voice, even before she introduced herself as Detective Ashley Larson. "Is Jackson here?" she asked.

"Yes. Come on in," Sam said, stepping to the side.

"Jackson. Oh my goodness, are you okay?"

"Hi, Ashley. Define okay."

"Still a smart aleck."

"Always," Sam said and they exchanged a quick, awkward glance.

"Uh, right. Sam, this is Detective Larson, as you just heard twelve seconds ago. Ashley, this is Sam, my nursemaid and hors d'oeuvres chef for the day."

They each uttered a quick "Nice to meet you." Ashley turned back to Jackson. "I couldn't believe they discharged you already."

"I was persistent. How'd you hear, anyhow?"

"Dylan and Detective Loyola's husband hang out, watch ballgames. They talked, he heard your name and called me."

"Dylan's her partner," Jackson transcribed for Sam.

"The one you rescued this summer?"

Jackson nodded.

"Of course," Sam said with a smile. "Shay."

"Like, totally," Ashley said with a dippy shrug. It seemed to break the ice.

"Can I get you something to drink, some snacks? I think Jackson left a few smokeys."

"I'm fine, thanks." Ashley sat on the coffee table. "Tell me about it."

He recounted the shooting as best he could remember it. She listened intently while Sam took a seat on the other end of the couch and half-listened, half-watched the muted Iowa Hawkeye marching band.

"Any ideas who did it?" Ashley asked.

"I already gave a statement to the detectives assigned to the case," Jackson said with a wink.

"That's cute. He's also very cute," she said to Sam.

"Or so he thinks."

Ashley now winked back at Jackson.

"Wasn't that stalker guy you mentioned a while back. was it?"

"I told you about that?"

"Mm-hmm. You called and asked about pulling prints off a vase or something."

"Oh, right. I tracked him down myself."

"I'm sorry," Sam said. "Stalker?"

"I didn't tell you?"

"Nope."

"When I was working on the set of *Twenty Something*, one of the actresses had a stalker. She asked me to track him down, help her take out a restraining order. He violated it and get sentenced to thirty days in County. He's locked up till tomorrow," he said, looking back to Ashley.

"Wait, wait, wait. Back up a second. What's this about *Twenty Something*?"

"You know it?"

"Dylan is addicted to it."

"He does get addicted, doesn't he?"

She raised an eyebrow.

"Just a joke, Ash. Lighten up." He looked to Sam, then back to Ashley with a shrug. "I worked as a gofer for the director for a little while, while they were shooting in L.A."

"Are you serious? Is he serious?"

Sam nodded.

"You didn't tell me you were chasing down the stalker of a Hollywood actress."

Jackson shrugged again. "You should watch it with him."

"Please."

"Seriously. Some night on a stakeout, cue up episode one-six, 'Past Sins.' Pay careful attention to Grayson."

Ashley just stared at him.

"Trust me."

She shook her head. "So if not the stalker, who? Is it about the rat?"

"Rat?" Sam asked.

"I don't know. L.A.'s finest are working on it. And gossiping about it, apparently. I'm not too worried."

"So I see. Well," Ashley said, slapping her legs as she stood. "Looks like you're in good hands. Call if you need anything."

"Will do. Thanks for stopping by."

She smiled at Sam, they exchanged pleasantries again, and Ashley let herself out.

"She's pretty," Sam said when she was gone.

Jackson nodded. "Meaning?"

"Meaning she's pretty."

"Yeah, and white and short and a little ornery, all of which you failed to mention."

"You called her Ash."

"Short for Ash-ley. Kind of a nickname sort of deal. Like say, calling a Samantha 'Sam.'"

"Relax, Jackson, I'm just messing with you."

"Thanks, I appreciate it." He sighed. "You were saying before she arrived?"

"It can wait. Halftime's almost over now."

"Good. Because I have to hit the head before kickoff."

"Um, Jackson."

"Yeah."

"Should I ask about the rat?"

He shook his head.

"That's what I thought."

*   *   *

Thursday, December 27
10:36 a.m.

THE BOWL games were getting marginally better. Marginally. Even so, Jackson had no qualms about instantly muting the TV when Josh Groban starting singing, "Noël, Noël, O night, O night divine." (It was a bit on the nose, but the best he had been able to come up with for Noelle's ringtone.)

"Hey," he said, realizing it was about the dumbest greeting ever.

"Hi, Jackson. I'm not waking you, am I?"

He had no idea what time it was, but considering he'd slept till noon two days ago, it wasn't an absurd question. He told her no, then asked what was up. Another stupid thing to say.

"We talked last week about maybe getting together, and I wondered if you were free tonight."

"Yeah, sure."

"I wouldn't ask on such short notice, but plans changed, and now Seth and I are headed down to see Dad tomorrow through Wednesday, and I don't know yet when Viggo wants us back on the set, so it might be now or never."

"Tonight works great. You have a place in mind?"

"How about Café Montana? Say, seven?"

"Sure. Want me to pick you up?"

"You don't have to do that."

"It's no trouble."

He could almost hear her smile through the phone. "Okay, sure. Make it six-thirty then. I'll call for a table."

"Great. I'll see you then."

They said goodbye and he closed his phone. He was still smiling with the TV muted when the theme from *Cagney & Lacey* startled him. He quickly flipped the phone back open and offered a much craftier greeting this time.

"Hey, Ash."

"Hey. Don't get excited, I don't have much."

"I'll take anything."

"I spoke to a friend at the FBI," she said. "This is between the three of us."

"And Maggie?"

Ashley sighed. "Four of us."

"Deal."

"They traced the package back to the Farley Building in New York City."

"That an office complex?"

"It's the main post office," Ashley answered.

"So was it mailed from there or just postmarked there? I assume a lot of mail from New York State flows out of New York City."

"I'm not Benjamin Franklin," she said.

"Fair enough."

"They also have the toxicology back on the rat. This is so disgusting."

"Go ahead."

"A lot of odds and ends, mostly pieces of commercial food—I'm not going to list them—what you might expect in a dumpster. That's what my friend told me. That and enough rat poison to kill an entire pack."

"Thanks, Ashley."

"Anything else?"

"No. Thanks again."

She hung up first, and Jackson mulled for a moment before scrolling past calls on his phone to retrieve the number for the FBI Field Office in Albany, New York. It took five minutes before he was speaking with Special Agent Jamie Joseph.

"Mr. Douglas. You got a lead on another crime syndicate for me?"

"A small favor, actually."

"What is it?"

"Not sure if it crossed your desk, but last night, my friend Maggie got a suspicious package. A dead rat in a box, throat cut."

"I hadn't heard," Joseph said.

"Local cops passed it onto the FBI here in L.A., and they determined the package was sent from New York City."

"You think it might have been Maxim Baby's doing?"

"Actually, I had another thought. They did an autopsy on the rat and found a lot of human food and rat poison in its stomach."

"No big surprise."

"No. I'm wondering if you can find out who out here might have handled the investigation and ask them to test for another substance."

"I can make a call," Joseph said. "Given the circumstances, I don't think it's out of line. What substance?"

"That's where I need the real favor. I need you to run to Kingston and order a burger from Troika. Make sure they give you the special house sauce."

"The Troika special sauce. You think the rat is from Troika?"

"I think my gut's going to rumble until I know for sure."

"Why not," Joseph said. "I'll see what I can do. You deserve one favor."

"Thanks. I appreciate it."

*   *   *

Tuesday, January 1
5:07 p.m.

THE PESKY Iowa Hawkeyes would not go away. USC extended their halftime lead by seven, to 34-7. But Iowa responded with back to back touchdowns, sandwiched around a very well-executed onside kick. The Trojans kicked a field goal early in the fourth quarter to stretch the lead back to 37-21, but Iowa came marching down the field again for yet another touchdown. With over nine minutes still remaining, Jackson was getting nervous.

"Relax," Sam said. "They're still up by ten."

"And leaking like the *Titanic*."

"Maybe we should turn it off. High blood pressure isn't great for gunshot victims."

"Is that doctor's orders, because if so, you're fired."

Sam smiled. "Doesn't work that way, I'm afraid. And no, it's not an order. But it is a strong recommendation."

"Noted."

Two plays later, USC's tailback broke a tackle and bolted for daylight. Jackson jumped off the couch as he streaked across the midfield rose logo and across an empty field for a touchdown.

"Jackson Douglas!" Sam shouted. "Sit down."

He could not resist a fist pump, painful as it was, as the tailback was mobbed in the end zone. He slowly sat back down.

Sam's eyes blazed, albeit with a hint of a smile. "What do I have to do, sit on you to keep you from moving around?"

"Whatever you feel is necessary," he said with a smirk. She slapped his knee.

The extra point pushed the margin back to seventeen.

"Sam, I know as a UCLA grad you can't relate, but winning the Rose Bowl is huge. It's the dream of every little boy—"

"Who has just been shot in the shoulder. Practically the neck. And I understand how much this means to you—although I don't know that I get this fascination with one game—"

"Look at it, Sam. The sunset," he said, nodding at the TV but also gesturing out his window at the real thing, "the colors in the sky, the lights, the field. It doesn't get any better than this."

"This isn't about football, is it?"

"Huh?"

"I mean, it's football, but it's the moment, isn't it? It's not about winning, it's about winning *this* game . . . because of this right now," she said, also pointing at the TV. A panoramic shot showed the teams lined up for kickoff, lights bathing the field, and the final pink glow of sunlight highlighting the San Gabriel Mountains in the background.

Jackson nodded. "Yeah."

"You're a romantic."

Iowa returned the kick to the thirty-eight, and Jackson's thoughts were far from romance. But he nodded to make her happy.

The Hawkeyes scored one more time, but when they failed to recover a second onside kick, the fight went out of them and the game was all but over. The final few minutes were a coronation. Final score, USC 44, Iowa 34.

Jackson took Sam by the hand and pulled himself close enough to graze her cheek with his lips. "Thank you."

She smiled. "You're welcome."

He sat back. "I think I need my nurse now."

"Oh?"

"Adrenaline's wearing off. Can I get something for the pain?"

"Is it bad?"

"Medium."

She nodded and patted his knee. "I'll get you a Percocet."

He reclined against the arm of the sofa as she headed to the kitchen. Behind her, through an otherwise dark house so as not to ruin the environment on TV, Jackson was convinced he could see one final streak of color in the western sky.

Sam returned and he downed his pill, then reclined his head against the arm of the couch and smiled. It had been the perfect Rose Bowl, played on an immaculate field on a splendid day, and ending with another glorious triumph for the Men of Troy.

"So, as I was starting to say earlier," Sam said, and Jackson opened his eyes. "I think we should talk . . . about the kiss."

Jackson studied her beautiful blue eyes. In all the excitement of getting out of the hospital and the Rose Bowl and smokeys, he had forgotten what had been paramount on his mind throughout the previous night—truth be told, even before he had been shot—their romantic interlude on Christmas Eve.

"Okay," he said. "What do you want to talk about? And which kiss? As I recall, there were two."

Sam laughed nervously. "Yes there were. Both of them, then."

He nodded, waiting.

She knelt down beside him, resting on her heels. "I tried to work this out the entire way back from Frisco, and no matter how I say it, it isn't going to sound right, so I'll just say it. I don't think we should kiss again."

"If it's because I had tenderloin on my breath . . ."

"Jackson, please."

"Right, no smart aleck. How come?"

"Because . . . This is hard to explain and complicated, and the shortest version is that I'm not the kind of girl who kisses random guys."

"I'm a random guy?"

"No. That's not what I mean."

He just looked at her.

Sam sighed in frustration and bit her lip.

Jackson reached for her hand. "Sam, just say it. It can't be a worse shot than the one I took last night."

She exhaled. "Kissing isn't something I take lightly, and I don't want to kiss just a friend or even just a boyfriend. Kissing is something I want to save for someone I'm serious about, and who's serious about me."

Jackson nodded.

"And I'm not trying to force you into anything, because I don't know if you're ready for a serious relationship and I'm not sure I'm ready for a serious relationship. But until that day comes . . . I don't think we should kiss anymore."

He nodded again.

"And I know you're probably wondering why if I'm that type of a girl I didn't act like that type of girl, like people who make racist comments and then say they're not a racist. But . . . it was the moment and you and . . ." She put her hand on her forehead. "I know that's not an excuse, but I feel silly for losing control and I'm scared that I lost control, and . . ."

"Sam, I agree."

Sam looked up. "You do?"

"Yes. I know our relationship status is a little vague, and frankly, that's fine with me. And if we make a habit of kissing, that vagary will disappear, and I don't think kissing is the appropriate reason to take vague to serious."

Sam's eyes closed as she smiled and sighed. "I'm so glad you agree." She opened her eyes suddenly. "You do agree, don't you? You're not just saying what I want to hear and inside dreading that we'll never kiss again?"

"I give you my word, Sam. I agree."

She sighed one last time.

"And for the record, we never did say never," Jackson said. "Just not for now."

"Right."

His turn to sigh. "But, I will have to give Ashley a call back."

"Why?"

"I want a victory kiss."

As she stood, she elbowed him in the ribs far harder than a nurse ever should an ailing patient.

Chapter Fifty-Four

Thursday, December 27
6:28 p.m.

NOELLE WORE A white floral blouse, dark faded jeans, and heels when Jackson picked her up at her apartment. A silver locket glistened around her neck, only half as bright as her smile. They discussed their Christmases on the way to Café Montana, where they were promptly seated at a table by a window. For a few minutes, they busied themselves with their menus. After they ordered, Jackson reached for his iced tea and asked, "So how's the old crew?"

"You didn't hear?"

"Hear what?"

"Jess is off the show."

"What?"

"It all started with her getting sick. She missed the first days of shooting in Vancouver but a couple of specialists couldn't find anything wrong with her. She insisted she needed treatment and wanted all sorts of provisions made for her. And from what I hear, Viggo basically told her to tough it out. It just got worse and worse and he finally had her character written out."

"How?"

"He wanted to write some grand scene where she gave her life to help unravel the mystery, which in itself would have been a huge script overhaul, but she wouldn't go for it. She refused to act unless it was under her terms, so he just killed her off. She was so distressed she OD'd on cocaine. Cate, not Jess."

"Wow." He sat back. "All my fault."

"Hardly."

"If I hadn't suggested we shoot in the rain . . ."

"Jess would have found something else to gripe about. This isn't the first time she's had 'creative differences' with a writer or director. She's a diva."

"Will the show survive without her?"

Noelle leaned forward. "Can you keep a secret?"

"If it's juicy."

"We're taking on cast members."

"Oh?"

"The plan has always been to add another series regular when we get to Vancouver, an insider who has knowledge about Mr X. But now I've heard rumors that Cassidy Hightower might be taking Jess's spot. I have no idea how."

"Cassidy Hightower? Sassy Cassy Hightower?"

"You a fan?"

"I may or may not have had a teenage crush on her when she was on *Over the Edge*."

"Maybe I can get you invited back on set, so you can meet her."

"I'm going to start stammering just thinking about it." He took a drink. "How are the frat brothers?"

"Driving Viggo nuts."

"How's Vancouver treating you?"

"Good. I know it's another soapy serial drama, but I'm having a blast shooting *Twenty Something*. There's something about a character so different from my own—it's really challenging but kind of freeing too." She reached for her glass of ice water. "And my agent called last week with two motion picture offers. *Twenty Something* is starting to look like my big break."

"That's great, Noelle. You haven't stopped smiling all night, or at the airport, for that matter. I assumed things were going well."

She looked down. "That isn't all *Twenty Something*."

"No?"

"No." Blushing slightly, she raised her head. "Taylor and I are seeing each other."

"The Taylor I know?"

She nodded.

"A crew person?" he teased.

"I know, I know. And I don't even know how it came about. Over the last two weeks in Vancouver, we just, I don't know " She shrugged. "It's just—I can't stop smiling every time I think about it, which is all the time."

"I'm happy for you," he said genuinely.

"I have you to thank."

"Me?"

"Yes. The whole deal with Finley. After he was caught . . . I don't know, I felt free like I haven't before. Like a cloud over my head was gone. I'm not sure I would have been willing to get involved with someone. I don't know, I can't explain it."

"Well, you're more than welcome. I'm glad things are going well for you."

"Thanks."

"And I'm glad it's Taylor. From my experience, most actors are knuckleheads. You've got your head on straight, so I'm glad you're not dating some crazy actor."

"Me too."

The waiter brought soup, salad, and bread.

"So where is Taylor for the holidays?" Jackson asked when he was gone. He crumbled some crackers into his soup.

"He's originally from Idaho, so he's visiting family there. We agreed it was a little too soon to be meeting families over Christmas."

Jackson tried a spoonful of soup. Hot and flavorful. "Well that's good. I hope things work out."

"What about you?" she asked. "How have you been doing?"

"Better," he answered. "I've been busy."

"Oh?"

He recapped events with Maggie, from rescuing her in Mexico over Thanksgiving—which was news to Noelle—to the reason behind his trip to New York to the rat Maggie had received in the mail. Noelle was awestruck as he recounted their adventures. His narrative carried them into dinner—chicken stir fry for her, a New York steak for him. He kept the details of the slit-throat rat to a minimum.

"Where do you get the courage to do all that?" she asked. "People trying to kill you?"

Jackson shrugged. "I just do what I have to, I guess. And death doesn't really scare me."

"It doesn't?"

"No. Death is a curtain, a veil between this life and eternity. Frankly, I'm ready for eternity to start."

"Aren't you scared though? I hate to even think about it."

"Sometimes. I get pangs of fear like everybody. It's an unknown, but I have a constant. God, through Jesus, has forgiven my sins. He's promised me eternal life with Him."

"Reminds me of Sunday school when I was a little girl."

"You can learn a lot from Sunday school."

"I remember we used to sing this one song every Sunday, 'Jesus Loves the Little Children.'" She wrinkled her nose. "Do you think that includes Shawn Thomas?"

"Yes I do. God is an equal-opportunity lover. Kind of baffling, sometimes. I can't stand most people."

"I don't believe that."

He shrugged. "Maybe the irritable ones just stick out."

"Like Shawn Thomas."

"Oddly enough, I kind of like Shawn Thomas. Can't explain why, but . . ."

They finished dinner with more talk about life on the set of *Twenty Something*. Noelle gave Jackson a few spoilers, and assured him his brief acting stint had been just fine. After a while, they ordered dessert, lingering over tiramisu and coffee.

Hers almost gone, Noelle leaned forward, resting her arms on the table. "So what are you going to do?" she asked.

"How do you mean?"

"I mean, what's your future hold? What are you going to do with yourself?"

"You mean wife and kids future, or how am I going to kill time?"

She shrugged. "Either." The smile faded. "I'm concerned about you, Jackson. You told me about your family, about everything that happened in Nevada. Are you going to be okay?"

He took a deep breath. "I think so."

Noelle stared at him, but didn't speak.

"You ever play video games?" he asked.

"I've played *Guitar Hero* with Seth and his friends a few times."

"Real musicians play *Guitar Hero*?"

"Why do you ask?"

"You play these shooter games, you've got a health meter, right? And you can only take so much damage before you die. Most games your screen starts to go dim or your controller shakes when you're almost dead. But if you can get away or kill whoever's coming after you, you stop taking damage and start healing. And I think that might be where I am. The screen's faded and the controller's still shaking, but . . . I think I might just be far enough away that I'm not taking damage anymore."

Noelle swallowed hard. "I wish I could help."

"You have."

"How?"

Jackson paused for a moment, making sure he said what he wanted to say. "By being you. Noelle, you've been a breath of fresh air, a sweet and sincere person in a world that had become like a violent video game. I see Shawn Thomas and Jess and Viggo, and I don't mean to knock them, but you're different. And that, in a way I can't explain, has been a help."

She smiled, beautifully. "Well, consider it a small payment for what you did for me."

"Friends don't pay friends, Noelle."

"Still, thank you's seem inadequate."

"Not at all."

A waitress hovered. "More coffee?"

"I'm good, thanks," Jackson said.

She looked to Noelle, then back to Jackson. "You two need anything else?"

Jackson glanced across the table at Noelle, then shook his head. "No, we're all set."

The waitress drifted off. Jackson and Noelle's eyes met again. "Seriously, Noelle, in my book we are more than even. It's not a platitude—I was happy to help."

Her smile waned. "I just hope he stays away."

"Stints in County tend to change a guy's mindset."

"Being in Vancouver will help, I suppose."

Jackson nodded and drained his coffee. "And the restraining order is still in effect, and if he violates it again, he'll really get slammed. For someone like Finley, I have a feeling that's a powerful deterrent."

"I guess that's something."

The rain that had fallen most of the afternoon had stopped, leaving a foggy mist in its wake. But by the time they reached Noelle's apartment, it had resumed again. Jackson walked her to the door to her building anyhow.

"I guess this is goodbye," she said, pausing under a canopy outside the door. "I'll be in Vancouver for who knows how long, and then if *Twenty Something* isn't renewed, I don't know where I'll be."

"Is that a real possibility, it not getting renewed?"

"That's the scuttlebutt. Depends how strong we are in the spring."

"I suppose."

"Let's try to stay in touch, either way."

"Okay."

"Maybe Viggo will have a cast party at the end of the year."

"If he does, I'll be there."

"You can meet Cassidy."

"A guy can dream."

She smiled. "Thank you for everything, Jackson." She reached up and hugged him.

"You're welcome, Noelle." He let go. "You take care."

"I will," she said. "You too."

She smiled and entered the building, and Jackson trudged through the rain. Sprinkles really.

His relationship with Noelle had never turned romantic—maybe hinted at it now and again, but which male-female friendship didn't? And yet, he couldn't help but think she had changed him. She was sweet in a workplace that was salty, precious in a world that was insignificant. She was radiant in his life that had been so dark. He didn't buy into a bunch of cosmic humanist crap about the evolution of the soul, and he still gave credit to God for his improved outlook. But maybe, just maybe, God had used a petite little actress, at least in part, to help return Jackson to something of emotional normalcy. She balanced the scales when they were tipping the other way.

The question now was, who would keep balancing?

Since he wasn't far from her place, Jackson swung over to Maggie's apartment. She opened the door in jeans and an orange tank top, her hair in a stub of a ponytail. Her face registered a smile tinged with confusion. "Jack, what are you doing here?"

"Just wanted to check in. I was in the neighborhood. Ish."

"Come in," she said, stepping aside.

"What you working on?" he asked, nodding at her laptop open on her coffee table.

"My first column. Can't live off Mexico forever."

"I suppose not."

"Thirsty?"

"No, thanks. You happen to hear anything from Nichols?"

Maggie shook her head.

"I asked Ashley to see what they've found."

"Your lady detective friend?"

"You forgot cute."

"And what did your cute lady detective friend say?"

"They actually passed it on to the feds, who traced the rat back to the main New York City post office."

Maggie shrugged. "That's not news really, is it?"

"No. The feds also did a toxicology report on the contents of the rat's stomach. Sounds like a dumpster diver."

"Aren't all rats?"

"I suppose, but I meant more like a restaurant dumpster."

"You sound like you've thought of something."

He paused, not wanting to mention his Troika suspicion unless it panned out. "Maybe. If it turns into anything, I'll let you know."

"Okay." Maggie's mouth turned up in a lopsided smile. "And you came all the way over here just to tell me that?"

"I figured if Nichols hadn't updated you, I should. And like I said, I was in the area. I wanted to check in."

"That's very nice of you."

"Yeah, well."

"Want to stay a while? I baked cookies today."

"You baked cookies?"

She whacked him with the back of her hand. "What's that supposed to mean?"

"Nothing."

"You don't think I can bake?"

"You've never baked for me before."

She raised her eyebrows.

"Not that you can't. I just don't see you as the puttering around in the kitchen in an apron kind."

"You want some cookies or not?"

He enjoyed her evil eye for just a second. "What kind?"

"Oatmeal raisin."

"I'd love some. Maybe some milk or coffee."

"Sit down," she said, pointing at the loveseat.

Smirking, he did.

Fifteen seconds later, a cookie bounced off his head.

Chapter Fifty-Five

Tuesday, January 1
7:49 p.m.

STRICTLY AS HIS nurse, Sam helped Jackson slip out of his shirt. He sat on the coffee table, and she carefully and as gingerly as possible removed the bandages on both the entrance and exit wounds. She had mastered the ability to work quickly and yet delicately, but some things just hurt no matter what. Fortunately, Jackson was in such pain already that he didn't really notice the new measure of discomfort.

"I still can't believe you were shot," Sam said as she gently dabbed around the wound on his back.

"I'd tell you to put your finger where the bullet hole is, but I hate to risk infection."

She ignored his attempt at humor. "I mean, I know your profession can lead to danger . . ."

"But you always think it's going to happen to somebody else?"

Sam discarded the cloth she had been using. "Yes."

She took a break and came around to face him, sitting on the couch. Behind him, the Fiesta Bowl had long-since gotten boring, with Oklahoma clobbering some undeserving team from a lesser conference. Reggie had come and gone, bringing them dinner and visiting for a while, and they were alone in an otherwise dark house, save for Sam's operating lights.

"You really aren't on a case right now?"

"Nope."

"Not a favor for a friend case, or something small?"

"Not anymore."

"And you don't think it has to do with what happened in Mexico, or the stalker Detective Larson mentioned?"

"No reason to think so. I didn't recognize the shooter so I have no idea who it was or why they shot me."

"How'd he get your gun?" she asked, beginning to dab the wound at the top of his chest.

Jackson winced. "How'd you know it was mine?"

"You made some comment about it somewhere along the line. Said he shot you with your own gun."

"I brought . . ."

"Jackson?"

Memories were starting to come back. He ignored them for the moment, focusing on answering her. "I brought it along for safety . . . just in case." He shrugged, which caused her dab to be a little off, which caused pain to shoot through his upper body. He sucked in his breath and winced again. "There was a struggle. He got it."

"Did he surprise you?"

"More or less. I had a chance to shoot him."

"And you didn't?"

"No."

Sam stopped again. "How come?"

He looked into her eyes. "I'm sick of shooting people."

After a moment, she resumed working. She suggested he let the wounds breathe for a little while before she bandaged them again. In that case, Jackson asked, would she mind terribly making some coffee. There was a draft.

With a small smile she headed into the kitchen and Jackson, with much grimacing, turned around to watch Oklahoma smack their opponent around. It was 31-3 in the third quarter and, after the excitement of the Rose Bowl, just wasn't appealing to him. He tried to remember what had been at the edge of his brain, what had eluded him all day, his reason for being at the cemetery. But it had floated away, just out of reach.

Sam returned just as "Boomer Sooner" rang out to celebrate another Oklahoma touchdown. "It's decaf," she said, handing him a cup. She too held a cup, likely tea since she didn't drink coffee. She sat down on the couch, facing him as he sat back on the coffee table so as not to touch the open wound to anything.

"How is it?" she asked.

"Hot. Thanks."

She took a drink. "When a woman asks how the food or drink is, temperature isn't exactly what she's going for."

"Sam, I feel like I should be wearing a poncho and saddling my burro right now."

She eyed him and took another sip. "What are you going to do?"

"Wait until you're not looking and down some more meds."

"I meant about the shooting?"

"Duck next time."

"I'm serious."

He shrugged, winced, and took a drink.

"Whoever did this is still out there," she said. "What if he comes back to finish the job?"

"Well, the police have the Glock, but the SPAS-12 is upstairs in the closet. You know, I've always been partial to a girl with a shotgun. Do you happen to have a pair of boots?"

"Enough joking."

"What do you want me to say? The cops are looking for the guy. I have nothing else to go on."

"I'm worried about you, Jackson. Somebody tried to kill you."

"So you keep reminding me."

"And you honestly have no clue who it is?"

"I have a list of possible suspects, but it's just a list. There's nothing to make me think it's any of them any more than it's some deranged psycho."

She took another drink. "What about after this is all over? What about the next time you're trying to 'bust some baddies'? You're not invincible, Jackson."

"I know."

"Do you?"

"Yeah. What's gotten into you, Sam? You never worry about anything."

She knelt down in front of him and set her cup on the table beside him. "You have gotten to me, Jackson. I know when you look back on this past year, you see all the things you did, or could have done. But I see all the things that could have happened to you. It sends shivers down my spine."

"Have some more tea."

She shook her head and stood up. "Why do I bother?"

"I'm sorry, Sam. What do you want me to say?"

"I don't know. Maybe that you'll be more careful."

"I am careful. But sometimes you've got to throw caution to the wind if you want to save the day."

"Spoken like a true action hero."

He shrugged again. It hurt again, and he made a mental note to stop shrugging.

She sighed. "How's the pain?"

"Bearable."

"Bad?"

"About the same."

"You think you can hold out for half an hour while I run home and get some clothes."

"Yeah. Why?"

"I don't think you should be alone overnight, and I didn't bring anything to change into."

"I'll survive half an hour," he said.

"You won't do anything stupid like chugging a bottle of Percocet?"

"No, ma'am."

Sam went into the kitchen and got his phone off the table. "Here's your cell. Call me—or 9-1-1—if you feel the least bit off."

"You mean besides having a tunnel through my body?"

"Besides that. I'll put on a new dressing when I get back, and we can figure out what to do about tomorrow."

"How so?"

"I have to work at seven."

"And I'll sleep till noon. It'll be perfect."

"I'll be back," she said. She pointed at the phone. "Call me if anything happens. Don't be a tough guy."

"I won't."

She headed for the door.

"Hey, Sam."

She stopped. "Yeah?"

"Don't forget that pair of boots."

*　　　　　　*　　　　　　*

Friday, December 28
3:30 p.m.

"YOU SURE you don't want to come?" Reggie asked. "Last call, man."

"You're going to get killed by Oregon, you know that right?"

His big friend grinned. Behind him, his black H3 idled in Jackson's driveway. Last minute, Reggie had scored a pair of tickets to the Holiday Bowl in San Diego to see his Nebraska Cornhuskers take on the Oregon Ducks.

"Word is they're not motivated. Crazy things happen in bowl games, bro."

Normally, Jackson would have jumped at the chance to join him, but despite the fact that he'd grown sick of sitting around his house and watching the rain, he just didn't quite feel up to it. He couldn't explain the lethargy, unless it was the rain. And even that had thinned, with the skies promising some actual sunshine and a little warmth. Maybe it was Christmas blues in the absence of his family. Or dead rats in the mail. At any rate, he didn't much feel up for activities.

"Another time, man," he said.

"All right." Reggie banged his fist and turned to go.

"Hope you keep them under fifty."

"Funny."

Jackson stood in the doorway and watched Reggie leave, then frowned as a white Honda Civic turned into his driveway. The driver's side door opened and a petite woman with short auburn hair got out. Jackson had only seen it held at the back of her neck in a chignon before, not hanging in wisps on her shoulders. For that matter, they had only ever been covered in epaulets instead of an orange peasant blouse.

"This is the right house," she said, sweeping her door shut.

Jackson forced words to his tongue. "Lieutenant Paige."

"I'm off duty. Call me Alison. I'm sorry to drop in unannounced. I called a half hour or so ago and just got voicemail."

"Yeah I was on the phone." Reggie's initial sales pitch. "What brings you out here?"

"To L.A., a road trip with a friend to visit her folks over the weekend. Here specifically, I've got some news for you."

"Come on in," Jackson said, stepping out of the way so the JAG lawyer could enter his living room. Fortunately, he'd kicked some things into corners recently and vacuumed in the last month. "Can I get you something to drink?" he asked.

"No. Thanks."

"Have a seat," he said, motioning toward the couch. Paige sat, and Jackson dropped onto the edge of his chair.

"I like your place," she said. "Not what I was expecting."

"Oh?"

She wrinkled her nose. "Maybe it's too much time around airmen, but I was picturing remnants and boxes for furniture." She smiled, then turned serious. "How have you been?"

He nodded. "Okay. It was rough at first. But, yeah, I'm . . . I'm hanging in there."

"Have you heard from Secretary Wittingham?"

"Should I have?"

"I told him I was coming out this way and said I'd get in touch with you, but I thought he might have called anyhow."

Jackson shook his head.

"I don't have all the details," Paige said, "but the DOJ and DOD, along with the Air Force, Army, CIA, FBI, and probably a host of other agencies, have continued to investigate what went on at Blane Air Force Base as part of Project Golden Dawn. Their findings have further corroborated your testimony at the hearing back in September and exonerated you and Miss McKenzie."

Jackson nodded, taking it all in stride. Exoneration implied innocence, and whether or not he was charged with any crimes or not, Jackson couldn't bundle his actions into a bag of innocence.

"Pursuant to those findings and their investigation, they have authorized the termination of your probation, and the reinstatement of your license effective January 1."

Jackson nodded again.

Paige raised her eyebrows. "Isn't that good news?"

"No, it is. I just hadn't given a whole lot of thought to my career as a private eye. Wasn't sure it would be something I could ever do again, or would ever want to."

"You still struggling with guilt?"

"How'd you know?"

"I've been there. Not to this degree, but . . ." She looked down. "In college, before I joined the Air Force, a guy tried to rape me on my way home from work one night. He picked the wrong girl," she said with a little smile. "My father trained me in self-defense. I fought back. I elbowed him in the neck and fractured his larynx. I got away and the police arrested him forty minutes later when he showed up at a walk-in all-night clinic. He's in prison for several other rapes, and to this day, he can barely make a sound."

"He had it coming."

"Yeah, he did. But still, every once in a while, I get tremors of guilt. The oddest things set it off, like hearing a beautiful vocalist at a concert or buttoning

428

my shirt and seeing my own neck and throat." She shrugged. "Anyhow, on a much smaller scale, I understand. It does get better."

"I appreciate that, Lieu . . . Alison."

She smiled, then explained a few more details that had been uncovered in the investigation into Golden Dawn—what she could legally reveal. She informed him Wyatt Quinn had been removed as sheriff in Kingman, Nevada, where he had served as a "warden" in charge of the citizens of the town, many of whom had been affected by the experiments of Silver Dawn and Golden Dawn. Along with three of his deputies, he was awaiting trial. The town itself was being examined by a variety of government agencies in an effort to determine what to do with its "infected" inhabitants.

She also said that Isaac Cutler, one of the rogue CIA operatives responsible for Golden Dawn, had been indicted in federal court on a range of charges from treason to murder. Senator Carson Moore had resigned his position and was currently under indictment on a bevy of similar charges, most of which were being kept out of the news for obvious reasons.

"What about General Reynolds?" Jackson asked.

Paige looked at him warily. "You heard about his death?"

"Yes."

"Officially, it was a suicide."

"And unofficially?"

"Unofficially, who's General Reynolds?"

"Ah-ha."

"The circle of people who know the whole truth is very small, and I assure you, I'm not part of it."

Jackson nodded. "I appreciate your coming out here. You know you could have just called."

"Tried, remember?"

"You could have tried again."

"I wanted to see you, see how you were doing. And some news should be delivered in person anyhow."

He nodded and took a chance. "You have dinner plans for tonight?"

"As a matter of fact, no. My friend and her folks are driving down to Anaheim to visit her brother, so I'm on my own tonight, with her car as a loaner."

"Could I buy you an early dinner?" Jackson asked. "Call it a way to say thank you for all you did for me."

"That isn't necessary," Paige said with a smile. "But yes, you can."

Chapter Fifty-Six

5:19 p.m.

THE RAIN HAD indeed subsided for good, replaced by warm, albeit quickly fading, sunshine. Jackson guessed—correctly, she informed him—that Lieutenant Alison Paige would be just as happy with diner food as at a fancy sit-down place, and guided her to the Santa Monica Pier. They had burgers, fries, and shakes at Pier Burger while watching the sunset play out across the beach and Malibu coastline. Jackson filled her in on events in Mexico and New York (she didn't scold him for "investigating" without a license), as well as on the trauma that had robbed him of his parents and brother a little more than a year and a half ago. She told him more about life in the JAG Corps, what had led her there, and her plans for the future.

The sun had set by the time they finished, leaving just a bluish glaze in the southwestern sky. They exited the restaurant and walked out farther onto the pier. The night was still, and without the sun, cool but not cold. At the end of the pier, they turned around and leaned against the railing, admiring the lights of Pacific Park and the rest of the pier, as well as Santa Monica and downtown in the distance.

"My brother served in Iraq," Paige said after a few minutes of both of them taking in the view in silence. "He always told the story about when he came back to the States after his tour was over. There was a small group in the airport to welcome them back, mostly family members—typical, I'm sure. But there was one old man, wearing a blazer, flight cap, a flag pin right here," she said, making a circle with her thumb and finger and tapping an imaginary lapel. "This guy was a World War II vet, ninety years old if he was a day, to hear my brother tell it. And he hobbled toward him, clasped my brother's hand between both of his, and thanked him for his service and his sacrifice."

Paige looked down at the dark water, lapping gently against the pylon. She swallowed. "He said—my brother, I mean—that almost made it all worth it."

Jackson watched the horizon until the lights blurred. He turned to Paige. "Why'd you tell me that?"

"Because I can see how what happened in Nevada—in Mexico—how it weighs on you. In your holding cell and the conference room three months ago and in your living room and in the booth just now. And I figured that maybe it might help, just a little, make it just a little bit worth it, if somebody thanked you."

She extended her hand.

Jackson looked down at it, very slowly starting to shake his head. "No. No, I don't deserve that."

"Exactly what my brother thought when the World War II vet took his hand."

Jackson continued to shake his head. "Your brother served. You're serving. I don't . . ." He shook some more.

"You did a horrible job that had to be done," Paige said. "A job that made a small corner of the world a better place. I've never been in war, so to speak, but I have seen what it does to people. No matter what we tell ourselves, the blacks and whites turn gray. Lines get blurred, right or wrong. But I know, Jackson, just from the little bit I've known you, that everything you did that fateful day you did with one purpose in mind—saving Miss McKenzie. And you did save her, and in the process took down a ring of corrupt government employees, a radical paramilitary group, and a crooked U.S. senator. And now you've suffered nothing but guilt for it for three months. Yeah, you deserve it."

She reached down to grab his hand and shook it.

Jackson sniffed away would-be tears, looking away for a second. He turned back and found her bright green eyes, reflecting the lights of Los Angeles. "Thank you, Alison."

Paige nodded and they started walking back

"You know," she said, "I looked at your jacket, saw you spent two years at USC, another semester at San Diego, so this probably comes as no surprise."

They took a few steps.

"But in my years at college, and now in the military, I've been around a lot of guys, Jackson. And whether it's my genetic makeup or my training with the Corps, I've become pretty good at reading them, seeing through the veneer." She shook her head. "Most guys, there just isn't that much there. But you, you're what my dad would call 'good people.' You're real. And I know nothing I say can change what happened or maybe even make a difference, but just know this—as someone who's a decent judge of character, I'd vouch for you any day."

They strolled leisurely along the pier and back to Jackson's car. Mostly in silence, they drove back to his place.

"Thanks again for coming, Alison," Jackson said in his driveway, standing beside her car as she leaned on the open driver's door. He'd invited her in for coffee, but she'd said she should be getting back. It hadn't seemed like a brush-off.

"You're welcome." She reached into her purse and withdrew a business card. "Don't be a stranger, okay?"

Jackson took the card and looked down at it. "A business card, not some infrared Bluetooth phone syncing?"

"I guessed it was more your style."

"That it is," he said with a grin.

"I'll see you, Jackson."

"Hey, Alison," he said, stopping her before she sat down. "You were wrong about one thing."

"What's that?"

"Out on the pier, you said what you said wouldn't make a difference. But it does."

With a smile, she slid down into the driver's seat and closed her door. Jackson waved as she backed out of the driveway and watched as she drove away. He turned and headed inside, feeling his phone vibrate in his pocket as he did so. He fished it out and flipped it open without checking the incoming number.

"Hello?"

"Mr. Douglas, it's Special Agent Joseph."

"Agent Joseph. You're working awfully late. You find something?"

"You want to join the Bureau? We could use a psychic."

"There a match?"

"Just heard from the lab. The rat's stomach tested positive for the special ingredient used in the sauce at Troika."

Jackson digested the news. "So what's the next step?"

"L.A. has coordinated with us. We'll question the KKK, family members, employees. We'll find out who did this."

"I appreciate it, Agent Joseph."

"You get any more hunches, give me a call."

"I will. Thanks. Oh, Agent Joseph?"

No answer. He'd already hung up and Jackson blew out a breath of air. He'd wanted to know what the special ingredient in the sauce was.

He called Maggie to break the news, and they talked for a quarter of an hour, pondering who might be responsible. They both concluded it could be anybody.

After saying goodbye, Jackson flipped on the TV, already tuned to ESPN. Immediately, he started laughing. The Holiday Bowl was less than eight minutes old, but Oregon already led Nebraska 22-0.

*   *   *

Wednesday, January 2
6:23 a.m.

ONLY A few specks of light managed to penetrate the canopy of trees in the center of the cemetery. It was enough to reflect off the barrel of the Glock 19 pistol trained on Jackson, but not for him to identify the figure holding the gun or make out facial features.

Time stopped. Both of them panted for breath, staring at each other like gunfighters in an old Western. Only Jackson couldn't see the grit in his opponent's eye, and he didn't have a six-shooter strapped at his waist.

He licked his lip, tasting blood. And rain. It had been falling steadily all night, and succeeded where the light failed in making its way through the tree cover overhead. The drops that didn't fall directly through found their way onto leaves and branches, then dripped in syncopation on the road below. All around the little canopy, the rain fell with perfect rhythm, pelting the grave markers while drowning out any ambient noise.

Jackson considered his options. He was at least a dozen feet away from the gun. To his right or left, he had just as much ground to cover to reach the slightest shelter. Beyond the tree line, there was nothing but open ground and small headstones. He had only one choice.

Jackson exhaled slowly. "You don't have to do this."

"Oh, but I do," rasped a voice. The hand not holding the gun reached up and pulled back the hood . . .

"Jackson!"

He sat up straight, pain shooting through his shoulder.

"Jackson, calm down. You were having a nightmare."

He tried to swallow, then turned to see Sam kneeling beside him. His adrenaline dropped and his breathing regulated. "I was . . . I was about to see the shooter," he said.

"What?"

"In my dream. He was taking off the hood."

Sam shook her head. "You didn't see a face?"

"No. What time is it?"

"Morning. I'm off to work."

Morning. At last. He'd woken up at least a dozen times, in and out of pain, pleading with the clock to move. It hadn't obliged.

"I need to check your bandage first," she said.

Jackson sat up and spun to the side of the bed, and Sam flipped on the light, blindingly bright. She was already in her scrubs. "How do you feel?" she asked.

"Okay. Sore."

"Sore is good."

"Yeah, wait till you get shot."

Sam smiled as she peeled back the bandage. "I'm just going to change it," she announced.

"Sure."

She made quick work, then announced that she had arranged for someone to cover the last part of her shift and would be by a little after three to check in on him. "If you need anything, call," she said. "Don't be a hero."

"Right."

She turned to go but Jackson grabbed her wrist. "Thank you, Sam."

Smiling, she gently eased him back down. She kissed his forehead. "Get some more sleep."

He closed his eyes, and his thoughts went back to the shooter. Try as he might, he couldn't force the hood back to see the face. The voice had been masculine, sort of. Raspy, so hard to tell. Then again, it was a dream. Albeit a realistic one.

Thinking about the shooting was getting him wired, and likely preventing sleep. So he thought about Sam instead, his last memory before he dozed off their Christmas Eve kiss on the beach.

Chapter Fifty-Seven

Monday, December 31
12:17 p.m.

GRAY SKIES AND drizzle had returned, delaying Leroy's flight from Houston and thus wasting a few hours of Jackson's morning. He'd dropped his grandpa off at home thirty minutes ago, leaving him to nap. Now, as he flipped on his TV with another look out at the overcast skies, he hoped the weather cleared before kickoff of the Rose Bowl the following day.

It was not raining in El Paso, Texas, where Clemson and UCLA were battling in the Sun Bowl. Rather, brilliant sunlight shone from a blue sky, highlighting a magnificent contrast between the orange helmets and pants of the Clemson Tigers and the powder blue jerseys of the UCLA Bruins. Jackson chuckled every time he saw the cross-town rival of his USC Trojans. Their biggest claim to football fame was that their jerseys were a pretty color.

The shrill chirp of his phone interrupted the telecast.

"Hello?"

"Mr. Douglas, it's Special Agent Joseph."

"Even got you working holidays, huh?"

"It never ends. I've got good news and bad news."

"Okay."

"Good news is, we're pretty sure that Kasper's daughter Valerie Benson is the one who sent the rat."

"Valerie? Why her?"

"A number of factors. She majored in zoology at SUNY, so she's familiar with animals, poisons, probably cut up a bunch of fetal pigs and dissected frogs in biology classes for four years. Her prints were found on a doorpost in a storage shed behind the restaurant, which is odd because she doesn't work at Troika. A shed where we found several rat traps, by the way. We know from several sources that she made a trip into New York City on Monday the 24th, and she was seen

435

on a hotel security camera just a few blocks from the Farley Building. And it was her cousin who died—in her eyes because of Maggie's article—and her father who has the most to lose and the most time to serve by going to jail."

"Because of, originally, Maggie's article."

"Right."

"Okay, what's the bad news?"

"She's in the wind. We sent agents to her house to question her this morning, and her husband said she was at work. When the agents went to the animal shelter where she works, they were told she hadn't come in. Nobody's seen her since last night, in fact, when her husband said she went to bed early with a headache. They sleep in separate bedrooms, and I won't bore you with any more on that subject."

"You put out an APB or a BOLO for her or something?"

"We have, as a suspect. Hers isn't the most heinous of crimes, but considering her family and what just went down, and, frankly, since you were a big help to us, I'm making sure it gets high priority."

"You think she's a danger to Maggie?"

Joseph sighed. "She shouldn't be taken lightly, but to be candid, no, I don't. From everything we've looked at—her history, psych profile, the rather cowardly act of sending a dead rat—I'm guessing she won't act on her convictions. Or, I should say, won't act further. But, don't hold me to that."

"Fair enough. Thanks, Agent Joseph."

"I'll keep you posted if I hear anything more."

"I appreciate it."

Jackson lowered the phone and looked back at the TV. UCLA was driving, and he considered that just cause for a diversion. He paced to the dining room and called Maggie to update her.

"Valerie?" she said.

"Uh-huh."

"I didn't think that precious snowflake had the guts for something like this. Then again, last time I saw her she was sixteen."

"Agent Joseph sounded pretty sure."

"Okay."

"You all right?"

"I'm fine. It's not like she's coming here."

Jackson nodded to himself.

"Jack?"

436

"Yeah."

"What, you're worried she is?"

"Excuse me for saying it, but I'm not taking anything for granted with your crazy family."

"No excuse needed, but relax. Valerie doesn't scare me."

"Okay."

"I gotta go, Jack. A group of us from work are going out tonight, and I've got a draft to get done beforehand."

"I won't keep you. Later, Maggie."

"Later, Jack."

*   *   *

Wednesday, January 2
9:54 a.m.

JACKSON OPENED the front door as Reggie reached to knock. He stood there a moment. "Hey, man, how you doing?"

"I'm wandering around the house with no shoes and no shirt. Unless this is the Caymans, not great."

"Keeping that positive attitude, I see."

Jackson nodded for Reggie to come in.

"It hurt?"

"Yeah. You bring me something?" he asked, eyeing a paper bag in Reggie's hand.

"Lunch. Club on white bread, fries."

"You must have gotten up early, dude. It's ten o'clock."

"I've got a lunch date. I figured it can keep in the fridge."

"A date?"

"Business."

Jackson nodded. "Thanks. I actually like cold fries."

"I know you do."

Reggie placed Jackson's lunch in the refrigerator, then joined him at the dining room table. "So how you doing, up here?" he asked, tapping his head.

"Fine, I guess. Still no idea who shot me."

"Not the pipsqueak stalker, not a Mexican banger. Some mobster from New York?"

"I don't know. I don't think I'd have ever seen the shooter in that case."

"He'd have double-tapped you with his own gun before you got the chance."

"Yeah, and that's the thing. He wasn't strapped. It was my gun. So whoever it was didn't come there aiming to kill me. I think he—or she—shot more out of fear than anything."

"Don't scare him next time, man."

"That's a great idea, Reg. Thanks."

The big man grinned. "So who's looking after you, anyhow? Or you on your own recognizance."

"Sam spent the night. She's coming back later, I think."

"That's a good woman, man."

"You mean, a kind, virtuous, someday deaconess good woman, or you gonna hawk one into the spittoon as you hitch up your britches and tell me I should start a'courtin' her?"

"I'm just saying."

Jackson grinned.

"And if you're holding back because you think you're a bad man, well, I got news on that front."

"That's not it, Reg."

"All right."

"Grandpa's always poking, Mom before she died kept nudging me toward 'settling down.' The whole world wants to give me love advice," Jackson muttered.

"That tell you anything?"

"When did you say that lunch of yours was?"

Reggie smiled. "You know a near-death experience is supposed to make you reevaluate your life, make some changes, you know?"

"I thought maybe I'd let the flesh close over before I do anything drastic like propose marriage."

"Fair enough, man. I'm just messing with you anyhow."

"I would expect nothing less."

"And I do have to run. But I can rearrange stuff the next few days. You need anything, you call."

"Anything but a hot lunch, you mean."

"Next time," Reggie said as he stood, "I hope you get shot in the cynicism. Later, bro."

Jackson nodded, watching Reggie to the door. "Thanks for lunch, Hoss."

Reggie waved without turning back, and Jackson contemplated how to kill the rest of his morning.

∗   ∗   ∗

Monday, December 31
1:19 p.m.

FROM THE general vicinity of the end table beside his chair, the chorus of "By Heart" began to play. Jackson muted the Sun Bowl, flipped open his phone, and put it to his ear with a smile.

"Hey, Sam."

"Hi, Jackson."

Hearing her voice brought back the memory of their kiss. Or, rather, kisses. He remembered the smell of her perfume, the softness of her lips, her taste, the warmth of her body against his on a drizzly, rainy night. Like tonight?

"Jackson?"

"Hey, yeah. Sorry. How was San Francisco?"

"Good. Really good. Way too short, but that's always the case. How was your week?"

"Interesting."

"That sounds vague."

"And complicated. I can give you the CliffsNotes sometime." CliffsNotes being his edited, scrubbed version.

"Well you want to tell me about it later tonight?" Sam asked. "I have to work till ten-thirty or eleven. We could meet up after my shift and ring in the New Year together?"

"I would love to."

"You didn't have other plans, did you?"

"Well, now that Dick Clark's dead the ball drop just isn't the same, and besides, that happens at nine anyhow."

"Great," Sam said, her smile translating through her voice. "I'll call you when I get off, and we can sort of go from there."

"Sounds good," Jackson said. "I'll be here."

"Great," she said again. "Till later . . ."

He closed his phone and held it for a minute, watching the silenced TV. So if the ball dropped in New York at nine Pacific, did that mean that, technically,

439

they'd be getting together for an after party? And might it end like the last one had? It was raining, a little cool, the eve of an important holiday . . .

He let his mind play with the possibilities for a few minutes, then turned the sound back on. Clemson was about to score, and sunny El Paso was a definite improvement over soggy Los Angeles.

*   *   *

Wednesday, January 2
3:08 p.m.

FOR MUCH of the afternoon, Jackson drifted in and out of sleep, trying to make up for the previous two nights. His doorbell woke him.

Sitting up, blinking a few times, he looked at the clock. Was it after three already? Hadn't Sam said she worked until three? Was she here?

He pushed himself up, groaning at the pain, and trudged to the door. First order for the nurse, more painkillers, please.

Maggie stood on his stoop. "I ought to slug you."

"Nice to see you too."

"How could you not call me?"

"Did I not?"

"Or at least return my call yesterday?"

"Rose Bowl, Maggie."

"Reggie had to tell me you'd been shot. Are you okay?"

"I'm mending."

"I ought to slug you."

"You want to come in, Slugger?"

Maggie stepped through the door. "Seriously, you're okay?"

"It hurts, but yeah, I'll survive."

"What happened?"

He directed her to the couch, gingerly sat beside her, and briefly explained the details. Her eyes grew wider by the minute. "Is this because of me?" she asked when he was finished.

"I don't think so. I don't know."

"You haven't heard anything from Agent Joseph?"

"No."

"It couldn't have been Valerie."

"You convincing me or yourself?"

Maggie gave him her best evil eye.

"I don't think so either," Jackson said. "Joseph said he didn't think she was the kind to act on her threats. Although . . ."

"What?"

Jackson shook his head. "The shooter didn't come to shoot."

"What?"

"He—or she—didn't come with the intention of shooting me."

"How do you know?"

"Because he shot me with my gun."

"How'd you let that happen, Ace?"

He gave her his best evil eye. "I screwed up."

"So if not Valerie, who? Are the cops looking into it?"

"Along with a few drive-bys, stabbings, rapes, convenience store robberies, jay-walkings."

"So what are you going to do?"

"Work on my quick draw."

"Jackson!"

He shrugged. "What do you want me to say?"

The doorbell interrupted her. Jackson started to stand, but Maggie beat him to it. "You rest. I'll get the door."

Jackson prayed it wasn't Sam.

"Hi," a soft feminine voice said when Maggie opened the door.

Sam.

"Hi," Maggie's husky voice replied.

"I'm Sam."

"Maggie."

Jackson wished the bullet had been a few inches higher and to the side, right in the head.

"Hi, Sam," he called before they could continue the discourse. He had to think fast and talk slow, a difficult combination. He stood as they both turned to face him, the same question in each of their eyes: Who's she?

"Bandage time?" he asked.

Sam nodded. Maggie did too as she stepped to the side.

"How are you feeling?" Sam asked.

"Okay," Jackson said, hoping the conversation stayed medical. Explaining the presence of the "other woman" was hard enough when she wasn't standing right there. Damage control, he said to himself.

"Better or worse?"

"I'm low on meds right now," Jackson said. "Time for another dose."

"Are they down here?" Maggie asked.

"No, in the bathroom upstairs. Only bottle."

She started for the steps, looking back once as Sam helped Jackson remove his shirt. Sam didn't say a word, but her eyes searched Jackson's.

"I told you I had an interesting week," he said quietly.

"Let me guess, a client? Ahem, ahem, seeing as how you haven't been licensed for three months."

He nodded, since technically Maggie had been a client. Of sorts.

Sam nodded too and began the process of removing the old bandage. Jackson kept his wincing to a minimum. Was it possible Sam didn't read the *Times* and didn't recognize Maggie? Then again, Maggie's hair was in a ponytail, messy from being under a motorcycle helmet, and she was dressed down a little from the photo the paper used.

Maggie returned with the bottle of Percocet and retrieved a glass of water from the refrigerator. When Sam had removed the bandage, Maggie handed them both to Jackson, and he downed a pill. "Thank you."

Maggie nodded, glanced at Sam, and took the glass back to the kitchen.

Sam watched her go without asking how a client knew her way around Jackson's house so well, and then applied the new bandages, both front and back. "That should be good for another twenty-four hours," she said. "Otherwise you're feeling okay?"

"Yeah, thanks."

"Okay. Then I'll see you tomorrow."

"Thanks, Sam."

"Call if you need anything." She smiled, first at Jackson, then at Maggie. "It was nice to meet you."

"You too," Maggie said, walking Sam to the door. She closed it behind her and Jackson took the opportunity to let out a deep breath.

Maggie walked back to Jackson, who was struggling back into his shirt. When he peeked his head through, she was grinning at him. "You drew a cute nurse."

"Two of them, it seems."

"A friend of yours?"

"She goes to my church," Jackson replied. Another not untruth.

Maggie nodded. "And that's why she makes house calls?"

"Well, that and my charming grin."

Maggie faked a laugh. "Must be some church."

"You're cute when you're jealous."

She waited a moment, then changed tacks. "I'm off for the day. Do you have dinner plans?"

"No. Unless Connie's brewing a surprise. She's been quiet."

"I'll make you something."

"Please, I'm sick enough."

Maggie bit down on her tongue, which was firmly embedded in her cheek. But she said nothing as she flopped onto the couch, and he down beside her. That's when she punched him in the thigh so hard that his eyes watered.

Chapter Fifty-Eight

VIRGINIA AND SOUTH Carolina were knotted at 17, late in the fourth quarter of some corporately sponsored bowl game. Jackson couldn't keep up with them anymore. Besides, only one really mattered, the "Granddaddy of Them All," the Rose Bowl. It was less than twenty-four hours away, and with his Trojans in position for a solid win, his excitement was building.

In fact, Jackson's mood in general was trending toward happy. The rain was still there, with an occasional rumble of thunder, but the forecast assured him it would be gone by tomorrow. Noelle's personality, coupled with Lieutenant Paige's words, had impacted him in a way he hadn't expected possible, and he felt himself burgeoning out of a three-month period of doldrums. Plus, Paige's news that his license would be reinstated had him considering once-forgotten possibilities.

And Sam would be off in three hours. Jackson couldn't help think about their Christmas Eve kiss. He knew that it had been a spontaneous thing, driven by the moment. Sam wasn't his girlfriend, and he knew that theirs had not progressed to a kissing relationship. And yet, her lips had been like sugar, and he wanted more.

South Carolina missed a field goal, and the game teetered toward overtime. Immediately afterwards, at midnight Eastern, some idiot was going to jump a motorcycle off the Coronado Bridge in San Diego and onto a barge floating beside it. Jackson figured it would make for some good television.

Miami marched to midfield, stalled, and the game went to overtime. And Jackson's phone rang. He swiped it off the coffee table.

"Hello?"

"Jackson Douglas?" The voice was muffled.

"Yeah. Who's this?"

444

"I have info about your girlfriend."

Jackson sat up straight. The voice was hoarse, slow and measured, neither masculine nor feminine. Jackson couldn't place it. "What kind of info?" he asked.

"The kind you'll want to know about."

"Okay, I'm listening."

A short, raspy laugh. Still unfamiliar. Disguised or distorted, perhaps? Jackson ran through all the people he'd dealt with recently. Maggie's relatives, Maxim Baby and his associates, father and son Vasquez, Rod Finley, members of the *Twenty Something* cast and crew. None of them were a match. Not even close.

"Not on the phone. Meet me at Woodlawn Cemetery. Main entrance, off 14th. Walk toward the pavilion. I will be waiting."

"Who are you?"

"Ten o'clock tonight," the voice answered. "Don't be late. Your girlfriend's life depends on it."

The line went dead, and Jackson immediately checked the number. Then he dialed Mouse, who didn't answer. Probably working. Else mad that Jackson hadn't spent any of his "Christmas vacation" playing video games with him. Jackson thought about calling the police, but stopped short. What would they do?

Instead, he replayed the conversation. Info about his girlfriend? Who? Sam? Maggie? Had someone spotted him with Noelle or Lieutenant Paige and made an assumption? And who was it anyhow? What info did they have? Were they purposefully disguising their voice, or was it unfamiliar to him. And what about that last part—"Your girlfriend's life depends on it"?

Jackson had no answers, no clues. His only option was to wait until ten o'clock.

*   *   *

Wednesday, January 2
7:34 p.m.

MAGGIE MADE a hamburger and tater tot casserole, one she claimed was easy and for which Jackson had the ingredients. He told her it was good, which it was, and because she would have pulverized his other leg if he hadn't.

She'd left after dinner when Jackson had fallen asleep during the Sugar Bowl. He'd woken up long enough to tell her he'd call her later and to thank her for her concern and again for dinner. And to witness Reggie returning his Granada, an event that felt like a dream to him now. Then he'd promptly fallen asleep again. When he woke up the second time, LSU was leading Texas by two touchdowns and his shoulder was throbbing.

A commercial came on for a new action thriller, lots of babes and bullets. The gunplay reminded Jackson of his shooting, and he tried to probe the deep recesses of his brain for a clue. Who had shot him?

Throughout the evening, he'd slowly remembered the phone call that had led him to the cemetery. The specific words had come back to him bit by bit, then in waves, until he could recall them verbatim and could hear the voice as if it was in the room with him. But he still couldn't identify it, despite repeating the conversation over and over.

"Jackson Douglas? . . . I have info about your girlfriend . . . The kind you'll want to know about." . . . A short, raspy laugh. . . . "Not on the phone. Meet me at Woodlawn Cemetery. Main entrance, off 14th. Walk toward the pavilion. I will be waiting. . . . Ten o'clock tonight. Don't be late. Your girlfriend's life depends on it."

Jackson stood and paced as the LSU Tigers kicked off. Two phrases stuck in his head. The way he stressed "the kind you'll want to know about" and "I will be waiting." What was it about them? A familiarity in those phrases. What could it be?

He paced some more. Texas' quarterback rolled out and threw an interception.

The first phrase was an audible clue. "You'll want to know about." Jackson said it a dozen times, until his inflection matched his memory. Something in the word "want" stood out—something with how it had been said. Similar to how it had been said once before?

The second phrase screaming in his brain was familiar, but he couldn't place why. "I will be waiting," he said to himself. "I will be waiting. I will be waiting."

LSU scored again. Jackson muted the TV. He was so close. He could feel it. Like when he saw a familiar face on TV, and every time he looked at it, a gear tumbled in his brain until he realized where he had seen it before.

"I will be waiting." Not "I'll be waiting." No contraction. Why? And where had he heard that particular phrase before, without the contraction?

He turned off the TV completely and paced some more. Then he stopped, eyes closed, and thought back to the shooting.

Only a few specks of light managed to penetrate the canopy of trees in the center of the cemetery. It was enough to reflect off the barrel of the Glock 19 pistol trained on Jackson, but not for him to identify the figure holding the gun or make out facial features. He saw only a rough shape, as might be formed by baggy pants and a sweatshirt with the hood pulled up. That, and the unmistakable polymer barrel of the gun.

Before that.

Jackson closed his eyes harder.

Rain was falling as he drove to the cemetery, and as he parked, got out, and surveyed the landscape. He didn't see anything.

Headlights. He remembered headlights.

He waited for a truck to pass, then crossed the road. The gate was ajar, and he began walking down the path toward the pavilion, trees lining either side of the pavement. They filtered the rain while making it sound twice as loud. Eyes alert, Jackson walked slowly, his hand at his waist, ready to reach for the Glock jammed into the back of his jeans.

Still, he saw nothing.

Jackson opened his eyes. The refrigerator had kicked into gear, humming, bringing him out of the trance. He was so close. It was like a voice shouting him out of a dream. He could hear the words, but they were slurred. He closed his eyes again.

A minute ago, the gun had been in Jackson's hand. Like now, he had been unable to identify more than the general shape of the figure in front of him. Unlike now, the two of them had been separated by only a few paces, close enough that a slight moment's hesitation had cost Jackson.

The gun. It had been tucked inside the waistband of his jeans. The shooter had been in front of him? Or had he?

No. He appeared from the trees to the right.

Baggy pants. Sweatshirt with hood. No eyes.

The figure lunged, throwing a wild right hook that Jackson dodged. Instead of the jaw, it caught his lip. A second later, the shooter's body collided with Jackson's shoulder, and the two of them fell to the ground.

They grappled for a few moments on the wet pavement, both struggling to gain the upper hand in the dark, both throwing punches that didn't land. Jackson found a place to put his foot and kicked, at the same time pushing the shooter away. Jackson somersaulted backwards and popped to his feet, drawing his gun. He leveled it as the shooter rose, less than ten feet away.

The hood was cockeyed now, but still obscured the face.

"Who are you?" Jackson asked.

The figure took a step closer.

Jackson steadied the gun, leveling it between the eyes. "What do you want?"

Another step.

Jackson's finger curled around the trigger.

He saw himself shooting. But he wasn't in the rain-soaked cemetery any longer.

He was on a boat. In Marina del Rey. And his bullet plugged into the chest of a drug dealer named Sanders.

He blinked away the image. The darkness returned, and with it a warehouse. He was shooting again, multiple times, repeatedly. He remembered blood oozing across the concrete.

Another step.

Jackson fired again, and again, and again. Now he was shooting an automatic weapon, in the darkened desert. Then on another boat. Bodies were piling up. Killing after killing after killing after killing.

The gun in Jackson's hand began to shake. Rain spattered through the trees into his face, blurring his vision.

The figure lunged again, knocking the gun from Jackson's hand. He heard it clatter on the pavement, felt a blow graze his chin, and instinctively lashed out. They fought again, rolling, grunting, grabbing. An elbow caught Jackson in the stomach, momentarily slowing him. He saw a kick coming for his head and rolled back from it. When he turned around, the figure had risen to his feet. Jackson stood, looking for the gun. Too late, he saw it was in the figure's hand.

Jackson licked his lip, tasting blood. And rain. He exhaled slowly. "You don't have to do this."

The gun didn't waver.

Jackson swallowed. "We can work this out."

He shuffled his foot a half step forward. If he could close the gap in half, he'd have a chance to make a lunge. With some skill and a little bit of luck, he could avoid being shot altogether, or at least take a bullet in the arm or leg instead of the heart or head. Assuming the figure was a decent shot.

And capable of actually pulling the trigger.

Jackson exhaled again and took another small step, hoping the rain would muffle any sound and the darkness would obscure his tiny movement. In front of him, the figure was like granite. Like another tombstone in the graveyard.

Shaking his head ever so slightly, Jackson inched his foot forward again. "Why don't you put the gun down? Tell me—"

The gun discharged, emitting a brilliant white flash and a deafening report. Jackson's mind processed both the sight and sound in the instant before he felt a bullet tear into his flesh, commanding all of his brain's attention.

He spun backwards from the blow, staggered once, and fell to the ground. His brain was pummeled by neurons that jostled for position to announce new and unheard of levels of physical pain. Despite the agony, he was aware of three things as he rolled onto his back.

His Glock had clacked on the pavement.

The shooter had darted across the cemetery lawn and disappeared into the shadows.

And the rain fell with renewed intensity and complete apathy.

Wait! There was more.

The Glock had clacked on the pavement.

The shooter had disappeared into the shadows.

And—No, between that.

Clack. Clack. Clack.

A voice.

Raspy, like on the phone.

What had it said?

Clack, voice.

Clack, voice.

Clack . . . "Live by the sword . . ."

Jackson's eyes snapped open. Alone in his quiet house, dark with the TV turned off, his heart began to pound.

He knew who the shooter was.

Chapter Fifty-Nine

7:51 p.m.

IT WAS TIME for more drugs.

Or maybe it was time for less.

Now that Jackson knew who the shooter was, all the pieces clicked into place.

But could he be wrong? Could it be anyone else?

There was one way to find out. He looked for his phone, found it, and began making calls. It took several to find the right person, on a weeknight, no less. All the while, the clues thundered in his head, like a river that had been steadily plunging toward a precipice, and was now plummeting down a waterfall.

"*. . . your girlfriend.*"

"*The kind you'll want to know about.*"

"*I want to talk to her.*"

"*I will be waiting.*"

I will be waiting.

"*Live by the sword . . .*"

The minutes ticked by as Jackson waited on hold. Finally, he confirmed what he already knew. He ended the call and immediately dialed another number. "Pick up," he pleaded. But she did not pick up.

Jackson dialed again, and while waiting, hurried up the stairs to his bedroom. The police still had his Glock, held as evidence in his own shooting. He fingered his SPAS-12 shotgun, considering whether or not to bring it with him. It had one purpose—to kill—and he wasn't sure he was ready for that. Not again.

He grabbed it anyhow and took the stairs two at a time, ignoring the pain in his shoulder. Reggie had parked the Granada in the garage, and Jackson nearly tore off a mirror backing it out, then almost took out a jogger on the sidewalk. He waved an apology, checked for traffic, and squealed tires as he turned onto the street.

The Granada's fuel gauge indicator blinked on almost immediately. Jackson ignored it. He had enough to get where he was going.

He sped across town, seatbelt off because it would rub his wound. He spent his time alternating between trying her phone again and praying. What was the biblical position on prayers for wisdom and safety when they came while careening across the city with a loaded shotgun riding shotgun?

Jackson's shoulder was throbbing as he swerved to the curb in front of her apartment. He looked around, saw nobody, and grabbed the shotgun off the seat. He hurried to the front door, knowing there was probably a security camera that would spot the shotgun, but likely nobody manning the monitor 24/7 so as to do anything about it.

The night had cooled, a breeze blowing off the ocean. Palm trees beside the building flapped nonchalantly, unconcerned.

Jackson took the steps two at a time, heart pounding almost as much as the fears in his head. It had been forty-six hours, plus or minus a few minutes, since the shooting. So what made him worry that she was in danger right now? Was it because he had just figured things out? Likely. But she wasn't answering her phone, and that was cause for concern. Better safe than sorry, he reasoned as he pushed through the stairway door and into her hallway.

It was quiet, and he hurried forward, hiding the gun beside his leg as he reached for the doorbell.

He could hear it echo throughout the apartment, but nothing happened. For good measure, he banged on the door. Maybe she was gone? But that didn't mean she was safe.

Jackson considered his options. He couldn't just wait in the hallway, shotgun on his lap, until she returned. Sooner or later a neighbor would come by, and he'd be busted. Besides, what if she wasn't coming home tonight?

He was about to leave, to head down to the car, when he heard a noise. Nothing loud, just a soft exclamation. A whimper, maybe. Jackson turned and pressed his ear to the door. He knocked again, listened again. He tried calling her name, and heard the whimper again. A few decibels louder this time, and more urgent.

It came a third time, cut off suddenly. Jackson knew he wasn't imagining things. He stepped back, ready to knock down the door. Then he remembered his shoulder, the deadbolts, and the SPAS-12 in his hand. Mentally laying out the interior of the apartment in his head, he stepped to the side and took aim, down at the lock.

"Lord, please," he breathed.

And fired.

The kick of the shotgun tore at his right shoulder, but the pain was felt in his left. Gritting his teeth, he kicked the door. The last deadbolt tore away, and the door swung open. Jackson charged in, SPAS ready.

Noelle sat on the couch, wearing a black bathrobe. Her eyes were wide with terror, framed by crinkled damp hair pulled back to make room for a strip of cloth covering her mouth. Her hands were in her lap, bound. Rod Finley stood behind the couch, a knife in his hand. It was less than an inch from her throat.

He was shirtless, sweating, green eyes wild.

Jackson knew he couldn't shoot—not with the shotgun. Noelle would be in the way. And judging by the smile on Finley's face, he knew it too.

"Drop the gun," he said.

"I thought you loved her," Jackson said.

"I do."

"Then you don't want to hurt her."

"I don't want to . . ."

"Then don't."

"It's not that simple."

"Yeah it is. Drop the knife."

"Then what's to stop you from shooting me?"

"I'm going to shoot you either way," Jackson said. "But you have a chance to save Noelle."

Finley looked down at her, then back at Jackson. "No. You aren't going to shoot me. You didn't shoot me in the cemetery, and you aren't going to shoot me now."

Jackson ground his teeth. And leveled the gun.

"I'm not buying the bluff," Finley said, smirking. "Put the gun down."

Jackson's internal turmoil played out on his face. Then he slowly raised the gun. "Safety on," he said, clicking it for Finley to see. "Setting it down." He began to lower it, then suddenly hurled it across the room at Finley. He ducked, causing him to remove the knife from Noelle's neck. She immediately fell sideways on the couch as Jackson charged. He launched himself over the corner of the couch, in the general direction of Finley, determined that whatever it took, Finely was not getting up.

Jackson knocked Finley to the floor, landing on top of him before rolling into a stool by the counter. He nearly passed out from the pain in his shoulder, but composed himself enough to see Finley clambering on all fours and reaching for the knife he had apparently dropped. Jackson kicked out at Finley's wrist, sending the knife flying across the room. With a sneer on his face, Finley crawled forward and jabbed his fist at Jackson's chest, landing a blow just below the bullet hole.

Jackson growled in pain and rolled away from another blow, cracking his shoulder against the wall in the process. He thought he might literally die from the pain, but again pulled it together and got up as Finley stepped back and picked up the shotgun. He had the smarts to turn off the safety, but that action cost him. Jackson, bleeding and almost beside himself with pain, charged again. With his good arm, he reached for the shotgun, turning it to the side as Finley pulled the trigger. The blast exploded into the kitchen, and the kick knocked Finley over.

Jackson seized the gun by the barrel, and as Finley staggered to his feet, Jackson swung, the butt of the shotgun clocking Finley on the side of the head. He sprawled, and Jackson fell to the ground and dropped the gun. The torque from the swing had been the final straw, and he instinctively reached out for his shoulder.

Finley rolled several times, holding his head. When he realized he wasn't dead, he got on hands and knees, looked around, and spotted the knife. He clutched it, stood wobbly, and turned toward the couch, where Noelle was curled into a ball, shrieking.

Jackson felt for the SPAS, grabbed it, and took aim as Finley staggered toward Noelle. From his seat on the floor, Jackson fired. The kick knocked him backwards, but he was still able to see Finley fall.

He'd seen the movies. It wasn't over. Almost crying from the pain, Jackson forced himself to get up, using the gun as a crutch. He trudged around the couch and saw Finley splayed back against the TV cart. Blood covered his face and chest, and the half of his neck that was still there.

Jackson looked at Noelle, her face buried in the couch. He took off his blood-soaked shirt and draped it over the carnage that had been Rod Finley. Then he collapsed on the floor.

*   *   *

9:32 p.m.

FLICKERING RED lights pierced an otherwise dark night. Jackson sat on the curb, still shirtless, but covered with enough gauze and bandages to keep him warm. He had fought not to be readmitted to the hospital, and won. The bleeding had been stopped, and his only real problem was pain. And that was starting to grow on him.

A shadow blocked the light for a moment, then disappeared as a small figure joined him on the curb.

Noelle, in sweatpants and a hoodie. Jackson turned to her. "Are you all right?" they asked each other almost simultaneously.

She emitted a nervous chuckle. He grinned. "I'm okay. Are you all right?"

"I am now," she answered. "But if you hadn't . . . How did you know?"

"I didn't," he said. "I just finally figured out Finley was the one who shot me. When he called me the other night, he said something about my girlfriend. I figured he somehow concluded we were dating, and if he was mad enough to shoot me, I didn't know what he might to do you. I tried calling you, but you didn't answer. So I came over."

"I just got back from San Diego tonight," she said. "I didn't even unpack, just drew a bath and planned to go to bed early. I stepped out of the bathroom and he was laying . . ." She gulped. "In my bed."

Jackson had to ask. "Did he . . ."

"Rape me? No. Before he could do anything, the doorbell rang. That's when he brought out the knife. He . . . he gagged me, forced me into the living room. The rest . . ."

"I'm sorry you had to go through all that. I had no idea he was even out of jail until tonight. They gave him credit for time served before the sentencing. He was actually released Monday."

"I just can't believe it. How does someone get so delusional?"

"I don't know." Jackson winced and tried to adjust the way his shoulder was resting. He couldn't find a comfortable place.

"Are you sure you're okay?" Noelle asked, touching his good shoulder.

"Nothing I won't survive."

"I think I owe you another steak dinner," she said with a smile.

"No. No, this one was personal."

She turned as the ambulance holding Finley's body pulled away. "How did you know it was him?"

"A couple of things," Jackson said. "For one, the way he said, 'the kind you'll *want* to know about' when he called me. It struck me, something in his tone or inflection, it was the same as when he said, 'I *want* to see her,' at Seth's concert."

"Really?"

He nodded. "He also used the phrase, 'I will be waiting.' Not 'I'll' but 'I will.'"

"Same as at the end of the erotic poem he wrote me."

Jackson nodded again. "The clincher was when I remembered he'd said something after shooting me. 'Live by the sword . . .' I remembered his online handle, 2EdgedPen. Two-edged pen, double-edged sword, live by the sword/die by the sword. That's when I made a few phone calls and found out he'd been released from jail Monday. I called you, got no answer, and came over."

"Wow."

He shrugged. It hurt.

Noelle waited until he looked her direction. "I'm sorry you had to do that. Kill him. After everything . . ." She stared into his eyes for several very long seconds. "I don't suppose Taylor would like it very much if I kissed you on the lips, so . . ." She leaned in and very gingerly, very softly, very slowly kissed his cheek, at the same time rubbing the back of his neck with her hand.

"Thank you for saving my life," she said when she pulled back. "Thank you for doing . . . for doing what you had to do to save my life."

Jackson suddenly flashed back to the Santa Monica Pier and his conversation with Lieutenant Paige. How a thank you from an old World War II vet almost made it all worth it for her brother. And he smiled.

"You're welcome, Noelle."

She rubbed his shoulder—the good one. "Do you want to come inside? Kendra's letting me stay at her place tonight since mine's a crime scene, and I'm sure she won't mind. It's getting kind of cold out here."

"Thanks, but I should be getting home. To bed. Before the cops change their mind and want to ask me more questions tonight."

"Are you okay to drive? I can take you home."

"I'll make it. You should relax, as much as possible."

"Are you sure?"

"Yeah. I'll be fine."

Noelle nodded. "Will you call me when you're rested?" she said. "Turns out I've got a few days before I head out to Vancouver. Maybe we could get together, talk. After everything . . . I don't know."

"I'll call you," Jackson said.

They said goodbye, and Jackson hobbled stiffly to his car, trying to keep his upper body from moving as he walked. Noelle and the dissipating crowd of onlookers and the remaining cops and medics were all behind him, the lights still flashing, casting a long shadow on the street in front of him.

He'd done it again. Killed. Nearly blown a man's head off. Gruesome, graphic, gross stuff.

But he had saved Noelle's life from a crazy, deranged psychopath.

He had done what he needed to do. Maybe that was his calling. The guy who did the dirty work.

Maybe this was even God's calling. Somebody had to shoot bad guys before they stabbed or raped or tortured beautiful young women. Soldiers killed to protect freedom. Cops killed to protect civilization. Sometimes, the bad guys fell through the cracks, and the only defense against their crimes was a private citizen with means and opportunity. And who better than Jackson, a guy whose life had already been scarred by death and tragedy?

Let the blame and the guilt fall on his shoulders. Let him carry the burden for society. The guy who did what needed to be done, no matter what. All for the greater good.

Maybe.

He stopped at the door to the Granada, pausing for a moment to look at the scene behind him. Noelle was gone. A few onlookers remained. Another police car pulled away.

Maybe this was his calling.

And maybe he could live with that.

Acknowledgements

FOR A NUMBER of reasons—mostly repeated plot revisions—this was the most challenging novel I've ever written, and I couldn't have done it without a lot of help.

My wife, Sierra, was once again instrumental with her support, reassurance, and patience with my many ideas and questions. As usual, my parents provided initial reviews of my manuscript, and then did so again when I rewrote it. In addition to proofing drafts, Mark and Tiffany Robinson gave advice and input along the way (especially in regard to cover design), and never tired of serving as sounding boards. And Chris Hembel provided some much-needed, last-minute tweaks, and did so quickly and eagerly. If, after all these proofing efforts, mistakes still exist, they are undoubtedly on me.

Muchas gracias to Joseph Botana for his assistance with translating. It was needed, as I speak even less Spanish than my protagonist.

A special thanks to my aunt C.J. Grace for lending her medical expertise to the novel, and for excusing me when I disregarded "doctor's orders" for the sake of plot.

Lastly, thanks to those of you who've been with me from the beginning. Your encouragement and enthusiasm keep me going.